What people are saying about

Malibu Motel

Malibu Motel explores the darkest places one is willing to go to when all they care about is money. Having it. Possessing it. Living a good life and not wanting to work for it. Dark and seedy, this is a cautionary tale and the writing portrays that mood perfectly...This isn't a story you read to your children at night. This is a story I would recommend only to those brave enough to delve into the dark.
Southern Today Gone Tomorrow

A compelling read that perfectly captures the frailty of human nature.
January Gray Reviews

An intensely readable riches-to-rags story, *Malibu Motel* will have you gripped till the last page.
Bridget McNulty, Now Novel

In the world of money, sex, drugs, and plastic friends, being the big fish doesn't put you in charge of the pond, it makes you the mark.
Joseph Spuckler, Evilcyclist

Chaunceton Bird has created a fantastic story in *Malibu Motel*... A stunning and visceral look into the high stakes world of big money and the risks taken by the wealthy elite.
Anthony Avina, Edge of Sanity

It's true what they say: the higher you climb, the harder you fall. A gripping novel based on true events that will keep you

engrossed until the last page.
Amy Williams, Tomes with Tea

Absolutely Fantastic! Definitely worth the read!
Erik McManus, Breakeven Books

Exquisite is an understatement.
Tee Wai, Biblichor

Malibu Motel is an unflinching account of life lived in the fast lane; a true modern-day rags to riches and back again story. Caish Calloway is the absolute opposite of a traditional hero—a selfish, entitled individual who thinks of little more than money, sex, drugs, and alcohol. Despite these obvious problems, you still can't help but wish Caish luck in the quest to reclaim former wealth and escape the clutches of extreme poverty. From start to finish, *Malibu Motel* is a real roller coaster ride and a story that keeps you turning page after page!
Lorna Holland, The Writing Greyhound

Brilliantly Entertaining. A story that will show you that greed really can cost too much.
Stacey Garrity, Whispering Stories

Malibu Motel is an absorbing read that explores the murky depths of society and humanity. The writing in *Malibu Motel* is agile, and intersperses simple liveliness of style with passages that are dark and reflective. It's the kind of book you can't put down.
Kalyan Panja, Travtasy

Malibu
Motel

A Novel Based on a True Story

Malibu
Motel

A Novel Based on a True Story

Chaunceton Bird

Winchester, UK
Washington, USA

JOHN HUNT PUBLISHING

First published by Zero Books, 2019
Zero Books is an imprint of John Hunt Publishing Ltd., No. 3 East St., Alresford,
Hampshire SO24 9EE, UK
office@jhpbooks.com
www.johnhuntpublishing.com
www.zero-books.net

For distributor details and how to order please visit the 'Ordering' section on our website.

Text copyright: Chaunceton Bird 2018

ISBN: 978 1 78904 172 9
978 1 78904 173 6 (ebook)
Library of Congress Control Number: 2018946923

A CIP catalogue record for this book is available from the British Library.

Design: Stuart Davies

UK: Printed and bound by CPI Group (UK) Ltd, Croydon, CR0 4YY
US: Printed and bound by Thomson-Shore, 7300 West Joy Road, Dexter, MI 48130

We operate a distinctive and ethical publishing philosophy in
all areas of our business, from our global network of authors to
production and worldwide distribution.

To Averie

One ship drives east and another drives west
With the self-same winds that blow;
'Tis the set of the sails
And not the gales
That tells them the way to go.

Like the winds of the sea are the winds of fate,
As we voyage along through the life;
'Tis the set of the soul
That decides its goal,
And not the calm or the strife.

Ella Wheeler Wilcox

1

Money can buy happiness. Money is happiness. Money gives happiness a run for its money.

Don't let the poor tell you differently. Enough money can buy long-lasting comfort, security, and liberty. People just don't realize how much happiness costs. So, when their tiny budgets can't afford it, they tell themselves and others that the only ways to true happiness are through religion and having babies that mercilessly scream through the night and soil themselves hourly. "Oh but the good times outweigh the bad," they say with bags under their bloodshot eyes, disheveled in every way, hair turning gray.

What they mean to say is, a *little bit* of money can't buy happiness: a $50,000 car payment and a $500,000 mortgage is not happiness, it's slavery. But a $15,000,000 mansion and a stable full of exotic cars, without a drop of debt, that is happiness. Who better to speak on the link between money and happiness than me—who once lived with nothing, and now pays servants to wipe the ocean's salt off my beachfront house? I've been poor and I've been rich, and I can honestly say I am happier rich.

Which is why I'm anxious about today's meeting with Jamie T. Lowell, founder and managing partner of Green Mountain Investment Group. Lately, I've had a pinch of bad luck. Some of my businesses have entered into dire financial straits, and I may have overreached on a few recent car purchases. My accountant, Mindy, has done nothing to help my deteriorating financial condition (other than the trite advice to stop spending money), and my hope has been waning. But then I met Penn. Her name is actually Penelope, but, as I have repeatedly told her, four syllables in a first name is offensive, and I refuse to entertain such nonsense.

We met a couple weeks ago at a house party. Just bumped into each other. She asked, so I told her about my financial problems. As chance would have it, she had the solution. She told me about this new investment venture called Green Mountain that had given her remarkable returns. As a prudent investor, I wanted to spend time googling Green Mountain and several financial terms (searches like "what in God's name is a put option?") before making any serious decisions. Green Mountain's Wikipedia page showed that Green Mountain was a Fortune 500 company with hundreds of millions of dollars in annual net income. Most of the listed executives did not have their own Wikipedia entries, but the entry for founder and managing partner, Jamie T. Lowell, was thorough and impressive.

I also ran the opportunity past Mindy. She advised against it, but then that's what I had come to expect from her. Mindy is the type of conformist who goes to UCLA because society tells her she needs a college degree to make money, then spends the rest of her mediocre life advising us changemakers how not to spend ours. I was wise enough to avoid college entirely. Mindy's advice was to not invest with Green Mountain because she hadn't heard of it. As if she is a financial oracle who knows of all legitimate investment management corporations. She's not even an investment expert, she's an accountant. I don't know why I brought it up in the first place.

The bottom line is that I am hemorrhaging cash, and Penn presented an opportunity to reverse that.

One cannot simply call Green Mountain and set up an appointment. It's all very prestigious. Invite only. And Penn was my way in. A few days ago we went to lunch at Neptune's Net and I got what I needed: a one-on-one appointment with Jamie T. Lowell.

Penn was eager to tell me about Green Mountain's platinum-plated package of low-risk double-digit returns and money-back guarantees—which, I admit, seemed too good to be true. A money-back guarantee for any unrealized gain in the first six months? What in the hell kind of investment firm would guarantee your money back? Penn said that it was the company's way of expressing their confidence. Green Mountain was unsinkable, and had such substantial capital reserves that they would always be able to buoy up a client through any unlikely loss. And I knew she wasn't lying because I read the same thing on Green Mountain's Wikipedia page (almost word-for-word the way Penn described it). Green Mountain really was making more money than the Federal Reserve.

But how much of Green Mountain's earnings do investors see? I asked Penn for some hard numbers.

She told me that she started two years ago with a $500,000 investment in a Green Mountain "long-short" hedge fund. Within a year, her initial investment had grown to $825,000, so she added another $500,000. To date, after just over two years, she has made well over half a million dollars. Penn even pulled up Green Mountain's Investment Tracker App on her phone and showed me proof of these incredible gains. Lots of green lines, triangles, and numbers showed me that she wasn't lying.

At the end of our lunch, Penn offered to call Green Mountain and line me up with Jamie T. Lowell.

Which brings me to today. This morning I put on my most expensive clothes and my best pair of Louis Vuitton shoes. It's important to make a positive first impression with any distinguished individual. Jamie T. Lowell is just such a person. I might make a lot of money with Green Mountain, and I don't want to leave anything to chance.

At 11:07 a.m. I pull into a parking garage underneath a Los Angeles high rise and park close to a wall so that I won't get doored by some prick in a BMW. The elevator takes me to the forty-fifth floor. The elevator doors open, and the smell of sawdust and the buzzing and clanking of drilling and hammering assault me. I walk through some glass doors and a receptionist greets me and apologizes for the construction. He tells me to have a seat while he lets Jamie know I'm here. While I wait, I have a look around. The walls are bare and the office is empty. By the time Jamie arrives, I have only seen the receptionist, Jamie, and two construction workers.

"Caish Calloway! Sorry about the dust, we are in the middle of a renovation," Jamie offers an extended hand. "Glad you could make it."

"Oh the pleasure is mine, I'm excited to get started."

Jamie T. Lowell is a beautiful human being. There's no other way of saying it. The symmetry of Jamie's face is stunning. Each feature is flawless; proportionally sized and sharply shaped. Flawless skin. Jamie's hair, which is drawn back in a loose, low ponytail, is near-black, and has just enough gray to prove that the rest of the vibrant color is natural. Jamie's eyes are seawater green with a shimmering gleam. Although Jamie's frame is somewhat petite, it's obvious that Jamie hasn't missed a gym day in a while. Jamie's clothes look tailored and extremely expensive. Yet, no jewelry. Not so much as a wedding ring (which I only looked for out of habit).

Jamie leads me back to a corner office with "Jamie T. Lowell, CFA, MMF" etched into a brass plaque mounted on the glass door. The office is huge and minimally furnished. The ceiling has to be fifteen feet high. All of the walls are glass. Jamie's desk is white marble and completely bare except for an iMac, a few papers, and a silver pen.

"Please, have a seat," Jamie says, motioning to the black leather chairs in front of the desk. "How's the traffic out there this morning?"

"Not too bad, there was an accident at the 110 interchange, but other than that it wasn't bad." As I sit, the receptionist peaks in and asks, "Can I get you anything? Would you like something to drink?"

"No thanks," I gesture.

"Did you take the ten in?" Jamie asks.

"Yeah, usually it's bearable."

"I agree. So, remind me, Caish, how did you first hear about Green Mountain?" Jamie says while situating papers and typing something on the computer.

"Um, it was through a friend of mine, Penelope Perez. We were talking about money and Green Mountain came up." For the first time in a long time I'm a little nervous. I'm not quite sure why, but my voice feels shaky and my legs are jittery.

"Oh, that's right. She called a couple days ago, mentioned that you were interested in one of our long-short hedge funds, is that right?"

"Yeah."

"Great. Before we discuss the details of those funds, let's talk about your financial goals." Jamie is still typing. "Where do you hope to be in five years?"

"Richer." My forced laugh comes out too loud and I feel blood rushing to my face to announce my embarrassment. Jamie gives what seems to be a sincere chuckle at my feeble joke and eases my embarrassment.

"Any specific goals?" Jamie asks.

"Well, in all honesty," I say, "I just want to shore up my financial independence, buy a yacht, maybe a few more cars, and a home in Monaco. Then I'll be set."

"You've come to the right place. How about your current financial position, how would you describe that?"

"Rich." Except this time I try to be more couth in my joke and opt for a grin.

"That's good to hear. On this front, though, we need to be more particular. What is your annual income?"

"Tough to say, really. I have an accountant that keeps an eye on my money, and she files my taxes and everything, and I don't really keep an eye on what it turns out to be."

"Perhaps you could give me a ballpark?"

"Well, maybe a couple hundred thousand dollars a year? I

am an entrepreneur, so I don't have a set salary. In the past few years some of the businesses I've started haven't really panned out, so my annual take is lower than it has been in the past."

"I see." Jamie seems disappointed. "And what about your net worth?"

"Mmm. I'd say probably around thirty-five million dollars." Jamie's disappointment vanished. Encouraged, I add, "I have a house in Malibu worth just shy of twenty million—which is paid off—and a car collection worth several million. I also own lots of furniture, art work, and clothing that is worth a few million."

"Okay, and what kind of liquid assets do you have?"

"Um, I have… well, what do you mean by liquid assets?"

Jamie rephrases the question, "Well as in cash on hand, any stocks or bonds, etcetera."

"Oh right, right. So, I've never been one to put money into the stock market, and with the recent business difficulties I mentioned, I only have around a hundred thousand in the bank." At this admission my confidence falters. Shame washes over me. Surely Jamie will kindly ask me to take my empty bank account and get the hell out. What did I expect? Of course an investment advisor was going to ask about my money. I just hoped Jamie wouldn't be so specific. "My hope was that it would be enough to get my feet back under me. Especially if I reinvest most my earnings."

After Jamie finished noting my response, Jamie's charismatic smile soothes my worries.

"Look," Jamie says, "we here at Green Mountain don't judge. Regardless of your current financial situation, we're here to help. Even if your bank account isn't where you want it to be right now, you have more than enough assets to get started."

"I was hoping to get started without having to sell anything, would $50,000 be enough to open an account?" I ask.

"Caish. We want you to make serious money. Real money. And we can't make you serious money with a $50,000 investment.

Our minimum buy-in is $500,000."

My heart sinks into my stomach, which begins digesting it. Hopes dashed.

Jamie goes on, "But look, I understand your situation. Let me talk to the other partners and see if we can make an exception for you. I might be able to get you in for a little less than that."

"I dunno. Maybe this isn't the right time for me to be investing more. I was sort of hoping I wouldn't have to sell anything."

"You don't have to sell anything Caish, but something tells me you will. You don't strike me as the type of person who enjoys living on a budget. You also don't look to be the type of person who enjoys worrying about whether the next startup will finally be the one that makes you some serious money. Correct me if I'm wrong, but I'm willing to bet you have not always been a millionaire." Jamie is now standing and looking down on Los Angeles through the fifteen-foot-tall transparent wall.

"You're right," I say, "I was born into a working class family in Missoula, Montana."

"I knew it. You have a determination about you that people born into wealth rarely have. You know what it's like to live without, and you're not willing to go back to that lifestyle. We're quite alike, Caish. I'm the youngest of six children, born in Salt Lake City into abject poverty. Purely proletarian. I studied hard, worked in a bowling alley until I was twenty-two, and starved through college so that I could make some money as a financial consultant." At this point, Jamie is pacing and becoming more animated.

"But the problem was," Jamie continues, "I didn't have enough capital to gain the respect of serious investors. Unless I wanted to be a slave at E-Trade for the rest of my life, I had to do something. So I began to work hard at the California state lottery."

No way. I never meet other winners.

I cut in, "Don't tell me you actually won?"

"I did." Jamie paused. "I won upwards of forty million dollars. But I earned it. Winning the lottery is no cakewalk. Constantly spending all my money on tickets, always getting my hopes up, never winning. Week after week. Month after month. All my friends and family telling me I was throwing my life away, criticizing me for my foolish hopes of winning. But I kept my resolve and played the lottery as if my life depended on it. Because I knew, with enough effort and perseverance, I could win that thing. And without that money, I would never be respected as I should be. And I won. I proved everybody wrong, and I won the California state lottery."

"Jamie," I began, "I haven't told many people this, but I am also a winner of the California state lottery."

Jamie lit up, "I knew it! There's just something about you, Caish, I knew I could see it. How much did you win?"

"One hundred and twenty-four million dollars, but you know how brutal taxes are."

"Wow, I bet you earned it though."

"Oh you bet; winning it wasn't easy. I've always been drawn to California, it's hard to explain, but it was like a magnet constantly tugging at me until I finally moved down. But I came here with a purpose, the weather was just a perk. I came here to win the lottery. Everybody told me I'd never win, I suffered through years of gas station clerks telling me that the ticket is a loser. You know how it is. What you said is exactly what it was like for me. But, I knew I could win it. Ya know, the universe is always balanced. Karma. And I knew that with all the bad luck in my life, one day it would balance out and I would win," I say. Jamie is nodding along.

"I knew it, Caish. I knew it. You are a fighter. You're a wolf, not a sheep. You work hard because you know that without hard work there is no success. I know you well because I know myself well. I know that people like us don't give up when life gets tough. We recognize when the stakes are high and we rise to the challenge. And Caish, that's how I know that you are going to sacrifice to get capital for your Green Mountain investment. You know what needs to be done. You know that with a strong investment, you will get strong returns. You have to pay to play, Caish, you know that. Look, I can tell you're pretty sharp, let me show you exactly how this works." Jamie reaches into a desk drawer, pulls out a green dry erase marker, and begins filling the glass wall with numbers, lines, and squiggles. "Hypothetically, and for easy math, let's say you start out with a ten million-dollar investment..." is Jamie's opening line into this investment session.

Over the next half hour, Jamie outlines exactly how the hedge funds at Green Mountain work, and why it's such a sure bet that each investment will be successful. The numbers and lines on the glass multiplied and soon we were onto the next wall. I can't really follow the math, but I can see the writing on the wall: Green Mountain is basically manufacturing money, and each extra dollar I invest up front will give me exponential returns.

"So. Here's what I recommend," Jamie continues, "mortgage your house and get started with a million. That way you don't have to sell anything, and you still have some spending cash in the bank. Then, when you see how big your returns are, sell a few cars—make it sting—because by putting everything you have into this, you will come out on top. In a big way. Remember that feeling when you first won the lottery? Like there's no possible way you will ever need to worry about money again? You can get that feeling back. Yachts, helicopters, rare art, a place in Monaco. Green Mountain can give you that in just a few years if you're willing to work for it."

"Okay, I'm in. Let me talk to the bank concerning mortgaging my place. But, Jamie, I'm going to do more than a million. Let's start with ten million."

Jamie's smile beams confidence. There was a dignity about Jamie's face that made me want to up my investment commitment to fifteen million, but I figured I better not bet the farm until I made back enough to prove that Green Mountain was legitimate. This was going to work. If I reap anywhere near the figures and rates that Jamie had outlined and that Penn had experienced, my days of decline would be behind me as soon as the money was transferred.

"I knew you'd make the right decision Caish. We are going to make a lot of money."

We hammer out a few more details regarding how the Green Mountain website worked, how to use the app, and collect all the paperwork I'll need to fill out.

"I can't thank you enough, Jamie. Thank you for this opportunity."

"My pleasure, your success is my success."

"Okay so I'll call you in the next few days about the first deposit after I've met with the bank," I say as I walk toward the door. Jamie beats me there and gets the door.

"Sounds good, I look forward to hearing from you. Maybe just swing in and we'll get it all hammered out in person. Whatever makes you feel best."

The receptionist is still at his computer when we enter the lobby.

Then Jamie adds, "Hey, Caish, I don't mean to be imposing, and I have every intention of keeping our relationship professional, but how would you feel about a Dodgers game tonight? I have box seats and my date fell through."

Going to Dodgers games is one of my favorite pastimes.

"Absolutely," I say, "I love the Dodgers."

"Great, how about we meet back here at… six? That should give us enough time to get over there and grab a bite to eat," Jamie said.

"Perfect. I'll see you then."

What an unexpected bonus. Jamie is awfully attractive, but I hadn't given any thought to the possibility of hooking up. Well, maybe a tiny bit of a thought. My main squeeze wasn't cutting it lately, so this would be a much-needed change of scenery.

I'm late for a lunch meeting with some app designers, but compared to the money I stand to make at Green Mountain, this meeting seems unnecessary. There is a brief pause when I walk in and take my place at the conference table. Somebody I haven't seen before is clicking through a PowerPoint. The meeting is a brainstorming session about whether people would use an app that helped them with public speaking. Ten months ago I had an idea for an app that started your car for you, but it didn't work out because the auto manufacturers wouldn't cooperate (or even return our emails). Then some of the developers talked me into investing in the company. "APParatus, Inc." So, I gave APParatus $250,000 and received ten percent equity in the company. Business was good for a little while, but now my investment was worth less than $80,000. In the last four months this place has imploded. It won't be long until the corporation is dissolved and we all lose our money to creditors. Unless, the engineers will remind you, the next app they design is the next Twitter. Jesus. How could I have been so foolish? And this was one of the investments that Mindy actually checked off on. Come to think of it, I should probably give her a call. I excuse myself and step into the hall.

"Hello, this is Mindy."

"Hey Mindy, it's Caish, how are you?"

"Hi Caish, I'm doing well, how are you?"

"Really great, thanks. Look, Mindy, I appreciate everything you've done for me, but I no longer need your services."

Mindy doesn't say anything for a few seconds, then asks, "Caish, can I meet you somewhere for lunch so we can talk about this?"

"Um, nah. I don't think that would be productive. It's nothing personal, Mindy, I'm just at a different place in life now, and I no longer need your accounting work. But don't worry, I'll still come to you for my taxes."

"Caish, you don't fire your pilot just because of some turbulence. If this has something to do with those Green Mountain people you were telling me about, I think this is a terrible idea."

"Yeah, well, we'll see. Okay, anyway, talk to you next April."

"If you say so, but please don't hesitate to call if you need anything. I'm as much your friend as I am your accountant."

"Sounds good. Thanks Mindy."

"No problem, you know I mean it."

"Okay, talk to you later."

"G'bye."

"K, see ya later."

"Bye."

I hate phone calls.

After the pointless APParatus meeting (certainly my last), I have a few hours to kill before meeting up with Jamie. I can't make it to Malibu and back in time, so I go shopping instead. I love The Grove and I've been meaning to check out the new Michael Kors.

At 6:00 p.m. Jamie and I meet in the lobby of Green Mountain's building. Jamie is wearing the same clothes from earlier in the day, but now also has a chic camel coat that looks custom. I offer to drive, but Jamie tells me that the reserved spot needs Jamie's license plate and adds, "You know how they are at Dodger Stadium, they'd probably give even your Lamborghini a ticket."

"How'd you know I drive a Lamborghini?"

"Guessed. I figured, a person of your regard would probably own a few fine Italian automobiles," Jamie said while melting my insides with a smile warmer than sunbaked sand.

"Am I fine leaving my car—I mean my *Italian automobile*—in the garage here?"

"Definitely, security here is top-notch."

Jamie leads the way down an escalator to P2 and we find Jamie's BMW parked less than a foot from the wall.

Jamie apologizes for the tight fit on my side, "If you don't park close to a wall in these caves, Neanderthals will door the shit out of your car."

"I know exactly what you're talking about," I say. "And taking up two spots is an open invitation for the Neanderthals to key new pinstripes into your car."

Small talk isn't my strong suit, but Jamie guides us down conversation channel like a seasoned gondola guide. Traffic thickens as we drive past Chinatown, so we have plenty of time to get to know each other. We agree with everything the other says, and we're surprised at how much we have in common. My anxiety from this afternoon was just beginning to ebb when the excitement of something new—of some*one* new—returns my nerves in spades. Apparently Jamie notices.

"Everything okay Caish? You seem restive."

"Yeah, definitely," (I insert the best fake laugh I can muster) "it's just been a while since I've been to a Dodgers game. I'm excited. This is gonna be a blast."

Jamie's smirk tells me my bluff has been called. Jamie's eyes say that Jamie knows the real reason why I'm nervous.

"Yeah, it's been a while for me too," Jamie says. Then, after a brief silence, "Caish, you have every reason to have a few butterflies right now. This afternoon you learned that all your money problems are going away, and now you're on a smokin' hot date with a wealthy admirer whose intentions are yet undisclosed."

"Ha! Is that what it is? Your fancy company and smoldering good looks are just too much for me to handle?"

But Jamie was right. And we know it.

"Yeah," Jamie said with unashamed smugness, "that's part of it." Our shared smile confirmed we were on the same page.

"I thought tonight was strictly business," I mumble.

In the quiet that followed, Jamie reached over and delicately took hold of my hand. I look at Jamie in surprise, but don't pull away. Jamie's hand is soft, dry, and meticulously well groomed. Warm but not hot, ideally sized, and holding just tight enough to show emotion, but not so tight as to cause alarm. Usually I won't hold hands with somebody until after I sleep with them, but this feels right. I squeeze back. Jamie is in control.

The Dodgers demolish the Diamondbacks for most of the game. In the ninth inning the Diamondbacks scored three runs that brought the game within a point. The entire stadium was on its feet when Jansen struck out Herrmann to end the game. I don't remember the last time I had this much fun. I take plenty of pictures for Facebook.

Jamie offers to drive me home and have somebody bring my car by in the morning. When we arrive, I invite Jamie in for wine and cheese. Jamie has an eye for art and is drawn to a Pollock painting in my entryway. It isn't one of Pollock's major works, but it's still a good painting. I'm not really a connoisseur; I just admire art for its ability to strike up conversations. Plus, it helps to let visitors know that I have good taste and lots of money. This particular painting has always been a harmless collection of colorful splatters that reminded me of tadpoles in a pond during rush hour.

"Jackson Pollock is one of my favorite artists, and yet I have never seen this incredible painting," Jamie says.

"Yeah it's not one of his more popular pieces, but I like it."

"I can see why, there is such grace and balance in this piece. And the chaos of most Pollocks seems to be smoothed out by this warm canvas color."

"My thoughts exactly," I add.

If it hasn't already, that piece of art is now earning its keep.

Jamie is also drawn to my piano. I don't play, but growing up I always wanted a black grand piano. So, naturally I bought the best black grand piano money can buy.

"Wow, this is beautiful, Caish," Jamie remarks while taking a seat at the piano and examining the fine woodwork. "I've never sat at a Hamburg Steinway before. This is quite the experience."

"Do you play?" I ask.

"A little."

And with that, Jamie eases into that one song from *Ocean's 11*. The one that's playing at the end while they look at the Bellagio fountain. And it's perfect. I sink into a loveseat and watch as Jamie gets lost in the keys.

When Jamie stops playing I feel like you feel when a massage ends. I beg for another song, and Jamie keeps playing. I pour Jamie a glass of Champagne on ice and place it near the piano. Jamie has a few sips and keeps playing. I get through three cigarettes by the time Jamie stops serenading me.

After a few drinks we walk out on my deck and look out to sea. The water is as black as the night sky.

"Do you see many fireworks out there this time of year?" Jamie asks.

"Almost every night." I move closer. "I'm sure there will be some tonight."

Jamie's voice is soft, "Ever light your own?"

Then there are fireworks. Fireworks with long, meandering fuses whose sparkle and crackle are a spectacle of their own. The fuses burn with delicacy as their sizzle slithers toward explosives. Some fuses are shorter than others, causing surges of combustion flaming up with welcomed surprise. But most take their time. When the sparks finally penetrate the firework housings a rush of flames propel the pack of gunpowder into the crisp night sky. Some scream on their way up; some take off with little more than a gasp. Then comes the explosion of color. Scarlets, oranges, and yellows with vibrancy and brilliance that seem to make the moon blush. Each blast is accompanied by a boom that reverberates deep in the diaphragm. Each ball of flame hangs in the sky before collapsing into smoke, leaving only the smell of smolder and gunpowder. And there are lulls. Soothing interludes of calm in the echoes of synthetic thunder.

Then the candle's flame licks the next fuse. The interval between each blast begins to shorten. Like a heart on adrenaline the pace of each burst quickens. In a breathtaking chaos of sound loud enough to feel and color bright enough to blind, the fireworks erupt in a fountain of flames. The geyser of fire is topped by a supernova explosion of blended colors creating a white light that seems to be coming from both sides of the eyelid. Time and place cease to exist. The climax of the fireworks is so immense that the mind is wiped of any straggling thought. Tranquility through pandemonium. The last few pops and snaps are felt more than seen. Slowly at first, then suddenly, awareness returns. The air is still, having just been pummeled into a daze.

2

"Caish. How do you like your eggs?"

There are worse ways to wake up. "Mmm. Scrambled, please."

"And your coffee?"

"Sugar and cream. Like you mean it."

Breakfast is delicious. The weather is sunny. 74 degrees. Beams of sunshine saunter through the kitchen's skylights and give Jamie an angelic glow. Jamie mentions something about needing to get back to work and leaves around mid-morning. As I walk Jamie out, a young man drives my Lamborghini down the driveway toward my garages. He hands me the key and I tell him to wait while I grab a tip. $500 ought to cover it.

That afternoon I swing into the bank and discuss mortgaging my house. Normally I would never go into debt like this. I get queasy thinking about paying a bank to lend me money. And the twenty thousand questions from the twenty-something year-old loan officer don't help. But, I have money to make. If leveraging my house and selling a few paintings is the way to conquer these money problems, then so be it.

After the initial volley of questions the loan officer transfers me to a more senior banker who will continue the barrage. The senior banker, Aaron D. Valentini, is incredibly energetic and nimble for his immense size. Throughout the conversation I keep scooting back to resist the pull of his gravity. Mr. Valentini speaks quick. Faster than most Californians, which means he is skirting the line of incomprehensibility. He's clearly the type of gentleman that grinds and snorts his allergy pills so they'll work faster. I initial and sign a pile of papers and we're done in under an hour. Mr. Valentini tells me that in a few days the house will be mortgaged and the money will be in my accounts.

I spend the rest of the week calling art and car dealers setting up consignments. I get sentimental with my cars, so choosing which of them to sell is a painful exercise. I part with a Mercedes Gullwing and a Koenigsegg Agera. Both cars are incredible, but they are two of my most valuable, and I can always buy replacements later.

The artwork is an easier choice. I have a Warhol, a few Rothkos, and a Barnett Newman that I don't care about and that are worth, collectively, a few million dollars. I never understood any of that abstract expressionism (or whatever the hell it's called) anyway; I seriously doubt that anybody actually does. The Pollock, however, stays. Jamie likes it. And since I own it, and picked it, that means Jamie likes part of me. The praise Jamie gives the painting is praise of my fine taste and shrewd eye.

By the end of the week I'm back in Jamie's office transferring ten million dollars into a Green Mountain hedge fund. Later that evening we celebrate with dinner at Melisse and polish off the night with cocaine-fueled sex. I'm sleeping much better these days.

Gull calls and the low hum of fog horns lift me out of late morning dreams. Late morning on a Sunday. Or is it Wednesday? Doesn't matter. Half an hour later I sit up on the side of my plush pillow-top king size bed and stare out across the Pacific. This could be heaven. Not far off surfers are bobbing, waiting for the next swell. Further out a small pod of dolphins is taking its time moving up the coast.

The squeak of Sergio's squeegee snaps me out of my trance. Sergio and his crew clean the sea salt off my windows every Friday morning (ah, Friday, that settles it). Pulling on a robe and stepping into sandals, I make my way out to the deck and offer Sergio a cigarette. He declines, as usual, and scorns me for "sucking death's verga." Friendly words from a friendly man, he even delivers them with a chuckle. After a few more pleasantries I leave him to clean in peace and mosey downstairs for coffee.

I check my Green Mountain investment app and see green

numbers and climbing lines. It's only been four months since my initial investment and I've already made several hundred thousand dollars.

Being that it's a Friday, that means I have a busy day ahead. More often than not I have a weekly lunch with the team at GrabBags, a luggage company I started three years ago. The company is doomed, but I still show up to the meetings. Then, at around 7:00 p.m., a few of my friends from the Malibu Ferrari Club get together for an evening cruise down the Pacific Coast Highway and get sushi at Nobu. After that (and I haven't checked on this detail yet but I am confident this is the case), I will party. The party is normally at some socialite's house, but occasionally a B-list celebrity or a trust fund beneficiary will host the soirée. I don't judge them for not having earned their money, it's not as if anybody would turn down millions of dollars. And I speak from experience—although mine was earned. Finally, I'll wrap up the night by flying to my vacation house in Monterey. Monterey has a certain elegance that I can't get enough of, so I bought a little place up there a few years ago. I try and make it up every other weekend.

The sun is shining through the overcast by the time I get out the door, so I decide to take the Cobra. There is nothing like a Shelby Cobra, but mine is particularly unique. The car was built for racing in Europe in 1966, and is one of only twenty-three "Super Snake" roadsters with a 427. It's also one of five Super Snakes to have black paint, a black that, to this day, is as deep as space itself. It won several races early in its life, then was shipped to California and converted to a street legal racer. Fifty years later I bought the car at an auction. Now the Cobra spends most of its days parked next to an Aston Martin DB4 and a Porsche 930 in the classics section of my garage.

The sound of the Cobra starting up is an electric whirl followed by a roaring bass drum rhythm that could startle a fart out of a deaf person. While I wait for the car to warm up I scroll through my Facebook feed. From the looks of it, I had an eventful night last night. My memory is foggy, but I distinctly remember getting together with some friends on one of their yachts. Kelsey's yacht. We met at the marina in Oxnard and went for an evening trip out to the Channel Islands. Facebook videos remind me that the outing became eventful when, at around midnight, we convinced the second officer to try a few magic mushrooms. She then mistook the lights of a distant cruise ship for floating gold coins and was convinced that we needed to "make like Mario" and go jump through them. After she tried to wrest control of the yacht from the captain she was restrained and subdued. The best friends are those with character. And yachts.

I need a yacht of my own.

I ease the car out of the garage and wave to Isabella and the other gardeners on my way up the driveway toward the gate. My yard looks incredible. Recently-mowed grass, groomed palm trees, and colorful, well-pruned flowers that I don't know the names of. Even the fountain has been freshly polished. Isabella and her team have earned one hell of a tip this week.

On the open road the Cobra rumbles along like galloping thunder. If roads could talk, they would thank me. Cruising down the coastal highway, cool wind in my hair, I light a cigarette and find my zen. Sun rays glisten on the ocean and heat the beach. Do seagulls know how well they have it?

I pull into the Chevron by Malibu Point to get some smokes and top off the tank.

Society has five-star hotels, five-diamond resorts, and fine dining at Michelin-starred restaurants, but no luxury gas stations. Chevron is as close as it gets. Whatever car you drive, whatever your status, you have to fill up with the other commoners. Which is fine. There are usually a couple people who get excited over what I'm driving, and I'm happy to make their day. Gas stations also give me an opportunity to take stock on the status of humanity. Here we all are. If there's a case to be made against democracy, it is made at the gas station. These are the people choosing our presidents.

The teller rings me up for two packs of cigarettes, an Arizona Iced Tea, and six Superlotto tickets. I usually play the MegaMillions, the Powerball, and the Scratchers. Statistically I'm more likely to win a second time than I am a first, so I buy tickets every time I fill up. If winning has taught me anything, it's that you can't win without playing. Plus, it's only a few bucks, and the returns are in the millions. It's a no-brainer.

The GrabBags meeting is short. The hope is that we're going to save the company by starting a few crowdfunding campaigns. Definitely doomed.

After a few errands I make it home with enough time for a nap next to my infinity pool. My seizuring phone wakes me up at 7:40 p.m. Mia is wondering where I'm at. Last week at sushi I mentioned a newly-restored Ferrari 330 that I just bought, and she was looking forward to seeing it. I text back saying I'm on my way.

I text an invite to Jamie, who has been busy at work lately. As expected, Jamie is too busy to make it tonight, but suggests we get together sometime next week. I'm not the type of person who gets attached to other people, but something about Jamie has drawn me in. I miss Jamie. It's been weeks since we last talked, and even then it was just about Green Mountain.

I change into evening finery, put on a couple of my favorite rings, and freshen up for tonight's festivities. As I'm putting on my jacket and walking out the door, I glance up at my Pollock painting and a feeling of foreboding creeps up, seemingly from the shadows of my soul. The thought crosses my mind, is Jamie letting me down easy? Was what we had just a way to get me to invest? No. Can't be. I had already committed to investing before Jamie invited me to the Dodgers game. I'm probably overthinking it.

The Ferrari revs to life in much the same way as the Cobra, but the Ferrari's V12 engine has a more dignified hum. It's near 8:30 p.m. and I've missed the group drive, so I drive straight for Nobu.

The parking lot is full, so I park across the street at McDonalds. That's better anyway. I feel like Nobu and its parking lot are so close to the ocean that they could be swept away without warning at Poseidon's whim.

The host takes me back to the deck where the others are already enjoying sushi. A couple of them look up at me, then go back to their conversation. I scan the group for a friend and see Mia with an open spot next to her. This isn't a big group of people, maybe ten or fifteen of us, but I'm relatively new to the club, so I don't know most of them. Mia sees me coming her way and stands to greet me with a hug.

"We thought you weren't gonna make it!" Mia has mastered the ability to smile and speak simultaneously. "Some of us were beginning to think we'd never see the 330."

A couple familiar, nameless faces look up and simulate smiles. I return the gesture and sit next to Mia. I survey the rest of the group as Mia tells me about the group drive. Most of these folks come from old money, so we don't have much in common. Others made their money through business, finance, law, medicine, or some other occupation that they think makes them valuable to society. They all dress and act ostentatiously, especially toward each other. I mostly associate with the club because I like the cars; the silver-haired professionals tend to look down on us new money mortals. Mia also comes from old money, but she isn't snobby about it.

I met Mia Cortez at a spa resort in Japan last year. We were drawn to each other by our shared nationality. Our friendship grew like bamboo as we soaked in hot springs, steamed in saunas, and spent evenings sipping sake. We were both recovering divorcees that lived in Malibu—Mia being a lifetime resident, myself having just moved in six years earlier. We both knew what it was like to have wealth and how difficult it is to fend off freeloaders and gold diggers. As children our parents neglected us, and we both had siblings who had grown up to be monsters. The list of shared experiences seemed endless as we explored each other's lives. Right down to our shared love of cars and the struggle of protecting them from the ocean's salt. In fact, it was Mia who invited me to the Malibu Ferrari Club.

When the conversation lulls, I ask Mia what parties are going on tonight. Usually my phone receives more invitations than I can scroll through by this time of night, but I haven't heard anything from the usual crowd. Although Mia doesn't party as often as the rest of us, she always seems to know who's hosting what.

"Hmm. Ya know I haven't heard anything," Mia replies. "Lemme check."

While she scrolls through her phone I figure I'll dispel some of the silence on our end of the table. I look at the gentleman sitting across from us with his plastic wife. They're looking toward a conversation happening a few seats over, but neither has said anything in a few minutes. Might as well break the ice.

"Hi, Jack, right?" I offer.

"Roger," Roger says.

"Oh, for some reason I thought it was Jack, sorry about that."

"It is Jack, I was just saying 'rodger' as in affirmative," Jack says.

"Oh yeah okay I see. Cause I was gonna say," I force a chuckle, "I thought it was Jack."

"Sounds like you said it anyway."

Okay, so Jack is a jackass. No problem. Plenty of people are like that at first.

Round two: "So what do you drive?" I ask.

"The Ferrari. It's the red one," Jack says with a straight face.

"Well I figured you drove a Ferrari, but which one?"

Jack shifted in his chair to show his annoyance in as subtle-yet-still-obvious a way as possible. "The red LaFerrari. There are two Ferrari LaFerraris in the group, one is yellow, one is red. Mine is the red LaFerrari."

"Oh you said *La*Ferrari, I thought you just said *the* Ferrari. Okay, wow, well done. That's a beautiful car." I pause to give Jack a chance to ask me what I drive.

Jack courtesy smiles and takes a sip of his wine, then looks back toward a nearby conversation.

I turn to Mia, who is texting. "Any luck?" I ask.

"Nothing yet," she says. "Might just be a club night for you."

"For me? Are you not partying tonight?"

"No, I have my daughters this weekend. I'm going straight back to my place after this."

"Oh yeah I forgot," I say. "Well give them my best. Don't worry about me, I'll find something to do tonight."

We both scroll on our phones for a while until Mia asks, "What about Jamie? I thought you'd be having steamy dates in Paris by now."

"I wish," I grumble. "Jamie is either avoiding me or is the busiest person on earth. Either way, I fear the worst."

"Caish, don't be so dramatic. Jamie probably just needs some space, you know how that goes. Just find somebody to fill the time until Jamie comes around," Mia counsels.

"Yeah, I know. It's just tough sometimes."

Back to our phones.

The evening's conversation ambles along, assisted by countless bottles of wine and chocolate bento boxes. I thought after dessert we'd stand out in the parking lot and geek out over each other's cars for a while, but when we reached the parking lot most people just started leaving. A dozen of Italy's finest contributions to the world stir to life and fill the evening air with divine melodies. There goes Jack in his red LaFerrari.

I turn to Mia, "Do you want to see my 330? It's in the McDonalds parking lot right there." I point across the street.

"Oh definitely," she says, "but I really should be getting back. I told the sitter I'd be back by nine thirty and it's almost ten thirty. Why don't you swing by tomorrow afternoon and let me see it in the daylight?"

"This weekend I'll be in Monterey, but maybe I'll come by Monday evening," I say.

"Sounds like a plan, drive safe."

"Will do. See ya later Mia."

The 330 is right where I left it. A few young guys are taking selfies with it when I walk up.

"Damn! Is this yours?" one of them shouts as if I'm still across the street.

"Sure is."

"Ho. Ly. Shit. I have never seen a Ferrari 330 GT in the flesh. What year is it? '65?"

Wow, this guy knows his stuff. "Yeah, 1965." I can tell by the way he dresses and his uncouth enthusiasm that he doesn't own anything near this, so I don't ask what he drives (spare him the embarrassment). But I was like these guys (without wealth, that is), and I remember how exciting it used to be to see cars of this caliber, so I'm happy to let them enjoy this incredible piece of art and machinery. I pop the hood and they're all but hypnotized.

"Did you do the restoration yourself?" they ask, almost in unison.

"No, I bought this right after it was restored," I say. "I've restored other cars, but I figured I'd leave any Ferrari restoration to the professionals."

"Oh yeah, good call. So do you own an auto body shop or something?"

"No, I'm an entrepreneur. But I worked as a mechanic for almost fifteen years, so I know my way around an engine."

"How does it feel to drive something like this?" the younger one asks.

"Nothing too special. You get used to it," I say.

"Really? I guess a whaler's wonder wanes, right?"

"What?"

"Ya know, Moby Dick? It's like 'in a whaler wonders soon wane,' or something like that."

"Oh yeah, probably," I say. I have no idea what this kid is talking about.

"So is this the original 400 Superamerica 4 liter V12 engine?"

The questions continue this way for ten or fifteen minutes. Sometimes I can't tell if people are really curious about certain details of the car, or if they just want to find something I don't know so they can go home and tell their friends they saw a Ferrari and knew more about it than the owner. Either way, I field their questions and we conclude cordially with handshakes and first-name introductions. They ask for my number ("ya know, so we can invite you to some car shows coming up"), but I'm smart enough to avoid giving any personal information to random lurkers. Their swooning resumes when I start the engine and they take pictures and videos as I pull away.

The night is new and I don't have plans. I have a few hours before I need to get to the airport and I'm not one to waste time. There aren't many clubs in Malibu, so I decide to drive to Santa Monica. But before I do, I need to hustle home and change cars. If I'm driving around looking for a good time I need to be in something exotic. Classics don't get nearly the attention as my cocaine-white Lamborghini Aventador. When I get home I spend a couple of minutes in front of the mirror, then I get the night started with some blow—just a couple lines though, all things in moderation. Alert, energized, and ready to rock, I hop in the Lambo and break the sound barrier on my way down PCH.

I slow down when I pass Ocean Boulevard and drive just over a walking pace when I get to Santa Monica Boulevard. I scan the packed sidewalk for people that I'd like to spend the night with. While I'm waiting at the light on Third Street, a couple interested passersby glance at me with hungry eyes. Their bodies and clothes tell me all I need to know and I wave them over. One of them leans on the passenger door and looks in at me.

I keep it light: "Evening. Any plans for the night?"

"Yeah, actually. You?" Hungry Eyes says.

"Nothing that can't be rescheduled. Where you two goin'?"

"A little later we are hittin' up Hyde."

"Bullshit, you can't get into Hyde," I say politely. Nobody unfamous or not rich strolls into one of LA's most renowned nightclubs on a Friday night, not even with the looks of Hungry Eyes.

"Yeah, actually, we can. Anyway, have a good night Lamborghini Bambini."

"Woah hey hold on, I can get you in," I say, reeling them back in. At this point the traffic light had turned green and a few cars had the gumption to honk. They can go around.

Hungry Eyes smirked and said, "Whatever, we're getting in without you. But if you want to tag along I guess that'd be chill."

"Where are you parked?"

"We're ubering. And if you plan on partying with us, you probably should too."

This was sounding good. "I'll cross that bridge when I come to it," I say. "I'll drive, let your friend catch up with us at Hyde."

"Thanks, but our Uber is the one honking at you. We'll meet you there."

They get in the car behind me and I drive toward Hollywood. I drive slow so the Uber will pass me (I'd rather not drive all the way to Hyde if they aren't really going), then follow it to Hyde.

When we arrive a valet approaches and I tell him to clear a spot for me and that I will be parking my own car. The valet runs to a nearby car and drives it out of the way and I park within eyesight of Hyde's entrance. The bouncer needs to see me in my car, it's the only sure way I'll get in, and I need to be extra sure tonight or I might not be able to get Hungry Eyes in. I rev a couple times before I turn the car off, just for good measure. I step out and light a cigarette while I wait for Hungry Eyes to come over, friend in tow. But instead, Hungry Eyes walks straight to the bouncer, glances back at me briefly, then walks right in. I flick the barely smoked cigarette into oblivion and walk toward the entrance. Having made eye contact with the bouncer several times at this point (both while in the car and standing next to it), I feel good about my chances. Sure enough, after a few formalities ("sorry, your name is not on the list, back of the line") I slip him a hundred and he lets me in.

Like any nightclub, the music is loud, the light is low, alcohol is everywhere, and most people are on their phones. Unlike most nightclubs, Hyde is packed with rich, influential people. And there are often a few famous people stashed away in private rooms. People are packed in tight, and getting a seat at the bar is not an option. I open a tab with shouts and reaches and take my cocktail on a scouting mission to find Hungry Eyes or any other familiar face. I'm in no hurry though, at a place like this I'm among my peers.

Several people recognize me and we make small talk. As small groups form, we don't so much talk with each other as we talk while standing by each other. Each person looks up from their phone to make passing eye contact with whoever's talking, scans the room, then looks back down at their phone. Each scan is conducted as casually as possible. We all pay just enough attention to the conversation to make it seem as if we care about what each other is saying. While I'm scanning the room and considering who I could hook up with, I spot Hungry Eyes moving back to a private area. I excuse myself and snake through the crowd. By the time I get to where I saw Hungry Eyes, security stops me. I try most of the usual "do you know who I am" phrases but to no avail. I even offer him a Franklin. Security tells me not to make problems and to enjoy the rest of the club.

Heading back to the place I was before, I find the chatting with has moved to the dancefloor. I set my and move into the sea of pulsing people.

We drink, "dance," and dabble in drugs and debauchery. I catch glimpses of Hungry Eyes throughout the night, even making eye contact a couple of times, but we never talk. What a tease. Whatever, I'm over it. Besides, I should get going, I have a flight to catch.

I close my tab, step out, and call Sergio to come drive me home. Sergio, a man of humble circumstances, loves exotic cars. One morning, while he was cleaning my windows, I offered him an opportunity to drive the cars he loves so much. Here was the deal: he could drive my cars whenever I needed to get home but was too... let's say incapacitated. It was a win-win. I trusted him and needed somebody to drive me and my car home, and he always wanted an opportunity to drive sports cars. It was a little after 1:00 a.m., and Sergio sounded groggy. But he was at Hyde in no time (I think he lives in Inglewood, so he had to have broken speed limits). I nap on the way home and wake up when he shifts into park.

Looks like his wife followed us over. I tip them both for their time, then wobble inside and pack for my weekend in Monterey.

I would never drive myself to the airport, even if I do have a hangar to park in. Sometimes it's better to be driven than to drive. My chauffeur, Miles, is a few minutes early. He loads my luggage into the trunk of the Mercedes Maybach S600 and waits by the car as I tidy up. When I step out of the house Miles puts out his cigarette on the ground, pulls out a small canister (like the ones used to hold a roll of film) and places the cigarette into the container for later disposal. He then opens the passenger-side rear door and I slide into the most comfortable hand-tailored topstitched Nappa leather seat on the planet. I love this car. Even the refined sound of the door closing has been thoughtfully engineered. LEDs provide the cabin with a soft moonlight glow. Wood and leather cover every surface and are offset by brushed aluminum accents. I stretch out my legs and recline the seat as Miles guides us up the driveway. Without music playing the cabin of an S600 is virtually silent, so Miles puts on some Van Halen at a low volume. He knows me well.

As we travel toward the 101, I pull out my phone and make sure the house is all buttoned up. Using a smart home app I close two windows, turn off all the interior lights (the exterior lights are automated), lock the doors, windows, and gate, and set the alarm. I text the pilots to make sure we're on for our 3:00 a.m. flight to Monterey and they report they are running pre-flight checks. I check the Green Mountain app to see how quickly my wealth is multiplying. The green lines are steep; all is well.

I must have drifted off because suddenly we're pulling into a well-lit hangar and I can hear the hum of jet engines. When Miles opens my door the sound jolts me back to full alertness. The Gulfstream G500's twin jets are warming up just outside of the hangar. Miles and a flight attendant carry my bags to the plane while one of the pilots greets me with a vigorous handshake. I haven't met this pilot before. He says the weather looks good and he's excited to get in the air.

We walk out of the hangar and across the tarmac. I climb the airstair and find my way to a leather couch in the cabin. Most G500s are pretty similar, but this is the first time I've seen this interior layout. It seems more spacious than usual. I don't own this private jet; I pay a yearly membership fee to a charter organization and I fly wherever I want, whenever I want, without having to deal with the hassle of ownership. We taxi to the runway and the cabin lights dim. After a brief announcement, the pilots put the lever to the metal and g-forces, sound, and speed increase in tandem. We skip down the runway then the ground drops away.

After a few minutes of climbing, the steward approaches

me and asks if I'd like anything to drink. The flight attendant's pressed white uniform and tidy hair seem out of place at three o'clock in the morning. Too clear eyed. As if this poor service industry slave hasn't had nearly the night one deserves. A name badge pinned to the flight attendant's shirt has "Taylor" etched between two golden wings.

"I'll have whatever you're having, Taylor," I say.

Taylor hardly blushes, "I wasn't planning on having anything. But I would be happy to make recommendations."

"In that case," I say, "I'll have two glasses of your finest Pinot Noir."

"I don't drink while I'm at work, but I appreciate the gesture," Taylor states.

"Well then clock out."

I think Taylor's smirk turned into a smile as Taylor turned and walked away. The glance back over the shoulder confirms my suspicion. Taylor's eyes say all that needs to be said.

Taylor is not wearing a ring and we are the only two people in this flying island (besides the two pilots—who are presently occupied). I know that behind the back partition there is a bed and a shower. Flying from Van Nuys to Monterey only takes an hour, so we don't have time for games. I would never force anything, but if we're both on the same page, why wait?

After a few minutes I realize that Taylor is not coming back with the wine. I see it as an invitation to join Taylor in back. I remove my shoes and walk through the softly-lit cabin toward the partition door. The door slides opens without a squeak. This room is just as dimly lit as the rest of the cabin, but the lighting in here is warmer. The bed takes up nearly all the floor space, with only a small walkway running along one of its sides leading to the bathroom. The curved walls have white leather stitched to them and the three windows on either side of the room have their shades open to the black outside. Two glasses of red wine are sitting on a small table next to the head of the bed. On the bed is a dark plush comforter. On the comforter is a light flush Taylor. Once again, our eyes do most the talking. Then, for the second time that evening, g-forces, sound, and speed increase in tandem.

I'm thinking about Hungry Eyes and Jamie the whole time. Not that Taylor isn't every bit as bangin' as Hungry Eyes (and just shy of Jamie), I just can't get Hungry Eyes out of my head or Jamie out of my heart.

Before we land Taylor and I exchange numbers that we both know won't be used. Not that the inflight entertainment wasn't worth repeating, we're just realists. My huge tip will make it awkward because Taylor won't be sure which service I'm paying for.

I'm putting on my shoes and buckling up for landing when Taylor, looking as fresh as ever, walks over to my seat.

"I'm embarrassed I didn't ask earlier, but what is your name?" Taylor asks.

"Caish."

"Quiche?"

"*Cai*sh, like cake. Caish Calloway."

3

Every summer I drive in the Bullrun Rally. It's an underground car rally (invitation only) with a $20,000 admission fee. Networking with the right people is crucial if you want to be successful, so I see the admission fee as an investment. This will be my first year with my Lamborghini, and I want to make a lasting impression. I take the car to the Beverly Hills Lamborghini dealership and have them give it their best treatment. A full detail, service, and inspection will run me well over a thousand dollars, but those small nominations are the sort of cash I still have plenty of.

The morning of the rally gets off to a rough start. I wake up to the blaring beep of a flatbed tow truck backing down my driveway. I must have left the gate open. Jesus Christ. These people are relentless. I'm sure they're here for the Porsche. I bought it several months back on credit, and I may have missed the past four payments. Buying on credit has never been my style, but times have been tight, so I didn't have a choice. If they could just wait a few months, I'll be able to make my first withdrawal from the Green Mountain account without incurring penalties and pay off these loans.

I stagger out of my room, down the stairs, and out the side door to handle this situation. I step onto the warm cement of my driveway barefooted and find a husky gentleman holding a clipboard having a look around.

Without a trace of annoyance, I ask, "Excuse me, can I help you? Are you lost?"

"Good morning, are you Caish Calloway?"

"Yes, how can I help you?" Again, I'm laying on the kindness here. I even offer the brute a cigarette as I light one of my own. He declines.

"My name is Rob Tugly and I'm here with Tugly Ugly Repo & Tow on behalf of Aston Martin of Beverly Hills. Are you aware that you have defaulted on your payment agreement to Aston Martin of Beverly Hills?"

Damn. I forgot about the Aston Martin. I may have missed a few payments there as well.

"That doesn't sound right... seems like they would have sent some sort of notification if that were the case," I say with a sincere look of consternation. Rob is just a pawn for his company. He doesn't really care about taking my car. I bet he earns $25,000 a year and lives in a two-room, one-bath hovel in Hawthorne. People like this, which is to say most people, can easily be persuaded with a little incentive. Rob is just like all the other lazy lower- and middle-class citizens of this country. He probably wakes up, does the minimum amount required of him, and goes home to his screaming children and mindless sitcoms.

"They have sent notifications," Rob states, "and you received them. They sent the notifications via certified mail, and you signed for them. Either way, that's not really the point. I need to take your Aston Martin DB4, California license plate IAM DB4."

"Mm. Nah, I'd rather not allow you to do that." What did Rob expect? I add, "And I know my rights, you can't take it. But let's not get mired down in all the prickly details of your job. How about this: I'll make it worth your while to go back to Tug-One-Out and tell them that the car wasn't here and neither was I."

"It's Tugly Ugly Repo & Tow," Rob says.

"Yeah. Look, how about $500 to forget about the whole thing?"

"Are you aware of what a secured transaction is?" Rob asks, clearly missing my point.

"No, but that's not what we're talking about right now."

"It is, though. Ya see, a few months back, when you purchased your Aston Martin, do you remember whose money you used to purchase it?"

"My own, of course."

"Close, but not quite. You borrowed $715,810 from Aston

Martin of Beverly Hills to buy this car. To secure their loan, the dealership asked you to agree to use the car for collateral, that means that—"

"Yeah look, Rob, whatever, I get it. But what I'm saying doesn't concern Aston Martin of Beverly Hills. It's just me and you Rob. Me, you, and, let's make it $1000 cash."

"No, this is not between me and you. In fact, I have nothing to do with this. I am just doing my job. Now, I don't mean to take up much of your time, could you please pull the DB4 out of the garage and park it about fifteen feet behind my truck?"

"Sorry Rob, I can't do that." I have to put my foot down. I've paid the dealership over two hundred thousand dollars so far, and they have no right to come take my car just because I'm sort of behind on payments. Especially since I can pay off the loan in a few months.

"Let me get you to look at something here for me," Rob says and steps toward me with the clipboard out in front of him. "Does that look like your signature?" He points to a squiggle.

"Yes."

"What you signed here is an agreement to allow Aston Martin to—"

"Rob, fuck that. I know. You don't have to keep telling me. But I'm not going to open the garage. I have enough money to become current on my payments, I just haven't gotten it to the dealership yet. They'll have their money, and I'll keep my car. Trust me, everything is under control Rob. You can leave."

Rob looked disappointed. I was finally getting through to him.

"Caish, if you don't open that garage, the dealership will go to court and have the sheriff come take your car. The police will force you to relinquish the vehicle."

"Well then let them try to force me to *relinquish the vehicle*. It's my car and they're not taking it. Goodbye Rob."

Without another word, Rob smiled, tipped his hat, and drove

his truck up and out of my driveway. And to think, he could have done the exact same thing but with $1000, had he been willing to see reason. Had he been more entrepreneurial. He may have even made more if he was an enterprising negotiator. It just goes to show you why he's not one of us. Why he goes home to peasant blue-collar squalor and I go home to 8,000 square feet of beachfront heaven. Because I am a hustler. I have ambition that Rob will never have. What does he know about hard work? About sacrificing to make your dreams come true? Obviously nothing. If he had any real desire to amount to anything, he would have his own tow truck business and stop taking orders from other people. He would see an opportunity when it was staring him in the face, instead of blindly following the orders of superiors.

Whatever, I don't have time to think about that. Let the sheriff try to take my Aston Martin. I'll move it to a storage unit later today. I'll tell the authorities it was stolen if it comes to that. But for now, I have a rally to get to. Registration starts in an hour and I'm two hours away.

I change into a T-shirt and jeans that say I'm casual and laid back, yet extremely rich. I put on my Gucci driving shoes, put a few carats worth of diamond studs into each ear, and grab my driving gloves on my way out the door. Last night I packed my bespoke Lamborghini suitcases with everything I'll need on the rally, so I'm ready to go.

I all but begged Jamie to come with me, but I guess this is still a busy time of year for investment advisors and hedge fund managers. Having a co-driver is an essential part of any rally, so, when Jamie turned me down, I called Mia. She said she couldn't take a couple weeks off work. I decide to let Riley Hammon be my co-driver. Riley is young enough to be reckless, but old enough to be legal—right in the sweet spot. Riley is a blonde model with a small frame, a big ego, and complete disregard for authority. Riley wasn't my first choice because I'd rather not go on a road trip with an immature talk box who won't stop telling me about who said what to who. But I figure if we party early into every morning, Riley will sleep while we drive.

Riley is on the curb and ready to go when I pull up to Empire Apartments. We arrive at the rally with plenty of time to spare and get registered. The Bullrun is an exhibition of the finest mechanical engineering money can buy. Over a hundred exotic cars, many of them modified, dominating over three thousand miles of highway. Most drivers know how to have a good time, so it ends up being a week of nonstop racing and partying. Registration is a pre-party of re-meeting last year's drivers and checking out any new cars.

After we get our wristbands, grab bags, and paperwork (all quite official), we work our way back to the Lamborghini to make sure we're all set. That's when I hear the unmistakable voice of Tim Rayburn.

"Hey Mud Duck, you can't park there!"

I turn to see Tim, about fifty feet down the parking lot, laughing and walking toward me. Tim drives a blue Lamborghini Aventador SV with Selina, his wife, as his co-pilot. We met a few years back at this rally and hit it off when we discovered that we were both lottery winners (up until Jamie, he was the only other winner I'd met). Tim made his way through the crowd and greeted me with a half-hug and giggles he could hardly contain.

"Caish, you missed it!" Tim's cigarette seems to defy physics as it clings to his lower lip. "Just before you got here, haha, there was this Oscar Meyer Wienermobile doing fuckin' burnouts! Ah haha, you'd have laughed so hard! Hahaha. Oh God. You know, the big ass hotdog cars? Oh, sweet Jesus. Just picture it, this fuckin' thing's got like a supercharged Chevy 570 pushin' over 700 horses and nobody knows it. Probably turbocharged too. It pulls into the parking lot and everybody's makin' fun of it and talkin' shit. Haha, then, Caish, I shit you not, the dude just lets it rip and does one of the longest fuckin' burn outs I've ever seen. All sorts of donuts and shit. And, haha, he's got his arm out the window flipping everybody off. The smoke cloud was so fuckin' thick, haha, people were chokin' and running for air. Pluggin' their ears and yellin' at him. Haha, I don't know how the dude's tires didn't blow out. And then he just fuckin' drove away. Haha, oh my God Caish, you'd of loved it."

"Haha, dammit, nobody asked him to come on the rally with us?"

"We couldn't, he just fuckin' rolled up, burned rubber, and peeled out of here. Haha, a fuckin' Oscar Meyer Wienermobile! Oh God. Anyway, how've you been Caish? You look great, everything going alright?"

"Yeah man, everything is going great, how about you? How's Selina? She still your co-driver?"

"Yeah she is, and she's doing great. You wouldn't believe how good she's looking these days. Damn. Oh there she is right there. Selina!" Tim yells across the parking lot, "Hey, Selina, look it's Caish! Com'ere! Here she comes."

Selina is indeed looking great. Her hair is as blond as the sun's corona and she looks like she just walked off the set of a movie. Her new breasts look as natural as her tan. She must be 37 years old or something, but she looks 25. To date, I'm not sure I have ever met somebody who smiles and laughs more than Selina. Her and Tim are apt examples of how much happiness money can buy. On the rally, if you pass Tim's Lamborghini (or, more likely, when Tim passes you), you will hear two things: the roar of a Lamborghini V12, and classic rock almost as loud. And you'll see four things: Tim's smiling face, Tim's middle finger, Selina head-banging, and both of Selina's hands in the air telling you to rock on.

"Caish! Long time no see! How are you baby?" Selina says with arms out, reeling in a hug.

"I am really great, how about you?"

"Never been better! Who's this gorgeous co-driver you've got with you this year?"

I had completely forgotten about Riley, who was scrolling through Twitter in the passenger seat.

"Hey Riley, come meet two of my favorite people," I say, motioning to Tim and Selina. Riley pockets the phone and walks around to the front of the car.

"Riley, this is Selina Rayburn and her husband Tim. No doubt they will be the best people you meet on the rally. Tim, Selina, this is Riley Hammon. Riley knows how to have a good time and was available on last-minute notice to come along."

Riley offers a limp handshake to the Rayburns and says, "Nice to meet you, I look forward to partying with you." Despite Riley's weak first impression, I'm sure the Rayburns will see Riley as I do: a young beauty with a tight body and a high tolerance for controlled substances.

"Hell yeah Riley," Tim says, "we look forward to wearin' you out. How are your cocaine supplies?"

Riley blushes and laughs nervously. "What?"

"Ya know," Tim continues, "Bolivian marching powder, blow, California corn flakes? Surely you brought a couple weeks' supply?"

Riley glances at me suggesting I take it from here. So I do. "Yeah we're all stocked up. But we know where to go if we run low."

An organizer on a bullhorn announces the beginning of the rally and people start filing into their cars.

"Well good stuff, this is going to be a fuckin' rally to remember. We'll see you two on the road! Oh, by the way, did you hear about Mario Andretti?" Tim adds.

"No, what's up?" I ask.

"He's here! I shit you not. He'll be rallying with us. They say near the end of the rally he's gonna choose one of his favorite cars and drive it."

"Like, drive one of our cars?"

"Yeah, isn't that bitchin?"

"Hell yeah that's bitchin. See you out there Tim!"

Riley and I slide into the Lambo and add to the symphony of starting engines. The Italian V12 (well, I guess sort of German these days, but whatever) gives me chills every time I start it. The pedals feel firm under my Guccis. The smooth vibration of the engine massages us through the seats.

Riley asks, "Should we do a couple lines to start things off?"

"Not a bad idea," I say, "but I always get coke all over the place when I try and snort in the car. It's like eating in the car for me. So let's hold off until our first checkpoint."

"Fair enough," Riley responds. Then, "Tim and Selina seem nice. Are they always that high?"

"Oh they weren't high, Riley. That's just how happy they are naturally. You'll know when they're wired."

"No fuckin' way. Nobody is that happy sober," Riley says with bewilderment.

"Really, I'm not kidding. They're just properly rich. Find them in the morning, they'll be smiling and laughing just as much. Maybe wait 'til they've had their coffee and a few cigarettes, but they'll be just as chipper."

"That doesn't mean they're sober," Riley replies, "maybe they put coke in their coffee instead of sugar."

"We'll get breakfast with them tomorrow and you can see for yourself. Will you grab that checklist and see what our first challenge is? We need to stop by my place on our way out of town, but if there's something we can do on the way we might as well." And like that, we're off. We take off toward my place to move the Aston Martin. Riley will help.

My gate is open. I get a pit in my stomach. I know I closed my gate. Rob has been here since I left. I know it. The sneaky bastard must have been watching the place. Fuck. How could I forget to set the alarm? Sure enough, the DB4 is gone. That motherfucker broke into my garage and stole my DB4. I'm calling my lawyer, this is bullshit.

"Good afternoon, thank you for calling Morely, Black, and Associates, how may I direct your call?"

"To Gabriella Rodriguez."

"Transferring you now, please hold." No hold music is better than any hold music.

"Gabriella speaking."

"Hey Gabby, this is Caish."

"Good afternoon Caish, everything going alright with that settlement?"

"Yeah it's great, thanks for your work on that. But I'm calling about something else. A repo guy just broke into my garage and stole one of my cars. I want my car back, and that asshole arrested."

"That doesn't sound good. Were you home when he broke in?"

"No."

"Is the garage attached to your house?"

"No, this is one of the detached garages."

"Was the stolen vehicle used as collateral for a loan?"

"Yes, but Gabby the guy broke into my fucking garage and stole my car. That car is worth like a million dollars."

Gabby is quiet for a moment. "Okay, what is the vehicle's year, make, and model, where did you buy it from, and who was your lender? Also, do you know the name of the repo company?"

I give Gabby the details lawyers need and she tells me she'll call me back tomorrow with some options.

"Well, no need to call back," I say, "just handle it. I will be on the road for the next two weeks, and I want that car back in my garage by the time I get back. An added bonus would be for Rob, the repo truck fucker, to be in jail. When that happens maybe just shoot me a text letting me know everything's taken care of. Twelve hundred an hour for your time, right?"

"Yeah, the billing rate hasn't changed, but, Caish, it may not be possible to get your vehicle back that easily," Gabby says. "It sounds like you entered into a purchase money security agreement with Aston Martin of Beverly Hills, and they may be within their rights to take it back if you have defaulted on your loan. That said, I'm going to do everything the law allows to get your Aston Martin back, I just want to make sure your expectations are in the right place."

"Yeah I get it, everything takes forever. Either way, please just handle this."

"Sounds good, Caish. I'll start making phone calls as soon as we hang up." Then she hung up. I don't think I have ever heard Gabby say "goodbye" or anything like it. She doesn't have time for that. That's why I work with her. She's a hustler, like me. She's also rich like me, so I'm sure we have a similar understanding of reality. She won't let some schmuck like Rob do this to one of us. The poor can steal cars from each other until the cows come home and nobody cares. Hell, they probably enjoy the added drama in their pointless lives. But stealing from one of us has swift consequences. We have the full weight of the justice system behind us. Rob doesn't stand a chance.

"Everything alright?" Riley asks when I get back in the car.

"No. Some asshole repo fucker just broke into my garage and stole my Aston Martin DB4."

"Holy shit! Caish that's terrible," Riley says while scrolling through Instagram, "sorry to hear it. What a goddamn tragedy. Was that your only Aston Martin?"

I see Riley grinning, as if to say, "Really? You mean you only have sixteen cars now? Whatever will you do?"

"Oh fuck off Riley. You know what it's like to lose something you've worked for? Something worth a million dollars?"

"I'm just kidding, Caish, chill out. That sucks your car was stolen."

"Yeah. Well since we're here, wanna swing in and do a couple lines before we get out on the road again?"

"Definitely," Riley answers almost before I'm done asking. "Wanna fuck too, or do you think we have time for that? Looks like we need to be in Vegas by 9:00 p.m."

"What time is it now? Fiveish?"

"Yeah right around there."

"I think we have time, but let's hurry."

Soon we're back on the road. Windows down, heart-rates up, bobbing and weaving through traffic like Muhammad Ali rumbling in the jungle. When we transfer from the 405 to I-15 we settle into our cruising speed. Road trips in exotic cars can be quite a challenge. Discomfort sets in about an hour into the trip. The seats are so firm, the suspension is so stiff, and the tires are so thin, that crosswalk lines turn into speed bumps. Desert highways aren't exactly glassy smooth, and the slightest crack at 90 mph can become a teeth-rattling chasm. Sure, the Lamborghini has a comfort mode on the suspension, but that hardly helps. Then there's the constant battle to avoid rock chips, to stay out of blind spots (the car's low profile seems to make it invisible), and not get tangled up with rubberneckers gawking at the car. A road trip in a Lamborghini takes incredible focus and resolve.

The first checkpoint is at the base of the Baker thermometer. I'm told that it's the tallest thermometer in the world, and that it was built after Baker's temperature reached 134 degrees Fahrenheit. You'd think they'd have spent the money on the world's biggest air conditioner. But then I never have understood these desert folk. Growing up in Missoula was no metropolis, but at least we had basic amenities. What do the desert folk eat? Where do they shop? What do they do all day? What opportunities are there for the children to become rich and make a difference in the world? But, I guess it's their choice. Being poor is as much a choice as being rich. This is America. If they want money, it is there for the taking. If somebody is poor, it is because they want to be poor. Anybody can start a business and become rich, it just takes some grit.

One of the many reasons I enjoy these rallies so much is that it allows us to inspire kids. Take these kids in Baker, for example. Every day they probably lay around in the desert sand methed out of their minds looking for UFOs with no end (or beginning?) in sight. But then, when Ferraris, Porsches, Maybachs, and Bentleys roll into their baked city, suddenly these kids see something to aspire to. As a mechanic, exposure to high-end luxury cars inspired me to play the lottery; maybe I can inspire the next generation to do the same.

The cars in the rally surround the gas station like a camel caravan at a watering hole. I'd be surprised if the place had any premium fuel left after we're all tanked up. Riley and I arrive with just enough time to fill up and set off with the last group of cars. The rest of the rally has already set out for Vegas. But there's no rush. A rally isn't a race, it's fundamentally a road party. With the sun setting at our backs we set off for the city of sin.

Las Vegas, the world's greatest pinball machine. The marvel of millions of flashing bulbs and the orchestra of slot machines, car horns, and electric bells create an atmosphere of sensory ecstasy. The roads are lined with palm trees and hookers. The sidewalks are bustling with tourists and street performers. And the gutters are cluttered with cans, cups, leaflets, and drunks. Unfortunately, city officials have done a lot in recent years to "clean up" Vegas. Apparently the government thinks they can run a city better than the mafia. But, that said, there is still plenty of real Vegas left for a good time.

With my luck, a trip to Vegas is a fun-filled payday. I have a Midas touch when it comes to slots and craps tables. On a bad night I'll break even. On a good night I'll triple my money and get laid.

Riley and I decide to stop by the hotel and check in before meeting up with the rest of the crew at Tao—the club where tonight's festivities are taking place. We pull into the reception area of the Palms Resort and toss the keys to a lucky valet (chauffeurs will handle the driving for the rest of the night). Bellhops take care of the few bags we brought, and, after a brief visit at reception, we go to the room to spruce up for the evening.

Our suite is Penthouse B (not that B is any less luxurious than A, I just prefer B).

"Everything look alright?" the concierge asks after showing us around the suite.

"Everything looks splendid," Riley says without breaking eye contact with the concierge. During the tour of the penthouse, I could tell Riley was already making plans with the concierge. I can't say I disagreed; the concierge was a fine specimen.

"Superb. In that case, I'll leave you two to your room. Please don't hesitate to ask for anything, we are at your beck and call. Just pick up the phone, say 'concierge,' and tell us what you'd like."

"And what if the concierge is what we'd like?" Riley says, looking the concierge from top to toe and adding as much sauce as possible to the question.

This concierge gave enough of a blush to signal flattery, but not so much as to suggest that the proposal was offensive. "Well," the concierge replied, "when you say 'concierge' into the phone, the resort concierge is automatically put on the line, then from there we handle the request."

Yeah right. This concierge knew what Riley meant. But a little banter never hurt anyone. I figure I'll back up Riley on this one.

"I think you know what we meant," I say, "what if we want you? All of you. And maybe a few of your friends. Do we simply pick up the phone, say 'concierge,' and make our request?"

In the pause that followed, you could tell the concierge was thinking about hiding behind something like, "I am flattered by your offer, but as a concierge for the Palms Resort, I am obligated to decline those types of offers from our guests." But, instead, said, "I get off at 2:00 a.m., is that past your bedtime?"

"Absolutely not. By that time we should have a few more open-minded friends up here and plenty of everything you could ever want."

"Great, see you in a few hours."

This is one of the small bonuses of money. Not that I couldn't have seduced the concierge with my wit and stunning physique alone, but that concierge knows that I have more to offer than just great sex. Obviously I'm rich, which means that I travel with enough cocaine to fuel a small regiment through several nights of heavy partying. It also means that I'm well-connected, that I share my winnings generously, and that hard liquors and fine wines will be flowing like the Colorado River. Not to mention free rides in exotic cars, free gambling, and free five-star food and rooms. The concierge knows the score.

After changing clothes and relaxing in the suite, Riley and I replenish our bloodstreams with more coke and bounce down to the casino. Cue the Tom Jones.

Golden elevator doors swing open and Riley and I step into the array of the gambler's fray. No windows, no clocks, and no clear way out. Clouds of tobacco smoke filled with the lightening of jackpots. I take it all in. The rhythm of the machines, the hope of their operators. Dealers in their uniforms, pit bosses in their suits, servers in their skimpy outfits. Clinking coins cascade into trays; mini waterfalls of metal money. Ringing slots, beeping games, and singing Elvises. Dice bounce across tables, balls spin around wheels, and cards are dealt. But it's not a passive experience. The gambler can be in control. Those that allow themselves to be acted upon in this place lose money, those of us who act upon, make money. See the symbolism? It's as if all of life were packed into one stimulating simulated room.

While Riley and I pull the levers on a few slot machines (word to the wise, the loose machines are always in areas of high foot traffic), I check my Green Mountain app. It's nice to know that even if I have a rare bout of bad luck, I'll still be making thousands of dollars an hour. But the app glitches and shuts off every time I try and open it. I'll restart my phone later.

One of Riley's machines goes wild and coughs up a few hundred bucks in the clinking clanking clatter of the gambler's victory.

"What's the deal? Thought you guys weren't going to make it!" Tim yells over the thumping music.

"Yeah we were a little late getting to the hotel, we had to stop at my place on our way out of town," I half-shout.

"Oh yeah? Everything alright?" Tim is bouncing with the music and his eyes are half closed. His drink is sloshing over the edges of the glass, down his hand, and trickling toward his seventy thousand dollar Patek Philippe, but he doesn't seem to notice.

"Yeah I think so, just some car stuff, you know how that goes."

"Oh definitely. Well hey, now is the time to forget about the bullshit. Rodney is already sloshed as fuck, and he's buying shots for everybody. Here," Tim hands me his drink, "get started with this. Have you had some coke lately? You feeling alright?"

"Yeah Tim, seriously I'm good. Honestly, I've never been better."

Tim probably didn't catch that. He was bobbing off into the crowd toward the bar. Tao always puts on a good show when the Bullrun is in town, and tonight is no different. The DJ tonight is somebody famous (DJ Ex-Scratch) and the crowd is turned up. Confetti cannons keep blasting paper into the air (and our drinks), and fog from the smoke machines amplify the effect of the countless strobe lights and lasers. The music is loud enough to hear with your chest. If a pilgrim from the 1500s discovered time travel and teleported into this room at this time, they would instantly explode. It would be a goddamn mess. Riley and I indulge in a dab of ecstasy and plenty of alcohol at the club, then recruit the best looking people to join us in our penthouse. At the penthouse things get a little wild, but not too wild. Enough wild not to get my deposit back, but not so wild as to be banned from future stays. The concierge shows up with a few friends just after 2:30 a.m. and we give them the best night of their lives. At one point, we recreate sex on the beach but with cocaine instead of sand.

The next morning (well, early afternoon) we need a few gallons of coffee to get up and running, then we repeat the same routine every night for two weeks. Sometimes the parties are more eventful (meaning more drugs, liquor, sex, and property damage), and some nights they are more relaxing (maybe just some weed, lounging, and sex in hot tubs and saunas). Riley and I meet lots of new friends along the way, some of which may become future business associates, most of which will probably just be one-night stands.

The Lamborghini handles the rally like the champion that it is. We were only pulled over once on the entire rally, and it was for going 158 mph in a 65 mph zone. I couldn't help myself. It was on a stretch of desert road through Utah that probably hadn't seen a car in decades and needed some excitement (as a side note, the goal was 200 mph, and I had plenty of road left to make it happen). The cop was cool about it though, saying something like, "Well I can't say as I blame ya, shoot, if I had me a vehicle as fine as this here specimen I may be tempted from time to time to see what she was capable of." The cop made it clear that he could give me a reckless driving citation, tow my car, and even jail me. But, with good ol' fashioned coaxing the officer showed me some friendly western hospitality and only gave me a ticket for 30 mph over and sent us on our way.

Throughout the rally the Lamborghini garnered plenty of attention, but there was a Bugatti Chiron and a Porsche 918 that always drew larger crowds. Which is understandable, I guess. Both of those cars cost around two or three million dollars, whereas my humble Lambo costs just over half a million. Any person with a bit of scratch can afford a Lamborghini, but owning a Bugatti takes real wealth. And people with real wealth know that. I've known for a while that it was time to upgrade into a higher class of vehicle—a higher class of existence—but my recent financial misfortunes have made it difficult. It's not as simple as just selling all your cars and buying a Bugatti. If a Bugatti is the only car you own, it sends a clear signal that you are stretching to look wealthier than you are. I have to keep my collection at the size that it is and add a Bugatti.

I have discussed this and other financial goals with Jamie, and we are on track to be making that sort of money in a few years. I'll finally be able to have a home in the French Riviera and a yacht with which to get there.

The Bullrun Rally comes to a close at the same place it started: Los Angeles. On the final day Mario Andretti chooses to drive Tim's Lamborghini; likely because by the end of the rally they're best buds. There is one final night of partying (this time with champagne instead of vodka) and an awards ceremony, then we all return to our regular routines. The next morning I drop Riley off at the Empire Apartments and we say goodbye with a quickie. When I get home, my Aston Martin is not in my driveway. I'll call Gabby tomorrow. I'll probably sleep for a few days straight. Then it's time to get back to business. The rally has stoked my burning need to become truly wealthy. My days of making money from little startup businesses and side projects are behind me.

In the past few months Green Mountain has done everything Jamie said it would. Steady returns of nearly ten percent *a month*, no losses, and low administrative fees. After I'm rested up I'm going to sell my equity in all the businesses and go all in with Green Mountain.

4

Jamie doesn't answer. I leave a message saying that I'm ready to go all in. A few seconds later Jamie calls back and apologizes for missing my call.

"So, you're ready to take it to the next level?" Jamie asks.

"Definitely. My days of mediocre wealth are numbered. I'm ready to join the ranks of the truly rich. This week I'm going to have my businesses buy me out and I'm going to slide all my chips across the table, so to speak."

"Well, that sounds great, Caish. This is exciting. But, I do just want to caution you against jumping into anything one hundred percent. We do recommend diversification and cash reserves in case the worse were to happen. We can work out the details in person, but let's plan on investing the new money into various Green Mountain accounts. We have lots of options."

"Yeah, sounds good. Either way, I trust your judgment. Diversify it in whatever way you think is best," I say.

There is a brief pause on Jamie's side.

"So how much new money are we talking about here, Caish?" Jamie asks.

"I think I'll do the other ten million that I have from mortgaging the house, and I can probably get a couple million from my business equity. I'll also sell a few more things around the house that I don't need, and that might be another million or so. I haven't sat down with a calculator and figured it all out yet, I just called you first so it could be on your radar."

"Very good, Caish. Very exciting. How about you get the money together, then swing down to my office and we'll take care of all the details. No rush. I'll provide you with all the information you'll need on your new investment portfolio when the money is transferred and diversified."

"Bitchin'. I look forward to it."

"Oh, and Caish, how about dinner afterwards? On me," Jamie adds. I can feel my heartbeat in my ears. I almost choke on my elation.

"That's, er, you... I thought you'd never ask! Yeah, let's definitely plan on it," I manage.

"Great, I look forward to seeing you. Just give me a couple days' notice before you swing down. It's a busy time and I don't want to keep you waiting."

"Perfect. Okay thanks Jamie, see you soon!"

I'm not sure what I'm more excited about, making tens of millions of dollars, or supper and sex with Jamie. We haven't seen each other in months, and I long for Jamie in a way I normally don't feel toward other people. Usually if I don't get what I want out of somebody, I just go to a party, club, or roadside and get it from somebody else. It's similar to a gas station running out of Marlboros so you buy Pall Malls instead. But with Jamie there's something different. I don't think it's just sex appeal; Jamie may be among the most attractive people I've ever seen (and can fuck like a young lion), but I can get great sex from physically perfect eighteen and nineteen year olds any time I want. And it can't be the money: I've never been to Jamie's house, and we haven't been on any trips together, so I only have vague ideas of Jamie's worth. Whatever the reason, I can't wait for our date.

My office is one of my favorite rooms in my house. It's a corner room facing the ocean on the second story of my house. Natural light floods the room through the skylights and the glass walls. The walls that aren't glass are stark eggshell white, and the floor is a grayish hardwood. The furniture in the room is all mid-century modern. My desk is a modern obsidian-top desk with silver legs, my chair is custom built by Fiorano Furnishers using the best black Italian leather, and my shelving and cabinets are a charcoal colored wood behind a lightly frosted glass layer. I flew in Tosca Giacosa (one of the world's most renowned interior decorators) from New York to design and decorate the house, and this room was also her favorite. As a business oriented individual I knew I would spend lots of time in this room, so I was scrupulous. The final touch was an Eames lounge chair. As with all the rooms in my house that face the ocean, the glass walls open up to the deck that runs half the length of the house.

After plenty of coffee, I settle down in the office, light a cigarette, and get to work. My phone calls start with APParatus and Bambooze and throughout the day I work my way down to SomethingSmart and Whimbley's. Most of the companies understand. As if they were waiting for the day this call would come. Others, like Canberra Organics, are quite upset. Whatever, if they can't make it without my money, they don't deserve to make it. Anybody can run a business and become successful. If they have failed to make money (which virtually all of them do) it is because of their own lack of effort. My attorney, Gabby, handles the paperwork associated with wrapping up my business investments. She tells me that it will only take a few weeks to take care of everything.

I call Mindy and tell her she was wrong about Green Mountain. In spite of my newly acquired wealth, she still tells me it's a bad idea. This is what a college education gets you.

Throughout the rest of the week I spend most of my time in my office. All day I'm on the phone and computer lining up sales and consignments. I'm well-connected and I've been hustling since my broke days, so I get top dollar for everything I sell. The next week I drive to dealers, jewelers, brokers, and even pawners to sell gold, jewelry, antiques, clothes, sports memorabilia, art, shoes, and other valuables I find around the house. Near the end of the month my bank accounts are looking healthier than they have in years.

From the equity in my seventeen businesses I earn two million. I make another three-and-a-half million selling art (but not the Pollock), and four million from selling nine of my cars. I make about two million from my stash of diamonds and jewelry.

Selling furniture, antiques, and a few bars of gold brings in another one-and-half million. Add that to the other ten million that I have from mortgaging my house, and that brings my total new cash to almost twenty-three million dollars. Adding my initial Green Mountain investment, plus the interest I've earned on that so far, and my total investment will be almost thirty-five million dollars.

That will leave me two million in the bank. I can pay my mortgage and living expenses with the interest I make from Green Mountain, and everything else I have is paid off. After I get this money to Jamie, I'll sit back and watch my wealth, power, and status grow. This is how rich people make money. Working is for the poor. It won't be long now until problems are a thing of the past for me. True, even the wealthy have mishaps that no amount of money will prevent. Wine doesn't care how expensive your carpet is, and nails puncture the tires of Ferraris and Fords alike. Plus, some problems can't be stamped out; relationship drama, illness, and aging are here to stay ("wealth can't buy health" in the words of Pusha T). But even then, would you rather be sad and dying in a grimy shack in the heart of Mexico City, or in a villa in Monte Carlo? Fact is, money is power against adversity. A bastion against Hopelessness. Obviously people can be happy without achieving great wealth. But wealthless happiness is delicate, fickle, and prone to annihilation at the first signs of strife. Happiness backed by greenbacks is impervious to life's costly trivialities. But I digress.

Jamie and I agree to meet this Friday at four o'clock. Jamie says that will give us plenty of time to get everything situated before dinner. Friday is two days away. Two days to sit around with over twenty million dollars in my bank account.

After setting up the meeting with Jamie, I mosey out back and sit on my diving board with my feet dangling over the ninety-two-degree water. I pop in a cigarette and find that I left my Zippo inside. Dammit. When I'm making money again, I think

I'll hire a butler. I have a small house staff, but they mostly just clean. What I need is somebody who can go get my Zippo when I leave it inside. Seems like the type of job for a butler. And if I'm buying a butler, I might as well buy a Batmobile too. No half-measures.

Having returned from retrieving my lighter, I lie on the diving board, light a smoke, and drift in and out of sleep. I can hear waves below beating against the cliffs. Sounds from the ocean are the most soothing sounds on earth. Probably because we came from the ocean (life, that is). I'm not very religious, but I've heard God started it all in the sea because he was a fisher of men. Or something like that. I wonder if when he hooked women he just threw them back. Catch and release or something.

The diving board starts to itch my back, so I strip down and slink into the pool. I float over to an inflatable doll that somebody left from a party and slide it under my back so I can stay afloat without any effort. In all my wiggling my cigarette dipped in the water, so I drift back to the diving board and light another. Hours waft by without a single movement. Even when I pee, I just lay there without stirring. My ears are underwater, so I only hear the occasional muffled seagull squawk and the whir of the earth. Floating in this lovely place, soaking in this bliss, it seems as if life couldn't get any better. But that's wrong. Floating in a pool in Monte Carlo is better than floating in a pool in Malibu. Or better yet, floating in a pool on a yacht parked on the coast of Monte Carlo.

From where I float, on my left I look over the edge of the infinity pool and across the Pacific, which, forty or fifty feet below, massages the rocks that support my piece of Malibu. To my right, I can see into the ground level of my house, and I can see my piano. Memories of Jamie playing on our first night together consume my thoughts. It was incredible. The night was perfect. So, why was Jamie drifting away? How in the hell could anybody not want to be with me? It sounds conceited to ask, but the question stumps me. I'm sure everybody thinks they are irresistible, but, in all honesty, it's actually the case with me. Yet, I just can't land Jamie. I don't want to bring it up on Friday because I don't want to seem needy or desperate. But I have to do something. Maybe things will change when I get a place in Monte Carlo. I can't wait that long, though.

The next couple of days I spend in roughly the same way. I invite Riley over for late-night sex on Wednesday, and on Thursday I almost buy a French Bulldog. But other than that I just relax, go on drives, and watch Netflix.

On Friday I pull into Green Mountain's parking garage a few minutes early—traffic was lighter than I expected. The elevator takes me to the forty-fifth floor and when the doors slide open I step out into the familiar sights of construction work, but I don't hear any hammering or drilling. It looks like nobody has lifted a hammer in months.

Jamie is waiting for me in the reception area. "Caish! Welcome back. It has been too long."

"Hi Jamie, how are you?"

"I am doing really well, thank you. How are you, Caish? Excited?"

"Yeah, definitely. Little nervous, but mostly excited."

"Good, it's a big day. Let's go to my office." Jamie leads the way.

"When is your construction going to be finished?"

"What's that?"

"I said when are they going to be done with the construction?"

"Oh, yeah sorry about that. Longshoreman's strike or something. Nothing to worry about."

Jamie's office hasn't changed in the months since my first visit. I plop down into the same black chair I sat in last time and look at Jamie. Jamie pours two glasses of Scotch.

"Where is everybody?" I ask.

"It's late on a Friday afternoon, I let everybody leave early.

That is one of the perks, as you know, of working for yourself. To celebrate our growth I've been closing the office at noon every Friday for the past year or so."

"Hm."

Jamie leaned forward, "Caish, check your Green Mountain app. Just have a look."

I pulled out my phone and opened the app. Nothing out of the ordinary, just more green lines and triangles. More money made.

"Am I supposed to be seeing something?" I ask.

"Only that you have made over a million dollars since your first investment just a few months ago. Do you see that?" Jamie is pointing at my phone, "Right there on top. See those numbers?"

Sure enough, I have made over a million already.

"I understand if you're nervous, Caish. And if you can't trust me and Green Mountain, maybe you'd be better taking your money somewhere else. But I can guarantee you that you will not be making nearly the amount of money with any other firm." Jamie had a good point. I am feeling anxious, but the money is really my primary concern.

Jamie went on: "Fear and uncertainty are what keep the poor from making the kind of money we make. They are so afraid of failure that they never try. What if Steve Jobs had taken a job as a salesperson with Microsoft instead of starting Apple? What if he let his fears get the better of him? I'll tell you one thing, Caish, he would not have bought that hundred million-dollar yacht. Let alone changed the world. You just have to ask yourself, are you going to let natural feelings of apprehension keep you from making tens of millions of dollars?" Jamie took a sip of Scotch and looked at me with a look of genuine concern. "You already have proof that Green Mountain will make you rich. Don't let a few nerves stop you from getting your place in Monte Carlo."

"You're right," I reply, "what do you think I came down here to do?"

"Oh, I know. Sorry if that came off wrong. I'm just sensing some nerves on your part, and I wanted to respond to that. You're being vigilant. That's one of the things I love about you. You are always keeping an eye on the details."

"Yeah. Okay we don't have to keep talking about it," I say, "let's get down to business."

Then, after a few phone calls and verifications, Jamie gives me the account number to which I am to wire my twenty-three million dollars. Jamie walks me through the different accounts that my money will go into and specifies exactly how the funds will be diversified. We set up an income plan where my interest will pay me $200,000 a month for the first two years, then $350,000 a month every month after that. Green Mountain's conservative estimation is that within ten years I will have well over two hundred million dollars. At that point I can take out fifty million to live on, and let the other one hundred and fifty million keep making interest. By the time I reach retirement age, that one hundred and fifty mil' will have grown into several billion dollars. Several *billion* dollars. Jamie shows me the math a few times in simple terms to make sure I understand it all. After a few more signatures, Jamie drives us to the bank to make the transfer. The bank's top brass show up for the transfer, and I sign a few more pieces of paper. Then the bank transfers the money. My bank account now has $2,102,313.03 in it, and my total Green Mountain investment is $35,689,917.97.

"Congratulations, Caish! This is huge. Now, let's go celebrate." Jamie motions toward the door.

We shake the bankers' hands, offer a few more pleasantries, then hop in Jamie's BMW and head for WP24 in the Ritz Carlton. On the way over, Jamie is gripping my hand quite tightly.

"Jamie, you seem nervous."

"Not at all," Jamie replies, "quite the opposite. You must be misreading my excitement."

"In either case, could you loosen your grip? My fingers are

starting to tingle."

"Oh! Sorry. I didn't notice." Jamie says, letting up. After a brief silence, Jamie adds, "It's just that, with your investment the entire firm stands to make a lot of money. You, of course, will make the most, but all of us at Green Mountain will benefit from your investment. We have had a few other big investments this year, and I am thrilled about where the firm is heading. We are going to have a very good year. So I'm just excited, that's all."

"You're not alone," I respond, gazing out of the passenger window. "After years of working toward my financial goals, I'm finally about to accomplish them. In a few years I'll be able to buy a Bugatti Chiron, a few years after that I'll buy that place in Monte Carlo, and then, at last, I will buy my own yacht."

Jamie smiles and gives me a sideways glance, "Tell me about the yacht."

"Have you ever seen the yacht Steve Jobs built? I think it's called Venus or something."

"Ooooh yeah, I've seen it. It's so minimal and perfect. That's the design you're thinking?"

"Yeah, except mine will be black."

"Classy," Jamie says softly, "but, that's a pretty pricey yacht."

"Not when you're a billionaire."

"Ah, very true, Caish. Wow, what an exciting time. This is really great."

I give Jamie more details about the yacht and then about my place in Monte Carlo. When we arrive at the Ritz Carlton, a valet takes care of the car and we ride the elevator up to the twenty-fourth floor. WP24 is chic, low-lit, and filled with some of the finest citizens in Los Angeles. The floor space is huge, and the ceilings are high, yet there's a coziness to the place. The outside walls are floor to ceiling glass, giving the restaurant a sweeping view of the Los Angeles skyline, which, at the moment, is warmly lit by a tangerine sunset. A piano player is filling the room with a soft melody, and the guests' conversations join in a low murmur — as if most of them are discussing hushed mafia operations.

Jamie arranged for us to have a table next to a window wall, and for a little while after we are shown to our seats, we stare out at the skyline in silence. I've never been sure why the settlers of this city named it Los Angeles. I don't speak Spanish, but I know it means "The Angels." Why name a city "The Angels" instead of just "Heaven"?

"Jamie," I break our silence, "why do you think the settlers of this city named it Los Angeles?"

"Hm. Good question."

A server approaches our table with waters and Jamie orders us a bottle of wine with a name that I can't pronounce. Jamie also orders lobster spring rolls to give us something to snack on while we peruse the menus.

"Maybe the settlers saw angels here when they first arrived," Jamie answers.

"You don't think they were referring to themselves?"

"What do you mean?"

"Well," I say, "maybe they thought they were angels for having established such an important place. Like, they were angels bringing the rest of the world a gift from heaven."

"Maybe," Jamie says, "or maybe it's just angel ridden. We could always Google it."

"Nah, let's not get our phones out. I just want to experience this. This view. This dinner. This night — a night I'm sure we'll think back on for the rest of our lives."

"You're absolutely right," Jamie says, raising a glass, "it calls for a toast. To your bravery in investing, to your ambition in living, and to the rest of your wealthy life."

"Our wealthy lives," I correct. "I want you to be there too Jamie."

We drink to the toast. The wine tastes sweet, almost like dried cherries.

"You know I will be, Caish. I'm not going anywhere," Jamie declared. "I'm sorry I have been distant lately, but that shouldn't cause you worry. You met me at a strange time in my life, but that's all behind me now. After this weekend I'll have a lot more free time."

"What is strange about your life?" I ask.

"I'll explain it all later," Jamie responds. "We'll have plenty of time to talk. But, I'm with you. Let's live in the moment tonight and not be distracted by our pasts. By the way, do you have plans this weekend?"

"Not really, why?"

"Because, like I mentioned, this weekend I'm still pretty busy, but after this weekend I'll have a lot of free time. As a token of my apology for being unavailable, I bought you a suite here at the Ritz for the weekend. All expenses paid, have whatever you want, enjoy their spa, room service, and whatever else you'd like through Monday morning. Then—"

"Jamie, I don't need you to buy me—"

"Well just hold on, Caish, there's more. Then, on Wednesday, I am flying us to Villa Corallina in Tahiti, where we can relax and get to know each other a little better. Right now I have a booking for two weeks, but we can stay longer if you want."

That does it. All my hopes are becoming reality.

Jamie, probably sensing that my emotions have the better of me, doesn't let the silence get uncomfortable. Reaching across the table, Jamie takes my hand, and, with a gentle squeeze, says, "Let's start over, Caish. This time, no business. No Green Mountain between us. We'll move your account over to another one of our senior executives and you and I can focus on us. Your money will blossom into something beyond your imagination; my hope is that our love can do the same."

"Love?" I squawk.

"Let's stop acting. We know what this is. Maybe it's not there yet, but it's well on its way. I know you've been feeling what I have. When you lay in bed, plug in your phone, and roll over into the darkness, whose face do you see?"

"Yours."

"Caish, when I'm not with you, my heart literally feels heavy. As if it's weighed down by your absence. I know I'm not the only one feeling this way. Tell me you feel it to."

"I do," I manage to control my emotions enough to turn some thoughts into words, "of course I do. Jamie, you have no idea how much this means to me. For months now I thought I was going to have to learn how to live without you. It seems childish for me to have such a yearning for somebody I have only spent one night with, but there's something about you, Jamie. There's something about us."

"I know. And we start tonight," Jamie says. "Then—just give me the weekend—then on Wednesday we'll begin the rest of our lives. Enjoy your stay here at the Ritz. Lose yourself in their amenities and let your problems dissolve away. Don't think about any bills, forget about the repossessions, and let the Ritz Carlton take you to heaven."

"How do you know about the repossession?"

"You mentioned it a couple weeks ago. Your Aston Martin, you said."

"Hm. Weird, I didn't think I mentioned that." In fact, I'm sure of it. I would never tell Jamie that one of my cars was repossessed, and I *certainly* would not mention that another may soon be repossessed. Jamie must have seen it in one of the financial checks they do at Green Mountain.

"Yeah, you said something about it," Jamie says. "But anyway, don't worry about it. Don't think about it this weekend, enjoy yourself. Then on Wednesday we'll take a real vacation."

"What about my car? My Lamborghini is still parked in your building. I'm not sure I want to leave it there all weekend."

"Just leave the keys with me and I'll have our runner drop it off tonight or tomorrow morning. The same guy that did it last time. You can trust him."

"Let's just go back tonight and bring it to the hotel. It's what, a couple miles away?"

"Nah," Jamie says, "I don't want to interrupt our evening. I'll take care of it tomorrow."

"But it would be nice to have my car here for the weekend, in case I want to go anywhere."

"No, you don't want that hassle. Ubering will be easier. Plus, valets, even at the Ritz, are still valets. You don't want them having access to your car. You'll feel better about your car being parked safely in your driveway. Trust me."

"But I won't be home to open the gate. Your runner won't be able to get it into the driveway."

"I'll just text you when he's there and you can open the gate for him. Your smart home app works at any distance, right?"

"Yeah..."

"Great, then it's as easy as that. Don't worry about it, Caish. Really, I'll take care of everything. After all this, do you still not trust me?"

"No, no, it's not that. I do trust you. Here, here's the key."

"And the garage door opener is in the car?"

"No, I use the app for that too. Plus, I may trust your runner to drive my car home, but not to have access to my garage and house."

"Oh I agree, Caish, I just wanted to make sure it was parked where you want it," Jamie says. "Now, can we stop discussing minutiae and enjoy the evening?"

"Yes, please," I say.

"Excellent. I propose another toast," Jamie says. We raise our glasses and Jamie continues, "To you, Caish, who has the knowledge to know when to act, the courage to make money, and the wherewithal to know who to trust. And to us, the most important couple in Los Angeles. Cheers!"

"Cheers!"

"Tonight we're going to learn why they call this city the City of Angels."

If I have had a better night in my life, I do not remember it. The night I won the lottery was outstanding, but this is a whole 'nother category of joy. Jamie and I talk about my past, my present, and our future. For the first time in my life, I feel a real connection. This must be what love feels like. Real love, not love for a parent or a dog or a child. Like wealth, there are varying levels of love. Real, adult to adult, passionate, lust-filled, trusting love is what we have. Real love has finally arrived in my life. And it's all thanks to the greatest match-maker of all: money.

We dine on steak that tastes like it was prepared by God himself. The wine hardly tastes sour, our desserts are delicately sweet, and the Louis XIII cognac polishes off the meal with a remarkable richness.

After dinner we go shopping for swimsuits and clothes for my weekend at the Ritz. Then we go back to the hotel and head to the rooftop pool. The glittering lights of LA completely surround the Ritz Carlton, but the sounds of the city barely make it past the glass walls surrounding the pool. We relax on the patio furniture for a while and talk about socialites who don't deserve their money, then step into the pool. Hotel pools are usually too cold, but the temperature of this water is perfect. Probably the exact temperature of my pool.

In the pool, and later in the hot tub, we can't keep our hands off each other. Jamie and I tug at each other's swimsuits, but refrain from getting too carried away in front of the other guests. We curse the transparency of water. The second time Jamie's hand slips below my waistline we know it's time to put on our robes and get to the room.

Jamie's robe drops in the elevator, and mine falls somewhere in the hallway. Had we left the room key at the pool, we likely would have fucked right there in the hall. Luckily that isn't the case and we make it inside just in time. Our swimsuits are the last pieces of cloth blocking the expressway to ecstasy. Jamie tears my swimsuit off with an almost feral ferocity. The time for foreplay passed along with our self-control back in the elevator, and we are well on our way before we hit the bed. When we finally fuck, my toes are pointing so hard I get charlie horses in both calves. Our fingers dig like claws into each other's backs. Our skin wets with sweat and our bodies clap to our dance. We gasp, groan, and scream, vocalizing our savagery. Barbarians didn't fuck this hard. Jamie's stamina rivals mine. After several orgasms we sense each other closing in on the final climax. Jamie is on top. We cling tighter, thrust harder, and yell louder. Speed and movement give way to rigid tension as every muscle flexes. A few tremors move through us in the final seconds of rapture. Jamie collapses onto me and we lay on the bed, hearts thumping.

As we lay, other than our panting and a few "hoooly fuck"s under our breath, it's quiet. Then we hear the elevator bell ring and laughter down the hall. Exhausted, I crawl to the end of the bed and look toward the door. Light from the hallway shines through the room's entryway. My sprawling robe is holding the door open.

5

The Los Angeles Ritz Carlton is an oasis inside of an oasis. Which is always how I've thought of my house, but being in the heart of LA in this kind of comfort is a special experience. In Malibu it's easy to forget how rich you are because everybody else is just as rich. But downtown, you are constantly reminded of your status by the ever-present froth of homeless riffraff. With Jamie back in the office for the weekend, I have some time to explore the city alone. And, as if I didn't already feel like I was on top of the world, the denizens of Los Angeles remind me just how high above them I am.

It's best not to look directly at them, but sometimes it's hard to resist the unwholesome urge to stare at these vermin. Especially when they're yelling things like "Thazz it! Puzzy gawd dammit! Whad I tell ya 'bout dem bagel shoez!? Huh!? I says *Brenda* would—ya hear me!?—*Brenda* gon' be drivin' south t'morrow! Repent! Only through Lawrd gawd Jayzuz can ya enter inta paradise! Caaaaamel's eye!" And they gesture like possessed Italians: fingers snapping, arms flailing, head twisting and twitching, eyes rolling every which way (and not always in unison), and a slouched crooked walk on the brink of collapse. Their hair usually looks like something pulled out of a shower drain. Their dirt-caked clothing probably has entire communities of undiscovered plant and animal life. Oh and the smell—medieval stenches that could kill canaries.

I don't understand why LA puts up with this shit. Why not just send them all to Baker? Give them a free ticket to the desert and teach them to farm the land. Let them be self-sufficient out there. I heard there are over fifty thousand homeless people in Los Angeles alone. That's more than the total population of most cities. Fifty thousand vagrants crawling through the streets, bringing violence, filth, and drugs—and not the good kind—

to all who happen to work or live in their path. Their march is slow, like a glacier of trash, tarps, and shopping carts moving through canyons of buildings. And it's completely hopeless. When Reagan cut funding for California's mental hospitals the state drained the bedlam out of the institutions and into the gutters. So there's nothing to be done except to ship them out. It's either that, or let the city's foundation continue to rot. If I haven't already moved to Monaco in a few years maybe I'll become mayor and clean this place out.

I get back to the hotel around two or three in the afternoon. The day's shopping has exhausted me. I eat gourmet room service and relax by the pool, then go to the spa for a full body massage. The therapist asks if I have any soreness or tight spots, then gets to work.

I put my face into the strange donut pillow and just before I close my eyes I notice a tile mosaic on the floor. It's a detailed mosaic of the earth. It's detailed enough to have wispy clouds and different shades of green and brown. I'm right over China. This must be what God's view is like. Actually, this is surely exactly what it's like to be God. Angels probably give pretty good massages. God. What a weird guy. Some say God is angry at the world and that things are worse now than they've ever been. These are the same type of people who claim money can't buy happiness. I can see where they're coming from. God never helped me, I've had to work for everything I have. I earned it myself. Truth is (and I am sure there are statistics to support this) the world is better now than it has ever been. The standard of living around the world is higher now than ever before. Just check Facebook for proof of that. We're doing great. Old ladies complain that the decline in society's morals is evidence that the apocalypse is at our doorstep. They forget that selling sex is the oldest profession in the world. If anything, society's morals are improving; everybody is always clamoring to donate to some bullshit relief fund or feed-the-poor program. Sure, maybe climate change will wipe us all out in a few years, but I doubt it. The world isn't ending anytime soon. And I know a lot of religious people can't stomach that, because they're positive that Jesus is going to descend from the clouds and they'll never have to die and they can tell all their friends, "see you bunch a sinners, I told you I was right about Jesus saving me and not you." But Jesus is only coming if the world is ending, so these people point to every flake of bad news as evidence that the world is ending and that Jesus is coming and avoid acknowledging all the good news that outweighs the bad ten to one. Bunch of short-sighted, narrow-minded zealots that would give anything to have their prophecies come true, but wouldn't pay a dime for the truth.

"Is that too much pressure?"

The massage therapist's elbow is making circling motions in my lower back.

"Ah... no, that's just right."

After an hour or so, while the therapist is massaging my legs, I slip into a dreamless sleep. The therapist wakes me up with "Caish, we're all done. Would you like to relax in here for a little while?"

"No thanks, I'll get going. Phew, I must have slipped off there. That was very relaxing."

"Don't worry about it, you're not the first." Then, as the therapist is walking out the door, "There is coffee, water, and snacks in the lounge. Have a wonderful day, we hope to see you again soon."

I take my time putting my robe back on, then check out the lounge. While sipping on the Ritz's exceptionally brewed coffee, I browse the colorful—heavy on the yellow—pamphlets advertising attractions for tourists. It's fun to see how tourists experience my city. Trips to Santa Catalina Island, whale watching, swimming with dolphins, jet ski rentals, bus tours, celebrity tours, and all the other activities you'd expect. There are even biplane tours.

"Perfect for the traveler looking for the thrill of a lifetime!" the pamphlet tells me. "Get a bird's-eye view from an open cockpit of Los Angeles, Laguna Beach, Hollywood, Malibu, and more! Day and night tours available, call ahead for available times and booking." Why not? I fly all the time, but I've never flown in a biplane. The wind in my hair and the divine view of my city sounds like the perfect way to spend my evening. I take the pamphlet back to my room. After a steamy shower that may have lasted an hour, I call the number on the pamphlet and set up a ride for tonight's Sunset Special.

I tan by the pool for an hour then freshen up for my first biplane ride. Jamie had my car delivered back to my house, so I take a cab to Fullerton Airport. The tour company's little tin shack hardly hides the yellow biplane parked behind it. My insides braid themselves into a knot of nerves at the first sight of that old bird. There's a yellow banner on the side of the shack with the words "Fly LA *By* Plane" in bold cheesy letters. Before I can fly I have to go through the rigmarole that lawyers have created. First, I am subjected to an orientation video, then a safety lesson. Then I have to sign a bunch of forms and pay the thousand dollars or whatever it costs. And even after that, I'm still given an abbreviated safety refresher after I sign the forms.

The pilot, who could pass as Chuck Yeager's son, meets me as I walk onto the runway and asks me about any specific requests.

"I have a house on the coast in Malibu, could we fly low over that?"

"Absolutely, our flight path tracks right up the coast. We'll be close enough for your neighbors to see you wavin'. Maybe even close enough for a brief chat. Why don't you text 'em and tell 'em to look out for us in about forty-five minutes."

"Oh, nah. I don't really know my neighbors that well."

"New to the area are we?"

"Sort of, yeah."

"Well, if you were ever in need of an ice breaker, this autta do it. Let's suit up."

We put on period-correct flight suits, headsets, and leather helmets. We even have those goggles that have two pieces of straight glass for each eye. The pièce de résistance is a black ascot tied around my neck. The plane is a two seater, and I get the front seat, just a few feet back from the massive propeller. I climb onto the wing and clamber into the cockpit. The pilot makes sure my belts are tight and checks the radio.

"Now just as a reminder, we'll be able to hear each other perfectly fine up there," the pilot says, tapping the ear of his headset, "so if you need anything, just ask. Also, should you feel airsick, this here bag to your left is going to be the best place to blow chow. I'll be just behind you, so if you blow chow into the wind, I'm not gonna be a happy camper. Lastly, let me know if you get light headed. Don't want you passin' out and missin' the views!"

Satisfied that I'm not going to become a lawsuit, the pilot hoists himself into the cockpit behind me and, from the sounds of it, starts pressing buttons and pulling knobs.

"You ready to go up there, Caish?"

"Yes, sir!"

"Alrighty, sit back and enjoy the ride!"

With that, a starter motor kicks and with a few pops, sputters, and bangs, the propeller starts to spin. The smells of the vintage airplane vanish in the gale wind sent back from the propeller. It's loud, but not as loud as I expected. The plane nudges forward, and I tense up with excitement. My knot gets tighter. It all feels slightly rickety. Far from safe. The back of the plane swivels back and forth as we taxi around the runway. We wait for a few minutes while a private-plane lands, then move out to another runway. I've been on a lot of runways in my life, but never has one looked so large than from the cockpit of this little airplane. We're like a tiny toy plane on a freeway.

"Ready for take-off?" The pilot's southern voice comes

through my headphones without a crackle.

I give him a thumbs up, then return my hand to its iron grip on the handhold by my legs. The propeller's rotation speeds up and our acceleration is about as dramatic as that of a Volkswagen Beetle. The rear of the plane lifts into the air and the plane is level. The trip down the runway lasts for all of ten seconds and we're already climbing into the air. It seems like we're going way too slow.

The wind shoves my microphone into my lips and I almost swallow it when I open my mouth to shout, "Are we going fast enough?" We're flying at less than freeway speeds. I drive faster than this.

"Yup! These little fellas don't need nearly as much speed as large commercial aircraft. Also, no need to yell, I can hear you loud and clear."

"Just seems like paper airplanes need more speed than this to fly."

"Haha, maybe so, Caish, but, nonetheless, here we are at about three hundred feet and climbin'. Never in all my days have I seen a paper airplane do that."

The air is warm and clear. The old machine carries us up toward the pastel clouds with just enough shake to keep me on edge. I'm white-knuckling the leather-wrapped grips as I watch the ground shrink away. We bank hard and fly southish over the ocean along the shoreline. The little people down on the beach seem even less significant from this height. From up here I can't see their sunburns or the brand of swimsuit they're wearing, just that they are there. Sitting or walking, swimming or bobbing, sleeping or talking, just people. Thousands of them. Tiny dots with all their own webs of trivial drama and meaningless futures. Each one of them sure that they are unique. That they are above average in every way. That God knows their name and helps them find a parking spot when they are running late to their toddler's dance recital.

I take a picture for Facebook and caption it "Tiny People, Tiny Problems. #nofilter." Oh, Mia just posted. Looks like she's back from her scuba-diving trip in Cozumel. Wow, it looks beautiful. Such clear water. Maybe I'll go there later this summer. And Mia's girls look wonderful. They have been posting ten selfies a day every day of their trip. Don't blame them. Selina posted a video of her and Tim driving down PCH with the top down in one of Tim's Ferraris. Ah man, looks like a few friends went out on Kelsey's yacht last night without inviting me. Not that I would have joined, but what the hell? No invitation? New notifications. Invited to like another photography page. Three likes already on my picture of those tiny people. I'll post it to Instagram too. "Tiny People, Tiny #firstworldproblems #malibulife." New notifications. I have six new followers. Tim just posted a picture of his Ferrari at Mugu Point. Mia's daughters are blowing up Instagram too. Oh God, I don't know whose French Bulldog this is (@frenchfryfinny), but this video of the little pup taking a bath is the single cutest thing on this planet.

"Alrighty, Caish, we have reached our cruisin' altitude for the evenin'. We're gonna head down to San Clemente then make our way up the coast until we get to Oxnard, then we'll fly on back. 'Course we'll wiggle our wings at your house on our way through Malibu. As we fly by Manhattan Beach we'll take a lil' detour and go look around the City of Angels. The sun should be settin' just as we arrive downtown. Sound like a good plan?"

"Sounds good!"

"And how ya feelin' up there? Nauseous or anything?"

"Nope, feelin' great," I say. "Any peanuts or beverages?"

"Haha, I'm afraid not on this flight, although we'll have plenty of refreshments waitin' for you back at the airport."

The little plane takes us down the coast at a leisurely pace. We turn around above Laguna Beach. The sun is setting on our left, and I can already see the glimmer of LA's skyline. When we fly into the city the sun has just dipped into the ocean. A hundred shades of orange fill the sky and reflect off the city's glass. The buildings themselves light up the evening with the yellows and whites of millions of fluorescent bulbs. Downtown looks like a bunch of megaliths put on their best glass and got together for cocktails. Static giants chatting about their human infestations.

We make a long sweeping turn over Dodger Stadium to fly back to the coast. I remember my first night with Jamie. The passion each time we've been together is more than I've ever felt with anybody else. Our future is all I can think about. Well, that and money, of course. I take a picture and text it to Jamie.

"Dodgers fan?" the pilot asks.

"Sure am, and I have some great memories from that stadium."

"Well don't be shy with that camera, plenty of views up here I wouldn't blame you for wantin' to remember."

The pilot makes a good point. These will look great on Facebook and Instagram.

The sun has now sunk into the ocean, but the sky is still full of fading oranges and purples.

"That's my place right there on that cliff," I point down to my palace.

"That big white one?"

"Yup!"

"Not bad! Let's get a closer look."

We fly over my house low enough to make out the blow-up doll in my pool. Jesus. My house is the best. Modern architecture tastefully designed to complement the natural surroundings. My automated lights have turned on, so the pool, yard, and exterior of the house are lit such that passersby are forced to recognize the house's beauty twenty-four hours a day. Like me, my house is perfectly manicured. Not so much as a blade of grass out of order. You can tell almost everything you need to know about a person just by looking at the car they drive and the house they live in.

Speaking of which, where is my Lamborghini? It's not in the

driveway. I realize Jamie never text me asking me to open the gate.

The pilot wiggles the wings and his southern voice comes on over the headset, "Now you be sure and let your neighbors know that we were the ones buzzin' your neighborhood. If they mention your name when they fly with us we'll give you twenty-five percent off your next ride."

"Oh that's great. Yeah I'll be sure and mention it" if I ever talk to them.

I text Jamie again (still no response to the Dodger Stadium text): "Jamie, I just flew over my house. Lambo not in driveway. What's up?"

This time Jamie texts back right away, "Wow! That looks like fun! Great pictures! Your car is fine, I took it to the Lamborghini dealership in Newport for a full detail. Just wanted to surprise you. I'll get it back before we leave to Tahiti. Trust me."

"Alright, but you gotta tell me about shit like that."

"You just need to trust me, Caish. I trust you, you should trust me."

"Okay. You're right. See you Wednesday."

"Can't wait."

On our way back to the airport I text Mia to see if she will come enjoy the Ritz Carlton with me tonight.

"What time does the pool close?" she asks.

"I don't know, but even if the pool closes, you should still come down. For the room service alone."

"K. ttyl."

The biplane lands in on its front wheels, then bounces back onto its back wheel before squatting onto all of its wheels and slowing down.

"Thank you choosin' Fly LA By Plane tonight," the pilot says as we taxi back to the shack. "We have just touched down in Fullerton Airport where the weather is a balmy 82 degrees and the local time is 8:48 p.m."

"Haha, thank you sir, it was my pleasure."

"Help yourself to the refreshments back at home base. I wish I could stay and chat, but I've got a night tour startin' in about twenty minutes."

"Sounds good, thanks for the great flight!"

After returning the company's clothes and goggles, I take a cab back to the Ritz. I change and get ready for the evening. Reception tells me that the pool is open daily from 7:00 a.m. to 10:00 p.m. It's 9:32 p.m. I text Mia and let her know that the pool closes in a half hour. She says in that case she'll come down tomorrow. And that's what she does.

The next day I meet Mia and her daughters in the hotel lobby at about 8:00 p.m. Her daughters, about 7 and 10, are pattering around looking crosswise at the art and guests hanging around the lobby. The seven-year-old is already wearing her goggles and snorkel. She makes a honking noise through her snorkel as she duck-walks in circles around Mia. We take the elevator to the twenty-sixth floor. When the elevator doors slide open Mia's giggling daughters blast out and nearly bowl over a group of retirees. Mia yells after her daughters to come back and apologize but they're already cannonballing into the pool, so Mia apologizes with a shrug and a face that says, "You know how kids are, don't blame me, what are you gonna do?"

Mia and I relax poolside before getting into the hot tub.

"So, I don't think I ever asked," Mia says, "why are you staying at the Ritz Carlton this weekend? Isn't this a Monterey weekend for you?"

"Yeah, it normally would be, but Jamie surprised me with a weekend here."

"Ooooooo, Jamie huh?" Mia was all smiles—elementary school recess gossip smiles. "So is Jamie finally making all of your dreams come true? It's about damn time, Caish."

"Haha, you're telling me. It looks like it's finally moving in that direction."

"K, for real, Caish, give me the deets."

After a refresher on how Jamie and I met and all the time between then and now, I tell her about Friday night and our plans in Tahiti.

"Damn," Mia says as she nudges suds. "Jamie said love?"

"Yeah, that was the word. Love."

"And what do you think? You buy that?"

"What do you mean?"

"I dunno, I mean, you've been with Jamie what, three or four times? Over the span of four or five months?"

"So?" What is Mia suggesting? Just because she can't find love none of the rest of us can?

"I'm just saying," Mia says, "doesn't it seem a little quick? Has Jamie been to Monterey with you yet?"

"Not yet, but we'll go as soon as we get back from Tahiti."

"So has Jamie even met Mark?"

"Not yet, but—"

"Does Jamie even know about Mark?"

"Um, I think I've mentioned him, yeah. But—"

"Caish, you think you may have mentioned in passing that you have a son in Monterey?"

"I just can't remember if we've talked about it yet, but I don't see how that changes anything."

Mia stands up and sits on the edge of the hot tub, leaving her feet and shins in the water. A portly man eases into the hot tub and smiles at us as if to say, "Great night for a conversation with strangers in a hot tub, right?" We give him a smile that says, "Sorry, no thank you."

"Either way, why are you so concerned about it?"

"I'm not concerned," Mia says, "I'm just surprised you're so head-over-heels for somebody you hardly know and who hasn't met your son. I guess it makes sense if Jamie is fuck-you rich, but it still seems quick. Does Mark know about Jamie?"

"Mia, it's not like we're getting married, Jamie just labeled a feeling between us. In Jamie's opinion it's love, and I don't think that's such a bad thing."

The portly man was now staring into the suds, his face said, "Dammit."

"Maybe not, but being blinded by passion for a rich attractive person is what ended my career as a real estate agent and started my career as a single mom. From your perspective I can see... well, never mind."

"Mom, watch!" One of the Cortez children shouts. Looks like the seven year old has just learned how to do backflips off the side of the pool. "Very nice sweetie, just remember to jump far out from the edge. Don't want to bonk your noggin."

"What were you going to say?" I ask.

"Nothing, I was just gonna say I can see where you wouldn't have learned that lesson yet."

"What lesson?" I ask. I crawl up and sit on the edge of the hot tub. The portly man takes his leave with a smile that says, "Okay nice chat, have a nice night."

"Just that life isn't easy for the ones left holding the bag."

"Holding the bag?"

"Yeah." Mia walks over to a lounge chair and dries off.

"Mia, what's that supposed to mean?" I follow her to the chair and dry off. "Are you jealous or something?"

"No, Caish, I'm not jealous. Forget I asked, I'm just surprised that things are moving so fast with somebody you hardly know and who you haven't introduced to your son."

I have an even temperament, so I keep smiling. I'm not going to let Mia get to me. Not sure why she feels the need to be so goddamn matriarchal at the moment. But, I can see why she's bitter. I would envy me too. I drop it and we watch her daughters without speaking. After a little while I figure I'll dispel some of this tension.

"Mia, have you called Green Mountain yet? I told you about

them right?"

"You sure have. That's where Jamie works, and that's how your making so much money right now."

"Yeah, have you still not called them?"

"I called a few months back when you were first telling me about it, but they never answer my calls."

"They're always swamped, I'll talk to Jamie. Do you have at least $500,000 to get started?"

"Yeah, I think. I can always sell some stock if I need to. Is that some sort of minimum buy-in?"

"Yeah, otherwise it's not worth their time."

"Hm."

"You're missing out on mega money as long as you're not investing with them."

Mia, leaning toward the pool, "Honey don't spit the water. Don't put that water in your mouth, it's disgusting. You've probably already peed in that, and now you're drinking it. Don't do that. Seriously. Disgusting." She leans back on the chair and continues, "You think it's all legit, huh?"

"I've made hundreds of thousands of dollars already."

"Don't such big returns make you nervous?"

"Nope, that's just how Green Mountain does things. Plus, Penn—have you met Penn?"

"No."

"Oh, but I've talked about her before, right?"

"Um, yeah I think. Is she the one that got you into Green Mountain?"

"Yeah, that's Penn, anyway, Penn has made a shit ton of money with Green Mountain too. So it's not just me. I'll text Penn and see if she wants to come down, you can talk to her about it."

While I'm searching through our pile of belongings for my phone, Mia says, "Oh don't worry about it, I should get the kids back."

"What do you mean? You haven't even seen my room yet."

"We're not leaving right now, but I probably won't be around long enough for Penn to get here, and I'm not really in the mood for a financial seminar right now."

"Okay, I won't text Penn, never mind. But why not stay the night? My room has a king size bed and one of those pull-out couch/bed things. We can have a slumber party with your daughters, they'd love it."

"Sounds like a good time, but Ryan" (Mia's ex) "will be at my place early tomorrow morning to pick up the girls. They're going to Disneyland tomorrow. Really we should be getting back soon." Then turning to her girls, "Alright kiddos, let's get dried off, it's getting late."

"Mia, I don't know if I hurt your feelings or something, but you don't need to leave, you've been here less than an hour. How about this: let me buy you and the girls a room here at the Ritz, get all the room service you want. My way of saying sorry about whatever it is you're upset about. It's been too long since we've spent time together, and I would hate to see you leave on a somber note."

"If I wanted to stay here I would buy my own room, I don't need you to buy things for me." Mia stands up and pulls her sweater on over her swimsuit. "I'm not leaving because I'm bugged, Caish, I forgot about the early morning tomorrow."

"Come on, Mia, what's up? What did I say?"

"Really, nothing."

"It's Jamie, isn't it? You're jealous of Jamie."

"Oh for Christ's sake, Caish."

"What? I'm right, right? We kind of had a thing for a while, two struggling single parents with financial problems on the horizon. And now that I'm—"

"Ha! Single parent?" Mia was now drying off her daughters with enough rigor to wipe the fuzz off their skin. "You think just because you have a son and you're single that you're a single parent?"

I stood up and helped Mia gather her things, "Well... that seems to make sense to me, but—"

"Caish, you have no idea what it's like to be a parent. And you have no idea what it's like to be single. You are not a single parent. You have to be a parent first. You can't just buy a house for your ex and your son and call yourself a good parent."

"I have bought Mark a lot more than just that house. And he is a very grateful son."

"When was the last time you even talked to Mark?"

"It has been a little while, but that's just because my place in Monterey is getting renovated." Which was mostly true. I'm adding a garage.

"Are there no hotels in Monterey?"

"I—"

"Doesn't matter, Caish. Don't bother." Mia was now walking toward the exit. I start to follow but decide against it. Mia and her daughters (who's wide eyes show they sense trouble) march inside and out of sight. I sit back down on the lawn chair and check my phone. Few notifications. I set my phone down and look around. There's the portly guy. Now his face says, "Yeesh."

This is my last night at the Ritz and I'm not going to let Mia's temper tantrum spoil it.

Texting, "Riley, I'm at the Ritz Carlton downtown, you up for a good time?"

No response.

Still no response.

"Riley?"

"Sry, busy 2nite."

Looks like I'm ordering out. Selina Rayburn gave me the number of a high-end escort service that I've been meaning to check out. I have more than enough yeyo for two (or three...) and I'll be damned if I squander the night feeling sorry for Mia. This is one of my last nights being single, I'm going to make it a night to remember.

6

Monday. Two days to go until my much deserved vacation to Tahiti. The stay at the Ritz Carlton this past weekend was relaxing, but I need a break from Los Angeles. A change of scenery from this grind.

My taxi pulls through my opening gate, down my driveway, and parks in the roundabout next to my fountain. The driver hops out and lugs my bags out of the trunk and up to my front door (I had to buy new clothes for my stay at the Ritz, plus I picked up some new luggage and swimwear for Tahiti). I tip him $500 and head in for a nap. I'm always tuckered out after getting home from a trip.

My house is just how I left it. The Pollock painting in my entryway, looking more ominous than the last time I saw it. I'm going to shower, then nap, then catch up on business. The clack of my leather soles on the marble floor echoes through the 8,000 square feet of modern architecture and design. When all my windows, doors, and walls are closed it's alarmingly quiet in here. I clack over to my sweeping staircase, clack up the hardwood stairs, and clack down the hall to my room. After a half-hour, scalding-hot shower and a couple-hour nap I feel refreshed and ready for the afternoon.

First matters of business: order lunch and schedule the delivery of my Lamborghini. I haven't heard from Jamie since Saturday night's text, so I assume Beverly Hills Lamborghini is waiting for me to come pick it up.

"Yes? This is Ichiban Sushi."

"Hi, this is a delivery order. Bring me a sunrise roll, a crunchy spicy tuna roll, a lion king roll, and a nigiri platter. And a Coke. And an order of edamame. And can you include ponzu sauce on the side for the sunrise roll?"

"Okay, sunrise, crunchy spicy tuna, lion king, nigiri platter, and edamame with a Coke. That all?"

"Yeah, and the ponzu sauce on the side, right?"

"Yes, yes, ponzu sauce on the side."

I give them my card number and address and they give me the usual 30 to 40 minute delivery window. Which is really pretty quick when you consider that it's sushi they're delivering. Next order of business.

"Hello Lamborghini Beverly Hills, how may I direct your call?" said a lovely young receptionist. They must vet their receptionists based on how young and soothing their voices sound.

"My Lamborghini Aventador was dropped off on Saturday for a detailing, and I was just calling to have somebody drive the car back up to Malibu, or to have it trailered up."

"Okay, no problem, and what is your name?"

"Caish Calloway. C-A-I-S-H, C-A-L-L-O-W-A-Y."

"Great, just hold on a sec and I'll check on your car."

"K, thanks."

No hold music, thank the gods.

"Caish?"

"Yeah I'm still here."

"Did somebody else bring your car in, or would your car have been left under anybody else's name?"

"Oh yeah, sorry, Jamie Lowell. It's the cocaine-white Aventador. Saturday is when it was taken in."

"Alright, just one second... and you said Jamie dropped it off this Saturday?"

"Yeah, just a few days ago."

"Okay, hold on another second for me..." her voice trailed off. A second turned into ten, then thirty, then a minute or two crawled by. This was certainly out of the ordinary.

"Caish?"

"Yup. Still here."

"So Caish we don't have any record of a white Aventador

being dropped off for detailing any time within the past four weeks. There is no Jamie Lowell in our system. And the last service record we have for your vehicle is three months ago. Looks like we did a full service at that time."

"What do you mean?"

"I'm sorry?"

"What do you mean? Like, my car isn't there?"

"Correct. We don't have your vehicle here, and we don't have any record of it being here any time in the last three months."

"Is it possible that somebody did a full detail off the record? Like as a favor? Maybe they just didn't log it?"

"That's not likely, every intake is logged, even if the service is comped. Plus, we only have two client Aventadors here right now, and neither of those are your car."

"So you're positive my car isn't there?"

"That's correct. Would you like me to check with Lamborghini Newport? Is it possible your Aventador was taken to that dealership?"

"Oh! Dammit, yeah, you're right, I just remembered Jamie said the car was taken to the Newport dealership. Phew! Okay never mind, I'll give them a call."

"Would you like me to transfer you over there?"

"Oh, yeah that would be great. Thanks." After two rings an equally young soothing voice answered. "Hello Lamborghini Newport Beach, how may I direct your call?"

"My name is Caish Calloway, and somebody named Jamie Lowell, that's L-o-w-e-l-l, dropped my car off there for a detail on this most recent Saturday. It's a cocaine-white Lamborghini Aventador."

"Okay, please hold while I check on your vehicle."

The only thing worse than hold music: hold advertisements for the place you're on the phone with. Here I am, waiting to speak to people from the Lambo dealership, and they put me on hold and play a recording that tells me to call the Lambo dealership for this and that.

"Caish?"

"Yeah, I'm here."

"Your vehicle is not here and we don't have any record of servicing a white Aventador this past weekend."

"What?"

"Your Aventador is not here and we didn't service an Aventador this weekend."

"Are you absolutely positive there is not a white Aventador parked anywhere on your lot? Maybe somebody forgot to enter in the computer or something?"

"We are absolutely positive, Caish. Would you like me to call Lamborghini North Los Angeles and check with them? Maybe Jamie Lowell took it to that dealership?"

"No thanks, I'll call them myself." And I do, frantically. They say the same thing as Beverly Hills and Newport Beach: "Sorry, Caish, your vehicle is not here, and we don't have any record of your Aventador having been brought in."

I call Jamie. It rings once then a recording tells me, "We're sorry; you have reached a number that has been disconnected or is no longer in service. If you feel you have reached this recording in error, please check the number and try your call again." Oh God oh God oh God. Not good. What the hell. I call Green Mountain's main line. Same message. Disconnected. Fuck. I jog up to my office and look up the number I have for Green Mountain to make sure it's right. It is. Oh God no. I pull up the website and instead of seeing the Green Mountain homepage with scrolling green numbers, escalating green lines, and green triangles, I see:

This site can't be reached

www.greenmountainfinancefirm.com's server DNS address could not be found.

Search Google for greenmountainfinancefirm

ERR_NAME_NOT_RESOLVED

No no no. I snatch my phone and check the app. Every time I try to open the app the screen just flickers and closes immediately. I call Jamie again. "We're sorry; you have reached a—" this can't be happening. I text Jamie just in case texts somehow still get through: "Jamie, what the fuck is going on? Your number is disconnected? Call me ASAP!" Shit shit shit. What the hell is going on? Why would Jamie change numbers without telling me? And where the fuck is my Lamborghini? Okay. Let's see... Oh, Penn! She's friends with Jamie. I call Penn.

"We're sorry; you have reached a number that has been disconnected or is no longer—" no. I call again. "We're sorry; you have—" again, "We're sorry; you have—." Tears well up. I can't breathe, my chest is in a vice. I refresh the website and get the same message.

I have to get to Green Mountain. I'm going downtown. Now.

For the first time in my life, I fall down the stairs. Not all the stairs, just the bottom eight or nine. And it's not so much a fall as it is a slide into second base. My hip is throbbing as I scramble to my feet and peel out across the tile toward the garage. Never wear socks when you're in a hurry. At the garage door I pull on my Manolo Blahniks and pull the first key out of the key drawer that my hand touches. It's the Porsche 930 key. Good thing, the Porsche 930 is a 911 with a turbo that turns an already fast car into a ludicrously dangerous and almost uncontrollably fast car, which is exactly what I need. At this time of day it will take me nearly two hours to get to downtown LA, but with the 930 and an ample use of shoulder lanes, I might be able to get there in an hour. Yet, I still need to let the 930 warm up. I feather the throttle as it burbles to life and search Facebook, then Instagram, then Twitter, then Google for Jamie T. Lowell. Nothing. Penelope Perez? Nothing.

I leave my garage with a bit more gusto than usual and can't keep the car on the driveway. My perfect lawn now has Porsche 930 tracks. I accelerate toward the opening gate with rooster tails of grass and dirt coming out from behind the Porsche. When I get the car back onto the concrete the rubber bites in and sends me back in my seat. I let off the gas enough to make the turn out of my driveway and onto the road then lay into it when I get onto PCH. My hands are so shaky that I can't get a cigarette lit. Usually I don't smoke in the cars, but I need smoke in my lungs now more than ever. Every car I pass on the shoulder blasts their horn in a futile attempt to scold me. No time for these little people. A red light in the Parker Canyon area forces me to settle down for a few seconds. Finally I get the fucking cigarette lit. Again, not a good habit to get into—smoking in the car—but I don't have a choice. Ah shit, I forgot about my sushi delivery.

"Yes? This is Ichiban Sushi."

"Hi, this is Caish Calloway, I placed a delivery order a little while ago and I need to cancel it, an emergency came up."

"Okay, sorry we have already sent it to your house."

"I need to cancel the order."

"It will make your emergency better to have sushi."

"Yeah I appreciate that but I had to leave, nobody will be home to take the order, I need to cancel it."

"It is already sent to your house, you cannot cancel it."

"Okay that's fine, charge me for it, but just call your driver and tell him to eat the sushi."

"Our drivers cannot talk while they're driving. Neither should you."

I really don't have time for this shit.

"Look fine, I won't be there, do whatever."

More horns, more weaving, more turbo. When the shoulder is too small to pass on, or it's full of parked cars, I try honking and flashing my lights (the international signal for "this is a goddamn emergency, get the hell out of the way"), but in true California fashion, nobody gives a shit. Just middle fingers and honking back. So I wait. Hands shaking. Teeth tingling. Vision sparkling. Completely surrounded by cheap Toyotas and BMWs creeping down the highway. I feel like a sealed can of beer that has been shaken violently then set down, a flick away from explosion. This excruciating crawl lasts until I get to I-10, where I can take the shoulder again. After nearly two hours of molasses traffic I pull into Green Mountain's parking garage.

The elevator takes its time getting to the forty-fifth floor. When the doors finally slide open I step out into an empty lobby. The lights in the elevator lobby are on, but the rest of the lights on this floor are off. The glass door that leads into Green Mountain's office is locked. I call Jamie again. "We're sorry, you have reached —." I cup my hands on the glass wall and look into the reception area. No furniture, no Green Mountain brushed steel logo on the wall, no receptionist. Nothing. I bang on the glass and yell at a Jamie I know isn't there. I rattle the door and try to pull it off its hinges.

Nothing happens. The walls look on in silent embarrassment.

I turn and rest my back against the glass then crumple to the ground. I stare at my phone and think what to do next. My stomach and chest tense up, my eyes well, and I cry. Not a trickle, a full on shoulders-bobbing sob.

When my exhaustion overcomes my emotions, I try to collect myself and take stock of the situation. What is happening? What do I do? Where is my Lamborghini? Where is Jamie? Oh God. Where is my thirty-five million dollars? Who can I call? Mia. Mia doesn't answer. Oh! Gabby! Duh. Calling my lawyer should have been my first move.

"Good afternoon, thank you for calling Morely, Black, and Associates, how may I direct your call?"

"To Gabriella."

"Transferring you now, please hold."

"Gabriella speaking."

"Gabby this is Caish, do you remember Jamie Lowell and all that Green Mountain shit? Well I don't know what's going on but it's really bad Jamie's phone is disconnected and I don't know where my Lamborghini is and the app won't work and the website is down and Penn has gone ghost too and I'm scared and I drove down to the Green Mountain office and there's nobody here it's all empty and dark and—"

"Caish, calm down." Gabby's tone is sharp. "If you fear for your safety or think that you are the victim of a crime, you should hang up and call the police immediately."

"Just tell me what to do Gabby, I don't know what to do."

"I just told you what to do. Can you call the police? Do you want me to call them for you?"

"No, I can call them, okay I'll call them. What else should I do?"

"I'm an attorney Caish, not a police officer or detective. The first thing you need to do is find Jamie Lowell. We have some private investigators that work for the firm, but you need to be on the phone with the police right now."

"Okay I'll call them."

"Caish, pull yourself together. You need your wits. Call me after you've spoken with the police and let me know what I can do to help." As usual, Gabby hangs up halfway through my last word. I dial 9-1-1.

"Nine one one, what is your location?"

"Um, I can't remember the address. I'm in the big black building downtown."

"The Aon Center?"

"Uh, I don't know."

"Is the building on Wilshire?"

"Yeah, yeah, it's on Wilshire. I'm on the forty-fifth floor."

"Okay 707 Wilshire, we've got a unit on the way. What is your emergency?"

"I think I may have been robbed."

"Are you in immediate danger?"

"No."

"Are you injured?"

Financially? Probably. Emotionally, yes. Physically? "No."

"Are you safe where you're at on the forty-fifth floor?"

"I don't know, yes?"

"Can you get down to the lobby?"

"Um, yeah."

"Okay, take the elevator down to the lobby, police officers will be there in just a few minutes. Is there anybody around you?"

"No, I think this entire floor is empty." I push the elevator call button.

"Can you describe the person who robbed you?"

"Well, I mean I wasn't robbed at gunpoint or anything, I think that somebody tricked me into transferring my money to them and then disappeared. Oh and my car was stolen too." The elevator bings and the doors open to three young people in business casual staring at me.

"Okay I'm getting onto the elevator, I'll have to call you back."

"Let's stay on the line until you see the officers."

"No, it's okay, I'll call you back if I don't see them." Then I hang up. I realize it may have been impolite to the dispatcher, but it's so annoying to be on the elevator with somebody who is talking on their phone. Probably doubly so when the person is a hot mess talking to the police.

When I get to the lobby, people are bustling about as you'd expect at the end of a workday in one of these hives of industry. The lobby is huge, maybe I should have stayed on the phone with the dispatcher. I'll call her back... Oh, never mind, looks like those are the officers right over there. I wave and make my way toward them. There are two of them, both in black uniforms (including black ties), but neither of them have mustaches even though one of them is a male.

"Afternoon, you were the one who called?"

"Yeah, I think I've been robbed."

"Wha'd'ya mean ya think? Were ya robbed or not?"

"Well, I'm not sure. I think I've been scammed or something. I invested a bunch of money with Green Mountain and—well, have you heard of Green Mountain?"

"No, neva heard of it."

"Okay well I invested millions of dollars with them, over thirty million, and now they're gone. Phones off, website down, and their office on the forty-fifth floor is empty. I also think they stole my car. I mean I left it in the parking garage here and now it's gone."

"Have ya checked the parking garage?"

"Not yet, but I gave them the keys so they could take it back to my house, and now they won't answer my calls or anything."

"Ya gave 'em the keys to yur car?"

"Yeah, but not as a gift, just to get it back to my house."

"So ya think ya been conned?"

"Yeah, I guess, whatever you want to call it. But I need help. I have to get my car back. And my money."

"Okay, well are ya hurt or anything? How d'ya feel?"

"I'm not hurt. A little nauseous, but I'm not bleeding or anything."

"Okay good. Least yur not bleedin'. Well I'll tell ya right now this is gonna to be above our pay grade. We're beat cops, if ya was bein' robbed by some scumbag in a hoodie, we'd be able to cut that bastard down and get yur belongings back to ya. But this is a con, and cons are investigated by the Commercial Crimes Division of the LAPD. Martinez, ya wanna call this in and get somebody from CCD down here?" The younger officer nods, pulls a walkie-talkie the size of a brick out of her belt and steps away while speaking into the black brick. Officer no-mustache turned back toward me, "While we wait for them to get here, hows about we go check with building management and get all the records for the tenants of... a... what floor did ya say this Green Mountain outfit was on?"

"Forty-five."

"Yeah, we'll go get records of the tenants on the forty-fifth floor. CCD is gonna need those anyway. We'll get the ball rollin' on that and stick with ya until those detectives arrive."

We walk to the building reception area and the officer asks to speak with somebody from building management. Within a minute or two, an older man that looks like he's spent most of his life being a residential landlord in a rough neighborhood gets off the elevator and introduces himself as the building manager. He then steps behind the reception desk and scoots the receptionist out of the way to get to one of the computers. The officer tells him I am likely the victim of a crime and that he will need to review the tenant information for the forty-fifth floor, "Actually, let's make it the whole buildin', just to be thorough."

The building manager gave a look like he'd love to help but, alas, powers greater than he would not permit it. "I am sorry officer, as I am sure you are aware, tenant information is private, and I cannot release that information without a warrant."

"Oh come on," the officer says, "we both know we can and will get a warrant, just save us all some time and print out some records for us."

"Really officer, I am sorry. I cannot do that without a warrant."

"Jesus Christ. Can't get anything done these days. Okay, we'll get ya goddamn warrant. In the meantime, we need to check ya garage for a vehicle. It was stolen from your garage..." then, turning to me, "'scuse me, when di'j'ya say ya car was stolen?"

"I'm not sure, I left them the keys on Friday night. It could have been anytime over the weekend."

"Okay so it was stolen from this building's garage sometime over the weekend. We're gonna go have a look around down there. Ya got surveillance cameras down there in the garage?"

The building manager looks up from the computer and nods with the same look of helplessness.

"Lemme guess," the officer says, "ya gonna need to see a warrant for that too?"

"I do apologize, but that is the law, so, yes."

The officer, under his breath, says, "everybody's a fuckin' lawyer these days. Okay, let's go check out the garage, maybe we'll get lucky and find yur car is still there."

We aren't lucky. My Lamborghini is gone.

When we get back to the building lobby, Officer Martinez is speaking with two business-casual young men, one of which has a mustache, so at least now I know I'm dealing with real cops.

"Hello, my name is Detective Aaron Black, and this is Detective Paul O'Brien. We're with the Commercial Crimes Division of the Los Angeles Police Department. We've been told you believe that you are the victim of a financial crime, is that correct?"

"It is."

"And what is your name?"

"Caish Calloway."

"Caish?"

"Yeah, Caish."

"We have some questions to ask you, Caish, why don't we sit down?" Detective Black motions toward the lobby's couches and coffee tables. "Well if you two are on the case we'll leave ya to it," the beat cop says, then, to me, "good luck with all this, sorry to hear about ya loss."

Detective O'Brien tells me he'll be recording this conversation and places a small plastic device on the coffee table. Both of them pull small notepads from their jacket pockets and click open their pens in unison.

"Okay Caish, let's start from the beginning. Who took your money?"

"I think it was Jamie T. Lowell."

The officers ask for a detailed physical description. Not just height, weight, skin color, and all those basic attributes, but details about eyebrows, earlobes, teeth, jaw line, and on and on.

Detective Black then asks me to, "Explain in your own words

what happened." As if I could explain it with anybody else's words. I start by telling them about Penn, and they stop me there. "Penelope Perez." Another detailed description. They explain to me that Penn was likely a shill and briefed me on how these con operations sometimes work. Apparently a shill is somebody who acts impartial and uninterested in the con. They give the impression that the whole thing is on the up and up (like a magician asking for a volunteer from the audience and the "volunteer" being an accomplice of the magician). While I tell the detectives about how Penn and I met, and how Penn presented Green Mountain, they exchange glances like they've heard this story before. I tell them about Green Mountain and its website and app. I tell them about Jamie, but leave out the details of our personal relationship (I don't really see how that is going to help with their investigation). I also tell them everything I can remember about Green Mountain, including the office, receptionist, and construction. I give them specific numbers on how much I invested. When I say thirty-five million dollars both detectives stop scribbling and look up with open mouths and raised eyebrows.

"Caish, did you say *thirty-five million* dollars?"

"Yes, thirty-five million. Well it's like thirty-five million six hundred thousand or something."

"Caish, we need you to be completely truthful with us right now. You are telling us that you gave Jamie Lowell thirty-five *million* dollars?"

"Well, I guess. At the time I thought I was investing it in Green Mountain. Which, yeah, now I see where you might think that it's akin to just giving it to Jamie, but it was an honest, well-thought-out, well-researched investment in Green Mountain."

The officers stare at me for a few seconds, examining me, then look at each other, then back at me.

"Okay, Caish, we're going to get moving on this right away." Detective Black stood up and Detective O'Brien and I followed his lead. "We're going to get a warrant for all the records this place has of every tenant that has rented space in this building in the last couple years. Sometimes these people do things off the books, and we have our ways of looking into that as well. We are going to check surveillance footage and see what we can learn from that; both regarding your stolen vehicle and Jamie's physical appearance, license plate number, and any other information we can glean. We'll dust the forty-fifth floor for prints and see if we can learn the true identity of Jamie Lowell and Penelope Perez. Then—"

"True identities?" I cut in.

"They're names. We need to find out who they are. If we can lift a print, we'll run it in the FBI's database and see if we can learn their real names."

The realization that Jamie had given me a fake name hurt almost more than learning that Jamie had disappeared with $35,000,000 of my money.

"Anyway," Detective Black continues, "we'll also want to examine your phone and computers for any information relating to this matter. We're after any crumbs of data that might lead us to Jamie. We'll send over a forensic team to your house, if you don't mind, to collect those devices. We will only need them for a week or so. Also, you should know, although we will do everything in our power to keep this case, we may reach a point where the FBI wants to take it from us. If Jamie actually took thirty-five million from you, I bet the FBI will find some bullshit excuse to take it from us as soon as they sniff this investigation. With an amount that large, it is highly likely that Jamie has transferred your money across state and national borders. Probably several times by now. And that's where the FBI's jurisdiction kicks in. What will probably happen is that we will work with the FBI on it, but the feds are territorial, so don't be surprised if they take over the investigation entirely. In fact I'm going to call my contact with the FBI in just a few minutes. Anyway, none of that really matters to you. What matters is that we will dedicate all of our available department resources to getting your money back."

"Okay." I say.

"Okay." Detective O'Brien echoes. "What time is best for you that we send that team over to your place?"

"Tomorrow morning?" Truth is, if the LAPD and possibly the FBI are going to be digging through my phone and computers, I need a night to scrub them of anything that might make them think I'm not an upstanding citizen. Nothing too serious, just the usual drug and sex transactions that get law enforcement worked up. On top of that, I would feel better about having law enforcement in my home after I've had a chance to off-load a few pounds of cocaine I have laying around. I'll give Riley however much Riley wants, then flush the rest. Just to be on the safe side.

"Great, let's get your address and we'll send a team by around 8:00 a.m."

"Would eleven work? Eight is too early."

With the time nailed down, the detectives take my address and ask a few more questions. Then they give me an outline of how the investigation will proceed. First, as mentioned, they're going to get a warrant for all the records the Aon Center has and comb the forty-fifth floor for any evidence. Then, they will analyze my computers and electronic devices. They will run everything they find through their databases and "keep me posted."

"We're going to be honest with you, though, Caish. People like this—these professional conners—are pretty tough to track down. They cover their tracks well and move fast. You mentioned that you haven't seen Jamie since Friday, well that gives Jamie a three day head start on disappearing. Money these days is easy to transfer and hide if you know a good hacker that can move it through the system in ones and zeros."

"Okay. So... What? You're not going to get my money back?" I'm starting to feel dizzy.

"We're not saying that," Detective Black interjects, "we just want you to know that you need to consider arranging your finances in a way that doesn't necessarily count on getting this money back in the next few weeks. Or months. Hey, Caish, you're not lookin' too good, you feelin' alright?"

I don't have time to answer, I'm about to hurl and I need to get to a bathroom. I take four steps to my left and throw up a slop of stomach muck onto the carpet.

"Okay okay take it easy," Detective Black says. "Take a seat, here, come on back." The detective leads me back to the couch and sits me down. "Take it easy, Caish, here," Detective O'Brien sets a garbage can down at my side and jogs over to reception, says something and points toward me. The receptionist peaks up over the desk and has a perfectly normal reaction to seeing a puddle of vomit on carpet. The receptionist picks up a phone and probably says, "Hey, some asshole just puked all over the floor down here, you better send somebody to clean it up." The detective returns with a paper cup full of water.

"Here ya go, just try and relax. You're alright. Everything is gonna be fine."

"Detective O'Brien, I have just learned that I probably lost all of my money. All thirty-five million dollars of it, and you two just told me I might not get it back for months. I. Am. Not. Alright."

Detective O'Brien glances at Detective Black, then says, "You're right, the situation is not looking good. But I mean right now. You're okay right now. This seems like a big deal now, but, like my father always used to tell me, what seems like a big deal now, won't... well, forget it. Look, just take it easy. Baby steps for the next few days."

"And what about my car?" I ask.

"Oh yeah, let's get your license plate number and vehicle information and we'll check Long Beach to see if it shows up on any of the shipping manifests. We'll also flag it as a stolen vehicle so if these jackasses are dumb enough to drive it around,

LAPD will pick 'em up. But, again, Caish, don't get your hopes up too high. If these people are professionals, that thing was inside a crate headed for China yesterday listed on the ship's manifest as 'strawberries.'"

7

Tuesday. Tomorrow I am not going to Tahiti with Jamie. In fact, I'm not sure I will ever see Jamie again.

They aren't wearing blue blazers with yellow "FBI" lettering on the back, so I have to examine their badges to make sure they aren't imposters. Apparently the FBI took over the investigation sooner than expected. The new point man on the operation introduces himself as Agent Palmer, a tall, middle-aged, well-built sculpture of brawn and grit. At 11:00 a.m. sharp a team of four agents arrive and begin dismantling my office. They take my iMac, both my laptops, my phone, and my tablets. They don't say much. Just ask where my devices are and then if I have any more devices. They say they'll get my phone back to me in the next couple of days, and the rest of my computers within the next couple of weeks.

I walk them out then stand in my entryway. I stare at the back of the door for a spell, then turn and look at my Pollock painting. In hindsight, maybe it tried to warn me with its splotchy foreboding doom. It had once looked like a pond full of tadpoles, and now it looks like a tornado of chaos and killing. Of course Jamie liked it. I want nothing to do with it. I'll sell it right now. But, I realize I don't have my phone, so I hang up the idea. Not having a phone is as crippling as not having vocal cords. Not having computers is... well... like not having hands? Whatever. The point of the matter is that I can't get anything done. I decide to go for a drive to clear my head.

My garage is the biggest room in my house. At 5,000 square feet, my garage is almost as big as my house. Squeaky clean white epoxy floor, white limestone tiled walls, with a ten foot ceiling holding 130 can lights. Several parking spaces are vacant as a result of my recent sales and the theft of my Aston Martin and Lamborghini. My fleet has been gutted. I'm down to six cars.

But, as bad as things may get, I'll always have my cars. These are paid off. Well, most of these are paid off. And car insurance isn't a problem. It would cost thousands a month, but I bought a $50,000 surety bond with the DMV a few years back, and they count that as insurance.

For today's drive, I opt for the Porsche 930. The only good part about yesterday was driving the 930, might as well brighten today with the same machine. This 1986 Porsche 930 cost me about $182,500 — higher than most 930s go for in today's market, but it's because this one has an RWB body kit. Its satin black paint and black wheels give it a sinister look. The engine and suspension are from a 2015 911 Turbo. I still owe money on this car, but I'll pay it off. I can't part with it. I'll use my earnings from the Pollock to pay it off.

I drive for hours. I take PCH up to Santa Barbara, then get lost on side roads coming back through the valley. I know it's a bad habit, but I smoke through a pack of cigarettes on my drive. I make it a point to tell kids never to smoke in the car, but cigarettes help with this crushing anxiety. Without the income from my Green Mountain accounts, I'm not sure how I'm going to keep my realm from eroding. Until I get that thirty-five million back, I'm going to need to get creative. With my 5.92 percent interest rate, the mortgage payment on my fifteen-year, twenty-million dollar mortgage comes to just under $170,000. *A month*. And that's not my only expense. $1,200 a month for my landscapers, $900 for my utility bills, another $600 in maintenance and heating for the pool, and $1,500 for the cleaning crew for my house. $8,500 a month for my private jet charter membership. $1,600 a month for chauffeur services. $1,000 a month on car detailing. $150 to $200 on eating out every day (all three meals (I don't like cooking)), so that's another $5,000 a month. Depending on the market, cocaine costs around $70 a gram, and I go through roughly ten grams a day, so I guess that's another $20,000 a month. The little things add up too. Cigarettes (at a couple packs a day) cost me close to $500 a month, and gas is probably $300 to $500 (some of my cars only take race fuel). Clothes, a few thousand, clubs, maybe a couple thousand, and "escort services" range between five and ten thousand a month. Obviously I need a steady income. I have two million in the bank. That will keep me afloat for now, but I'm not blind; I'm basically broke. Time to circle the wagons, as my brother would say.

On Thursday, still phone-less and having not flown to Tahiti yesterday, I drive to the bank to discuss my mortgage with Mr. Aaron D. Valentini, the largest banker in town. Mr. Valentini invites me into his wood-paneled office and I brief him on my situation. When I get to the part about having a $170,000 monthly mortgage bill, two million in the bank, and no source of income, I slow down to give Mr. Valentini plenty of opportunities to jump into the conversation offering solutions. Instead, Mr. Valentini sits with his elbows on his desk and his interlocked fingers under his nose. His eyebrows have been furrowed since we sat down, and, aside from the pleasantries when I first walked in, he hasn't said a word. Then, mercifully, he interrupts.

"Let me stop you right there, Caish. What can we do for you?"

"That's what I came here to ask, what can you do for me?"

"Hm." And then he was back to brow furrowing.

"Maybe I could refinance?"

"Already? You financed just a couple months ago."

"Or, maybe just change it to a thirty-year loan to make the payments smaller?"

"That would be refinancing." Mr. Valentini takes his elbows off his desk and leans back in his chair. Do people who weigh four to five hundred pounds always worry that their chairs, beds, cars, floors, etc. are going to just give up and collapse? How much can Mr. Valentini's chair possibly take?

"So, is that an option?"

"I'm afraid not." Mr. Valentini says, looking more bored than afraid.

"Surely there is something you can do. Maybe we can push back the due date on my next payment?"

"Suspending payments is not a wise practice. Typically deferring repayment only compounds the problem by foregoing for another day what should be done today. At this juncture I suggest making your scheduled payments punctually. I am sure the FBI will apprehend this confidence artist and return your money to you with due haste." Mr. Valentini rotates in his chair and heaves his massive body onto his feet. "If the FBI has not made any progress in six-months' time, let's reconvene."

I take the long way home and stop by Riley's place. I don't remember the last time I knocked on a door. Riley answers with a look of confusion.

"Did you just knock on my door?" Riley opens the door wider and I walk into the entryway. Riley's apartment has high ceilings and white walls. Dark slate tile and modern furniture. Riley doesn't walk into the apartment and sit down. Instead, Riley keeps us in the entryway.

"Yeah, sorry, you busy?" I ask.

"Sort of, yeah. Why did you knock on my door? No text? You knock on doors now? Are you alright, Caish?"

"Yeah, I'm fine. Well, sort of. Actually I guess things are a little up in the air right now. Anyway, I don't have my phone right now and I was in the neighborhood so I figured I'd swing by and see what you were doing. Wanna grab a bite to eat?"

"You're asking me on a date?"

"No, no, not a date. We'll just go get food, maybe get some drinks afterward, do some coke, and maybe round off the night with sex. But not a date, no."

"Sounds fun, Caish, but I have a photoshoot early tomorrow and I can't be hung over."

"Just dinner then?"

"Sorry, I can't. I have other stuff going on tonight." Riley's eyes look left and Riley nods down the hall. I lean around the corner, look down the hall, and hear the shower running.

"Are you with somebody right now?" I ask.

"Yeah. Sorry," Riley says, "you don't mind do you?"

"Oh no, no, not at all, you know me, I'm way chill about that kind of stuff. All good. Okay have a great night." Get me out of here.

"Caish, really, this doesn't change anything."

"I know. It doesn't, Riley. Really, I'm good. There's just a lot going on right now. I'll call first next time."

"Well, text."

"Right, yeah, I'll text first next time. Like usual."

I always figured Riley had other relationships, but witnessing it isn't easy. It doesn't feel good. Who is Riley with? And is that person as attractive as me? Doubt it. As rich? Not likely. So what is Riley doing? Is it retaliation for something I did? Whatever, Riley is young and replaceable. There are hundreds of models that are just as hot that would kill to be with me. They're all down for anything as long as coke is available. Riley's loss.

The FBI returns my phone two weeks later. Two weeks without a phone or computer is Gulag-level isolation. I spent most of the time going on drives, floating in my pool, watching movies, and trying new restaurants. I was also very productive, I paid off the loan on my Porsche, and lined up a couple cars for consignment. At this point, my bank account was down to $1,682,004.27.

A few weeks later the FBI returns the rest of my electronics and gives me an update on the investigation. We meet in my office. Agent Palmer and I stand behind one of the FBI's computer people as she hooks up my computer.

They had not found any clues by reviewing surveillance video and rental records from Green Mountain's office building ("we suspect somebody at the building allowed them to rent space on a vacant floor using false names and taking payment off the books, we're still looking into that"). The forensics team that examined Green Mountain's floor didn't find so much as a hair. I told Agent Palmer that Jamie had played my piano, so maybe there were some fingerprints. His team dusted the keys, but they had been wiped clean. We tried a few other places that I was sure Jamie had touched, but again, wiped clean.

Agent Palmer also tells me that the computer forensics team couldn't find a trace of Jamie anywhere. He also tells me that what I was doing online wasn't technically illegal, and there was no reason to delete all that. He must have read the confusion on my face, because he gave me a short lesson on how nothing is ever actually deleted. But, either way, Jamie had apparently been successful in deleting Jamie from existence. The trails on the app and website ownership winded through several sham corporations with fake operating members. The way Agent Palmer tells it, all sorts of people who never existed set up corporations which then created other companies to build and host a website for a company that was created with the sole purpose of taking my money. After my money had been transferred, it was immediately divided into smaller denominations and transferred to at least fourteen thousand corporations that don't actually exist. They're just bits of information in server towers around the world. From there, the money — which was just zeros and ones flying through fiber optic cables under the ocean — went to thousands of offshore accounts to which the FBI cannot get access, or even find.

"Essentially, this person we've been referring to as Jamie scrambled your money and made it disappear using sophisticated computer hacking techniques," Agent Palmer told me. "But, we'll keep working the case from every angle we can."

"And what about my Lamborghini? Anything?"

"Nothing."

"Is it normal that there isn't even a ransom note or anything?" I asked.

"You mean for your car?" Agent Palmer seemed to stuff down a laugh.

"I don't know, yeah?"

"No Caish. These types aren't interested in ransoms, they took everything they wanted. No negotiation."

"So, when do you think you'll have my money back?"

"Well, that's the tough thing. At this point I can't really give you an estimate. You may want to adjust your lifestyle so that you can live comfortably with what you have left. We can't make any guarantees that we will be successful in recovering your money."

"What do you mean? Are you saying I might not get my money back?" I ask.

"Yes, that is exactly what I have been trying to tell you."

My face goes numb and I start to see little sparkles.

"Woah, Caish, you better have a seat, you're looking a little pale," Agent Palmer took my arm and guided me onto my Eames chair. "Can I get you something to drink, Caish? Let's open a window."

"Agent Palmer. You have to get my money back. It's your job."

"It absolutely is. And we're doing our best. We have a high success rate solving these types of crimes. I just want to be transparent with your regarding the sophistication that 'Jamie' and 'Jamie's' team used to defraud you." Each time Agent Palmer said "Jamie" he bent his index and middle finger to make air quotes. Every reminder that Jamie wasn't even Jamie stung. He continued, "I would hate for you to go on living a lifestyle that is no longer sustainable."

"What are you trying to say?"

"Easy, Caish. I am just letting you know. You know I have reviewed all of your financial records and bank accounts. If it were me, I'd sell this place and get something more... practical."

"Okay, thank you Agent Palmer. I appreciate the financial advice. But I think I can handle it. You think owning a place like this just happens? You don't think I know how to handle my own fuckin' money? Well you're wrong. I worked very hard for this house, and I'm not gonna sell it just because some assholes stole from me because they were too lazy to work for their own money. Now please, get back to doing your job."

There were a few awkward minutes while the technician finished setting up my computer, then I walked them to the door and showed them out. Then I called Gabby.

"Good afternoon, thank you for calling Morely, Black, and Associates, how may I direct your call?"

"To Gabriella Rodriguez."

"Transferring you now, please hold."

After making me wait for twenty minutes, I hear, "Gabriella speaking."

"Hi Gabby, it's Caish."

"Hello Caish, how are you this afternoon?"

"Not too good. I just met with the FBI and they told me they can't find Jamie or my money."

"Very sorry to hear that," Gabby said. "So, what can I do for you Caish?"

"I don't know. Can we sue the FBI for mishandling my case? Or can you have your private investigators find Jamie?"

"What evidence do you have that they have mishandled your case? Hasn't it only been a month?"

"Maybe, but they just told me they can't find Jamie or my money. They just said it's all gone and that I should sell my house and cars and buy a fucking Hyundai or some shit."

"Caish, before you go on, I have a very busy afternoon that I have to get back to. Before I can devote any more time to assisting you with legal counsel, you will need to become current on your bill. You haven't paid on last month's invoice." Which was true. Gabby billed me for twelve hours of legal work on that Aston Martin repo situation. But she didn't get the car back. Now she wanted me to pay her $14,500 for her time.

"Oh yeah," I said, "I meant to talk to you about that. Do you really think fifteen thousand dollars is reasonable for legal work that didn't get my car back? That just seems like too much."

"We can't guarantee success in every case, Caish, you know that. You pay for me to be your lawyer, not to solve all your problems. Get that bill paid and give me a call about this FBI thing when you have some evidence that they mishandled your case."

"Okay, sounds goo—" and Gabby hung up.

No evidence surfaced. Not for me against the FBI, and not for the FBI to get my money back. Not in the next few days, not in the next few weeks. In two months my bank account had somehow trickled down to $1,230,521.15. I consigned three more cars, which brought my total down to three: the Porsche 930, the Shelby Cobra, and my G Wagon. But the consigned cars just sat in the showrooms of the car dealers. Until they sold I would be having cash flow problems. My Pollock finally sold, so did my piano, which brought in some much-needed cash and removed some much-resented reminders of Jamie. Despite all that Jamie had done, I still longed to see that beautiful face again. I still sent texts every now and then, just in case this whole thing was a mistake, and maybe Jamie felt the same way about me as I felt about Jamie.

Last month I called the real estate agent who sold me my house seven years ago and told her that I needed to sell my place in Monterey. She sold that in a couple weeks and I made $500,000.

Then, a couple weeks ago, I called her again and told her I need to sell my house. Not my vacation house, my actual house. As painful as it is, I won't be able to make the mortgage payments for much longer, and Mr. Valentini refused to let me refinance. I don't have a choice. The agent told me she thinks we can get "thirty mil" for it. The market is booming right now, she said. Everybody who's anybody is crawling over each other to get into Malibu. Oh and your ocean view right on the cliff's edge? Thirty mil, no problem, she said. This news brightened my mood, and for the first time in weeks I went to a house party and got laid by some young Hollywood hopeful.

The next morning I felt like a new person. Maybe I should start investing in real estate. I had the good judgment to buy my current house, and I'm about to make a huge profit on the resale. Lots of people make money buying and selling property, I might as well do the same.

My house didn't sell for thirty million dollars. It sold for twenty-one million and some change. After taxes and fees I broke even. My cars also sold. I was no longer in debt, and I had enough cash to live on. My bank account had roughly two million dollars in it—the lowest since before I won the lottery. But, I had cash. And with the house and cars sold, I didn't have any debt. Plus, of the one hundred and twenty-five million that I won, California still owed me four million over the next five years. I didn't receive my earnings in a lump sum, the state paid me in front-loaded payouts. These last few are the smallest, but it should give me enough to either live off the interest (if I can learn to be more parsimonious, as Mr. Valentini has advised), or begin rebuilding what Jamie stole from me and get back on top. Six million is more than enough to stay happy.

In the spirit of frugality, I put my pride aside and bought a two million-dollar Spanish-tiled house in Spanish Hills, Camarillo. Since, at the moment, I didn't have much to spare, I bought the house with a loan. I have more than enough to cover the mortgage, I just wanted to stay liquid. The house is only four thousand square feet, only has a four-car garage, and the pool is just a regular pool in the ground without a view. No infinity about it. There's also a small hot tub in a gazebo. I still invite people over for parties, but I can't help but be a little embarrassed about the cheaper house. Even Mia, who also had to downsize, at least stayed in Malibu. Mia and I aren't as close as we used to be. I think the stress of moving and dealing with this "change in lifestyle" has put some distance between us. Same story with Riley. But that's how it is with people; in with the new, out with the old every few years.

To save money, I hired an interior design firm to help style my new house instead of going with Tosca Giacosa again. By going with Chip, from Kate Thompson Designs, I only paid $25,000 for interior designing instead of Tosca's quoted $95,000. Mr. Valentini would have been proud. Despite the downsize, I didn't have enough furniture to fill my new house. I sold most of the antique and designer pieces before the move. And my walls were bare since I sold most of my art. Chip selected new furniture sets and art that fit the feel of the house.

Then it got quiet. Most nights I ordered delivery and watched movies. I tried to read a book, but that turned out to be remarkably boring. I was actually surprised at how boring it was. I could only read a page or two before I found myself browsing Instagram. Not even cocaine made it interesting. Most nights I went for a drive and bought lottery tickets. I spent plenty of time floating in the pool, drinking in the hot tub, and tanning. Every now and then I would call the FBI to see if there was anything new with my case, but there hasn't been anything new in months. No names, no leads, no money.

Downtime is exactly what I need to clear my head and chart a course out of this small-time money. I'll lay low for a while, then put my plan back to wealth into motion.

8

One million dollars in cash makes a smaller pile than you'd think. A million dollars in one hundred-dollar bills fits comfortably into a duffle bag. Ten thousand dollars is a stack of one hundred one hundred-dollar bills and is only about half an inch thick. One hundred of those stacks, and there's a million. One thousand pieces of perfectly shaped, crisply printed pieces of paper. Stacked, one million dollars is three-and-a-half feet tall. Spread out on my king size bed, there are enough bands of ten thousand to cover most of my comforter.

Feeling forlorn, I boost my spirits with some warm soft cash. Withdrawing a million dollars from the bank isn't easy. There are several forms to fill out (even though it's your money), and, after days of waiting for the bank to let you take your cash, the FBI shows up to ask if you are making this withdrawal to pay a ransom. For days afterward the FBI follows you around just waiting for a drug deal. Some of us just need to occasionally feel the cash. To handle hundreds of stacks of ten thousand dollars. To hold power. To feel the texture of joy. Ever wonder what happiness smells like? Fan a ten thousand dollar stack of one hundred-dollar bills into your face and take a deep whiff. Money is happiness. Not just because of what it can buy, but because of what it means. The holder of this special paper is in charge. The wealthy call the shots and manipulate the masses.

The poor try to even the score by claiming, "Ya can't take it with ya when ya die," and, "I ain't never seen a U-Haul followin' a hearse." When really all they're saying is, "I reckon you're more successful than me now, but when we all die I'll have a bigger house in Heaven because God—Heaven's only developer—likes us poor folk better." Face it, a loser in life is a loser in death. Money is the point system in the game of life. The rich are winning. We are winning. I am winning. This is me. This is my success. I own it. I am it.

Nobody, not even Jamie and Penn, can change that. Just because most of my money was stolen from me does not mean that I am any less successful. I still have forty million dollars, even if thirty-five million of my dollars are being used by somebody else at the moment. Nothing can stop me from fighting my way back to the top. I went from a bank account of $112.87 to having $125 million in accounts receivable; it will be easy to get to $125 million with a starting balance of six million. I have the work ethic of the ambitious poor and the wisdom of the earned rich. I've been here, done this, and come out on top. My rebound starts here.

The million in cash has several purposes. First, it cheers me up. The weight of the bag holding the money, the sound of the money pouring onto my bed, the feel of the stacks as I organized them on the comforter, the crunch of the bills as I laid on top of them, and the smell of printed power. These are some of my favorite things.

Second, I need to have cash in a safe in case somebody tries to hack my bank account or steal money from me in the way Jamie did. A rainy day fund, if you will. Third, I need to see what I'm spending. I have lowered my cost of living substantially by cancelling my private jet membership, my chauffeur service, and all my cleaning services (both for the house and cars), and buying things in cash will help me keep an eye on where my money is going. Fourth and finally, I need cash for everything I have always needed to pay for in cash: cocaine, sex (only sometimes, and I have cut back on paying for this), and club expenses.

Just before the sunset, Tim and Selina Rayburn dropped by to check out my new place. I told them about the Green Mountain disaster and they offered to help in whatever way they could. Apparently they had been conned as well a few years back (as Tim put it, "a fuckin' sociopathic finance fuck") and knew what it was like to lose a several hundred thousand dollars. I told them that right now the best thing they could do to help would be to keep me company.

Tim's teeth-whitened smile radiated as he swung his legs out from underneath the door and clamored out of his Lamborghini. He had put on a few pounds since the last time we saw each other, but cocaine kept him spritely. Selina climbed up and out of the car with grace. If anything, Selina looked younger than she did on the Bullrun Rally. Turns out the fountain of youth is wealth.

"Caish! Ya goddamn mud duck, how have you been?" Tim said while giving me a side hug.

"All things considered, I've been great. How have you two been? Selina you're looking incredible as usual."

"We've been great too," Selina said. "You look happy, Caish, I'm glad to see that."

"Look at this fuckin' place!" Tim had his arms out like he was about to hug a giant. "This is beautiful, Caish. And you said you got this for only two million? That's a fuckin' bargain. Oh and check that out, a little gazebo, with, what is that? A hot tub in there? Oh hell yeah, Caish!"

After the tour we settled down on my back patio. The sunset had warmed the sky up to a glowing orange that reflected off the pool. This house wasn't on the beach, but it had a decent view of Ventura County. Besides a golf course there wasn't anything on the hill below my house. We had a clear view of strawberry fields, the 101, and, beyond that, Oxnard. The view was obstructed only by a few palm trees.

We relax with our cigarettes and wine and wax philosophical.

"So, where to from here, Caish?" Selina asked.

"Well," I said, pointing to the gazebo, "I'd like to plant a lemon tree right over there."

"Haha, I like it. Any long-term plans?"

"Tough to say."

"It is," Tim said, "we've also been kind of treadin' water

lately. Not sure which direction to swim."

"Seems like it would be best just to lay low for a while and get my bearings."

Tim lit his third cigarette. Coyotes yipped and howled in the distance and crickets creaked.

"And live off interest?" Tim asked.

"Yeah, I've heard that you can live comfortably off of the interest of just a couple million."

"Nah, it's not true," Tim said. "Maybe if you're a fuckin' austere peasant. Or a monk. If you get lucky and have six or seven percent interest rate—and I mean you'd have to be fuckin' lucky, most interest rates are like three or four percent—but even if it's seven percent, that's only seventy thousand a year for every million you've got. So for a couple million, you'd only be making a hundred and forty grand a year."

"But that seems doable."

"Ha! You really are a fuckin' mud duck, Caish. You buy this place with cash, or did you mortgage it?"

"Mortgage."

"And what are your payments?"

"Eleven thousand a month."

"So right there you've got, what? A hundred and ten grand a year?"

"More like over one hundred and thirty," Selina said.

"Yeah," Tim continued, "so there goes your hundred and forty grand a year. Not a lot left over for cars, cocaine, and the fuckin' Copacabana, if ya know what I mean. And remember, that was best case scenario. Fuckin' seven-percent-returns scenario. More likely is that you get four percent. Then you're making eighty K a year off your couple million, not even enough to cover half your fuckin' mortgage."

"Jesus." I sip my wine and think.

"It's the same problem we're in, Caish," Selina said. "We've only got a few million to work with and we're not getting nearly the interest rate we deserve."

"It's not all bleak though," Tim said. "As long as you have enough to pay off your house, which I think you said you did, and enough to buy a few cars, what else do you need? The tough part is that what happens in six or seven years when Lamborghini releases a new model and you don't have enough to buy it? Then you're putting around in an old model and everybody knows you don't have the scratch to play big league."

"Oh come on, Tim, it won't be like that," Selina said, "an Aventador will always be an Aventador, and a Lamborghini is still a Lamborghini."

"No, it's true, Selina," Tim said. "Ever see somebody driving a Diablo around? That was the Aventador of the nineties. See somebody in one of those and the first thing you think is, ah that poor fuck, can't afford a real super car so they buy a classic and try to be big league. We all know its minor league. We still think it's a bitchin' car, but it's fuckin minor league."

Tim was right. And my garage had two classics and a G Wagon in it. Tim looked at me and must have remembered that I was no longer big league. He amended, "Caish, you know what I mean. Your classics aren't a fuckin' Diablo though. Your Cobra is worth two Aventadors and your 930 is worth, what, five hundred thousand or something? Totally different." But the damage was done.

"God I miss my Aventador."

"We miss it too, Caish," Selina said, "we're excited to see your next one."

Then we let the Coyotes do the talking for a little while. The sky had darkened to a twinkling charcoal and a soft breeze made tiny ripples on the pool. My rope lights swayed in the wind. Tim lit another cigarette. Selina and I pulled our jackets around our shoulders.

"I can never remember, what do you two do?" I asked. "Professionally, I mean. Like what do you do for a living?"

"Tim buys and sells cars," Selina said.

"Well, I'm not a fuckin' used car salesman," Tim said. "It's more like, a broker of fine art."

"Haha, okay Tim. You're a broker of fine art." Selina rolled her eyes and took a sip of wine.

"It's true! Caish, ya know how for a lot of high-end cars you have to get an invite to buy it, and then you're on a waitlist to get your car? Like with the McLaren F1, you know?"

"Yeah."

"Okay, so Ferrari invites me to buy, for example, the Ferrari LaFerrari or whatever new model they come out with. I agree, and I am waitlisted after my hundred-grand deposit. Now, sometimes at this point I can sell my spot in line. Some fuckin' banker or lawyer wants the LaFerrari and didn't get invited to buy it or just can't wait another eight months or some shit. But usually I hold out, because if I can wait until I receive the car, then I can immediately resell it (subject to Ferrari's terms) for a pretty fuckin' good profit."

"But there are only so many opportunities like that, right? What do you do in the years that you aren't invited to buy a supercar?"

"Easy," Tim said, "I buy a regular sports car, like an Audi R8, and customize it in ways that people usually don't dare to, then I sell it for more than I bought it for."

"How do you customize them?" I asked.

"Oh all sorts of shit," Tim continued, "sound system, new paint, maybe some engine work. I have a shop downtown that does all the work for a good price. Lately I've been making some good money putting wide-body kits on Ferraris and Porsches. Like your 930. You can make good money putting an RWB kit on a 930. People are afraid to cut up a high-end car, but they love to buy a cut up high-end car. Weird shit, but I make good money."

"Millions?" I asked.

Selina sent a fake laugh to cut at Tim, then added "definitely not, but we make enough."

Tim let it slide.

"Hm. I gotta figure out something like that," I said, "all the businesses I started more or less flopped. Apps and shoes and bags and electronics and toothbrushes and all that other shit. None of it can bring in any real money."

"Yeah," Tim said, "well I'd be happy to help you get your start in my line of work. Rayburn Enterprises could use another partner."

"Maybe just until I get something else going. That'd be great. Thanks Tim."

"No fuckin' problem, Caish. We got you."

After the Rayburns left for the night I browsed James Edition, the duPont Registry, and Hemmings looking for a car to get started with. My budget was a couple hundred thousand and I wanted something with good resale potential. I settled on a 2015 Rolls-Royce Wraith and sent the necessary emails to have it purchased before the end of the week.

When the Rolls arrived, Tim got me in touch with his shop that did the customizations and I had them paint it with a chromaflair paint that changes colors from different angles. And not from orange to a slightly-more-red-orange, this paint goes from green to purple depending on your angle. Pretty bitchin'. I also replaced the twenty-one-inch wheels with twenty-three-inch wheels, per Tim's recommendation. I also put in new subwoofers. It took a few weeks to sell, and when all expenses were paid I only made $5,300. Tim explained that usually the margins were better, and that if I did that ten times a year, I could probably be making close to two hundred grand. Add that due to the interest I will be making off of the millions that California has yet to pay me, and I will be in a good position. Comfortable, at least.

But still far from a yacht and a place in Monte Carlo.

After a few months I settled into a routine. My place in Spanish Hills started to feel like home and I made more of an effort to get out and meet new people. I cut down on my drug use, and weaned my cocaine usage down to about five thousand dollars' worth a month. My monthly expenses were just my mortgage, my food, my drugs and alcohol, and gas. And a small budget for clubs and parties. Most of this was paid for using money from selling cars. I bought and sold one or two cars a month, and usually made around ten thousand a car. In the first year I only lost money on one car, but it was only ten or twenty thousand.

Unfortunately my bank account was not making much from interest. My total balance was just over six hundred thousand dollars. I put back $250,000 of the cash I withdrew. The interest on that was less than five K a month. Not even enough to cover half my mortgage. Tim was right. I was too broke to live off interest.

Then, a real opportunity came my way.

The Ferrari dealership in Thousand Oaks invited me to buy a new, limited edition Ferrari. Only 399 of these were going to be made, and demand was high. There would probably only be around fifty of these cars in California. The car would cost me $759,900. I didn't want to empty out my bank account and my cash reserves weren't enough to cover that (not even near enough to cover that), so I explained the opportunity to Aaron D. Valentini, and he agreed to front me the cash.

"But," the massive Mr. Valentini said, "this loan must be conditioned upon a security interest in the future lottery winnings payouts from California for the same amount. Surely you understand that I can't make a loan of nearly one million dollars without some sort of collateral."

"What about the Ferrari?" I asked. "Won't that be the collateral on the loan?"

"Oh it certainly will be, but you don't have a car right now, do you Caish? You are asking for money to buy a car that is not yet available, and which we cannot yet inspect. Thus, we will require a lean on your future earnings."

Not entirely understanding Mr. Valentini and wanting to get a move on with the loan, I agreed. So what if he had a lean on my future earnings? That would only happen if I lost money on the Ferrari, which wouldn't happen.

Well it did happen. But I didn't lose too much. Only about $22,000. And twenty grand is a drop in the bucket of four million. In fact, I realized that I should be leveraging my assets more aggressively. My money that the state hadn't disbursed was an asset that, at the time, was not doing anything for me. And as long as I didn't use that asset, I only had a million or so to work with. I didn't realize that I could borrow against my future payouts until Mr. Valentini pointed out the opportunity.

From that point forward, I financed all of my purchases with loans against the pile of gold California was holding from me. It kept my bank account healthy so that I could make at least some money off of the interest, and lowered the risk of cash flow problems.

It was difficult to deal with the anxiety associated with this change in lifestyle. I'd get headaches constantly and had trouble sleeping. I even had a panic attack. Gabby called to discuss her bill while I was cleaning my G Wagon and my legs went weak. I sat down with my back against one of the wheels then slid down further until just my head was propped up by the tire. I couldn't catch my breath and my heart was trying to break my ribs. The closest thing I had felt to this was in dreams where I am being chased by the guy from Texas Chainsaw Massacre but I can't run. Like I'm stuck in sap and my ghastly doom is closing in. I got dizzy and was sure that I was dying right there on my cobblestone driveway. The non-existent walls were closing in. Trapped, suffocating, vision getting spotty. Killed by a phone call from my attorney. Hose in hand. Suds all over.

The weight of the panic attack eventually lifted, but for

a few hours afterward I was still shaking. That was my only panic attack, but the anxiety never left. I tried taking Xanax and Valium, but they just didn't cut it, so I tried Vicodin and Oxycodone. Those helped. My headaches subsided and I slept like a sloth. Too much Oxy and I started to lumber like a tortoise. But, cocaine solved that problem. Checks and balances.

California finally gave me my money. On January 12th the state released 1.2 million into my coffers (it would have been 1.6, but Mr. Valentini took $400,000 to cover a few outstanding payments). This couldn't have come at a better time. Despite all I had done to cut back, I was still getting low on cash. But this 1.2 million was more than enough to last me until my next payment.

I stopped trying to flip cars when I lost almost forty thousand in a single month. It had been a rough year. That hurt. I decided I could live off of interest and future lottery wins. I'd just cut back in the meantime. No more flying, especially not on private jets. No more month-long ski vacations to Park City. No more weekend vacations to anywhere. No more resort stays. I even cut back on the little things: I try not to drive more than three hours a day to save on gas, I work on my own car when something breaks, I cut down to a pack of cigarettes a day, I cancelled most of my magazine subscriptions, and I stopped ordering and dining out for lunch. No more wine with every dinner, and when I did get wine, not the expensive stuff—and not a whole bottle. No more cocaine on Sundays, Mondays, Wednesdays, and Thursdays. No more shopping sprees (I cut down my shopping to only once a week, and for the most part I avoid stores like Dior, Dolce & Gabbana, and Louis Vuitton). No more buying anybody drinks at clubs. No more ecstasy. No more $500 tips. No more paying for sex. No more house cleaners, pool cleaners, or car detailers. I even mow my own goddamn lawn.

This new frugality freed up some cash. For the first time in far too long, I was in a good position to buy a new car. Not to sell to somebody else, but for myself. I missed my Lamborghini more than I missed Jamie. It was time to get another. A new Aventador was just outside of my price range, so I went with a beautiful gloss black Huracan that was for sale at Lamborghini Beverly Hills. It was love at first sight. Mr. Valentini financed it with another one of those leans on future earnings. Finally, after nearly three years of deprivation and sacrifice, I would be back behind the wheel of Italy's finest. Lamborghini sent a car to pick me up so that I could drive the Huracan out of the showroom.

We arrived at the dealership at noon on Friday. The saleswoman asked for a few signatures and then handed me the keys. I slid into the car as they opened the glass doors at the side of the dealership. The car's startup interrupted every phone call in the building. I eased it off of the showroom floor, through the parking lot, then onto the open road. The odometer had 159 miles on it (all testing miles from the factory). Before the day was through I would double that mileage.

I was back. The howl of the exhaust announced it. People on the sidewalk and in crosswalks stopped in their tracks and pulled their phones out. Every person in every car couldn't help but admire the perfect machine. Most of them saying, "Hey, nice car! I'll trade ya! Ahahaha!" They knew I was on top. My Facebook and Instagram got a lot of love when I posted a video of me going 100 mph. Every time I stopped a crowd formed. Riley wanted to go for a ride, so I swung by Empire Apartments. Riley then told me that Empire was old news, and that Riley had been living at a place in Thousand Oaks for the past year. After picking up Riley, we took the Huracan to the Rayburns' house. They loved it. Tim and I both knew that Huracans were minor league compared to Aventadors, but he didn't mention it. The Rayburns got in their Lamborghini and we all went for a drive that lasted late into the night. We drove down PCH, snaked up through Encinal Canyon, across Mulholland Highway all the way to Woodland Hills, then took the 101 back to my place.

After the Rayburns left, Riley and I had the best sex I'd had in months. Finally. Finally I was back. Finally I was happy again. Truly happy. Turns out even a couple million can buy happiness. A beautiful place in Spanish Hills, a Lamborghini, and a young model. Try getting any of those without millions of dollars.

9

The trouble was, and this really was quite troubling, I couldn't get my bank account above two million dollars. The car buying and selling hadn't done much, and interest on my money wasn't enough to live on. Another problem was that now I had payments to make. In addition to my mortgage, Gabby was leaning on me to pay her bill, so I agreed to a repayment plan that involved monthly payments (plus interest). I was also making payments on loans for my Huracan and a newly purchased Tesla. Both car loans were made by borrowing against my future lottery payouts. Then, when I missed a payment on the Huracan, they repossessed the car. Didn't even give me a chance to make good on the payment, just stole it when I wasn't home. Right out of my garage. Bastards.

After a few months, most of my cash was tied up in mortgage payments and I couldn't make payments on the Tesla anymore either, so that was repossessed too.

When California gave me my last lottery payout of $815,000, my total net worth was down to one and a half million. Less than what I owed on my house. I sold the G Wagon, figuring all I really needed was my Porsche, but that only brought in another hundred thousand. Being the entrepreneur that I am, I thought up a plan to thwart the impending blackness of poverty. I'd flip houses. I was no longer on good terms with the real estate agent that sold my other houses (her fee was unreasonable, so I didn't pay it, now she's suing me or whatever), so I called Hailey Preis.

Hailey and I met years ago at a beach party. She's a beautiful woman that doesn't look a day over fifty. Which isn't bad for a forty year old who has spent her entire life in event management. The night we met, Hailey was explaining that her gray hair (which was dyed black) was gray as a result of a Super Bowl halftime show she organized a couple years back ("Christ almighty, these fuckin' divas, they turned my hair gray and gave me congenital heart disease"). Her wrinkles came from the cigarettes she was forced to smoke to cope with the stress of her career, and the bags under her eyes came from her second gig of flipping houses. Her second gig was the reason I reached out to her.

As mentioned, my plan was to rebuild my empire buying and selling premiere real estate. I'd call my company Calloway Enterprises Inc. "The House You Want for the Price You Deserve." I paid a marketing studio in LA ten thousand dollars to develop that tagline, a logo, and a website for Calloway Enterprises. I rented some office space downtown and put together a team. Hailey Preis would manage the team, Matt Hollioak would be the salesperson, Zack Preswright would be the general contractor, and Nettie Ups would be our primary contact at BazookaMedia, the marketing studio taking care of our internet presence. If everything went as planned, this team would work without me having to micromanage them. I'd compensate them using a salary/commission system that Gabby drafted, then pay myself with whatever profits were remaining. On the advice of counsel, I incorporated Calloway Enterprises so that I wouldn't have any personal liability for the debts or losses of the company.

I also doubled down my efforts to win the lottery again. Moving forward, I would buy twice the normal amount of tickets every time I went to the gas station—which I did at least once a day. After the first three weeks, I won five hundred dollars from a Scratcher that only cost me a buck.

I organized a dinner party at Surasawa, America's most prestigious sushi restaurant, to make sure the Calloway Enterprises team knew our mission. I had pitched Calloway Enterprises to each of them before, but we had never met together as a team. Taking them to Surasawa was my way of demonstrating to them the kind of lifestyle Calloway Enterprises could give them. I had just closed out the first month of business and, although we had yet to make any purchases, we had some excellent leads on ideal aging estates in Hollywood and Bel Air.

Getting a reservation at Surasawa is nearly impossible, and I almost lost ours when I came down with a pretty bad flu. But I paid a bit extra and the owner let me bump our reservation back a week without any hassle. Nothing cash can't cure.

I picked up Matt and we met Zack and Hailey there. Surasawa is unassuming; it is on the second level of a newly developed brownstone building just off Rodeo Drive in Beverly Hills. The restaurant is reservation only, and only seats small parties. The dining area is relatively small, my master bedroom has more square footage. The Calloway Enterprises team sat at the sushi bar, and the four of us took up the entire bar space.

Haruki Surasawa, the two Michelin-starred chef that owns Surasawa, must be over ninety-seven years old. He stands at probably 5'2," fully extended, but has a hunch that puts him in the sub-five-foot range. Not a single hair anywhere on his head. He speaks with an accent that he probably keeps for authenticity sake (if I remember correctly, he has lived in California for at least ten years).

With our order placed, I get to business.

"Thank you all for coming out tonight, although I guess you should be thanking me." I smiled but I don't think they got it, because they just looked at me with blank faces. "Not just because I'm buying you the best sushi in the world, but because I am giving you all an opportunity to make lots of money." Still no reaction other than a couple small nods. "Like I said on the phone, I want to hire each of you to work with me at Calloway Enterprises. At Calloway Enterprises we will change the way houses are flipped and revolutionize the home buying process. You've each been selected because you're—"

"Because we're the best of the best of the best?" Hailey interrupted, "Come on Caish cut the melodrama. We're your friends and we know you're in a tight place and we want to help."

"Well, that's part of it, but this is something I've been thinking about for several years."

"Caish," Matt said, "Hailey's right, we're here because we want to help." Zack was nodding along with a sake to his lips.

"You think I'm asking for charity? That I'm buying you the most expensive sushi in the country because I'm broke?"

"That's not what we're saying," Hailey was saying. "We're saying that you don't need to waste our time talking about revolutionizing industries. If you wanna sell a few houses, great, we can help with that. But let's keep it real. Renovating houses is expensive work, and we're expensive people, so before we agree to any of this, we're going to need to talk numbers. And—"

"Yeah, got it. We'll talk numbers," I said, "I was just going to give you some context on why we're here and the direction I plan on going with this. I want to do more than sell a few houses. I want to create a company that reimagines the housing market and takes it from where it's at now, which is like, 1960s practices, and modernize everything. Change the way people think about buying a home."

"See, Caish," Zack chimed in, "this is what Hailey's talking about. You can put that preachy shit in Facebook ads, but when you tell it to us, it makes us feel like you think we're idiots. I mean, 'change the way people think about buying a home'? Come on Caish."

"What? Can we not do that? Can we not start a company that has new ideas and uses new tools? There are better ways of buying and selling houses than the frustrating process that we go through today."

"Okay, Caish, like what?" Hailey asked.

"Like, how about no more signing fifty thousand forms? How about being able to buy a home the same way people buy a computer? You can buy anything online, why not a house?"

My three future employees stared at me as if they were trying to solve a puzzle. Haruki placed our edamame in front of us.

"Are you serious?" Hailey asked.

"Yes, what's wrong with that? Why can't we do it? Imagine going to Zillow and being able to buy with one click. Like on Amazon."

"Because we're talking about a fucking *house*, not a book," Zack said.

"Yeah, Caish, people don't want to buy houses on the internet," Hailey added. "Even if they wanted to, nobody has enough money to buy a house. Regular people have to get loans to buy houses, and the process of convincing a financial institution to loan you the money takes time and inspections, both of the house and of the financial position of the borrower. And all those forms you want to do away with? Those are required by law."

They were missing the point.

"You guys are missing the point, there is money to be made in innovating new ways to buy and sell houses."

"So what's the new way, Caish?" Matt asked.

"Well, I don't have all the answers, I was hoping that by bringing together experts in the industry that we'd be able to figure something out."

"But you *do* have some idea of how *this* all works, right?" When he said "this" Matt swirled his finger around as if he were asking whether I knew how the building's ceiling worked.

"Absolutely," I said, "Hailey has decades of experience selling houses, Matt, you're one of the best salespeople in the valley, Zack, you're a recognized general contractor with an impressive record. I have a contact at BazookaMedia, Nettie, who is working the internet side of things. So, Hailey will manage us as a team, Matt will line up the buys and sells, and Zack will do the renovations. Then Hailey will sell the properties. All the while, Nettie will drive us online traffic and maybe make some sales just by posting the houses online. If we optimize our online presence—"

"Wait, so how do you make money?" Hailey asked.

"I'll take a salary out of the company's profits."

"You mean take a distributive share out of the revenue?"

"Tomato, tomato."

"No, Caish, not tomato tomato. Partners in a four-person corporation do not receive a salary from company profits. They take distributive shares, and it is an expense of the corporation, not a profit."

"I think we're getting lost in the weeds on this, Hailey," I said.

"Maybe," Matt said, "but I think what Hailey was asking is what is your role? What do you do to earn money from Caish Enterprises?"

"Calloway Enterprises."

"Yeah, Calloway Enterprises."

"I invest. I bring together the team, rent the office, pay for marketing."

"So what's your cut?" Zack asked.

"Well, we can talk numbers and figure out what the fairest way to structure this will be, but I was thinking since it's my company and I am the one bearing the risk, I would own fifty percent of the company and we'd split profits fifty-fifty."

Hailey looked like she was losing her patience. Thank God our first rolls of sushi arrived and distracted her before she could hone in on another tiny detail of what I said. After we divvied out the sushi, Hailey just said, "No."

"No?" I said, "No what?"

"No, that's not how it works. No, that is not equitable. No, I will not stop selling houses on my own, just so that I can sell houses for you and give you some of my take."

Zack agreed. "Yeah, I'm with Hailey, that's a pretty shitty deal, Caish. Without you even getting into details I can tell you've never run a business before, and although you may have a few good ideas, I'm making good money right now, and your vision kind of looks like a way for me to make less money and for you to earn my money."

Matt's head was nodding along with Zack. When Zack finished, Matt gave me a shrug, as if to say, "Yeah, they're right."

"Well you're wrong, Zack," I said, "I have run a business before, several businesses. And a few of them have been pretty successful."

"Creating an app is not a business. Neither is designing a new toothbrush and selling it online. Just because your lawyer has set up a corporation for you does not mean you've run a business. Do you know anything about operations management? Or the four Ps of marketing? Shit, Caish, I don't mean to bring you down, but your pitch sounds like what a landscaper tells to a bunch of high school students looking for a summer job. We make lots of money on our own, and you aren't presenting a way for us to make more."

"Look," I said, "I'm not trying to take your money, I am trying to invest in you. Think of how much more you can accomplish with real money at your disposal."

Hailey almost spat her sake out. "What?" she stated. "You're not actually patronizing us, are you?"

"No, no, of course not. I would never do that. Why?" I said.

"Because," Matt said as he poured soy sauce into a little dish next to his plate, "you're talking to us as if we have never seen a balance sheet. You're giving us platitudes that would make the layman cringe. You have just pitched a business model that is idealistically simple and proposed that you get fifty percent of the company's profits just for renting the office space."

"I said we could discuss numbers, that was just a ballpark."

"Caish," Matt leaned in, "you're not hearing me. Your grand plans are puerile. I hate to say it like that, but you don't know the first thing about running a business, and we'd have to be crazy to drop our businesses—which are very successful, I would add—to help you make money."

"Yeah, Caish," Zack added, "we're your friends, and we're

happy to help. We'll buy the next app you come out with or whatever, but for Christ's sake."

Then it was quiet for a little while. In a regular restaurant, the bustle of the kitchen and the hum of conversation soften the blow of awkward silences, but at Surasawa, the silence was brutal. Worst of all, I could tell from their faces that they felt bad for me. Like they just kicked a puppy and now they were thinking of a way of consoling it. Hailey spoke up, "Caish, run some numbers over the weekend. Put together a business plan—do you know what a business plan is?"

"Of course, yeah."

"Okay, put together a business plan, send it to us, then let's do this again. As is, it sounds like you've got a few ideas janglin' around in your noodle but haven't thought of practicalities." What she was really saying was, "Unless you know every single little detail of how to run a business, I won't join you." Which is exactly what I should have expected from somebody who went to college. I can't remember where she went, but I know she has a degree in something, and she thinks that makes her the smartest person in the room. I expected more from her.

"Sounds good." Which was my way of saying, fine. I fold. Gig is up. "But I still don't think you heard me out. And I've already rented the office space and paid a marketing company for a logo, a motto, and a website."

"You paid a place to make a motto?" Zack asked.

"Yeah."

"What is it?"

"The House You Want for the Price You Deserve."

"Hm." Zack raised his eyebrows then sipped his sake.

"Everything is ready to go," I said, "I have done all the legwork, all you guys need to do is show up to work and make money."

"We wish it were that easy," Matt said, "we wish we could help you, Caish. But next time pitch the company before paying to set anything up. Let's just enjoy the evening. Surasawa is quite the event, let's eat fancy sushi tonight and talk business after you've drafted a business plan."

Matt didn't think I was going to draft a business plan. None of them did. This was their way of turning me down but making it seem as if it is my fault that the business idea failed because I was the one who didn't draft the business plan. How hard could a business plan be to draft? It's probably just a plan for the business. I merely type up the type of business it is. Easy.

Over the next couple of days I drafted a business plan and emailed it to Matt, Hailey, and Zack. Hailey was the only one to respond. She said, "Looks good, Caish, but this isn't a business plan. This may pass as a mission statement, but it's not a business plan. A business plan includes an analysis of financial factors, operations plans, management layouts, marketing details, design and developments plans, etc. Also, be sure and include market strategies and a competitive analysis. Look forward to seeing it!"

Overcomplicating things isn't my style. Apparently it's Hailey's style. Wish I would have known that before buying her dinner. I called BazookaMedia and cancelled my contract. Of course there was an early termination fee.

A million dollars is almost enough to live on, but not when your house costs two million dollars. My options were dwindling. I no longer had enough wealth to make money for me, and I couldn't convince people to invest in my business ideas. Thank God for the California State Lottery, or Hopelessness would really be rearing its slimy head. The odds were on my side (since I had won before), and I had plenty of good karma stored up to tilt the scales of luck in my favor. Experts say that if you get lost in the wilderness, just stay put. The best course of action is to hunker down. I took the same course of action. Sure, my house costs two million dollars, but that two million dollars wasn't due any time soon. Thanks to Mr. Valentini, that wasn't due for thirty years. I still had more money than most people.

Most people are in debt. Especially in neighborhoods like Spanish Hills. Most of them can hardly make payments for their child's gymnastic lessons because they're spread so thin. They get the biggest mortgage they can qualify for (because square footage is one of the only sure signs of status these days), then lease the best Mercedes the rest of their money can buy. It doesn't leave much wiggle room, so as soon as little Janey needs braces the whole shtick caves in. Those people would kill to have a million in the bank. They hardly have enough to get from one day to the next. Me? I had enough to last years. Years to relax in my Spanish Hills estate while I waited for my next break. Whether that be through the lottery (which was most likely) or through a business or investing opportunity. Once again, money provided the security I needed to get through a tough time. A small rough patch paved over with golden asphalt.

In the years that followed, I settled into a sustainable routine. The Porsche was my only car, and I was fine with it. I bought a Lotus Elise to have as a backup car in case the Porsche broke down, but for the most part I just drove the Porsche. I made most my mortgage and Lotus payments on time, bought my usual batch of lottery tickets every morning, and refrained from buying much else. Instead of sushi and lobster, I ate burgers and tacos. Instead of designer shops, I shopped at department stores. I tried to replace cocaine with Focalin, but it just wasn't the same.

Downgrading hurts. Even with my Spanish Hills place and my Porsche, most of the people I considered friends abandoned me like sailors swimming away from a sinking ship. I wasn't invited to join prestigious groups, I wasn't tapped as a potential investor for any new startups, and I wasn't invited to house parties anymore. I still went to clubs and met new people. And I got back into dating. I even had good sex every now and then. But I was lonely.

10

I needed to reconnect with my son. Mark was born when I was young, and I was not in a good position to be a parent. Mark's upbringing has been financed by me, but my ex has been the one raising him. He's a handsome little boy with brilliantly blonde hair who likes to ride his bike. I think. It's been a few years since I've seen him. Before calling my ex, I do some research on how to be a parent. I google "how to be a parent" and read an article written by Alan Bradley, MS. "When human beings first start out," the article stated:

> we are, by nature, narcissistic, egocentric, amoral, and disloyal. Not to mention completely incompetent, gullible, and prone to unconstrained fits of violent rage. It takes an attentive, stalwart, patient parent to teach children how to be decent members of society, and this task often takes decades of diligence. Fraught with frequent failure, the difficulty leads many parents to give up and allow their young to grow up with the follies associated with children, thus leaving fully formed adults with the same immaturity and lack of development as toddlers. In past centuries, many parents turned to religion for help, relying on a fear of Hell to bridle their children. Although this is still practiced today, short-term threats are replacing religion with increased frequency (*e.g.* "Santa's watching," or "the Easter Bunny might not come if you are bad" (*see* Zhang Xiu Ying's work on threatening children)). Other parents have turned to drugs like methylphenidate (or "Ritalin"). But, by far the most used tactic is increased vocal volume and threats of deprivation of...

Yeesh. That's enough of that. This next article looks more practical, it's by Paul Lionetti, MS and it's titled, "How to Be

Moral Parents." The first paragraph reads:

> The moral limits of children's minds, although influenced by external stimuli, are ultimately set by the minds themselves. This is why, even after full development, some minds are able to sexually abuse children, carry out terrorist attacks, and torture animals. Broken minds produce perverse compulsions then fail to provide necessary limitations on behavior. Laws and punishment may dissuade those with conflicting tendencies toward anti-social behavior, but evidence suggests that no amount of detrimental consequence can prevent the lunacy of a broken mind from attempting to satisfy its insatiable hunger for grotesque, and often grisly, gratification...

What in the world? These college interneters are making a confusing mess out of a simple topic. Oh! I must have clicked on Google Scholar. That explains the hoity-toity articles. Having navigated back to Google proper, I found more promising articles. Articles like "10 Things Every Parent Should Know," "Why Kids Cry," and "12 Things You Didn't Know About Your Child—Number Two Will Blow You Away!" But even those articles were pretty worthless. Humans have been raising children for thousands of years without the help of this jargon, I'll be fine.

My ex answers the phone.

"Hello?"

"Hi, this is Caish, is Mark around?"

"Yeah, Mark's around."

"Will you give him the phone?"

"Why?"

"Why?"

"Yeah, why do you want to talk to Mark?"

"Because," I said, "Mark is my son and I have a right to talk to him."

"Oh you have that right? You can call and talk to your son whenever you want?"

"Yes. I do. So please hand the phone to Mark."

"Mark is busy doing homework right now, so maybe call back this weekend. I'll let him know you called. We have your number."

"Don't be like that, hand Mark the phone."

"Mark is busy right now."

"Have you forgotten who bought the house you and Mark are living in?"

And then the line went dead. So I called back. My ex answers again. "Caish, seriously, Mark is busy, call back this weekend."

"Don't hang up on me ever again. Give the phone to Mark."

"Okay, Caish, I am going to hang up. Try not to take it personally."

"I swear to God, if you—"

My ex hangs up. Okay. Fine. My ex has apparently forgotten that I have one of Los Angeles's best lawyers in my corner.

"Good afternoon, thank you for calling Morely, Black, and Associates, how may I direct your call?"

"To Gabby Rodriguez."

"Transferring you now, please hold..."

(Longer than usual wait.)

"Gabriella speaking."

"Gabby, this is Caish."

"Hi Caish, long time no talk. Another car get repossessed?"

"No, my ex isn't letting me talk to my son. Isn't that against the law?"

"I'm not a family law attorney, Caish, but I would be happy to refer you to an attorney in our family law practice group."

"Oh come on, didn't you go to law school? Is it illegal or not for a parent to keep another parent from speaking to their own child? Sounds pretty illegal to me."

"I am unfamiliar with your circumstances, Caish. It may be illegal in some cases, in others you may be violating a restraining order and by trying to reach out you may be the one committing an illegal act."

"What? My ex doesn't have a restraining order against me." What the hell Gabby?

"I didn't say that," I could hear Gabby straining to be patient with me. "I'm just using that as an example to point out that I don't have enough information to guess, and you don't want a guess anyway, so you should speak to somebody in our family law practice group."

"Gabby, are you passing the buck because I'm behind on my payments?"

"Caish, I am not passing the buck, I am telling you that your family law issue needs a family law attorney. But, since you mention it, yes, please get current on your bill."

"K, fine. Thanks Gabby." This time I hang up first.

I want to see my son, so I am going to see my son. I packed a few outfits into a leather duffle bag and tossed it in my Porsche. On my way out of town I stopped at In-N-Out to have dinner and collect my thoughts. My ex was keeping Mark from me, and my lawyer was unwilling to help. As a parent, it's my right to be with my son and to be involved in his life. It had been years since I'd seen him. I needed to drive to Monterey and spend quality time with Mark. The drive from Spanish Hills to Monterey takes about five hours, so I planned to drive to Pismo Beach and spend the night there, then pick Mark up from school the next day.

The drive to Pismo was therapeutic. It was near seventy-five degrees without a breeze. Windows down, stereo off. The 101 was congested through Santa Barbara, but otherwise the freeway was clear enough to let the Porsche run at Autobahn speeds.

I pulled into the Shorebird Resort a little after 10:00 p.m. "Resort" is optimistic. It's a cheap hotel by the ocean, priced high enough to make the middle-class think they're buying a luxury room. Picture a La Quinta Inn next to the beach with a decent pool. I would have stayed in a nicer hotel, but on such short notice this was all that was available. My room is a single-room suite with a view of the ocean. The last time I could see the ocean from my bed was two years ago. I fight off the surge of sadness that wells up when I remember my Malibu house. Two mini bottles of Smirnoff from the mini fridge help. It's Friday, and I'll be damned if I'm going to spend the night moping around this three hundred square foot poorly decorated cheaply furnished poorly-lit beige attempt at a hotel room.

There are several bars within walking distance of the Shorebird "Resort" but I take the Porsche. I don't know many people around here, and the Porsche is the best way to introduce myself. The Tar Bar looked like the place to be, so I rolled my window down and circled the block a couple times looking for a parking place. After a few laps a spot opened up and I parallel parked with speed and efficiency that impressed onlookers. I showed the doorman my ID and ducked into the Tar Bar.

This bar was like most bars, low lights, loud, and full of mostly youngish people glancing around, laughing, and acting drunker than they actually are. A live band was covering "Rock You Like a Hurricane" in the back corner, and the locals were making the most of the dance floor. I shouldered my way onto a bar stool and ordered a local pilsner and a shot of Jack Daniels. I also ordered spicy chicken wings. I hadn't eaten since Camarillo.

When my chicken wings arrive, a youngish local to my left leaned over and asked, "Excuse me, could I try one of those wings? Can't decide if that's what I wanna get." The local was thin, blonde, and looked like some famous person whose name I couldn't remember.

"Um. You want one of my buffalo wings?" I said.

"Yeah," the local said, completely unashamed. "Unless you're weirded out by that. Just wanna try one before I order a whole batch."

"Sure, yeah. I guess. Shit. I've never had a stranger ask to have one of my wings. Or even fries. But sure, here," I handed over a chicken wing. The local smiled, thanked me, dipped the wing in my Ranch dressing, and ate it with delicacy so as to spare the cheeks any stickiness. Those eyes... I had seen this person before.

"Mmm, those are super good. I appreciate it, thanks," the local said. Then the local hailed the bartender and ordered eight wings. "I can tell you're not from Pismo, huh?"

"No, I'm from here, I'm a California native," which I am at this point.

"Oh, yeah, okay. But I mean from Pismo. Are ya waitin' for anybody?"

"No, you?" I asked.

"Nope! I come down every now and then and try to make a friend out of a stranger."

"And I'm tonight's stranger?"

"Not if ya don't wanna be, but ya made me sad sittin' over here all alone and I figured, hell, maybe this tourist needs a friend."

"I'm not a tourist, I'm from California."

"Right, yeah, but I mean a tourist to Pismo Beach. I'm Jackie," the local said.

"I'm Caish, nice to meet you Jackie."

"How long ya been in town, Cash?"

"It's *Caish* like cake with an 'sh' at the end."

"Oh, *Caish*. How long ya been in town?"

"Just got here a couple hours ago."

"Hm. So, Caish, what's buggin' ya?"

"What?"

"Ya know, what's got ya down?" Jackie asked. "Seems like if the palm trees, warm weather, and local talent hasn't cheered ya up by this point, those buffalo wings would've. So, what's up?"

"Well, ya know, life can just be tough sometimes." I took a long swig of my beer and ate a few celery sticks, hoping Jackie would pick up on my hint that I didn't want to share my personal life with a stranger. That said, I didn't want to be rude. I hadn't had sex in weeks. Jackie was bangin' and obviously wanted to get with me—it was the hungry eyes that gave Jackie away. Hungry Eyes! That was it! Jackie was Hungry Eyes!

"Jackie! We've met before!" I nearly yelled.

"Haha, yeah? Jeez, must have been pretty good, huh?"

"Well we didn't really get to know each other, we met at a club and got separated before we had a chance to talk much."

"You remember me from bumping into me at a club? Quite the memory. What club?" Jackie asked.

"Hyde. It was a few years back. You were with a friend, and... Oh, actually we met before we got to the club. You were walking on like... or, in Santa Monica. You were walking in Santa Monica with a friend and I was in a white Lamborghini and you came over and started talking to me."

"Hmm, I usually don't approach people on the street, ya sure it was me?"

"Don't approach people on the street but you'll steal a stranger's chicken wing?"

"Sure, yeah. Pretty big difference. I know I wouldn't randomly approach a stranger's car in Santa Monica and start a conversation."

"Well you definitely did. I wouldn't forget those eyes," I sipped some beer at this point to let the words work their magic on Jackie. "Remember? You ubered over to Hyde, I was in a white Lamborghini and followed you over?"

"Oh! Haha, yeah! You're Lamborghini Bambini! What a trip!"

"Yeah, wow. What are the chances," I said, "it's a small world." This wasn't a coincidence. There's no such thing. God crossed our paths again for a reason.

"Yeah... I forgot all about that night. Oh, yeah, that was a *fun* night," Jackie said, grinning into the distance. Jackie was trying to make me jealous, which was a good sign. "But as I remember it," Jackie went on, "you yelled out to us from your Lambo. We didn't approach you."

"Mmm, I'm pretty sure you approached me," I said, "but it doesn't really matter. We got separated not long after and it sounds like we both had a pretty good time anyway."

"Sort of, yeah. So, Caish—it's Caish, right?—or should I call you Lamborghini Bambini?"

"Yeah, Caish. Let's stick with Caish for now."

"Okay, Caish, what brings ya up from Santa Monica? Did ya drive your Lamborghini up?" The bartender dropped off Jackie's chicken wings and set a new glass of beer in front of me. "Anything to drink?" the bartender asked Jackie. "Yeah, give me a water and whatever your best IPA is."

"Just vacationing," I answered, "but I'm actually from Malibu. I have a house on the coast sort of by Point Mugu. What about you? You act like a Pismo local, were you just visiting LA?"

"Yeah I'm from Pismo. But I have lots of friends in LA, so I'm down there all the time. You go to Hyde a lot?"

"Not a lot, probably once a month or so. If I remember correctly, and I do, you were in the VIP area all night when I was there. What's up with that? You have connections at Hyde, or what?"

"Just a lot of friends," Jackie said, "and I forgot, were you in the VIP area too?" Jackie already knew the answer.

"No, they wouldn't let me back there. Guess I'm just not fancy enough, even if I am a millionaire with a Lamborghini."

"Wow." Jackie's IPA and water arrived and Jackie took a gulp of beer before saying, "I'm surprised ya don't lead with that."

"What?"

"Ya know, 'I'm a millionaire with a Lamborghini.' That's a pretty good pick-up line."

"I didn't mean it like that, I'm just saying. They wouldn't let me back to the VIP area, so you must have quite the friends."

"Yeah, I guess, so, how long you in Pismo?"

"Depends, how long do you think I should be in Pismo?" I said. I figured it was probably time to get started with the hints. We had each other's names, what more did we need? Bodies like mine and Jackie's were meant to be together, if only for a few nights, and I had a feeling Jackie knew it.

"Hmm. So it's up to me?" Jackie asked.

"Should it be?"

"Depends."

"On what?" I asked.

"Well. If I don't get anything from it, then I don't think it should be up to me," Jackie was licking the sauce off of a chicken wing, "But, if there's somethin' in it for me, then it prob'ly should be up to me."

"I see what you're saying. I think you're safe assuming there's something in it for you."

"Oooo, a ride in Lamborghini Bambini's Lamborghini?"

"Play your cards right and there might be some candy too." That did it. Locked in. I'm sleeping with Jackie tonight. I'll finally land Hungry Eyes.

"Hm," Jackie said, acting deep in thought, "So, in that case, you should stay the weekend, feel out Pismo Beach, then, depending on how the weekend goes, stay the next week. Unless you have to get back to work or somethin'."

"I like that plan. When do you wanna go for a ride in my Lamborghini?"

"Let's have a few more drinks, on me—consider it a welcome gift—then go for a drive." Jackie ordered two shots of Fireball and we toasted to my stay in Pismo. Jackie's hungry eyes turned to starving eyes (in a good way) and I felt the fizz begin to build below the belt. The tingle that tells you it's time.

We had a few more shots, getting progressively more touchy, then I paid the bill and we capered out to the Porsche.

"Wait a minute, Lamborghini Bambini," Jackie was reaching for the door handle, then took a few steps away from the car, "I dunno much about cars, but I know this is not a Lambo. This wasn't the deal."

"My Lamborghini's still in Malibu," (God I wish it was) "I don't take it on road trips. But this Porsche is just as expensive as my Lamborghini."

"Mmmm, I really wanted a ride in a Lamborghini tonight, not some Batmobile Porsche."

"How about I sweeten the deal?" I asked.

"Can I drive?"

"No."

"Candy?"

"Yup. Hop in."

As soon as we were in the car, I reached into the glove box and pulled out a Ziploc bag of cocaine and a snuff spoon. "Care to do the honors?" I handed the bag and spoon to Jackie. Without asking any questions, Jackie peeled open the bag, loaded the spoon to maximum capacity, and inhaled it with the force of a reverse sneeze. We went back and forth until we both felt electric. I put the coke under my seat, lit a cigarette, and started the car. Again, I wouldn't usually smoke in the car, but it was important that I demonstrate to Jackie just how much of a badass I actually was. The cigarette was necessary.

"So, Porsche Bambini, where we hop bop boppin' off to?" Jackie turned toward me, sitting sideways in the seat, and Jackie's right hand slid around my knee.

"I've got a room at the Shorebird Resort, how about we take the long way back?"

"Oooo, the Shorebird, big spender."

"It was the only room available on short notice."

"Chill out, Bambi, I'm just givin' ya a hard time." Jackie's hand slid up the inside of my thigh. "Take me to your room Bambini. Bam Bambi Bambini. Bambi's jungle resort room…"

Jackie's hand cupped my crotch. "Or shall we begin here?" Jackie's hand slid up the front of my pants and nudged its way behind the top button. Jackie leaned across the seat and breathed into my ear, then whispered, "Maybe we should take the short way back." Jackie's fingers slid down into my pubic hair, and I snapped out of my trance with embarrassment for not having shaved.

From the parking spot, I smashed the gas pedal to the floor and might have clipped the car in front of me (no time to stop and check). Luckily there wasn't much traffic, so I didn't have to stop at red lights. Just slowed down, checked both ways, then did a burnout through the intersection when it was clear. By the third intersection, Jackie had unbuttoned my pants and was tugging at my underwear.

The Shorebird Resort was now in sight. I floored it and had to pass a car or two on the shoulder. The Porsche is good for that. The speed limit on that stretch of road was 40 miles-per-hour, and I was nearing 100 when I passed a squad car. The cop's lights went on immediately and my stomach plummeted.

"Fuuuuuuuuck. Fuck, fuck, fuck." I moaned.

"Yes, yes we will." Jackie said.

"Ah, shit. I don't think we will. God dammit." I let off the gas and started braking. "That was pretty fast and I've got a load on." I was buttoning up my pants and coming to a stop, pulling into the soft shoulder. The cop was right on my ass. I couldn't even see the cop car's headlights—just blinding flashes of blue and red. "I'll blow into one of those fucking breathalyzers, get arrested for a DUI, then they'll search the car and find coke. Fuck. Goddammit. All I wanted to do tonight was fuck you. Was that so much to ask?"

"Then lose the tail and fuck me."

"What?"

"If ya wanna fuck me, stop being a lil' bitch, lose the tail, and take me to your room. This is a Porsche, isn't it? Ya think that cop's in a Ferrari?"

"I can't run from the cops, are you kidding?"

"Not if you keep stalling. If he doesn't already, that cop is going to have your plate number in his system in a couple seconds."

The Porsche had just about come to a stop. A dust cloud from the shoulder surrounded our cars. In less than a second, I had a minute's worth of contemplation. I had two options. Option A: pull over and get fucked by the law, spend the rest of the night (and maybe longer) in jail. Option B: rabbit and get fucked by Jackie, spend the rest of the night in a hotel suite. If I chose option B and got caught, I would be formally fucked by the law. But, if I didn't get caught, I would get royally fucked by Jackie. Nothing to get the adrenaline running like a police chase. I once heard that participating in high-adrenaline activities is a good way to bond, but that's beside the point.

As the car came to a stop and rocked back, I made up my mind. I shifted into first, crammed the gas, and popped the clutch. After showering the cop car with sand and gravel, my tires met the pavement and squealed under the punishment of the Porsche's engine at full tilt. Jackie, seemingly oblivious to the stakes, yelled, "Yaaaasss! Lamborghini Bambini's gonna bam my bini me tonight!"

The Porsche launched into the darkness. The rearview showed me the squad car scrambling back onto the road, but not before we were well on our way. I killed the lights and made random turns headed toward the 101. When I couldn't see the squad car's lights anymore, I turned my lights back on. I pushed the Porsche beyond what I had ever tried. I kept my foot buried in the gas, letting off only to shift up or jam the brakes for corners. The engine roared and the exhaust barked flames on the down shifts. Finally we made it to the 101. I peeled out around the onramp corner and soared onto the freeway. We were weaving through traffic when, unbelievably, another set of cop-car lights lit up in the distance behind us. Now California Highway Patrol was giving chase. But the CHP car was too far back to get a read on my plates, so I was probably still in the clear. Still going to make it back to Shorebird, still going to land Hungry Eyes. It didn't take long to lose the CHP car. Their Dodge Chargers are no match for my Porsche.

We were flying at over 150 mph when Jackie yelled, "Shell Beach Road! Exit 191 B, this is you!" and pointed to the exit. I swerved into the exit, and put all my weight onto the brake pedal. The car's back end danced back and forth as we skidded down the exit ramp. A truck was stopped in the right lane, waiting to turn right onto Mattie Road, and a van blocked the left turn lane. I wasn't going to be able to stop in time, but needed to turn right. I veered into the shoulder to pass the truck. Just before I passed the truck, my passenger-side rear tire struck the curb on the side of the shoulder. The curb bucked the back end of the car up and out to the left. The entire car left the road and the back end slid along the side of the truck as the car rotated clockwise. Jackie let out a short, sharp yelp. When the car next met the road, the driver's side tires dug in and the car wrenched over onto its roof. The jolt was as loud as it was violent. Momentum kept the car rolling through the intersection and into a chain-linked fence. When it came to rest, the Porsche was upside-down with its hood buried in bushes and back tires spinning in the air.

My ears were ringing, and I'm not sure if I woke up or just stopped clenching. I opened my eyes and surveyed the damage. My seatbelt kept me hanging from what was now the top of the car. Luckily, this car was built to race, and had a roll cage, so the roof didn't cave in. The windshield was shattered. No airbags, but a four-point seat belt and bucket seat kept me planted. My left arm was broken. Unquestionably. There was a new joint between my elbow and wrist. I couldn't see my knees, but pain surged up through to my hips. Sirens whined in the distance. My vision was blurry. Something was in my eyes. Dust, tears, blood? It smelled like burning rubber. My arms were hanging down under my head and felt too heavy to move. I could hardly turn my head.

"Jackie, you alright?"

No response.

11

"Your honor, the defendant, Caish Calloway, was operating a vehicle in violation of California Code Section 23152(a), which provides that 'it is unlawful for a person who is under the influence of any alcoholic beverage to drive a vehicle.' The defendant also violated subsection (d), which states that 'it is unlawful for a person who is addicted to the use of any drug to drive a vehicle.' Not only was the defendant's blood alcohol level well over the .08 limit, a blood draw at the scene of the accident evidences that the defendant was also driving under the influence of cocaine. Further, by driving upon California's highways with a 'willful or wanton disregard for the safety of person or property' the defendant is guilty of reckless driving in violation of California Code Section 23103.

"That is why, your honor, the defendant is not guilty of vehicular manslaughter, but instead, of gross vehicular manslaughter while intoxicated, as provided in Section 191.5 of the California Penal Code. Said section provides, in relevant part, that 'gross vehicular manslaughter while intoxicated is the unlawful killing of a human being without malice aforethought, in the driving of a vehicle, where the driving was in violation of Section 23152 of the Vehicle Code, and the killing was either the proximate result of the commission of an unlawful act, not amounting to a felony, and with gross negligence.' Although Caish Calloway's unlawful actions amount to multiple felonies, the defendant is guilty of gross vehicular manslaughter while intoxicated because, while driving recklessly (which does not amount to a felony), the defendant operated a vehicle while intoxicated and caused the early, grisly death of Jackie Marquez.

"Moreover, your honor, by operating a motor vehicle with the intent to evade a peace officer, the defendant is guilty of violating Section 2800.1. By causing a death during flight from a pursuing peace officer, the defendant should be sentenced under Section 2800.3. Additionally, when police arrived at the scene of the accident, the defendant was observed attempting to throw what was later identified as a bag of cocaine away from the defendant's overturned car. The exact quantity of cocaine was unascertainable because as the defendant threw the bag, the bag ruptured and caused cocaine to vaporize into the air and disperse onto the defendant and the ground around the scene of the accident. However, there was enough cocaine observed on the defendant and collected from the scene to charge the defendant with transporting a designated controlled substance for sale in violation of Section 11352. The defendant was also charged with possession of a designated schedule II controlled substance in violation of California Code Section 11350. More cocaine was found at the defendant's Spanish Hills home in a subsequent FBI search.

"In conclusion, your honor, the defendant has been convicted of reckless endangerment, reckless driving, two counts of operating a vehicle while under the influence of intoxicating substances, three counts of evading a police officer, two counts of possession of a schedule II controlled substance, transportation of a controlled substance for the purpose of sale, and gross vehicular manslaughter. As these egregious facts are substantially similar to those in *People v. Boldter* and *People v. Thompson*, the prosecution and people of the State of California recommend the court impose a sentence of twenty-five years imprisonment and a fine of $200,000."

"Thank you counsel," Judge Peters said. Then, turning to the table where my attorney and I sat, said, "Counsel for the defense, you may proceed."

My attorney, Charlotte H. Dent (Gabby wouldn't take my call), walked to the lectern and laid out my defense. There were a number of "mitigating factors" that Ms. Dent needed to explain to the court. This part of the trial was what is referred to as the "sentencing phase." Ms. Dent assured me that she had the main trial under control, but the jury convicted me without more than an hour's deliberation. Ms. Dent did her best to convince the jury that I was acting out of character as a result of a sudden onset of immense anxiety associated with the last few years of my life. She emphasized my loss of money and relationships, and stressed my clean record. "First time offender," she said.

The jury wasn't having it. The prosecution was allowed to show them pictures of the scene of the accident. Ms. Dent objected to the evidence, saying that it was irrelevant and inadmissible under California Evidence Code Sections 350 and 351, that it was unduly prejudicial, and that the court should exercise its discretion and exclude it under Section 352. The judge disagreed, and the prosecution showed the jury photographs of Jackie laying in the road, twisted, road rashed, and dead. Jackie was thrown from the car while it was rolling and died from blunt force trauma. The jury also saw pictures of me completely covered in cocaine and blood, as well as the destroyed Porsche tangled in a heap of fence, bushes, and road signs.

As Ms. Dent earned my money trying to convince Judge Peters why a no-jail-time sentence was the most equitable outcome, I heard the last few years of my life recited in painful detail. Then I realized, when my Porsche came to rest on top of that fence, I hadn't been fucked by the law (and I certainly wouldn't be fucked by Jackie (rest in peace)), I had been fucked by bad luck. No other way of putting it. As if the universe were tipping the scales. Although I had to work hard to win, my lottery win also took a fair amount of good luck. These last few years were the universe's way of restoring balance. I didn't do anything to deserve this.

I heard Ms. Dent conclude, "That is why, your honor, the defense urges this court to sentence Caish to nothing more than time served and a fine of $50,000. Caish is not a criminal, and should not be punished as such. Thank you, your honor."

"And I understand the defendant would like to make a statement before I enter the sentencing order, is that correct?" the judge asked.

"Yes, it is," Ms. Dent said, turning toward me and inviting me to the lectern with an extended hand. "Remember," Ms. Dent whispered into my ear. She had counseled me before every hearing to, "show remorse, take responsibility, and stick to what we prepared." I nodded, then adjusted the microphone.

"Thank you, your honor," always good to stroke their pride, "I appreciate the opportunity to be in your court and address you directly. I acted poorly on the night of the horrific accident where Jackie died. I acted irrationally. I acted stupidly. But I did not act criminally. Your honor, I am not a criminal, and my actions that night do not represent who I am as a person. Sentencing me to prison would not rehabilitate me any more than the guilt I live with daily already does. Retribution is best served here with a fine and probation, not by adding me into California's crowded prison system. Your honor, God works in mysterious ways. And these trials, both the literal and the figurative, are God's way of humbling me, and teaching me the value of life, both mine and others. I take full responsibility for my actions, and I am deeply sorry to the Marquez family for the pain I have caused. I ask your honor for mercy and forgiveness. Thank you."

"Thank you for your comments," Judge Peters said without betraying any emotion, "but it is not within this court's purview to forgive you. I am ready to enter my sentence, do the parties have any other statements?" Judge Peters looked from the defense to the prosecution attorneys, both of whom stood and said, "No, your honor." "In that case," the judge continued, "I will proceed. I will note that I have received letters from Caish Calloway's ecclesiastical leaders, and a few friends discussing what an upstanding citizen Caish usually is. I have also received letters from the Marquez family telling me about the suffering caused by the loss of Jackie. Based on the crimes Caish has been convicted of and the equities in this case, I am going to impose a suspended prison sentence of five years with a mandatory fine of $175,000, payable with interest in a payment schedule to be determined at a later date. I am ordering probation for five years, and requiring regular random drug testing. Ms. Dent, will you draft a memorandum order reflecting this sentencing and circulate it to the prosecution before the end of the week?"

"Yes, your honor."

"Thank you, counsel. Is there anything else?"

"No, your honor," Ms. Dent said.

"No, your honor," the prosecutor said.

And then the bailiff said, "All rise," and Judge Peters walked through a back door without so much of a glance over her shoulder.

"Congratulations, Caish!" Ms. Dent said, extending her hand for a handshake.

"For what? Five years in prison? The fine of $175,000? Or the five years of drug testing?"

"Oh, Caish, no that's not your sentence. You received a *suspended* prison sentence of five years. Which means you don't have to go to prison. That's why the bailiff hasn't cuffed you and hauled you away. You're on probation for five years, and if you blow it, the judge will revoke the suspension and send you to prison, but if not, you're just on probation."

Oh praise God.

"Oh praise God Ms. Dent. I was on the verge of hyperventilating, I can't go to prison." The courtroom was emptying out. I looked around and caught a glance from the Marquez family that was intended to cut me to my soul. They still haven't been able to accept that it was Jackie's decision to go for a ride with me, and it was Jackie's decision not to buckle up. I'm not responsible for Jackie's actions.

"That's right, no prison time. Just fly right for five years and you're free as a bird. Easy, right?" Ms. Dent was smiling at me and putting files into her briefcase.

"Well, doesn't sound like that $175,000 fine is suspended though."

"No... it's not. Oh, and something else," Ms. Dent stopped what she was doing. "This was the criminal trial. The Marquez's will almost certainly bring a civil case against you for allegedly causing the wrongful death of Jackie."

"What? What about double jeopardy or whatever?"

"Double jeopardy means, generally speaking, that the state can't prosecute you for crimes that you've already been prosecuted for. It applies to criminal trials. This will be in the civil court."

"So what does that mean?" I ask. Leave it to an attorney to speak in confusing jargon.

"It means that the $175,000 isn't the last of it," Ms. Dent said, "The Marquez family will sue you and you will either need to pay an attorney to defend you, then pay a judgment—which you most certainly will have to because you have been convicted of the crime—or you will pay out a settlement, which could be a substantial amount of money."

And it was. After a year and a half of litigation and a two-month trial, the jury awarded the Marquez family three million dollars, all told. Not like they needed it. Mr. Marquez was a successful commercial property owner. Among his properties: Hyde. I appealed the judgment and Ms. Dent got the award down to $500,000 using some legal maneuvering and honing in on some obscure detail that the Marquez family attorney missed. All their money bought them a defective lawyer. Now they're bringing a malpractice suit against their attorney for the other $2,500,000. Fine by me.

My legal defense in the civil trial cost me $168,000, and my criminal defense cost me $215,000. Medical bills weren't as bad. I was insured and only had to pay $19,000 out of pocket. I had a broken radius and ulna, dislocated shoulder, fractured femur, bruised my saphenous nerve, and two sprained ankles.

Math isn't my strong suit, but the Pismo Beach trip cost me just over a million dollars and saddled me with five years of probation. All because Jackie wanted to try and outrun the police. Not to mention my Porsche 930 was totaled. It was a ball of mangled metal that they towed directly to the junkyard — which gave me three hundred dollars for the crumpled carcass. Although I was starting to get bored with the Porsche, nobody likes to see a car go like that. Insurance wouldn't replace it because I didn't have insurance. I withdrew my $50,000 insurance surety bond with the state to pay for some of this mess, but now I have to buy insurance for each car I own. Well, for the Lotus.

My seven-figure judgment debts were all payable in payments, so I didn't have any immediate cash-flow issues. I still had enough in the bank to live comfortably for many years.

But, just to be on the safe side, I sold my Spanish Hills house and moved back to Missoula, Montana. I made a good profit on the sale of that house. It wasn't an easy decision to make, but I needed a lower cost of living for a while. The Department of Corrections gave me permission to transfer my probation to Montana; Ms. Dent hammered out the details with the Montana criminal justice system. On the whole, things were looking up.

Checking out of California was incredibly difficult. Watching the moving service box up my belongings and load them into a truck bound for Montana moved me to tears. I broke down right there in my garage. Rubber knees, shaking hands, difficulty breathing. The whole scene. It's a cruel irony that at the time you most need a cigarette it's nearly impossible to light one. I collapsed into one of my dining room chairs that was about to be loaded into the truck and shook with sadness. Completely overcome with sorrow. Unlit cigarette hanging from my frown. Someday I would come back, but for now this would be the last time I inhaled California's air as a bonafide resident. The last time

I would have palm trees in my yard. The last time it would be seventy degrees in the middle of the night, and eighty at midday. The list of lasts was long. I would be returning to Montana. Snow-ridden, pine-filled, middle-of-nowhere Montana. Missoula, my hometown, has a smaller population than most Malibu house parties. Unless you want to be a surveyor or a logger, there aren't any opportunities to make money in Missoula. It's never easy leaving the center of the universe, but it's even harder leaving it for an uninhabited corner of the cosmos.

The movers didn't seem to notice my break down. I sat and sobbed, and they just kept loading everything I owned into the moving truck. I sat there for at least half an hour. Maybe they saw a lot of this. Rich people breaking down into tears when their wealth has been stolen from them. The wealthy realizing that there was always going to be an end to the money. That the vacuum of poverty sucks strong and relentlessly. The movers kept moving, and eventually I collected myself. When they finished packing, I got into my Lotus and followed the moving truck out of my driveway in Spanish Hills, through the palm-tree-lined streets of Camarillo, onto the 101 and 210 through Thousand Oaks, Glendale, and Rancho Cucamonga, then merged onto I-15 northbound toward Missoula, Montana. Toward fucking Missoula, Montana.

Hours and hours of empty land watched me leave my kingdom. The tumbleweeds stopped to stare at my convoy of despair. There were several opportunities for me to drive the Lotus off a bridge and put an end to it all, but I kept the car on the road. Suicidal thoughts kept me awake that night in the roadside motel. The next morning I lit a cigarette while I filled up at one of the gas stations in Idaho, but nobody seemed to notice, or care. Or maybe they were also hoping the place would explode. Anyway, the place didn't explode. As if the experience could get worse, it began to snow when we crossed the Montana border.

This was my first time back to Missoula since before I moved to Los Angeles over ten years ago. I bought the house we were driving to after finding it online and calling the real estate agent and rushing through the thousands of pointless forms. Given my recent bout of bad luck, I could only afford a small place on the east edge of town that cost $630,000. At that price, I could pay the mortgage and my other monthly bills and have enough left to live on. Three bedrooms, three bathrooms, and twenty-six hundred square feet. The house was built in a new development and had a three car garage for when I started rebuilding my fleet. For the time being, my Lotus had plenty of room. The back of the house opened up toward the water feature near the eighth hole of the Canyon River Golf Course. For such a low price it wasn't so bad. But, there was no mistaking it, I had slid back down to middle-class.

When the movers were unloading the last of my furniture, I realized I hadn't told my family I was moving back to town. Probably better that way. My dad and I hadn't talked in years. My sister, two brothers, and mom all resented me for not giving them more of my earnings, so we also weren't in the habit of communicating. I gave each of them a million (a million dollars! each!) and they hounded me for more. The nerve. They would create problems in their lives then come to me for money to solve them. "Caish, don't be selfish," they'd plead, "you got lucky and got more money than you're ever gonna be able to spend, I can't believe you ain't gon' just help out your own flesh and blood when we stand in need of help." So I'd float them a few hundred thousand more, then in a year they'd manage to spend it and ask for more. After a while I stopped paying their mortgages and told them to make their own money. At that point, all but my mom stopped asking. My mother was not deterred.

The tough thing about mothers is that they created you. Although fathers contribute an essential ingredient in the creation of life, mothers are the ones that build your body in their belly. And no matter what, for the rest of your life, you're indebted to them for that. Born in debt. And not just any debt, a debt that no matter what you do, no matter how many millions of dollars you give your mom, you will never pay off. Even if your gestation was the easiest nine months of all-you-can-eat, relax in bed, maternity leave in their lives, mothers will still hold it over your head for the rest of your life.

My mom was no different. When I was a kid it was always, "I gave birth to you, blah blah blah." And I'd say something like, "And did you have a wooden spoon in your mouth, or was that with an epidural? I forget." And then, "I had an epidural but it still wasn't no cakewalk." And back and forth until she would curse me with, "Someday you'll know what it's like to be a parent and deal with an ungrateful little shit." This never changed. When I became an adult the words changed but the message was the same. No matter what I did for her, it was never enough. And no matter how much money I gave her, she would always say something like: "So that's how you treat the woman who gave you life? The woman who brought you into this world and changed your diapers and gave you food and clothing and a roof to sleep under. This is how you treat me? By telling me you've given me enough? You're too selfish to give your down-and-out mom a few bucks out of your pile of gold?" Forever indebted.

So, five or six years ago, I blocked my mom's number and blocked her from all my social media accounts. My dad, who left our family two weeks into my life and visited infrequently, took his million and disappeared. He has always been mercifully absent. I had never been more grateful for that than now. If he were to learn that I was down to my last million and moved back to Missoula he'd probably want to come visit. In that visit, he's probably take subtle jabs by offering to help in whatever way he could. Reminding me that no matter how much I succeed in life, he will always be in a position to help. Always standing above me on the trail with his hand extended down.

My siblings, Catherine, Cormac, and Caleb (yeah, we were one of those families) thought I was selfish for not splitting my winnings between them and our mom. They always wanted more. I was closest to Catherine growing up, probably because we're closest in age. We were the perfect pair. Like a road and sidewalk. But even she had turned out to be a greedy bitch. About the same time I blocked out my mom, Catherine lost her cool at a Red Lobster and made a scene about me cutting her off. "After all I've helped you!" she yelled. "Everythin' I did for you, everythin' we been through, and you gon' make my kids go back to *public school*?" The other folks at the restaurant were staring at Catherine, who had risen to her feet and was leaning across the table pointing at my face. "You know we put them in Washington Private because you promised to help us! They got braces now! How we gon' pay for them? You fuckin' liar!" She picked up her plate, dumped what was left of her lobster and potatoes onto my lap, then frisbeed the plate through one of Red Lobster's windows. That last part may have been a tad more impulsive than what she had planned. She certainly looked surprised to see the window shatter. She stormed out of Red Lobster and I haven't seen or spoken to her since. Of course, I paid for her meal, the broken plate, the broken window, her plane ticket to and from Los Angeles, her hotel room at the Beverly Hills Wilshire, and her rented Mercedes. Being rich is a thankless occupation.

I spent my first day in Missoula unpacking boxes, sniffling through a cold, and drinking vodka. God I missed cocaine. The thought of not snorting a line for five years was almost more than I could bear.

In the evening I ordered sushi and watched Netflix. I tried to get my mind off money by watching porn before going to bed, but it was a depressing reminder of what used to be. An echoing ex. I had been reduced to a spectator. A professional athlete forced into early retirement by nothing more than bad luck.

Emptiness filled me. Tears rolled down my cheeks as if loneliness was literally draining me. How did it come to this? Never before had I been more aware of what joy and comfort wealth brought me. It's like when an air conditioner turns off, and you realize you've been listening to it all along, but never noticed, and the sudden silence pronounces its sound more noticeably than its own existence ever did. I was a clam without its pearl. I couldn't think about anything else. Everything reminded me of wealth. My comforter, of the times I slept on strewn cash. My leather jacket, of how rolls of cash used to feel in the pockets. My Lotus, of what it used to feel like to buy exotic cars in cash. I scrolled through my phone looking at pictures of us together. Me with power. Power with me. We had our ups and downs, but for the most part we were the perfect pair. Worst of all was seeing affluence with other people. My Instagram and Facebook were full of people I used to call friends hanging out on yachts and driving Italian sports cars.

I knew I couldn't give up on wealth, but I couldn't think of how to repair things. I tried my best to make things work, but forces beyond my control were always pulling us apart. I gave up everything and everybody for wealth. Now what?

I kept at the vodka until sleep subdued my pain.

12

Californians don't own snow shovels. There's no need for such a wretched tool. So, when I woke up to my first morning in Montana and saw a foot of snow had fallen through the night, with more still falling, my day's mission became clear: survive. To do so, I would need to get into town and buy equipment and supplies. If I was going to make it through a winter in Missoula, I needed a snow shovel, road salt, winter clothing, and snow tires—or a snow car. Something four-wheel drive.

After several cups of coffee and a couple cigarettes, I put on two pairs of pants, my leather jacket, my Dodgers hat, and my leather driving gloves. I went to my garage to see what I could use to clear my driveway. My Lotus sits low, and although our road looks well-plowed, I wouldn't make it there unless I could clear a path in my driveway. A push broom was the best I could manage. I opened the garage door and a three-foot wind drift fell into my garage floor. Sweeping sort of worked for the snow that fell into the garage, but the broom was no match for the hundreds of square feet of knee deep snow blanketing my driveway. Resigned to die in my socked in sepulcher, I closed the garage door and changed into sweats.

Then I heard the rumble of a snow blower. Out my front window I watched my neighbor clear his driveway and the sidewalk in front of his house. His snow blower was a massive orange machine that easily munched through the snow. When he was done clearing his property, he pushed his snow blower down the sidewalk in front of my house and began blowing the snow off of my driveway. A complete stranger, and he was clearing my driveway. Who is this guy? Does he want my money? He even cleared my front walk. Pulled out a little snow shovel and removed the snow right up to my front door.

Before he finished, I brewed him a cup of coffee and took

it out to him. His back was turned when I approached, and he apparently couldn't hear my shouts over the roar of the snow blower. I patted him on the shoulder. He gave such a start that he startled me. Some of the coffee spilled over the edge of the cup and scolded my hand. I dropped the mug. The mug fell to my freshly cleared driveway and shattered. Coffee splashed all over my neighbor's leg and nice orange snow blower.

When he turned off the snow blower I could hear him laughing underneath his ski mask. He pulled off the mask and said, "Quite the way to say hello!" He was a handsome man, maybe 45 years old. Bald with gray stubble around his square jaw line. Like Mr. Clean if he didn't shave for the weekend.

"Ah, God dammit," I said, "I'm so sorry. What do I owe you?"

"Ha! Whad'ya owe me? How 'bout a new cup a coffee?"

"Oh yeah, of course, I'll be right back. Just give me sec."

"Oh come on now, I'm just givin' ya a hard time. It was my fault. No need to brew another cup. My name's Kevin." He pulled off one of his gloves and extended his hand. His hand shake is exactly what you'd expect for a gruff Montana Mr. Clean: a vice grip with a single jarring whip of the arm.

"Very nice to meet you Kevin, and thanks a lot for clearing my driveway. I'm Caish."

"What's that? Quiche?"

"*Cai*sh, like cake but with an sh. Caish."

"Oooh, Citsch. Okay. Well that's quite a unique name. How'd your parents come up with that one?"

"To tell you the truth I have no idea," I said. "Been getting that question my entire life. Probably time I found the answer."

"I'd say," Kevin said, "well, welcome to the neighborhood Citsch. Where ya comin' from?"

"Malibu."

"Oh wow, okay. Big timer eh? Good f'r you. This your first time in Missoula?"

"I lived here a while back, but it's been quite some time."

"Okay, yeah? Well good. Welcome back then. Like I said, my name's Kevin, Kevin Grier, and me and my wife MaryAnn are your neighbors here to the west." Kevin flattened his arm and pointed down the street toward his house, then shifted and pointed the other direction. "To your east is the Black family, and—"

"The black family? What?"

"Yeah, Blacks, fine folks. You know 'em?"

"No. But Jesus. Just seems kind of racist to introduce a family based on their skin color."

"Haha!" Kevin almost keeled over in laughter. "No, no, Citsch. The *Black* family. As in, Mr. and Ms. Black. Black is their last name."

"Oh. Dammit. Sorry about that."

"Haha," Kevin continued, "ya shoulda seen your face Citsch. Ha, thinkin' I was some damn racist. Thinkin' 'ol Kevin was some Klansman. Haha. Anyway, beyond the Blacks are the Woods. Also a very nice family. Oh and I should mention that no, Citsch, they are not a family made of wood. They are a family with a last name *Wood*. Hahaha."

"Haha, okay yeah yeah," I said, "the Griers, the Blacks, and the Woods. Very good."

"And what is your last name?"

"Calloway. *Caish* Calloway."

"And did ya bring another Calloway with ya, or is it just you usin' up all that house?"

"Nope. Just me." No money, no spouse, no lover, no kids, no friends.

"Well that's just fine," Kevin said as he patted me on the shoulder like a father would when he told his child that dogs go to heaven too. "Missoula's a big town, I'm sure we'll find ya somebody."

"Oh, yeah, I'm fine, really. I'm not looking for a relationship." I was not about to have this conversation with Kevin. "So, Kevin, any recommendations on where I can get me some winter gear?" I probably knew this town better than him, but it was something to say.

"Sure! Yeah, 'course," Kevin said. "You got Google Maps on your phone?"

"Yeah."

"Great. Put in Grier's Hardware. That's g-r-i-e-r. Grier's is great because we can relate."

"Oh, very cool. You have your own hardware store?"

"You betcha," Kevin said, "finest shop in town. We'll even give ya a new resident discount."

"Oh no need for that, but I will definitely go stock up at Grier's."

"You need a ride? I saw ya pull in yesterday in a little sports car that doesn't look too fit to brave these here elements."

"Thanks for the offer, but I should be fine. I'd hate to interrupt your day any more than I already have. Plus, looks like the Blacks need their driveway cleared, and I've heard blacks aren't good at that type of thing."

Kevin gave me what was obviously a courtesy grin, then said, "Now Citsch, I don't care what your race is, we don't wanna be makin' those types a jokes."

"Well, no. I wasn't being racist, it's just what we were saying. Ya know, how I got it mixed up."

"Right," Kevin said, putting his glove back on, and reassured me with a smile. "I'm just sayin' for future instances. Anyhow, sure I can't talk ya into a ride?"

"I'm sure. Thanks for the offer. I'll get a more snow-appropriate car while I'm out runnin' errands. I don't suppose Grier's Hardware sells 4x4 trucks do they?"

"'Fraid not, but Albert's Automotive, which is just down the street from Grier's, has got the finest selection in town. I'd recommend stoppin' in there. Plus, they won't be givin' ya hassles about your credit, if that's somethin' you're worried about."

"That shouldn't be a problem," I said. But now that he mentioned it, my credit score had probably taken quite a beating in the past few years. "You've been a big help this morning Kevin, thanks a lot."

"Afternoon, you mean?"

"Oh, uh, I guess I'm not sure."

"Yeah, it's a couple hours past noon." Kevin put his ski mask back on. "Okay Citsch, pleasure meetin' ya. Tell the cashier at Grier's you're to receive twenty percent off your total purchase, courtesy of your new neighbor, Mr. Grier."

"Kind of you, thanks!" I said.

Kevin started up his snow blower and began blowing the snow off of the sidewalk leading up the street toward the Black's.

The Lotus didn't do well in the snow. Most rear-wheel drive cars struggle in the snow, but the Lotus seemed particularly ill-suited for the task. I had to get into town today and buy supplies; there was no telling how long this snow would keep falling, and the roads usually stay bad days after a storm passes. Plus, I'm not a procrastinator. The time to handle business is now.

The roads had been plowed, but they were still icy with a fresh frosting of snow. The Lotus's back end teased disaster with slips and shifts to the side anytime I pressed the gas or brake. I hadn't driven in snow in over a decade, but I was an excellent driver, so I was confident despite the conditions. Then, while I was making a right turn in the middle of town, the back end of the Lotus glided up around to the left and pulled the car into the opposite lane of traffic. Absolutely nothing I could do about it. I slammed on the brakes, but the car had become a granite stone sliding across a sheet of ice. The only thing missing was a curling team to sweep in front of where my car was heading. A truck in the opposite lane, driving too fast for conditions, couldn't stop in time and rammed into the driver's side rear of my Lotus. The collision tore off the rear bumper and dented up the driver's side of the car. The driver of the truck denied being at fault (of course). The police showed up and filed their report and we exchanged insurance information. The Lotus was still drivable, so I pressed on to Albert's Automotive.

As soon as I pulled into Albert's I knew what I would be buying. There was a late-model Chevy Suburban that had been lifted and had huge knobby tires. It was painted a metallic silver with purple ghost flames—not corny flames, these were tasteful. Definitely a professional airbrushing job. The flames had skulls painted into them that you could only see at certain angles. The shadow work was incredible. The Suburban also had a push bar and steel bumpers, with a rail light and all sorts of custom work. Exactly what I needed to get through a winter in Montana. Albert's agreed to take a trade-in for the Lotus, even though they don't usually buy damaged vehicles. I got $20,000 toward the Suburban by trading that in. After my bargaining I got what was originally marked for sale at $89,999.99 down to $75,000 and only had to put down $20,000. When all was said and done, I only had $35,000 worth of payments with an interest-free first year. I basically got a $100,000 Suburban for $35,000. The whole process only took a couple hours. That's how you hustle the system.

I drove the Suburban off the lot and over to Grier's Hardware. With four-wheel drive engaged it felt like I could tow a cattle trailer straight up an iceberg. Now I could drive at regular speeds despite the conditions.

Grier's Hardware was a small shop. It was a little white building with red accent paint and a sign that said, "Grier's is Great Because We Can Relate!" There was a small mountain of snow on one side of the parking lot, apparently where they had been plowing the snow. I parked on top of it.

I had made a list on my phone before I left: snow blower, snow pants, coat, beanie, gloves, snow boots, snow shovel, road salt, ice scraper, tire chains, and one of those kits you put in your car in case you slid off the road and got stranded in a storm. I probably didn't need the chains or the kit anymore, but I figured better safe than sorry.

The automatic doors slid open and a warm gust of lumber-scented wind welcomed me into Grier's. The shop didn't look any bigger inside than it did from the outside. There were only two cashiers, and they had their backs to me checking out patrons. Everybody had a vague familiarity about them. Missoula is a small town, and I knew it was only a matter of time until I heard, "Caish? Is that you?" and was pulled into a, "It's been so long," conversation. My stay in Montana was temporary, and I planned to keep a low profile. I pulled out a shopping cart and winded up and down the aisles.

Kevin was right, Grier's had everything I needed. They even had Sorel boots. They didn't have any name brand winter clothing though, so I grabbed off-brand stuff to last me until I could find something nicer. Name brands are important. The clothing is built better and lasts longer. Not to mention it's more stylish. I needed a Canada Goose parka. Not surprising that those aren't for sale at Grier's.

When I pushed my cart up to the cashier, my heart began to wallop.

Alex Rettig looked up at me from behind the cash register and, with a smile strained by ambivalence, said "Caish?"

Alex and I had dated during high school and a couple years after. We were each other's firsts. It was a complicated, messy relationship with ups of passionate sex and downs of torn up photos and drawn-out fights. When we were together it felt like we could conquer the world. Like we had discovered something that nobody else knew about. Everybody else thought they found love, but they had no idea. They had glowing charcoal, we had white-hot exploding jet fuel. In high school we skipped class together and snuck out every night. Alex's parents caught wind and tried to "ground" Alex, but that only upped the ante and made it more exciting. We did everything there was to do in Montana, then started exploring America. Long road trips filled with Bob Dylan, Twizzlers, sex in divey motel rooms, and, when we could get it, weed. Nothing could stop us. The full wrath of poverty, pestilence, or parents couldn't pull us apart. Come what may, our love would endure until the end of time.

Until it didn't. Alex had a habit of getting drunk at parties and hooking up with other people. The first couple times this happened, we wrote the instances off as drunken anomalies. On the third occasion, we had a fight that ended with Alex suggesting we try having an open relationship—which, at the time, I considered to be an absurd suggestion. A few months later we were back together, and the cycle repeated until I moved to California to embark upon the American Dream. We stayed in touch, but drifted apart when I married my ex. It got kind of painful there at the end. What's the saying? No good relationship ends well, but a bad relationship's end is better than its start? I can't remember. Whatever the case, we once had something incredible.

"Alex?" I replied.

"Yeah. It's me. Oh my God, Caish," Alex walked out from behind the cashier station and gave me a hug that lit my fuse. "How have you been?"

"I've been great, how about—"

"Where have you been?"

"Los Angeles, remember, I moved down a few years back. How are you?"

"Good, I'm doin' good. When did you—"

"So what's—oh sorry, go ahead."

"No, no you're fine, go ahead," Alex said.

"Well, I was just going to ask what's new?"

"Oh, yeah, well, lots I guess. When did you get into town?"

"Just last night. I bought a place over by Canyon River Golf Course," I said.

"Shut the fuck up. I live right next to that golf course. You know those apartments across the street from the clubhouse? That's where I'm at."

"Holy shit, what are the chances?"

"Haha, still sayin' that huh? What are the chances?" Alex's mouth did its best to restrain itself to a sociable smile, but the lips couldn't help but flicker back, pulling the sociable smile into a much more excited and emotional expression. That was it. That was the signal. I was sure of it. Alex wanted to get with me.

"Haha, I guess. Good to see you haven't aged a day," I said. Alex blushed. Just a shade, but there was definitely a blush. Yeah, tonight I was finally getting laid.

"Well, you're too kind. So," Alex looked into my cart, "looks like you're takin' this whole winter thing seriously. Lemme ring you up." Alex moved back around to the other side of the cashier counter and started scanning my items.

"Um, wanna grab a cup of coffee? Catch up?" I asked.

"Oh, I'd love to, but I gotta work. Maybe another time?"

"Sure, yeah. That's fine. When do you get off?"

"My shift ends at nine, but then I gotta get home to the kiddos."

Dammit. Kids. Ruining my life.

"Oh, you have kids?" I asked.

"Yeah, three of 'em. Ronnie, Shannon, and Michael. They're a handful."

"Wow, yeah. Any other major life events since we last talked?" Of course I was probing around to see what Alex's relationship status was.

"Hm..." Alex thought while scanning my Sorels, "well, you know I married Peyton Winward, right?"

"Oh wow, really? No I didn't. Jesus Christ. So I have missed a lot. Peyton?"

"Yeah, Caish, Peyton has changed a lot. I really think you two would get along great now that we're all adults. Let's go on a double date once you get settled in." Alex came out from behind the cashier counter for what I thought was going to be a heartfelt embrace where Alex would tell me how much I've been missed and how now that I was back a divorce was in order from goddamn Peyton Winward—one of the people who took advantage of drunk Alex at a party. But when I reached out for a hug, Alex gave an awkward chuckle and stooped down to my shopping cart to scan the bags of road salt and my snow shovel.

"Is that everything?" Alex asked.

"Yup. That should do it." I was humiliated. "Oh, actually I also wanted one of those big orange snow blowers, do you guys do delivery or something?"

"Yeah, definitely, do you remember which big orange snow blower it was, exactly?"

"No. Not like a model name or anything."

"No problem, let's walk on over and have a look at the one you want. We can have it dropped off by tomorrow morning. Is that soon enough?"

"Yeah, yup. That's great."

I followed Alex as we walked toward the snow blower section. I took the opportunity to examine Alex's figure. I wasn't lying when I said Alex hadn't aged a day. Alex was definitely still a cross-country runner with a strict diet. Ugh. I had to get with Alex. At this point my fuse was getting close to the powder keg, and Alex had to be feeling the same thing. Alex's face showed it. There was no mistaking it. The signs were there.

"You ever have to work late, Alex?" I asked. Without turning around, Alex said, "Not usually. Every now and then when we get a big batch of new inventory, but for the most part I leave on time." Hm. Alex didn't pick up that signal. I'll try another—

"This one?" Alex asked, pointing to a big orange snow blower.

"Yeah, that's the one."

Alex copied down some numbers from the snow blower's tag into a pocket notebook. "Great, let's get you rung up. We'll get your address for the delivery and have this on your doorstep tomorrow sometime between nine and noon," Alex said. Was that a signal? Rung up? Like, ring me up? Ring my up? Up my ring? Ring my bell? Hm. I followed Alex back to the cash register trying to solve the puzzle.

After I had paid for my goods, I figured I'd give it another shot. I knew Alex wanted me but was scared about what kind of ripples it would cause. At the same time, I knew from personal experience that Alex didn't place great value on fidelity.

"Alex," I said, "maybe just swing by my place on your way home. It's right by your apartment. I just want to catch up. Hear about your kids. Tell me about your life. Ya know? I've missed you. I think bumping into you today was more than just a coincidence. I mean, really, what are the chances?"

Alex thought about it (a good sign). Then, as another customer was walking up to the register, said, "I'll think about it."

"Should I text you my address?"

"I have it from the snow blower delivery info."

"Oh yeah. Okay. Well it was good seeing you. See you tonight."

Alex smiled and said, "Good seeing you too Caish, see you later."

See you later? As in, Alex will see me later because Alex is going to come to my house after work? Probably. Alex's emotions run hot, and what's more romantic than a long-lost lover coming back into town after having made millions in the big city? Ah, shit. Did I mention I was a millionaire? That would've helped. Alex probably already knew. Word gets around in these small towns, and news of one of its own making it big in Los Angeles had to have gotten back. All the more reason to think that Alex will come by tonight. Which means I had to get my house together. Or at least my room.

Kevin was taking down Christmas lights when I pulled up the

street. He paused, squinted at my new Suburban, then waved. I waved back. Kevin climbed down his ladder and was in my driveway almost before me. I opened the garage and parked in the driveway. I hadn't thought about the Suburban being too high to fit into the garage.

"Well Holy Hanna, Kit, this your new ride?" Kevin asked.

"Sure is, I figured it would be more appropriate for the conditions. Also, it's *Caish*. Like Cajun and cash. *Caish*."

"Oh! Shoot, sorry about that. Caish. I'm sorta hard at hearin' and terrible with names. But, now that ya liken it to Cajun chicken I won't soon forget it."

"Haha, oh no worries, you're not the first to struggle with it."

"So what'd j'ya do with your little sports car?"

"Well, I wrecked it, then traded it in for this," I said.

"Wrecked it! Haha, oh no, Caish. Are ya alright? I hope ya didn't hurt yourself." Kevin put his hand on my shoulder and turned me around, examining me up and down.

"Yeah, I'm fine, it was just a fender bender. Some guy in a truck was going too fast for conditions and slid into me. Happens."

"Sure does. Sheesh. Glad to hear you're alright. And glad to see ya got yourself somethin' more Montana appropriate." Kevin was checking out the Suburban as he talked, "So's this jalopy gonna fit in your garage? Looks like it's gonna be a *tiiiiiiiiiight* fit."

"Ya know, I hadn't thought of that. From here it looks like it'll be alright. Close, but it'll fit."

Kevin climbed up the back of the Suburban and looked toward the garage with his head sideways on the roof of the Suburban. "Yeah, I think you're in good shape. Tight but good. Tight is good, right?"

Wait. Gross. Was Kevin hitting on me? Was he not married? I guess that doesn't say too much about a person, but still. Oh, and was that a wink? Hell no.

"Yup, alrighty, thanks for checkin' that out. I'll pull it on in.

Good luck with those lights."

"Oh, yeah I appreciate it. Lemme know if I can help out with anything. I know movin' into a new place can be pretty tough." Kevin's smile was disarming, but his question about tightness echoed in my mind and kept me on guard.

"Will do. Thanks. Nice to know I have such kind neighbors," I said.

Kevin parted with a smile and I eased the Suburban into my garage. Sure enough, it was a tight fit. I unloaded my winter gear then got busy organizing my house. I started in my room, which would likely be the most important room of the night. I folded my bed tight enough to bounce a quarter off of the comforter. I put all my shoes and clothes away, then moved on throughout the house. I didn't have time to unbox everything, but I stacked the boxes in an orderly fashion and vacuumed. I put a few pillows on the couch and scooted a coffee table into place. After straightening up my kitchen I checked the clock. 8:52 p.m. Perfect timing. I pulled out the nicest of the four bottles of wine, and made sure my coffee maker was working properly in case Alex thought I was serious about the coffee. I put on some Gucci sweats and freshened up.

9:26 p.m., still no Alex. I didn't quite know what to do with myself while I waited. Do I watch a movie? Read a book? Snack on shrimp? I didn't want to start anything, but at the same time I didn't want it to seem like I was expecting any visitors. I opted for scrolling through Instagram. 10:00 p.m., still no Alex. Maybe Alex was actually working late. 10:32 p.m. No way Alex still at work. That settles it. I was wrong about Alex. Or maybe not. Maybe Alex is just putting the kids to bed. 11:16 p.m. I tell myself, "Okay fine, Alex isn't coming over, time to stop holding out hope," and agree with myself, but I stay hopeful. I can't turn hope off. I check my watch, check myself in front of the mirror, go over what I plan on saying, map out what the night will be like in my mind. 12:03 a.m. Maybe Alex is waiting until Peyton is asleep, and then is going to sneak out. Should I act asleep for when Alex comes over? That would make it look like I had forgotten and it was no big deal. Plus, I could say, "Yeah look, I'm just tired, let's go lay down for a minute." Then we'd cuddle, then hands would wander, and before you know it we're putting each other in our favorite positions. 1:09 a.m. I may have dozed off for a second, was that a knock at the door that woke me? Alex? I checked the front door, nobody there. Just darkness. 1:45 a.m. Still no Alex. I laid in bed scrolling through Instagram until my phone fell out of my hand and hit me in the face. I must have fallen asleep at about the same time.

11:21 a.m., still no Alex. Which was fine. Alex had moved on with life, and so had I. Probably better not to get anything started with Alex because I wasn't going to be here forever, and Alex probably wasn't ever leaving Montana. It would prevent a lot of heartache to put the candle out before it turned into a forest fire.

I woke up early because Grier's Hardware rang my doorbell at 11:21 a.m. to drop off my snow blower. The teenager making the delivery looked familiar, but I couldn't place him. Probably the offspring of some neighbor I had growing up. He was a kind person, and stuck around long enough to show me how to set up the snow blower. Last night it snowed another few inches, so I'd have an opportunity to try it out right away. But I needed gas and oil before I could run it. Which meant I'd need to buy a gas can. I hate buying gas cans at gas stations because they price them as if they were gold-plated. Not that I care about something being expensive, I just hate rewarding the gas station's opportunistic swindling. So I prefer to buy my gas cans at hardware stores. Looks like I needed to make another trip to Grier's.

The snow mountain in the parking lot had grown, but still was no match for my Suburban. I parked on top and jogged into Grier's.

As soon as I walked in I looked over at the cash registers. No

Alex.

I bought the biggest gas can they had and a five-quart jug of 5w-30 oil. I asked the cashier who checked me out whether Alex was working. "Nope, Colby is the manager on Thursdays." Hm. Probably better that way.

I filled up the gas can on my way home. By the time I got back Kevin had already cleared my driveway and walks. I went inside to do some online shopping.

My doorbell rang at around three o'clock and I ran into the bathroom to make sure I was presentable. I tried to control my breathing and focused on not smiling too big. I didn't want Alex to think I was desperate or anything. Which I wasn't. Oh but what was I going to say? I thought you'd come around? Better late than never? Do I joke? Play it straight? I'll just follow Alex's lead. Okay, nice and calm. But busy. I'm busy, not waiting, but calm.

When I opened the door I felt like a popped balloon. Two unfamiliar smiling faces introduced themselves as the Blacks.

"We wanted to introduce ourselves and welcome you to the neighborhood." They even brought me cookies.

"Oh, yeah, wow, thanks." After a brief pause, I remembered my manners and invited them in.

They couldn't stop talking about how wonderful my house was, likely because they had the exact same house. We settled into the kitchen where I made them coffee. I couldn't offer them any hors d'oeuvres because I didn't have any. They began telling me about our neighborhood and got visibly excited when they gave me the dirt. The Blacks were gossip goblins. I was inundated with who divorced who and how it was that this person was involved in that scandal. They lapped themselves up. On and on. I would have cared (a gobbet of gossip is good for the soul) except we were talking about people living in Missoula, Montana. Why would I care? Unless you have an inside scoop on Hollywood A-Listers I couldn't care less.

Eventually, when they were satisfied with their performance, the Blacks left and I went back to shopping. Little World Chinese food delivered my dinner and Facebook and Netflix provided the evening's entertainment. I stayed up until 2:00 a.m. waiting for Alex, but it was in vain. The only upside was that for the first time in years my mind was occupied with something other than money.

The next morning I woke up at about noon. I sipped coffee, smoked cigarettes, and scrolled through social media for a few hours. Looks like life in California was every bit as wonderful as it was when I left. It hadn't snowed overnight, so there was nothing new to snow blow. I take a cozy day to lick my wounds. I had been through more in the past few years than most people experience in a lifetime. I deserved a break. For dinner I ordered sushi, but Montana sushi just wasn't the same. I stayed up all night waiting for Alex, and still nothing.

After lunch the next day my doorbell rang, but I kept my cool. I figured it was just FedEx with my Canada Goose. Sure enough, just FedEx. A couple hours later, though, my doorbell rang again. Finally. This was it. And, praise God, it was.

Alex was standing on my doorstep looking around at my porch when I opened the door.

"Oh! Hey Alex, what up?" Dammit. All wrong. What the hell? Was I a teenager?

"Hi, Caish, is this a bad time? I just wanted to come say hi."

"No! No, not at all, please, come on in."

Alex stepped in and followed me to the main room area. The house had an open floor plan, and the kitchen was part of the main area. Alex took a seat at one of the kitchen stools while I made coffee.

"So, ya gettin' all settled in?" Alex asked.

"Yeah, everybody around here has been super nice. A few people have stopped by just to introduce themselves and welcome me to the neighborhood. Very small-towny."

"Well, what do you expect? It *is* a small town."

"True, yeah... it is."

"So—"

"Do you—"

"Oh, sorry—"

"Sorry, go ahead."

"No really, I didn't mean to interrupt, what were ya gonna say?"

"I was just going to ask about your work, do you usually work nights?" I asked.

"Lately, yeah. We just hired on a new—oh, do you need to get that?"

My phone had started ringing. It was a number I didn't recognize, so I ignored it. "No, sorry, probably wrong number. Either that or a telemarketer. There's no reason for anybody to call me. "

"Ugh, don't you hate that? They call me like twice a day."

"Yeah! Me too! Oh it's the worst. No, I don't need solar panels, haha."

"Serious." Alex chuckled. "They're the worst."

Then my phone rang again. "You should probably check it out," Alex said, "could be an emergency."

"Yeah, I guess you're right. Sorry, one sec," I said to Alex. Then, stepping out of the kitchen and answering my phone, "Hello?"

"Hello, is this Caish Calloway?"

"Yeah."

"Caish, my name is Jennifer Blanche, I'm your probation officer. How are you this afternoon?"

"I'm doing good. Thanks. But Jenny, could you—"

"It's Jennifer."

"What?"

"My name, it's Jennifer. I think you called me Jenny. I just wanted to clarify that my name is Jennifer. But sorry to cut you off, go ahead."

"Oh, yeah, *Jennifer*, could you call back a little later? Maybe tomorrow? I'm kind of busy right now."

"Sorry Caish, I can't do that. You need to come in right now and pee into a cup. I also need you to fill out some forms. Can you take down an address right now, or would you rather me text it to this number?"

"Look, Jennifer, I'm busy right now, I'll swing in tomorrow and pee into all the cups you want me to. I haven't used cocaine in months."

"Caish, maybe you don't understand our relationship. I am not asking you to swing by when it is convenient for you. I am not your friend. I am letting you know that you need to come into my office right this instant and pee into a cup or I will send the county sheriff to your house, and he will bring you in. Do you understand that?"

"Dammit Jennifer. You could not have called at a worst time. Why can't I come in tomorrow?"

"Caish. Listen to me. We do not negotiate. I give you orders, and you follow them. You do not plead, you do not bargain. You follow my orders. Come in right now, or I will send the sheriff to your house. Tell me you understand."

"I understand." Bitch. Fucking bitch.

"What do you understand?"

"That I have to drop what I'm doing, even if I am giving CPR to a dying child, and drive to your office to piss into a fucking cup."

"Watch your language, Caish. Would you like me to tell you the address, or text it to you?"

"Text it to me."

"Okay, I'll see you in about ten minutes. Don't be late." Jennifer said, then hung up.

I walked back into the kitchen where Alex was scrolling through Instagram. Alex looked up and asked: "Everything alright? Sounded kinda cross."

"Uh, yeah. Everything's fine I guess. But I gotta go."

"Oh, okay. Ya need to leave right now?" Alex asked.

"Yeah, I'm so sorry. Will you please come back later today?"

"Ah, I can't, Caish. Sorry. I pick up Michael from pre-school in a half-hour, from then on it's kinda hectic. Maybe another time."

I couldn't act coy anymore. I had to lay my cards on the table. Alex had to know. "Alex, will you *please* come back? Don't be weirded out by this, but I have been waiting by the door like a dog waiting for its owner for the past couple of days just waiting for you to come over. I can't stop thinking about you."

Alex's face looked sad. Like Alex was pained by what I said.

"I'm sorry," I said, "I know I shouldn't talk like that. But it's true. I miss you Alex." I almost added, "I moved back to Montana for you," but thought better of it. I didn't want to lay it on too thick. If things go well I'll add that in later.

"Maybe next Tuesday I'll come over and we can catch up," Alex said. "But, Caish, I'm married now. I have kids. Ya have to respect that."

"Of course, yeah. No of course. I wasn't suggesting anything else. I just miss you as a friend. Totally platonic. Definitely."

"Okay, I'll try to swing by next week. Are daytimes best for you? Are ya working anywhere yet?"

"Yeah daytimes are best." I thought about telling Alex that I was independently wealthy and didn't need to work, but figured that was a conversation for another time. That was a conversation for next Tuesday.

I walked Alex out and we parted with a hug. The type of hug where you lean in from the hips and sort of just touch shoulders, not the type of hug where your bodies touch from knee to chest. Alex was taking it slow. Something about a spouse and kids.

As soon as Alex drove away I scrambled to get myself together and bolted for the address Jenny texted me.

13

Jennifer Blanche looked like Miss Trunchbull from Matilda. Not to be trifled with. Her face dared you to test her. "Go ahead," it said, "see what happens." She definitely lifted weights. Not low weight, high repetitions—she wasn't interested in tone. High weight, low rep. She looked like at any given moment she might tie a rope to the front of a semi-truck and pull it across a parking lot. Her dark hair was drawn back in a tight ponytail. She wore a drab button down that was tucked into loose-fitting khaki pants. Her black military-style boots were laced high and tight.

"Glad you could make it," Jennifer said when I walked in. Her office was one of the many dreary rooms on the ground floor. The building was near the center of Missoula, right by the courthouse. Like most government buildings, this one was mostly windowless, poorly lit with fluorescent lights, and decorated with plastic plants and Monet prints. Jennifer's office door had a nameplate that said J. Blanche, Probation Officer. When I knocked, she opened the door and invited me to sit on one of the cheap chairs in front of her desk—which bore all the signs of an obsessive compulsive personality.

"Here's a cup, go into that bathroom," Jennifer was pointing with her thumb to the room next to her office, "and pee into it. When you're done, place it on the shelf above the toilet and come back in here. Are you going to use your own pee, or did you bring a bag of somebody else's pee?"

"What? No. I didn't bring a bag of pee with me."

"Okay, lift your shirt, let me see your waistband. Turn around."

I did as told.

"Good. If you ever bring in any pee, either your own or somebody else's, we will watch you pee into the cup for the rest of your probation," Jennifer Trunchbull said. "Any questions?"

"Nope." I took the cup from Jennifer and did as I was told. As I was doing my best not to pee on my fingers, it occurred to me that this was the first time I had to follow orders since before I won the lottery. With millions of dollars, nobody could tell me what to do. I had freedom from taking shit. I had freedom from even talking to other people. If I didn't want to, I didn't have to talk to anybody for any reason. Let alone take their small-minded orders. Now I was right back to following orders. Jennifer probably got picked on in high school, so she went into law enforcement, and now she thinks she's the boss. She's in charge, she tells herself, and she has the full weight of the law behind her, so you better do what she says. Classic inferiority complex.

As soon as I placed the urine-filled cup on the shelf above the toilet, a latex-gloved hand slid open a slot behind the shelf, reached through, and removed the cup. I washed up and returned to Jennifer's office.

"Everything go alright in there?" she asked.

"Yeah, it was fine."

"Good. We do onsite testing, so your results will be back in a few minutes. In the meantime, you need to fill out these forms. Don't lie. Don't try to get tricky. You can fill the forms out on the chairs in the hallway. I have a few phone calls to make so I can't have you in my office. Any questions?"

"No."

"Good. Here's a clipboard."

The forms asked for my name, address, birth date, phone number, social security number, and signature over and over again. Pages and pages of repetitive requests. Why not just have all of this on one form and have me enter my information once at the bottom? Bureaucracy, that's why. The government paid people to make these pointless forms, and people had jobs processing them. And Jennifer. Another cog in the machine. Treating me like a child. Like a sheep. Crowded into this dimly-lit hallway filling out pointless forms and peeing into a cup as if I were just another heroin addicted thief. A common low-life. As an added point of insult, I had to pay for this whole racket. They forced me to be on probation and to take piss tests, then charged me for it. My indignation about the entire situation was palpable. Is this how Jennifer would treat Bill Gates if he were in her office?

Having finished filling out the forms, I walked back into Jennifer's office. She looked up from her computer with a concerned face.

"Caish. You knock before you come in this office. You do not just barge in. You do not own this place. Do you understand?"

"Sure, but you told me to come back in when I was done with the forms," I said, sitting in one of the chairs across from her desk.

"No, I did not. Do not put words in my mouth. Even if I had, you knock, then wait for me to invite you in before you walk into this office." She reached across the table with an open hand. I placed the forms into her hand. She jogged the papers on her desk then flipped through them. Satisfied, she placed them in a neat pile next to another pile of evenly jogged papers.

"Okay, Caish. Here's how this works. You have been assigned a color. There are ten colors. Your color is green. Each day at 8:00 a.m. we do a random draw and pull out one of the colors. If your color is drawn, we text you (or, if you prefer, we can call you), and you immediately come in and pee into a cup. If you do not come in, we send a sheriff to bring you in. If you test positive for a controlled substance that is not prescribed to you, we take steps toward revoking your probation and invoking your prison sentence. So next time you find yourself sitting in front of a line of cocaine, think about whether it's worth five years in prison. Do you have questions about anything I just told you?"

"When my color is drawn, can I come in around noon? I'm not really a morning person."

"No. You come in within a half an hour of being told that your color was drawn. You live less than ten minutes away from this building, so you have no excuse for being late."

"But today you called in the afternoon."

"We were getting you set up in our system. From here on out, plan on eight o'clock."

"What if I sleep through the text?" I asked.

"Let's make a note here to call you instead of text. Do not sleep with your phone on silent. Any other questions?"

"No."

"Good. One last thing, I am not your counselor. If you would like a counselor, or if you would like to get involved in addiction recovery programs, here is a list of local help groups." Jennifer handed me a pamphlet with stock photos of happy diverse people walking through a grassy field. "Surprisingly, your probation does not require you be a part of any addiction recovery programs, but I would recommend you join anyway."

"I appreciate the offer, but I'm not addicted to drugs or alcohol."

"Oh, you're not?" Jennifer's tone was as mocking as she could make it.

"No, as a matter of fact I am not."

"Okay, Caish. Take the pamphlet anyway. There is contact information for social workers if you need them. Do you have any questions about anything we talked about today?"

"No."

"Good. Wait out in the hall for your urine test to come back. I will report the results. Shut the door on your way out."

I walked back out to the hall and sat in the same dingy chair. They wasted twenty more minutes of my day until Jennifer walked out and said, "Caish, you've been drinking. That's a violation of your probation."

"What? No, I just can't do drugs, I can still drink."

"No. You cannot. Drinking is a violation of your probation."

"No no no, it's not. Call my probation officer in California, or the judge or something. They said I could drink," I pleaded.

Jennifer said, "There's no probation on earth that would prohibit you from drugging and not prohibit you from drinking. Either you're lying, you misunderstood the terms of your probation, or the probation officer in California was incompetent."

"I swear to God Jennifer, I didn't know I couldn't drink. I won't do it again."

Jennifer mulled that over for a couple of seconds, then said, "Caish. As your probation officer I have great discretion over how to deal with a violation of your probation. Since this is your first violation, I will file a report and not take further action. I am not a merciful person, Caish. You need to understand that. I will hold you to the terms of your probation. Wait here." Jennifer walked back into her office, then reappeared with a sheet of paper in her hand. "Here are the terms of your probation. Read this sheet. There are certain employment restrictions and substance restrictions that you need to be aware of. Do you have any questions?"

"No. But really, I didn't know that I couldn't drink. Do you have to file a report? Can't this just be a warning?"

"I am filing a report. Any other questions?"

"No."

"Good. I recommend you do not violate the terms of your probation again. We'll see you next time your color is drawn."

After I escaped that hell hole, I drove around downtown—if you can call it that—looking for Red Bird restaurant. I needed a classic steak dinner with red wine. When I was a kid, Red Bird was too expensive. A group of us went there for our senior prom and it felt like we were royalty. I found the place on the corner of Front Street and Higgins. After finding a pile of snow to park on, I trudged through the Montana elements to get to Red Bird. My

Sorels kept my feet toasty and my Canada Goose kept my arms and torso at tropical temperatures. But the cold burrowed into my face. I tucked my mouth behind the top of my coat, but my eyeballs had nowhere to hide. They'd be balls of ice in no time.

Red Bird was closed. It was 4:27 p.m., and they didn't open until five.

I needed food and drink. Especially a drink. But what was I going to do about this new probation restriction? No alcohol? Christ. I can't smoke weed or drink alcohol. How am I supposed to relax? How am I supposed to socialize?

I was parked in front of Stockman's bar, so I figured I might as well eat there. Even though I couldn't drink.

Stockman's hadn't changed at all in the years I was away. Like most western-style bars, Stockman's was dim and stuffy. Hardwood floors, wood paneling, wooden bar, and wooden tables. The ceiling looked like a log book at the top of a mountain. Peasants from years past scrawled on the ceiling that they were here on such and such a date. Clever peasants drawing obscene pictures. It all felt quite egalitarian.

The bar was sparsely populated at this time of day. A bearded old man hunched over his Scotch at the bar watched me walk in and sit at one of the tables, then returned to his drink. A teenager that was probably related to the owner of the bar took my order of a bacon cheeseburger and fries and returned to the kitchen. I also ordered coke. Not *that* kind of coke, just a regular-carbonated-caffeinated-syrup coke. Nothing white about it. A few gentlemen in the back of the bar were playing poker and kept glancing at me. They recognized me; having become successful in Los Angeles, I am a bit of a hometown hero. I am surprised more people haven't recognized me. And although a lot of folks have a familiarity about them, I don't recognize many people either.

My burger and fries were everything you could ever ask of a burger and fries. Toasted bun, smoky bacon, melted cheddar, and a perfectly-spiced, evenly cooked, beef patty. Oh and the fries. Crisply fried with a soft center. Perfectly salted. Eating cheap may not be so bad after all.

As I ate, I thought about my situation. My bad luck may be coming to an end. There is a certain serendipity to Alex showing up in my life again, and that may be an omen of good things to come. There was still the problem of money, but that would solve itself with the lower cost of living in Montana and my personal prohibition from cocaine or alcohol. Other than the fact that I'd have to live off only food and soda for the next five years, things were looking up. Montana had a decent lottery, and I could probably get by on those earnings until I was in a position to move back to California. Nothing in my probation forbade me from playing the lottery, and I still had enough in the bank to buy a lot of lottery tickets. Even with my mortgage, judgment debt, legal fees, and now the Suburban payment, I still had enough to make it for a few years even if I didn't earn another penny in that time. Which was unlikely. I'd keep my ear to the ground for any opportunities and stay in touch with my California contacts for any new investment prospects.

When I got home that evening I got a call from a number I didn't recognize. I'd usually decline the call, but since it could be Jennifer Trunchbull calling from another number, I figured I better answer it.

"Hello?"

"Caish?"

"Yeah, this is Caish, who's this?"

"This is Caleb, what's up?" Caleb. The brother that took it upon himself to be the family's patriarch.

"Oh! Hi, Caleb, what's goin' on?" I said.

"Not much, just gettin' by, ya know."

"Yup. Yeah. I know."

"So, anyway, I heard you were back in town," Caleb said. It was only a matter of time. If Caleb knew, the family knew. If the family knew, the town knew.

"Yeah, for now. How'd ya hear?"

"You remember Dino? The guy with the chainsaw collection?"

"How could I forget the guy with the chainsaw collection?"

"Haha, yeah, probably right. Anyway, he called me up and said he saw ya at Stockman's earlier today." Ah. One of the poker players. Dino the saw collector. I don't think the guy is a serial killer, but in high school he used an oxy-acetylene torch to cut the roof off of our principal's car. The principal hadn't even pissed him off, Dino just liked cutting things apart and decided that the principal needed a convertible. Did it right in the school parking lot. He put the tanks and torch into a wheelbarrow, wheeled them over to the principal's car, dropped his welding mask over his face and got to work. Had the roof off before anybody noticed he hadn't come back from the bathroom.

"Oh, yeah?" I said, "Yeah I didn't recognize him, but now that you mention it, yeah that was definitely Dino. He hasn't killed anybody or anything yet, has he?"

"Haha, not yet. At least not that I know of." Then there was a brief silence. "So, were ya gonna call and let us know you were back in town or what? We should get together. Get lunch or somethin'."

"Yeah definitely," I lied, "just give me a couple weeks to get settled in. You know how busy a move can be."

"Sure, yeah, of course," Caleb said. "Either way though, you should call Mom. I'm sure she'd be happy to hear you're back."

"I bet she's already heard."

"Well. Yeah. But ya know, I'm sure she'd like to hear from you."

"Yeah, good point, I'll be sure and call her up," I said without any intention of ever calling that woman.

"Alrighty, Caish, I'll let ya go. Welcome back."

"Sounds good, thanks for the call, Caleb."

"Yup, see ya later."

"Bye."

"Bye."

I knew what they were thinking. Caleb, Cormac, Catherine, and my mom were probably on a conference call right this moment talking shit. A quartet of spite. Reveling in the fact that I had returned to a city that I had forsaken. The implication was clear, I had lost my millions and couldn't afford California anymore. In a way, Caleb's call was a shot across the bow. A way of letting me know that they know. That they have my number. That they will soon have my address. And that they are packing black powder into their drama canons right this moment.

Without wealth I felt vulnerable. I no longer had wealth to shield me from the vindictive sludge of humanity. Everybody who wished for my failure was mounting their attack. The murmurings had begun. Soon passive aggressive posts would pop up on Facebook. The first volley. Things like: "So happy that Caish finally came back to lil' ol' Missoula!" and, "Welcome back Caish, we always knew you'd be back someday!" Monsters. Every one of them. Then the direct messages on Facebook and Instagram, "Hey, Caish, I heard you're back, everything alright?" "Caish, what's up?" "Get tired of California?" My non-responses (which would be my only option) would affirm their suspicion; Caish Calloway has fallen from Mount Olympus.

Tuesday finally arrived. The only thing I could think about all weekend was being with Alex. Alex was my oasis and I was dying of thirst. In an attempt to calm myself down, I watched Netflix whenever I was awake. I ordered Chinese food and hunkered down. I found Alex on Facebook and studied every picture. Alex had a good life, I guess. As good as a life without wealth can be. Alex and Peyton went on a cruise last June and looked like they had a good time. Their bodies showed they could no longer find time for the gym, and their eyes broadcasted they had children. But still, Alex looked young and energetic. Vibrant, even. I couldn't find Alex on Instagram or Twitter.

On Monday I went shopping for the type of clothes that Alex and Peyton wore. Blue-collar clothing. Clothes that would show Alex I'm one of them. Clothes that make Alex comfortable. I also stopped by the pharmacy to buy more cold medicine. Tuesday morning I was up early. Sleep didn't come easy. Alex hadn't specified a visiting time, so I had to be ready all day. At 7:30 a.m. I drove to Einstein Brothers Bagels and picked up breakfast for two. I had coffee ready at 9:00 a.m. At ten o'clock, I put the breakfast in the fridge and changed out of my sweats and into my blue-collar Levis and sweatshirt. I checked myself in the mirror every hour or so to make sure I was presentable. At 11:00 a.m. I figured Alex probably had to take the kids to school and Peyton was at work, but maybe Alex had to swing into Grier's for something. At noon I ordered enough sushi for two and waited until 1:00 p.m. before I started eating. I ate slowly. I didn't stuff myself, lest I become lethargic. After two rolls I put the rest in the fridge. At 2:16 p.m. my doorbell rang. The butterflies in my stomach became frantic sparrows as I walked toward my front door.

Alex was looking toward the street when I opened the door. Hearing the door open, Alex turned toward me with a smile tinged by obvious consternation.

"Hey Alex, everything alright?" I asked.

"Yeah, yeah, everything is good."

"Oh. Okay. Good. Well, why don't you come in out of the cold?" I opened the door wider and stepped back.

"I would love to, I really would," Alex said, "but I think maybe I shouldn't."

"Haha, what do you mean?"

"Well. I dunno." Alex leaned against one of the pillars on my porch, arms folded. "Peyton probably wouldn't want me spending time in your house, and, to be honest, I think maybe things between us are best where we left them."

A lot depended on what I said next. I could not blow this. Alex came over to my house, which probably meant that Alex just needed to be talked into what we both knew was inevitable. I let the silence simmer, then gave it my best shot.

"Yeah, that's totally understandable," I said. "And I get it. I do. This isn't some Nicholas Sparks book. There are certain realities that we need to accept and respect, regardless of how we feel deep down. But I hope you know I just want to be friends. I just want to catch up on what has been going on in Missoula for the past decade from somebody I trust. But if you're uncomfortable, I get it."

Alex looked down, shifted, then said, "I'm glad you understand. And thanks for not making this harder than it has to be. In a different life I wonder how things would have been." Woah woah woah. Not good. Alex missed the subtext. I had one more card up my sleeve.

"Sounds good," I said, "but before you go, could you help me hang my microwave? It's just sitting on the counter and it should be mounted into the spot above my oven. But I can't do it alone and I don't trust my creepy neighbors yet. I promise this isn't some trick to get you in my house. I had just hoped you could help out." Alex couldn't resist a project. Truth is, I pulled the microwave off the mounts earlier this morning and unscrewed the mounting plates. Nothing wrong with hedging your bets.

"Ah, Caish, I really should go."

"If you really feel that way, I agree, you should go. But I don't think that's how you feel. You came here. I think that means something."

"I don't have your number."

"Let's fix that right now."

"Really, Caish. I dunno."

"Just help me hang the microwave, have a cup of coffee, and let's just catch up."

"Ah, alright. But no funny business, Caish. I'm serious."

"Of course not, Alex. There's nothing wrong with friendship. I think even Peyton would agree with that."

Alex finally stepped into my entryway. I led the way into the kitchen and pointed out how the holes had already been drilled, but that I needed help hoisting the microwave up onto the mounting plates once we put the mounting rack in place. I didn't have an electric drill (well I did, but it was lost in the move), so we used a screwdriver to install the plate (which had the added bonus of taking longer), then lifted the microwave into place. During the lift our arms brushed. Our conversation during the installation was limited to the proper installation of the microwave. Which was as I had planned. Alex just needed some time to build up the courage to ask me what Alex had been wanting to ask. After Alex asked, the top of this tension would blow off and wonderful things would happen.

After the microwave was installed, I convinced Alex to stick around for coffee. We sat across from each other at my breakfast table. It was in the midst of small talk that Alex asked, "Caish, why did you leave?" There it was.

"How long until Peyton gets off work?" I asked.

"I pick up the kids from school at three-thirty."

"So, we've got half an hour."

"What do you mean?"

"I left because California called. It's always calling. And I had to go become successful. Why didn't you come with?"

"Because I had a life here. I still have a life here. I couldn't just drop everything to go on adventures with you."

"And how has your life here been?" I asked.

"Oh fuck you, Caish. Just because I don't have money and fancy cars doesn't mean my life is shit. I am happy. Peyton and I are very happy."

I stood up and took my empty coffee cup to the kitchen sink. "I was being sincere, Alex. I'm not trying to be mean. Since you only have a few minutes, can I give you a tour of the place?"

Alex agreed to a tour. We bumped arms a few more times and I skipped most of the top story of the house and went straight to my room. On our way down the hallway our arms bumped again, and this time Alex reached for my hand. When our fingers interlocked I turned toward Alex and saw that the fight was over. Alex looked at me like Alex used to look at me. Like the time to live was now. I pulled Alex toward my bedroom.

I said, "And, finally, this is my—" but Alex held the back of my head and pulled me into a kiss that lasted until we fell onto my bed. We pulled each other's clothes off like they were on fire. One of my pant legs didn't come all the way off, but we didn't have time to fuss with it. We were breathing heavy from the first kiss. The fervor almost hurt. We gripped each other's backs and pulled. Familiarity blended with novelty. I couldn't get enough. I wanted more. Needed more. Faster, harder, deeper. Our bodies became slippery with sweat. We were sprinting, but couldn't pace ourselves. Passion swept us. Blinding, deafening, ecstasy. Time stopped. It wasn't until after we came that I noticed we hadn't used protection.

14

Alex and I laid in bed without talking. Just catching our breath. We were a naked, panting, sticky mess. I offered Alex a cigarette, and we smoked in silence. Then Alex said, "Goddammit, Caish. What did I tell you about respecting my family?"

"What?"

"You probably just ended my marriage. There's going to be an ugly divorce, custody hearings, alimony payments, and gossip for the rest of my life, just because you *had* to hook up with me. You just couldn't resist."

"Woah, Alex. *You* fucked *me*. I had no choice. You didn't even give me a chance to say, 'No, Alex, we shouldn't, think of your family.' Which of course is what I was trying to say."

Alex smirked.

"But," I continued, "this doesn't have to mean anything for the other parts of your life. We can keep it secret. I don't have anybody to tell. So unless your anxious to announce how incredible that sex was, our secret is safe, and so is your precious marriage." I put my cigarette out. "But, if that's the route you want to go, you better hop in the shower."

"Yeah, good call."

"Need any help in there?" I offered.

"I think I've had enough help for one day."

"You sure? My shower has two shower heads. One on each wall."

"Really?" Alex said. "Maybe you should just show me how it works. Other people's showers are impossible to figure out."

I pulled off the pant leg that had stubbornly held onto my ankle and led Alex to the bathroom. Alex's naked body wasn't perfect, but it hadn't aged a day since we were last together. Thin and scarless. There were four new tattoos.

I stepped into the shower and turned on both shower heads.

"Come on in, the water's warm," I said.

Then we were back at it. The shower had a grippy tiled floor, handles, and a shelf at knee height. We made the most of those as we held each other and wrestled out more orgasms. When exhaustion and satisfaction arrived, we held each other and let the water pour over us.

After a few minutes of this meditation, I said, "You probably shouldn't use my soap."

"Why not?"

"Peyton will smell it. I'd just rinse off really well. I'm going to dry off and get dressed. I'll have some coffee and cigarettes ready for you."

"Oh, shit! Caish, I have to pick up my kids!" Alex nearly ate shit slipping out of the shower. Alex grabbed a towel, dried off in seconds, and ran to my room to get dressed. I dried off and sauntered in, letting Alex get another look at my impressive physique.

"When are you coming back?" I asked.

"Ah, dammit, Caish. We can't have an affair. I can't cheat on my spouse. We can't do this. I can't do this."

"Alex, relax. First of all, we've already done this, and I think we both agree that it was one of the best decisions we've made in a long time. Second, nobody has to know. Seriously. I don't know anybody, I live outside of town, and my house is *completely* soundproof." I said that last bit with a wink.

Alex ran down the stairs and, when we were in the entryway, said, "I dunno, Caish. We fucked up. It's probably best if we forget this happened. We can't do this. It's not right."

"You know that's not true. This was more right than anything you've done in the past ten years. Come back when it feels right. I'll be waiting. Any time, day or night."

As Alex was walking out the door, I remembered that we didn't have each other's number and called after Alex, "Oh, Alex, we didn't get each other's number."

"It's probably better that way. See ya, Caish."

As I watched Alex drive away I realized I forgot to mention that I had a relentless cold and probably just shared it. But Alex had to have noticed and figured it was a risk worth taking. Whatever, nothing too serious. I'll mention it tomorrow. Or whenever Alex comes back.

I lit a cigarette and laid on my couch. Good Lord that went well. But how long would it take Alex to shake off that guilt and get back here for more? We have one life to live, you can't spend it worried about what other people think. If something or someone brings you happiness, indulge. Someday you'll be nearing one hundred years old, and you'll wish you would have lived more when you had the chance. Back when your body was tight, energetic, and rearing for more. If you aren't regularly having sex while your body still can, you are wasting God's greatest gift.

Alex still hadn't responded to my friend request on Facebook. For the next couple hours I browsed social media. Everybody's life in Malibu looked perfect. The house parties, yacht rides, and car rallies did not wait for my return. They marched on without me. I was cooped up in a cheap house in Montana, depressingly sober, and lonely. I had lost my house. My cars were gone. And, for the most part, so was my wealth. No money led to no Malibu. No Malibu led to no cocaine. And no cocaine led to no models. All stolen from me. Robbed by Jamie Fucking Lowell and Penelope Goddamn Perez. Worthless, despicable, con artists. Well, not entirely worthless. I guess at this point they were each worth about fifteen million dollars.

I called Agent Palmer for an update on my case. It had been several months since we last spoke, and a couple of years since Jamie and Penn robbed me.

"Agent Palmer, FBI," is how Agent Palmer answered his phone.

"Agent Palmer, this is Caish Calloway, how are you?"

"Hi, Caish, I'm doing well. How are you?"

"I'm hangin' in there."

"I heard you had a little incident in Pismo and that you're living in Montana now, is that right?" Of course Agent Palmer knew about that. We hadn't talked since before the accident but my face was all over the news. So was a video of the entire accident and its aftermath—including the part where I showered myself in cocaine attempting to throw that Ziploc bag into the bushes. Apparently the truck that was blocking the off ramp (and which was responsible for causing the accident) had a dash cam. All of the ingredients for a sensational story were there: millionaire + high-speed chase + cocaine + sex (everybody knew it was part of the equation) + dead Jackie = most exciting story of the year. For a couple of weeks news stations ran the story every half hour or so. The story resurfaced and had another cycle during my trial, but without the same juiciness as the fresh meat that the original story had. Agent Palmer also probably found out about it through his law enforcement connections. The cocaine on me at the accident led the FBI to search my house with German Shepherds. They found what they were looking for.

"Yeah, quite the little incident," I said, "things really spiraled out of control on that one."

"Haha, pun intended?"

"Oh, dammit. No. Anyway, I was calling for an update on my case. It's been a few months and I haven't heard from you."

"Well, Caish, you haven't heard from me because there haven't been any developments in your case. Like I said last time we talked, we have followed every lead available to us, and they are all dead ends. You were conned by professionals who were either genius hackers or who had genius hackers on their payroll."

I waited for Agent Palmer to say more, but he was silent.

"And the Lamborghini?" I asked.

"Gone, Caish. We sent you everything you needed to collect on insurance for that though, right?"

"Yeah, you did." But it didn't do anything because it wasn't insured. That bond I had with the DMV turned out to be another one of my bad investments.

I tried to think of something else to say. Something to tell Agent Palmer that would help. Or maybe a plea that he and his team try harder. But nothing came to mind. I had said it all before.

"Caish? You still there?"

"Yeah, yeah I'm here."

"I'm sorry for the bad news."

"So, what now?"

Agent Palmer thought for a moment, then said, "We move on. You, me, everybody involved."

"What?"

"There's nothing more we can do, we have to move on, Caish. So do you."

"Easy for you to say. Mr. FBI. Mr. Forty-Thousand-Dollars-A-Year. You don't have a dog in the fight. They stole thirty-five million dollars from me! And you're asking me to move on? You can't be serious."

"Caish," Agent Spineless said, "we do not have the ability to solve your problem. What happened to you was awful. You were robbed and the criminals who robbed you should pay. But we do not have the ability to make that happen. We have done everything we can. At this point, you need to move on. Sometimes we—"

"Send me everything you have on my case."

"Okay, we'll have a Google Drive folder created and send you the link. You still have the same email?"

"Yes."

"Okay, we'll get that to you in the next couple of days. And, Caish, this is—"

I hung up. I couldn't listen to that horse shit. The FBI is worthless. I should have handled this myself from the beginning. As soon as the FBI sent me my files I would sift through them and track down Jamie and Penn. The FBI couldn't find Jamie because they weren't thinking practically. The whole agency is full of people who went to college and learned some philosophical ideas that have nothing to do with the practicalities of finding a criminal.

Google pulled up tons of articles on how to track hackers and how to find stolen money. There were a few books on Amazon on the subject, so I bought those and selected overnight shipping. The FBI had wasted enough of my time, and it was time to get my money back. Worst case scenario, I would hire a private investigator to get my money back. I'd hire the best in the business. Price wouldn't be a problem because it would be an investment with thirty-five million dollars in returns. This felt great. The winds were changing. I would have my money back in a matter of months and be back in Malibu before the end of the year.

I ordered Chinese food and fell asleep watching Netflix. In the middle of the night I woke up coughing and walked down to the kitchen for a snack. I wanted cereal, but I didn't have any milk. Or cereal. My tissue supply was also running low. I put on my warmest clothes and hopped in the Suburban. While the Suburban was warming up, I checked Facebook and saw that Alex had accepted my friend request. This was a new level in our new relationship. Alex clearly wanted me, there was just the sticky situation of a spouse and children. I told Alex not to get married. I tried to help years ago, but Alex didn't listen and now look at the mess we're in.

The roads in Missoula were empty at this time of night. 3:16 a.m. It may as well be a ghost town with the lights left on. Walmart's parking lot was completely empty except for the snow piles that I would be parking on top of. But the place was closed. And they weren't the only cereal seller that was closed. Every grocery store in town was closed. Even 7-11s and CVSs were closed. There wasn't a single establishment in this tiny town that could sell me cereal and milk.

With the streets to myself, I let the Suburban show its strength. It had the torque of a dump truck and could climb any snow pile I came across. It was lifted pretty high, though, so I had to be careful not to let it tip over. Once, when I did a U turn at fifteen-miles-an-hour, the Suburban went up on two wheels and would have flipped if I didn't turn the wheel back in the direction of the roll. It pays to be a good driver. I blew through traffic lights and drove on a few sidewalks. Then I found myself driving by the Big Sky Equestrian Park and decided to see how the Suburban did off-road.

The ground was covered with a foot of snow, but the horse paths had been marked. The Suburban fishtailed as soon as I veered across the snow field. Which was wildly fun, but soon I lost traction all together, spun around, and became stuck in a rut. I examined the Suburban's dials and buttons, and found that it was in two-wheel drive. I shifted into four-wheel drive and floored it. The Suburban leapt out of the rut and blazed through the snow like a Siberian train.

I got onto the horse trial and sped toward the first obstacle, which looked like hay bales. I slowed down and the Suburban easily crawled over the wall of hay. The obstacles were not as fun as driving flat out across the open snow, so I gassed it and flew to the other side of the park. There was a small rise in the ground that I could get airborne off of if I went fast enough. So I went fast enough. In all my driving history, this was the first time I had ever jumped a car. I was beside myself in laughter. This was the most fun I'd had in years. I spun the SUV around, drove back the other direction, and jumped again. I could do this all night. Maybe middle-class life wouldn't be so bad. When

I was making my third lap red and blue lights flashed from the road across the field.. I tensed up and brought the Suburban to a stop.

Last time I ran from the police, things didn't go so well. But there was a lot of deep snow between me and that squad car. The cop would have to drive through a couple hundred yards of snow to get to me. There's no way. Unless the cop was also in a lifted 4x4. I rolled my window down. Jennifer Trunchbull would probably send me to prison if I was arrested for trespassing or whatever that cop wanted to get me for. And even if it was just a ticket that the cop had in mind, I was not in a financial position to be paying tickets. I turned the Suburban off so I could hear the cop. The cop wasn't on the bullhorn and wasn't driving out into the snow. Absolute silence. The cop turned on a spot light and pointed in my direction. It was a standoff.

Fuck it. I started the Suburban and floored it in the opposite direction of the cop car. I weaved around the obstacles in the horse path. When I left the path, I glided through the crystal sand at over sixty-miles-an-hour with a fifteen-foot tall snowbow in tow. In a matter of seconds I was back on the road and speeding through sleepy neighborhoods. I took random turns and drove through a few empty fields. When I was confident I had shaken the tail, I got back onto the side roads and drove at civil speeds. I tried to go through a drive through at a Taco Bell, but they were closed. The roads were still empty so I could have hauled ass, but I kept it slow in case another police officer spotted me.

I took the long way home, being careful to observe all traffic laws and stay off of the main streets. From the time I left the equestrian park until the time I shut my garage, I didn't see another police officer. The simple pleasures of small-town living. The LAPD would never have let me get away with that.

Leftover sushi and breakfast from Einstein's were the only things in my fridge, and the only food in my house. But I hate leftovers. I'd rather sleep on an empty stomach. I crashed into my bed without undressing. It felt like my eyes had just closed when my phone rang. I silenced it and rolled over. But it kept ringing.

"Hello?"

"Caish, your color has been drawn, report for urine testing."

I grumbled something.

"Caish. Green is today's color. Are you coming in or are we sending the sheriff to your house?"

"I'm coming in. I'll be there at eight."

"It's eight forty-five, Caish. Come in right now."

I pulled my phone away from my ear and checked. Sure enough, 8:42 a.m.

"Okay, yeah. On my way."

"Good. See you in ten minutes." Jennifer hung up.

I was drunk with sleepiness, but managed to get downtown without any incidents and peed drug- and alcohol-free urine into a plastic cup.

Now that I was out an about, I went to Walmart to buy cereal and milk. The last time I was in Walmart was over a decade ago. Missoula's Walmart is massive. Packed full of the cheapest products on earth with sweatshop pricing. All sorts of people were pushing around shopping carts full of chintzy cookware, tacky clothing, and worthless trinkets. Children screaming, flopping, and flailing on the linoleum floor. Teenagers meandering the isles with their friends, putting on hats and sunglasses from the racks, taking pictures of themselves, then laughing and looking around. Blue-vested employees preside over the entire mess with an exhausted surrender.

The grocery section was easy to find. With Cap'n Crunch in one hand and a gallon of milk in the other, I returned to the front of the store to find twenty-five cashier stations, with three of them operational. The self-check-out area was closed, and lines to the three cashiers were horrendous. Waiting in line was something I had forgotten about. When you have millions of dollars, lines are not part of your life. Occasionally things get a little backed up at a Lakers or Dodgers game, but for the most part, rich people don't wait in lines (unless you consider traffic to be a line, in which case everybody waits). What a complete waste of time. There I stood, shoulder to shoulder with the rest of America. The only thing to tell these commoners that I was of a higher ilk than them was my Canada Goose coat. But I doubt most of them knew what a Canada Goose coat was, let alone how much it cost.

After waiting in line for ten minutes, I remembered I needed more tissues. I asked the people behind me in line to hold my spot, but by the time I found the tissues and returned to the line, the people were gone. I explained my situation to the other people in the line, but they insisted I "wait like everybody else." They didn't get. I did wait like everybody else. I had just forgotten tissues.

Having braved the line (twice) and escaped that societal stew, I climbed into my Suburban and collected my thoughts. If I didn't win the lottery again soon, I'd be a regular in this place. My life would be stripped of quality and I would be forced to "shop the sales" and, God forbid, use coupons. I couldn't let that happen. I drove from Walmart straight to the gas station and bought two hundred dollars' worth of lottery tickets. Mega Millions, Powerball, and Scratchers. This was my new job, and I had to take it seriously.

My books from Amazon arrived, and I read up on how to track hackers and con artists. But reading is too tedious, so I called a professional investigator, Sara Thomas. She was expensive, but had a stellar track record. She was located in Los Angeles, so we Skyped and I granted her access to remote into my electronic devices. I gave her all of the information I could, and forwarded her the link to the FBI's file. She told me she would report back to me every Friday with updates on the case. It was refreshing to deal with a professional.

Weeks passed without Alex stopping by. I thought about stopping by Grier's, but I didn't want to be needy, so I waited. Another storm rolled through and I had a chance to use my new snow blower. Netflix released a new miniseries that kept me busy for a day. Kevin stopped by to see if I needed any help with removing my icicles. I went on another late-night tear in the Suburban, and this time was not spotted by Missoula's finest. Every time my color was called, I dutifully reported and deposited urine-filled cups into the bureaucracy. I bought more lottery tickets. I upgraded the sound system in the Suburban. I smoked a pack of cigarettes a day. Sometimes two packs. I bought more interesting books only to discover that it wasn't the content that made reading boring, it was reading that made reading boring.

The fog of boredom was crawling in. Depression's black cloud wasn't far behind. Missoula's winter months were besieging me.

Sara gave me the same runaround as the FBI. Every Friday she'd make up excuses about why she couldn't get me my money back. I stopped paying her and eventually the Friday reports stopped. Such a waste of money.

Alex finally came over and did the same "we shouldn't" routine. Something about, "Really, Caish, I just came over to talk." I knew what Alex wanted to say, "We should stop because of my family," and all that. It should have been much easier to get from the false-resistance phase to the smoking-after-sex phase, but Alex wouldn't budge.

"Well, come in and let's talk then," I said.

"Let's talk here," Alex said.

"Alex, it's like, negative a thousand degrees out here. Let's just step in where it's comfortable."

"Grab your jacket if you need to, but this shouldn't take long."

Alex's face looked hurt, something was wrong. I pulled out my pack of Newports, lit two, and gave Alex one. I pegged Alex as the Newport type and bought a pack for the next time we were smoking in bed. We took a few drags of our cigarettes in silence, standing shoulder to shoulder looking out from my front porch. The road was covered in bulletproof ice and flanked by three-foot berms of plowed snow. Past the road was a snow-covered clearing surrounded by naked trees. The sun was elbowing its way through the clouds and dancing off the white champagne powder. The entire observable world was locked in ice. How anything survived out there is beyond me.

Alex broke the silence, "Caish, really though, we can't keep doing this." Alex reached took my hand. "As much as I love it, and as much as I miss you, we can't do this."

"Why not?" I couldn't think of a good reason.

"You know why. If Peyton found out, I would be a single parent and all my family and friends would talk shit and resent me for being a cheater."

"Nobody is going to find out. I don't see why you're so afraid to let your heart do the thinking every now and then." Which is bullshit, we think with our brains, not our hearts. But I knew that Alex was a sucker for this kind of romantic soliloquy. "We have something special Alex. You know that. I know you don't feel this way with Peyton. And, judging by the last time you were here, I know Peyton isn't as good in bed."

Alex didn't say anything. I looked over and saw a tear rolling down Alex's cheek.

"Hey, woah, Alex, what's up? Don't cry."

"Caish. I have… uh…" Alex sat down on my porch steps. I sat next to Alex and tried not to show that I was freezing to death. My jeans did little to insulate me from the frozen cement steps. Alex went on, "I love Peyton, Caish. And look what you're making me do."

"Woah, Alex, I'm not forcing you to do anything. I thought we were both doing what felt right." I could see where Alex was coming from. It couldn't be easy being stuck in a shitty marriage and having kids to take care of, and then having a long-lost lover swing back into town with money and free tickets to Hot Sex City.

But at the same time, I couldn't understand why Alex was so worked up about it. Why not just explain it to Peyton. Tell Peyton that, sure, they were married, and Alex would like it to stay that way, but that Alex would like to have sex on the side with a far more attractive person. Peyton would probably be reasonable and understanding if Alex put it that way.

"Caish. My family isn't the only reason we shouldn't be doing this. I... uh..." Alex paused. "You should know that... um..."

"What's up, Alex?"

"So, um. A couple of weeks ago, like a few weeks after we had sex the first time, I got the flu."

No.

"Or at least what I thought was the flu."

God no.

"Caish." Alex was holding back tears. "You gave me HIV."

15

"No! That can't be," I said. "Did you give me HIV?"

"No, Caish! You gave it to me!" Alex's voice cracked and we both choked up. Not sobbing, but shaken. It didn't help that we were sitting on my porch in sub-zero temperatures.

"No way, Alex, I couldn't have. I always use protection. I don't have HIV."

"Caish, you gave me HIV."

"No, that's impossible. I don't have HIV."

"Have you been tested?"

"No, but I know I don't have it. Trust me. I'd know. I'm very careful about that sort of thing." And I was. I always used protection. Well, almost always. There was a time a few years back when I got a pretty bad flu, and I've had friends get HIV so I knew the symptoms, but I didn't get checked because I knew I didn't have it. There's just no way. I've been in perfect health.

"Have you ever done heroin?" Alex asked.

"No. Well, yeah, but I always used clean needles."

"How do you know they were clean? Were they your own needles that you got from a hospital or clinic?'

"No, but Alex, I'm rich. I'm not some back-alley junkie harpooning my arm with filthy needles. Any time I ever used a needle was at classy house parties. Clean places with clean people. Rich and famous people."

"Caish. I got tested. I have HIV. And I probably gave it to Peyton, but we haven't talked about it yet. I didn't have HIV before we had sex, and now I do. You gave me HIV."

"No, Alex—"

"This is the last time I will come to your house. I just came to say goodbye and to tell you to get tested. You have HIV and the sooner you can treat it the better." Alex stood up. "Don't freak out too much, it's not really terminal these days if you get treated."

I followed Alex down my walkway toward the curb where we folded into each other for what would be our last hug. I couldn't think of anything to say.

"You should also talk to anybody you've had sex with in the last few years. Tell them to get checked," Alex said. Then Alex got into a shitty middle-class car and drove away. The icy wind cut through my clothes as I stood staring in the direction Alex drove. Walking back toward my front door, I glanced at the Black's house and saw Ms. Black watching me through a window. A cracked window. Not cracked in the sense of being broken, cracked in the sense of being open a few inches despite the deathly cold. She was on her phone and stepped back as soon as I looked in her direction. There's no way she could have heard what Alex and I were talking about. Her house was at least a hundred feet from mine. But, other than the breeze, it was absolutely silent in this frozen tundra. I heard Ms. Black clack her window shut.

After a hot shower I bundled up and drove to St. Patrick Hospital. I wandered into the emergency room and told a nurse behind a desk that I needed to get tested for HIV. The nurse said, "Okay, no problem, let me just get you to fill out some forms here. Have you been to St. Patrick before?" as if I didn't just tell the nurse that I think I might have a life-threatening illness.

"Yeah. Um. I was born here," I muttered, looking through the forms.

"Oh, great," the nurse said, "Welcome back. You can fill out those forms right over there," the nurse pointed into a waiting area where several injured commoners were observing our conversation. "When you're done bring the forms back up here and we'll get your bloodwork started."

"Okay. Thanks."

"Oh, and do you have an insurance card with you?"

"I don't have medical insurance. I'll pay in cash."

"No problem. Let me know if you have any questions about those forms."

CNN played from a TV and a toddler made toddler noises. The only decoration was a fish tank. The room smelled sterile. The chair I chose was next to a coffee table full of old issues of People, InTouch, Time, and National Geographic. Two of the commoners were still staring at me, unashamed when I met their gaze. I worked through the forms, entering my name, birthdate, address, and phone number over and over again. When I finished, the nurse smiled and said they'll be right with me, again seeming to forget that I said that I think I have HIV.

Once again I was waiting in line. I arrived after these country bumkins, so I couldn't be helped until after they were. It didn't matter that my net worth was more than they'd make in their lifetimes. It didn't matter that I could be dying of HIV or AIDS. These people didn't know who I was. I let CNN tell me what to think until I heard, "Caish Calloway?"

"Yeah, right here," I said, getting up and walking over to the nurse.

"You can walk down this hallway right here and head into room E112. Dr. Clayton will be right with you."

Room E112 was small. I sat on wax paper that covered the padded bench/chair upon which Dr. Clayton would likely have me lay. I still hadn't taken off my Canada Goose coat; I couldn't stop shaking. The chills, probably. My breathing became shallow and irregular. My vision lost focus. An elephant was slowly sitting down on me and there was nothing I could do other than panic.

Dr. Clayton walked in looking at a clipboard, muttering something about, "So, looks like you've come in for some blood work." When Dr. Clayton looked up, her face went from friendly to solemn and she set her clipboard down.

"Cash, my name is Dr. Clayton. Let's get you out of that coat and lying down." We took off my coat and Dr. Clayton tossed it into one of the three chairs in the room. My movements were announced by the wax paper as I spun around and laid back. Dr. Clayton immediately began a cannonade of tests. Flashlight in my eyeballs, "Do you feel nauseous right now, Cash? Any dizziness?" Something plastic clicking in my ear, "Do you have the chills?" Stethoscope on my chest, "Any difficulty breathing?" A nurse came in and assisted Dr. Clayton. Forehead swabbed with something I'd never seen, "Are you taking any medications right now?" Upper arm strangled by a blood pressure machine, "Any allergies?" Mouth probed with a cotton swab that was bottled up and sent away, "Any soreness or pain anywhere on your body?"

"Just anxious," I said.

"You're a little pale, we want to make sure you're comfortable." Dr. Clayton pulled a fleece blanket from one of the cabinets and laid it on me. Suddenly I was seven years old being tucked in by my mom—before she turned into a greedy bitch. Tucking me in, kissing my forehead. Smiling with more warmth than my blankets. Jesus. What a woman she used to be. She tasted money and went off the deep end. It occurred to me that I was now living in the same city as her and became dizzy. But at least I was warm and being cared for. Dr. Clayton didn't kiss my forehead, though.

"Let's draw some of your blood and see what we're dealing with here, shall we?"

I didn't respond because I figured my approval went without saying.

Dr. Clayton said, "This is Raelynn, she's going to get that blood from you. I'll be back with the results in a few minutes. Are you comfortable?"

"Yeah, thanks."

Raelynn swabbed the crook of my elbow, said, "Little poke," then rammed a needle through my skin. She found the vein first try, and I watched my blood snake through a tube into a clear plastic bag. Satisfied with her take, she pulled the needle out and told me to hold a cotton ball over the excavation site. She buttoned things up, taped a new cotton ball to my arm, then walked out of the room saying something like, "Dr. Clayton will be back with your results in a few minutes."

An eternity later, Dr. Clayton walked in looking down at a clipboard. "Alright, Cash, you have tested positive for HIV —"

"Oh God oh God," I feel another anxiety attack coming on.

"*But*, before you ask any questions or get too worked up over that, let me tell you what that means and what that does not mean. First, and most importantly, you are not dying. Your T-cell count is low, but it's not devastatingly low. There are all sorts of treatments that we'll get you started on today that will get that T-cell count up again. In a few months you will be back to tip-top shape. Second, you do not have AIDS. HIV can cause AIDS, but you do not have that, and will not get AIDS because we are going to begin treating your HIV today. And third, since your T-cell count is low, you have been more susceptible to illness. A T-cell count measures your white blood cells, which are essentially the cells of the immune system. With a lower white blood cell count, your body is less able to defend you against infectious diseases. This would explain your cold-like symptoms, which is actually pneumonia. Regarding your —"

"Oh Christ, I have pneumonia too?"

"Yes, but that is also treatable and we'll begin treatment for that today."

"You mean chemotherapy?"

"Um, no. Pneumonia is a common lung infection. Not cancer."

"Oh, yeah. Okay. I sometimes mix pneumonia up with... what is it?"

"What is what?"

"Umm... leukemia! Sometimes I mix it up with leukemia. That's cancer, right?"

"Yes, but don't worry about that, you don't have leukemia,

which, you're right, is a type of cancer. But pneumonia is not. No chemotherapy necessary. We'll write you a prescription for the pneumonia and you'll likely have that kicked in a week or two. Your HIV regimen will be more intensive, and will take longer, but at your stage we usually see a high rate of success. We will—"

"So you can cure it?"

"Unfortunately there is not presently a cure for HIV, but with effective treatment you can live a full life without suffering from the side effects of HIV."

"But I'll still have it?"

"For now, yes. But HIV research has come a long way in recent years, and we are getting closer to a cure. Although you will still have HIV, after treatment you likely will not suffer from any of the side effects, and you will likely live a long life that will not be truncated by the disease," Dr. Clayton said. I thought about what she was saying. She studied me. Seeing that I didn't have any questions at the moment, she continued.

"Treatment will start today. We will get you on antiretroviral therapy, which is essentially a combination of medications that prevent the immunodeficiency virus from multiplying, which will give your immune system a chance to rebound and start fighting."

"Is this like, a handful of pills a day type of thing?"

"Not at all. Back in the 1990s it used to be that way, sort of a pill cocktail, but we've come a long way. Now it will be just a few pills once a day, plus the medication for your pneumonia."

"What are the side effects?"

"Of the medication?"

"Yeah."

"That varies from person to person, although most side effects are relatively mild. You may experience a headache or dizziness, and the medication may cause some stomach soreness. If your throat starts swelling or you begin vomiting, come back in immediately. Otherwise, I'll want to see you again next week, then every two weeks for the next two months, then monthly for the next six months. Here are your prescriptions." Dr. Clayton handed me a small slip of paper that had pre-printed medications on the top and handwritten medications on the bottom. "These prescriptions are for your HIV treatment, and this one here at the bottom is for your pneumonia. Somebody is bringing over the HIV medication right now, and you can get your pneumonia prescription filled here at the hospital or at your preferred pharmacy." There was a knock at the door. "Speak of the Devil," Dr. Clayton said. She opened the door and a nurse delivered a paper sack. "Here is your HIV medication. You absolutely must take this as prescribed. Here is a number to call if you have any questions."

Dr. Clayton sat and appraised the impact of her words. "I know this can be a lot, Cash, but you're going to be alright. That's the bottom line."

"It's Caish."

"I'm sorry?"

"My name. It's Caish."

"Oh, right. Sorry about that. What did I say? Cash?"

Night's darkness and temperature drop had settled in by the time I left the hospital. Or maybe this is just what the world is like when one is infected with HIV. Perhaps it's cold darkness from here on out. I drove home in a trance. I was HIV positive. My body was carrying HIV. And would carry HIV until the day I died. A cureless shadow lurking in my bloodstream for decades to come. Every decade I had left. My blood was laced with death. I carried poisonous blood. I was literally poisonous.

After ordering pizza and warming up next to my fireplace, I combed the internet for information on HIV. I remember Dr. Clayton talking to me, but I can hardly remember what she said. Most of the stuff online seems pretty hopeful. I found a story about a guy in Berlin who was cured of HIV, so a cure must exist. Given my situation (on the verge of broke and on probation), I was in no position to go to Germany. The trip would have to wait until I made back my money.

In the weeks after Alex broke the news about giving me HIV, I was recurrently dizzy. Like when you first wake up and stumble around, not sure what day it is or whether the dream you just had was real or not. I did as Dr. Clayton told me, and took all my medications when instructed. I kept my appointments with Dr. Clayton and reported my progress and side effects. Whenever my color was called, I continued to report and fill cups full of clean urine. Well, my urine had HIV, so maybe not completely clean.

My days turned into a routine of waking up around 8:00 a.m. (an ungodly hour), waiting for a phone call from Jennifer Trunchbull, showering, eating breakfast at a diner in town, swallowing my pills, then returning home to wallow in soberness for the rest of the day.

The HIV medication hurt. At first it felt like my insides were sunburned. Eating was painful and I had the runs. Dr. Clayton told me that quitting smoking would help with the side effects, but smoking was all I had left, so I passed on that advice. I went to Grier's Hardware every now and then to see how Alex was doing, but Alex was never there. Alex also blocked me on Facebook, which was unfair. It would have been nice to talk to somebody who was going through this, or who had been through this, but I was alone. People that used to be my friends didn't respond to my texts, wouldn't answer my calls, and acted like they didn't see my Facebook messages. I felt like an iceberg at sea. Once part of a mighty glacier, surrounded by majestic mountains of ice, now drifting into the open ocean. Slowly melting and falling apart, with fading memories of what it used to feel like to be part of the whole. Glaciers don't miss their icebergs.

The Rayburns, two of my closest friends, had drifted far from the glacier. Through Facebook I learned they had lost everything and moved back to Alaska to live with family. Tim was driving trucks and Selina was a manager at a Kohl's. They fell out of wealth's sparkling cloud and landed back in the mud with all the other commoners. Forced to slog their lives away for meager hourly pay. Well I guess Tim was probably paid by the mile, but still. Drudgery. A drudgery to which I refused to return. I earned my way out of that. I used to be a mechanic. I know what it's like to take orders from other peasants. Inconsequential tasks, meaningless deadlines, and pointless people are trifles that wealth insulates you from. Selina and Tim's story snapped me out of my self-pity and got me back down to the gas station to buy more lottery tickets. I had slacked off for a little while, distracted by the new drama in my life.

I needed money. I was running low. Ultra-low. Almost less than six digits in the bank account low. Walmart was selling these lottery gift baskets that had all sorts of lottery games in them. Over a hundred tickets from all sorts of games: Pirate's Treasure, Diamonds and Dollars, Super Cashword 17, BIG Money, Golden Casino, 10x Cash, Hot Cash, Pearls, Jewel 7$, Green, Flamingo, Mega Slots, Platinum Payout, Silver Spectacular. The list went on. A whole basket full. I bought three baskets, a few MegaMillions and Powerball tickets, a pack of frozen burritos, and a 24-pack of Diet Coke. Then I waited in line for twenty minutes.

Once home, I microwaved the burritos, turned on my fireplace and TV, and made myself a nest with blankets and pillows on the carpet next to the fireplace. I situated the pack of Diet Coke away from the fireplace, put two packs of cigarettes within reach of the nest, and cued up HBO (they just released a new original series). I brought my burritos over to my nest and started the show. God, HBO knew how to make quality productions. Finished with my burritos, I slid the plate across the carpet toward my kitchen and reached for the first of my three lottery baskets. I had hours of scratching ahead of me. But anybody who is not willing to work for their money doesn't deserve it.

I cracked open another Diet Coke and unwrapped the basket of tickets. I had hundreds of tickets to get through, HBO ready to play for hours, two full packs of cigarettes, and a fireplace with an infinite supply of natural gas. For the first time since sleeping with Alex months ago, I felt happy. The joy and excitement of money was at my fingertips. It was like wealth had finally sent me a text that said, "You up?"

Each lottery ticket could be my ticket out of Montana and back to the promised land. The first ticket I pulled out was a Make My Month ("Win Up To $50,000!"). I used my lucky quarter to scratch away the film hiding my winning numbers at the top of the ticket. 9, 2, 48. I started scratching through the fifteen prize spots looking for my numbers. As an added bonus, if I found a cash symbol I would automatically win whatever that prize was, if I got a bag of gold symbol, I would win five times the prize shown, and if I got a "MONTH" symbol, I would win all fifteen prizes. I got close on one of the prizes, but didn't win anything. The first ticket was not a winner. But that's what you have to expect with these. The odds of winning on the first ticket are slim. I work through the basket systematically and do all of the Make My Months first. Then I would move on to the Wild Cherry tickets, the Platinum Payouts, and the Super Cashwords.

Only ten tickets in and I won my first prize, twenty dollars. Not a huge win, but a good sign. And I only needed ten of those and the lottery gift basket paid for itself. I went into the kitchen to get a bowl for the winning tickets and a bowl for the losing tickets. Having returned to my nest and situated myself within arm's reach of all necessary parts of my operation, I lit a cigarette and got back to it.

I scratched and scratched. Ticket after ticket. Most tickets were losers, of course, but I was bringing in a fair amount of small wins. My winning ticket bowl was filling up. The first basket took me two episodes of HBO's new series to get through.

During my break, I heated up another burrito and kicked back on my couch with a Diet Coke. My bowl of winners was looking good. No big wins, but a lot of little wins and probably enough to pay off my initial investment in that basket. The burrito warmed my stomach. I pulled one of the blankets from my nest up onto the couch with me and began to drift off.

When I woke up, everything was exactly how I'd left it, except HBO had soldiered on without me. Four episodes passed during my nap. It was probably around two or three in the morning. I went back to the episode I left off on, rebuilt my nest, lit a cigarette, and got back to work. You have to be willing to work late nights if you want success.

Basket number two was a total loss. There were only thirteen winning tickets; twelve of them for $1. The thirteenth was for $5. Without taking a break between the second and third basket, I tore off the wrapping and kept scratching. I worked through the Golden Casinos and Green Flamingos without much luck. The Mega Slots gave me a few winners, one of which was $100. Momentum was building again, I could feel it. One of the Silver Spectacular's earned me $20. Several more $1 victories filled my winners bowl. With around fifty tickets to go, I started scratching off the Super Hot 7s.

My third ticket in and bells of wealth began to chime. On the fourth scratch area I revealed a "7" which means I won something. I scratched off the prize area below it to see what I had won: "$5000." I won five thousand dollars! That would cover this month's mortgage. And that ticket was only a one dollar scratch ticket. Five thousand dollars. I knew I still had it in me. A little perseverance goes a long way. If you dare to take risks, you can reap rewards that others are too afraid to try and harvest. These are the types of things they don't teach you in college.

With triumph I placed the $5000 Super Hot 7s ticket into the winner's bowl. I worked my way through the rest of the final basket and got a couple more small denomination winners. With my calculator app in hand, I added up my night's earnings. $5,212. And that was from a six hundred-dollar investment. Not to mention, I still had my MegaMillions and Powerball tickets to play later in the week.

The next morning, after peeing in a cup, I took my stack of winning tickets to the grocery store and cashed out. Holding thousands of dollars in cash felt good. The familiar feel of holding hands with money gave me goosebumps. I could have used the money to pay off some of my newly incurred credit card debt, or I could have put it toward my mortgage, but I decided to keep it. This was the first cash I had since spending the last of my million in cash during the whole Pismo disaster. This was the first money I had earned since moving to Montana. I didn't feel like parting with it so soon. Maybe I'd never part with it. Maybe this $5,212 would stay with me through thick and thin, through sickness and health. Money didn't care that I didn't live in Malibu anymore or that I drove a Suburban. It didn't care that I owned peasant clothes. It didn't care that I couldn't afford a yacht or a helicopter. Money didn't care that I had HIV.

16

Spring finally arrived and life returned to Montana. The field across from my house and the golf course out my back door went through a yellow and brown muddy phase, but are now blooming with vibrant greens. On the occasional sunny day I go for a drive, but the rain keeps me indoors most days. Well. The rain and the gossip.

Apparently Ms. Black heard every word (and then some) that Alex and I said on my porch, which could be distilled to the easily transferable news that Alex and I had sex, and now both had HIV. Ms. and Mr. Black were the wind behind the wildfire that carried the gossip. Missoula provided dry kindling for the fire: everybody knew each other, everybody knew the perpetrators, and everybody understood the consequences. Imagine the sensationalism:

"Oh my God, Mable, you ain't gon' believe this. You 'member Alex Rettig from high school?" Gossip Goblin would say.

"Umm. Oh yeah yeah," Rumor Rat would reply.

"And you 'member Caish Calloway?"

"How could I forget? Course I 'member Caish Calloway. Quite the looker. Talented too, and quite witty, if I 'member correctly."

"Okay, so Caish moved away shortly after high school to California. Left ol' Alex out to dry so Caish could go sun tan and make money or somethin'. Alex stayed in this here town, workin' and startin' a family. Married to Peyton somethin'-or-other."

"Right," Rumor Rat would say, "I think I seen Alex workin' at Grier's Hardware."

"Indeed ja have, that's Alex. Workin' hard. *Hwell*, meanwhile, Caish wins the lottery in California."

"Nah! Really?" So sensational! They'd be gripped by the story at this point. Locked in. Imagining the wonders of wealth and guessing at the means of tragedy that surely (hopefully?) lies at the end of this yarn.

"Yeah, really. I kid ja not. 'Member how all the Calloways bought all them big fancy houses and Corvettes? That's how. Caish gave 'em all millions."

"Well hot damn."

"But, didjya know Caish had come back to town?" Gossip Goblin would say, lowering his voice and leaning in, suggesting that the story was about to get a whole lot juicer.

"Really? Why'd ol' Caish come on back?"

"Caish came back, tail betwixt the legs, 'cause Caish ain't got no money left."

"Ya don't say. Spent through all the millions?"

"Spent it straight through. Dead broke."

"I'll be damned."

"Me too. Damn fool."

From what I could tell, news of the incident with my Porsche and Jackie at Pismo Beach had not yet arrived in Montana. If it had, Gossip Goblin would be sure and include it here. It was only a matter of time until the Blacks learned about that too, and would cash in that bit of information. The scandalmongers also wouldn't mention Jamie T. Lowell and Green Mountain. Even if they knew about that part, they'd keep it out because it either wouldn't make sense to them, or they wouldn't want to include "mitigating factors," as my attorney would say. Easier just to say I spent it all and think to themselves that they would have been wiser, and that, in their wisdom, they deserved the money more, but that the injustice of the universe gave it to fools like Caish Calloway instead of shrewd scholars like Gossip Goblin and Rumor Rat.

"Anyway," Gossip Goblin would continue, "Caish comes back to town and calls up lowly ol' Alex. Still have each other's numbers after all these years."

"Uh oh."

"Yeah, ya see where this here story is goin', don'tchya?"

"I'm supposin' so."

"Well, Caish and Alex get to talkin', and their loins get to burnin', and b'fore you can say in-fi-del-i-ty they're over there in Caish's new house messin' around."

Rumor Rat would be doing her best to hide her excitement behind a look of disapproval, as if to say, "I can't believe that such folks exist that would transgress God's holy laws and engage in such vile, awful, and downright selfish behavior."

"Well anyway, they're messin' around day after day, until without explanation, Alex stops goin' over to Caish's love nest."

"Trouble in sinner's paradise?"

"Indeed. Alex comes back a few weeks later and when Caish opens up the door, Alex refuses to enter. Somethin' about, I'm just here to talk."

"Uh oh. Alex was caught cheatin'? Came to end it?"

"If only." Gossip Goblin would look around and lower his voice to a near whisper at this point. Scanning their surroundings to ensure a safe environment existed for the transfer of such highly-sensitive confidential surreptitious secrets. Rumor Rat would glance around the room to show that she too was aware of that they were dealing in clandestine information.

"Alex, sobbing, pulls Caish close and says," Gossip Goblin again pauses for effect, then leans in and whispers, "I've got the AIDS."

"No!" Rumor Rat would shout. "You're pullin' my leg."

"Swear to God, Mable. I swear to our Lord Jesus Christ above, this is a true story."

"The AIDS?" Rumor Rat would ask, feigning to not fully grasp the implications so as to draw it out. Squeezing the story dry for every drop of blood.

"The goddamn AIDS. And that ain't even the worst part! It was Caish who gave Alex the AIDS." Gossip Goblin would lean back, probably sip a drink with raised eyebrows and watch Rumor Rat work out what exactly that meant. But before Rumor Rat could speak, Gossip Goblin would jump back in with: "Caish was messin' around with all sorts of them Southern California types, if ya know what I mean, and was injectin' heroin with the same company. Then, when the money was dried out, Caish came crawlin' back to Missoula to lick the wounds of foolishness."

"So what's Alex gonna do?"

"Well—and this is the real hum-dinger—after gettin' it from Caish, Alex gave the AIDS to Peyton. They have a few kids and are expectin' another. A bun in the oven as we speak."

"No!" And with that, Gossip Goblin and Rumor Rat would go back through the story, pulling out particular anecdotes and dissecting them. Asking rhetorical questions like, "How could ya possibly spend through all that money?" and, "How could you be so reckless?" They'd be confounded. Dumbstruck. But not quite speechless. Gossip Goblin would make it seem like a high price was paid for the information by saying something like, "But you can't tell anybody." Such an admonition added to the drama of it all. Rumor Rat would agree, "Oh no, of course not," with a face that said, "What? Do ya think I'm some sorta animal? 'Course I ain't gon' tell nobody." Rumor Rat would then tell the story to every person she knew, especially people she met at bars and parties, but with new and improved embellishments.

In a matter of days I was infamous. Everywhere I went people were looking over their shoulder and whispering to whoever they were with—who would then steal a glance and join in the whispering. Peyton and Alex's mother paid me a visit at my house, threatening to do this and that to me if I, "ever get near Alex again." That I should be ashamed of myself, and how could I live with myself. Shouting. Arms flailing. Leaning into my face. It was all quite a dramatic scene that I'm sure the Blacks ate right up. Not long after that, Peyton's parents came by and did about the same. Blaming me for everything. Another case of a family's failure to accept that their loved one, not me, was responsible for whatever harm they brought upon themselves.

It was Jackie and the Marquez family all over again. I bet if Alex contracted immortality from me they would say that Alex was responsible for that, and Alex alone. But since it was bad, they had to shift the blame. Not to mention, I'm still not convinced I had HIV before Alex and I hooked up. For all we know, Alex is the one who gave me HIV. But you don't see me waging war against Alex. I'm not enlisting my family to drive Alex out of town.

The only person that didn't send me scowls was Kevin, my friendly westward neighbor. He kept waving and smiling like always. The only difference these days was that he was looking up and waving from his lawn mower instead of his snow blower. He was either interested in me or was one of those religious types that are just waiting for an opportunity to invite you to their church. Which is probably one of those hip churches with electric guitars and lesbian preachers that wear shorts and sandals. I waved back and smiled, but closed my garage as soon as I pulled in and never walked over to talk. If I spent any time outside I'm sure he'd spring on me like a fox on a mouse. Facing the danger of Kevin talking to me, I mowed half my lawn once, then realized it was too big to mow myself and called a landscaping service. My house became my refuge.

Until my family learned my address.

The first to knock on my door was Caleb, who said that he was talking to a friend of Ms. Black's (which means that he was getting the dirt) and learned that I lived next to her. He said he was just coming over to make sure I was holding up alright and to see if I needed help with anything. It was a kind gesture, but I couldn't help but wonder if Caleb was just looking for a way into the heart of the drama. Just looking for more information so that next time Caleb was drinking with the rumor rats and gossip goblins he could sell the information for the only currency it was worth: increased status.

Caleb stayed for lunch. I ordered pizza, then Caleb insisted on paying the delivery boy. Again, a kind gesture, but a clear statement that he knew I was running low on money and that he was higher than me because paying for something like pizza was easier for him than me. A way for him to say (without actually saying), "Look Caish, you once had millions and thought you were ruler of the world, and now even me, Caleb, is in a better position to buy pizza."

Other than that the visit was relatively pleasant. Besides delivery drivers, cashiers, waiters, Kevin, and Jennifer Trunchbull, I didn't interact with other people. Having Caleb around brightened my mood. He seemed interested in my life. He asked about my place in Malibu, and I told him about my place in Spanish Hills. We talked cars for a couple hours (it was Caleb's 1969 Camaro that we credit as having given me the car bug). Caleb was the oldest of the four kids in the family, and had been working on cars for as long as I can remember. Cormac, the next oldest, liked tinkering with things, but was more drawn to construction than cars. Catherine was born six years after Cormac and did not have interest in anything mechanical. As a toddler and young child she only played kitchen. Always taking your order, returning to her plastic kitchen, and returning to you with a tray full of plastic food. Then she'd watch you act like you were eating the plastic food. If you didn't spend at least five minutes eating the plastic food, she'd get offended and go back to her kitchen and pout because you didn't like her cooking. I was born two years after Catherine and spent the better part of my toddlerhood pretending to enjoy Catherine's plastic hamburgers, drumsticks, french fries, potatoes, veggies, and weird orange roll-looking thing.

When I showed an interest in Caleb and Cormac's projects, like lawn mower rebuilding, fort building, box car racing, and rocket flying, Catherine did her best to learn to like those things too, lest she be left alone in her plastic kitchen for the rest of her life. The four of us were close, probably closer than most siblings due to our mother's laissez-faire parenting policy. Our father did one better by leaving the family a few weeks after I was born. He came back later to impregnate my mom with another, but she had an abortion. They didn't remarry and we hardly saw him. Our entire relationship with our mom was built on her telling us to clean the house and eat what was on the table. Occasionally she'd scorn us for not being grateful enough, or for being lazy, but for the most part she was out with her friends and we were left to live as we pleased. Caleb helped us with our homework, taught us the basics of how to tie our shoes, ride our bikes, and heat canned ravioli. When Catherine or I got sad, Caleb cheered us up. (Cormac seemed to never be either sad or happy, always just quiet and steady.)

I must have gotten caught up in sentimentality because I accepted an invitation to dinner at Caleb's house the next day. He said he'd invite Cormac and Catherine. I asked him not to, but he insisted.

"Caish, they really want to see you. We all miss you, and they really just want to reconnect."

"Did I ever tell you the story of when Catherine threw a plate through a window at Red Lobster?" I asked.

"Yes, you did. And I know we have all said things in greed that we didn't mean, but I think reconnecting will help us put that behind us and start fresh."

Caleb convinced me, gave me his address, and left with a hug and a pat on the shoulder. "Don't let the Missoula get you down, Caish. You know how great these folks are, they raised us. They mean well. They're just excited that something happened to this place for the first time since the gold rush." I smiled, nodded, and saw him to his car—some depressing Volvo with plastic hubcaps.

The small people of Missoula were not getting me down.

Honestly, I cared about as much for the people of Missoula as I cared about the ants in my backyard. Losing my money was getting me down. HIV was getting me down. Loneliness was getting me down. Hopelessness was getting me down. The list was long. Absent from the list were the tiny worthless citizens of Missoula.

Caleb's house was a 1970s two-story split-entry monstrosity. About as much curb appeal as the crumbling curb itself. Missoula was full of these slipshod dwellings. Whoever designed these houses should be shot, or at least forced to live in one of them. It had a rectangle facade with lopsided windows and faded brown plastic siding. The driveway sloped down toward a garage door that looked like it hadn't been opened in years. The driveway's slant had a steeper pitch than the house's roof, which wasn't flat enough to look mid-century modern, but wasn't steep enough to be respectable. A fifth wheel with cracked tires took up half the driveway. Caleb's sorry Volvo took up the other half. The lawn was splotchy and a grab bag of trees were planted randomly throughout the yard. The cement steps leading up to the house's front door were cracked and leaning. There was no porch, landing, or awning, just cracked cement stairs right up to the door. The front door, which was the best looking part of the whole mess, was a run-of-the-mill Home Depot door.

I knocked (a sticky note taped over the doorbell read "doorbell's fried, please knock"), and surveyed the other cars on the road that had arrived before me. Corvette, late-model Cadillac, and a G Wagon. Clearly the others had done better than Caleb at hanging on to the money I gave them. Caleb swung open the front door.

"Caish!" Caleb said, sounding surprised, "just in time!"

What the hell was that supposed to mean? I was right on time. The house smelled like cooking. A smell that hadn't filled my nostrils in years. Rolls baking on a cookie sheet; 375 degrees for twenty minutes. A roast in a crock pot, probably set to low and cooked since earlier this morning. Mashed potatoes, but not actual potatoes, dehydrated potato flakes with several cups of water, stirred regularly, no chives. Canned green beans poured into a bowl and microwaved. Caleb led me up the half-story flight of stairs and onto a landing where a black lab was beside itself in excitement.

Caleb patted the dog on the side, "This is Bobo, he loves people." Bobo was having a hard time keeping his front paws on the ground and was moving his head back and forth with almost as much pep as he was wagging his tail. Bobo was whining with excitement and jumped up to lick my face. "Bobo, down," Caleb said. Smiling to me, "Loves new people."

When we got to the top of the landing (which was carpeted in a God-awful '70s flower carpet that hadn't been vacuumed in months), the room opened up to the left and was crowded with people. Or at least it felt crowded. It was a small room full of mismatched cloth-covered furniture occupied by people. An outdated TV was playing in the corner. The walls were a bad beige and were filled with framed family photos and shelves installed to hold gimcrack trinkets. The ceiling was only eight feet high, and the room was dimly lit.

The person seated closest to me stood up, "Caish! Jeez it's been too long," and gave me a hug. It was Cormac. Fit as ever, but with less hair and more wrinkles. He looked great. His smile was one of the best I'd seen. Cormac's face should be in commercials. The others stood up as well and greeted me similarly. Catherine, then Catherine's husband, then Caleb's wife, then... dammit. Mom. She stood up and gave me a hug. Not with the same warmth as the others, but didn't say anything spiteful, so maybe things would be alright. Caleb didn't mention that she would be here. He'd say it was for the same reason that he didn't mention his wife would be there, he figured it was a given. But the real reason was that he knew I wouldn't have come. I should have known. That Cadillac was probably hers. This whole thing is probably just a set up to get the last of my money out of my bank account and into hers.

The front room opened up to the dining area. "Opened up to" may not be the right way to put it. It just sort of turned into the dining area, which consisted of a small table surrounded by an assortment of chairs. Next to the dining area, but separated from the front room, was the kitchen. Each area on this floor could have been expanded by three times and still felt too small.

Caleb took my jacket down the hall, then returned and announced dinner was ready. We squeezed in around the table and sat shoulder to shoulder. I sat between Cormac and Caleb's wife. The table was packed tight with plates, glasses, serving bowls full of vegetables, trays of meat, condiments, pitchers, and a bottle of Budweiser at each plate.

When we were all situated, Caleb, sitting at the head of the table, said, "Well, thank y'all for comin' out tonight. This is the first time we've all been together since we visited Caish in California about six years ago. I think I speak for all of us when I say we are truly overjoyed to have ya back, Caish. Tonight is particularly—"

"Caleb, let's say grace and catch up while we eat," Mom cut in.

"Great idea," Caleb said with a smile. Caleb lowered his head and closed his eyes. So did the rest of us. "Oh Lord, we thank thee for bringin' us all together on this beautiful spring evenin' to share one another's company and enjoy such a bountiful feast. We thank thee for..."

I heard the flick of a lighter and looked over to see Cormac lighting a cigarette.

"...and please bless that we can all travel home safely at the end of the evenin'. In the Lord Jesus' name we pray, amen."

"Amen" we all repeated. Except Cormac. Cormac just reached for the rolls, grabbed two, and put butter in them. Seeing that I was watching him, he turned to me and asked, "Want me to grab you a couple? You gotta get the butter in there before they cool off."

"Yeah, sure."

"Here ya go."

"Thanks."

"So, how you been, Caish? Seems like we haven't talked in years." In fact, it had been years. Six and a half. The rest of the table was still recovering from their amens and hadn't thought of anything to say, so they listened in on our conversation while dishing up food. Everybody scooped up whatever grub was in front of them, then passed to the left.

"I've been great. Some of the best years of my life. How about you?"

Cormac took his cigarette out to take a swig of his Budweiser. "Ya know, I've had some good years m'self. Here's the spuds. Ya mind passin' the gravy after you've had it? Thanks. But yeah I've been good. Ya know me and Bev split up?"

"Oh?" I said, not sure whether that was good news or bad. Beverly was a narcissistic asshole, but I think Cormac was into that kind of thing. Not that he himself was an asshole, but he seemed to like a bit of spice to whomever he was with. But marrying Beverly was one of the worst decisions anybody in this family had ever made.

"Yup. Just got the divorce finalized b'fore ya came back to town. Hey Caleb, can we feed Bobo?"

"Umm." Caleb's hesitation meant, "No, and please just volunteer not to feed him." But Cormac just kept looking at Caleb waiting for an answer. "We're trying to train him not to eat people food."

"Uh-huh. Can his trainin' take a break t'night? Kind of a special occasion and all, and he's just over here lookin' at me like a starvin' Ethiopian."

Caleb's wife said, "Maybe not right now."

Cormac let it rest and fed Bobo in secret. The noises of utensils sliding across plates and people chewing and swigging increased until Catherine's husband (whose name I could not remember) said, "Well anyway, welcome back, Caish. When was the last time you were in town?"

"It's been... I guess just over ten years. Maybe eleven."

"Have you seen the new fire station yet?"

"Not that I know of, is it nice?"

"Oh yeah, quite nice. And they got this new fire engine that is massive. One of those that has a hinge behind the main engine and the whole back ladder portion has a separate driver on the back of the truck, and that. Can ya picture it?"

"Yeah, I think so," I said. Catherine's husband smiled, nodded, and shoveled potatoes into his mouth. "What else is new in town?"

The family shrugged and continued eating. Then Caleb said, "Oh, well, ya know the Jacobs that used to live over on Russell Street?"

"Hmm..."

"Ya know, Albert Jacobs was Cormac's age. His dad had, like, big frizzy hair. Called him Einstein sometimes."

"Oh, yeah yeah. The Jacobs."

"Yeah, well anyway, ya know Albert married Peggie Desmond?"

"Right."

"Got 'er pregnant in high school, right?" Catherine's husband said.

"Yeah, anyway, they had like ten kids."

"Lord have mercy."

"Well anyway, they did one of those DNA testing things. Ya know, ya send them some of your DNA—"

"I'll send them some of my DNA," Cormac said, smirking with a cheek full of roast beef.

Caleb gave a courtesy chuckle and continued, "Ya *spit* into a little vile and send it into their lab, then they test your DNA and tell you where your heritage is from and who your relatives are and all that. Have ya heard of these things?"

"Yeah," I said.

"So everybody in the Jacobs family does it. Huge family. They all send in their saliva and a couple weeks go by and then they get their results back. Turns out, Albert is only the father of *one* of the kids! Only one! The oldest. All the rest are from different fathers. Something like six different men."

"No. Are you kiddin' me?" I said.

"No joke, turns out Peggie got around and the kids never knew, and neither did Albert."

Cormac asked, "I can't remember, do the tests say who the other fathers are?"

"No, not unless they've also done the DNA test and are in the databank. Just that they're not Albert's, and that each kid has a different dad than the others. Except for a couple."

A side conversation between Catherine's husband and Caleb's wife died of natural causes, and Catherine's husband asked, "So, what did Mr. Jacobs do?"

"Well that's the funny thing," Caleb continued, "they get the results back, and, ya know, he's readin' 'em and all that, and he just sets the results on the table, walks out to the garage, gets into his car, and drives away. This was a week ago and nobody's seen him since. Police are out lookin' and everything. Can you believe that?"

"Deserted his own children," Mom said, shaking her head.

"Poor guy," Catherine said, "I can't imagine the pain those other men caused him and that family. They had to have known that Peggie was married when they were fuckin' her."

"Watch your mouth!" Mom shouted at Catherine. The shout gave Bobo such a blench that the poor dog hit his head on the underside of the table hard enough to bounce spoons.

"Sorry, but really, how could they do something like that?"

Cormac swallowed everything in his mouth at once, took a swig of beer, then said, "Well come on Catherine, you tellin' me you've never thought about other men before?"

Catherine's husband, staring at Cormac, wrinkled his brow, tilted his head, and asked, "What?"

"Oh, nothin', I was just tellin' Catherine to lay off ol' Peggie. We ain't all saints."

"Yeah but Cormac," Catherine said, "surely you ain't condonin' adultery and homewreckin'."

"Certainly not. Nope. Just understandin' it is all. Sounds like it was consensual. Six times, that is—"

"She didn't—"

"I mean what, you're thinkin' her door was kicked in by six different rapists on nine different occasions and—"

"Those men took advantage of a woman in a difficult situation—"

"Variety is the spice of life, Cathy. Sounds to me like 'ol Peggie Sue was just lookin' for some spice—"

"They should be ashamed of themselves. They should be beggin' the Lord for forgiveness." Catherine's tone was sharp, but Cormac didn't care.

"Oh, so it's always the man's fault then, huh?" he asked.

"Absolutely not. It goes both ways. Women taking advantage of men and men taking advantage of women are two sides of the same filthy coin. Adulterers and fornicators come in both sexes. It's selfishness is what it is. That's why the Lord cursed them with the AIDS. It's a punishment for adulterers, fornicators, and, most especially, the gays. Says so in the Bible."

Caleb, ever the defuser, said, "I think the real interesting part of the story is where Albert could have gone. They have a cabin up in Calgary. That's my guess."

"Can't believe he just abandon his kids," Mom mumbled to herself, shaking her head and picking up her beer.

"Poor guy probably killed himself," Catherine said. "What

do you think, Caish?"

"Um, yeah. I dunno. Sounds pretty bad," I said.

"So, do you feel bad for Mr. Jacobs?" Catherine's husband asked, looking at me over the top of his beer bottle.

"I think we all do," Caleb said.

"Could I use your restroom, Caleb?" I asked.

"Yeah, yeah, sure. It's just down this hall, first door on the left."

Caleb's wife had to stand and scoot her chair out so that I could squeeze out of my spot on the table. She smiled at me with a smile that seemed to apologize. The hallway was three steps long. The bathroom door was a cheap pocket door, probably because a hinged door wouldn't fit back here. I slid the door open and almost tripped over the toilet on my way in. The toilet had a shag carpet cover on the lid. This had to have been a closet that was converted into a bathroom. If you didn't watch your step, your left foot would be in a litter box. I peed, then washed my face and checked their medicine cabinet. Lots of opioids. Caleb? No. Caleb has been a straight shooter his entire life. His wife must be addicted. Sad, really.

The bathroom was less than twenty feet away from the kitchen, and the door was pretty much made of cardboard, so despite their lowered voices, I could hear Caleb tell Catherine to cool her jets. Catherine said something about needing to address the elephant in the room, and Caleb said the elephant wouldn't be in the room if she hadn't dragged it in. They murmured for a couple minutes, then I heard Cormac say he didn't understand why he couldn't feed Bobo. "Dogs are meant to eat meat, that's what those big sharp teeth are for. Ya can't get mad at me for helpin' your dog be a dog."

I dried my hands on a hand towel that hadn't been washed in years and clicked off the two light bulbs on my way out.

Before I could get situated again, and while Caleb's wife was scooting her chair back in next to mine, Mom asked, "So, Caish, when am I going to see my grandchild again?"

"Mark? Well. Anytime you want. You could go right now. He's still living with my ex in that house in Monterey I bought them."

"I can't just fly to Monterey any time I want."

"Yeah? Hm. Yeah I dunno, I guess plan a trip or something."

"You need to bring Mark up to Missoula, Caish. Mark needs to see his family. All of us."

"Yeah," Catherine added, "it would be fun to have Mark up here sometime, show him how to rough it."

"Yeah," I said. I didn't know what else to say.

Mom looked at me with a concerned face. As if she had explained a math problem to me several times and I just wasn't getting it. "How is Mark?"

"He's good. Yeah. Doing really great in school and everything."

"What does he like to do?" Catherine asked.

"Just regular kid stuff. Ya know. Playing in the ocean and stuff."

"Playing in the ocean? In Monterey? Caish, that water is like fifty degrees. Mark would be hypothermic in minutes."

"Plus," Catherine's husband said, "are those pretty rough waters? I heard even experienced swimmers have died out there."

"Yeah," I said, "well ya know, just on the beach. He likes to play on the beach."

Mom dished up more mashed potatoes. "Do you have any pictures of him?"

"Yeah." I shifted in my chair, apologized for bumping Cormac, and pulled out my phone. I scrolled through to find a recent picture. "Here he is on his preschool graduation." I held the phone across the front of Cormac and Mom squinted at the phone.

"How long ago was that?" Catherine asked.

"Cormac, please stop feeding Bobo. It'll hurt his stomach,"

Caleb said after Caleb's wife nudged him for the third time. Cormac looked up with a resigned look that seemed to say, "Okay, fine, have it your way, but if this dog dies of starvation it's not on me." Caleb's wife whispered in my ear, "Could you please pass the green beans?"

I passed her the green beans then said to Catherine, "Oh, a couple years ago, I guess."

"Do you have a more recent picture of your son that you could show us?"

"Um. Let me see." I scrolled through my pictures, trying to think of an excuse for why I didn't have anything more recent. Then I realized that I wasn't a child anymore and didn't need to take this shit from Catherine. "No, I don't Catherine."

"Why not?" she asked.

"Because my ex keeps him from me and I'm a terrible parent that doesn't make enough of an effort to see my son. Is that what you're looking for?"

"I don't think that's what she meant," Caleb said, "we just wanted to see—"

"That's exactly what I was looking for, Caish," Catherine said. "Thanks." She leaned back with her beer. "By the way, you haven't touched your beer. Why's that?"

"Just don't feel like beer right now," I said.

Cormac glanced over. "Since when have ya not felt like beer, Caish?"

"If Caish doesn't feel like beer right now, that's fine," Caleb said. "Cormac, why don't you drink it, looks like you polished off yours a little while ago."

"I think Caish should drink it," Catherine said, staring across the rolls at me.

"Nah, no thanks. But thanks for the beer, Caleb. Here you go Cormac, knock yourself out."

"It's gonna take more than a couple a beers to knock me out, but I appreciate it."

The conversation continued like this for the rest of dinner. Caleb and his wife cleared the table (but told us to hang on to our forks) then brought over brownies and ice cream. Store-brand ice cream. Then coffee for me and more beer for everybody else. Mom and Catherine kept needling me questions and Caleb stepped in whenever he sensed the conversation was reaching a boiling point. Eventually people started leaving, but Caleb's wife, whispering, asked me for help with the dishes. I stood in the kitchen and relied on muscle memory to remind me how to wash a cookie sheet with brownie caked on it. When we were finished with the dishes, Caleb invited me to have a seat in their front room. Bobo hopped up on the couch and rested his head on my leg. I scratched him under his collar and told him that he was a good boy. He appreciated it.

"Thanks again for comin' over tonight, Caish. I know our family can be kind of hostile sometimes, but I think they're just havin' a hard time with all the change that's been happenin' lately."

"It's just Mom and Catherine. And Catherine's husband I guess. Cormac is fine."

"Yeah, Cormac has totally chilled out ever since he and Bev separated."

"Divorced," Caleb's wife added.

"Yeah, divorced now," Caleb corrected.

"Yeah, he seems great now. Hey, what is Catherine's husband's name again?"

"Joshua."

"Oh yeah! Joshua. And he hates to be called Josh, right?"

"Yeah, don't call him Josh." Caleb chuckled. I watched Caleb and waited for him to say whatever he wanted to say. Obviously he had something on his mind. Would he ask for more money? Obviously they had blown through what I gave them pretty thoroughly.

"Caish, Toni and I were talking"—Toni! That was Caleb's

wife's name, finally — "and we want to help out."

"What do you mean?"

"Well, we know about what you've been going through lately, and we want to do whatever we can to help." If they only knew.

"You've been talking to Victoria Black?"

Toni smiled and said, "We've been close friends since high school. So yeah, she's been bendin' our ear. But we've also been contacted by Jennifer Blanche." I tried not to show any reaction to that name, even though Toni gave me a pause in which to react. "She contacted us a couple of months ago and let us know that you were back in town, and why, and everything that happened in California."

"Don't you guys think Jennifer Blanche looks like Miss Trunchbull from Matilda?" I asked.

Caleb smiled, "We've actually never seen her, she just called."

"Oh. Yeah, she totally looks like Trunchbull from Matilda."

Caleb and Toni smiled. Then continued, "Anyway, Caish, we've been lookin' at different houses on the market, and we found one a couple blocks east of here. We found a lender that would give us a really low interest rate and wouldn't require anything down."

"Why would you guys move a couple blocks east into another house that's exactly the same as this house?"

"Well, not us, Caish," Caleb said, "you."

What in God's name?

"We will cover the mortgage for you until you can get back on your feet," Caleb said. Toni said, "And I have an uncle that runs an auto shop just off Higgins down by the river, he said he could use a hand. Maybe you could start there until you found somethin' else."

"What are you guys talking about?" I asked. "I don't need your help. I don't need another house. I have a house. A very nice house. Caleb, you've been to my house. And I don't need some dirty mechanic job."

"We know that you're strugglin', Caish, we just want to help you get back on your feet again."

"I don't know what you think you know about my financial position, but I'm doing great. Plus, I'm not sure you two are in much of a position to help. Looks like you've done a pretty good job of spending through everything I gave you."

Toni and Caleb were both looking at me like I was an upset teenager that didn't understand why I couldn't have the car. I turned the tables, "I gotta ask, what did you do with the money? I gave you over a million dollars, and what do you have to show for it?"

"Well, Caish, we are very grateful for what you've given us. You helped us, and now we want to help you."

"No, really, what did you spend it on? Where did it all go? How are you in a position to give me financial advice?"

"Well," Caleb said, looking at Toni, "we put most of what you gave us into a retirement account that we won't be able to touch until one of us is 65. And, you remember Miriam? Our oldest? Thanks to you she could afford to go to Brown. Graduated top of her class. And Edward? Our next oldest. He got into the University of Pennsylvania on a scholarship, but your gift paid his rent and living expenses for five years."

"That's it? You spent a million dollars on your kids' school?"

"Well, and our retirement," Toni added. "Plus we paid off this house, paid off the cars, and bought that fifth wheel you probably saw in our driveway."

"I guess what I'm saying is, if you two could make all that money disappear with only this place to show for it, you probably shouldn't be offering me charity and life coaching. Do you both still work?"

"We do, but, Caish, it's not like that," Caleb said. "We just—"

"Well but it is like that. You think that just because I've had some bad luck lately that I should return to living like you two. That I should become some peasant who uses coupons and drives a shitty car. That I should be eating leftovers from Tupperware and working a brainless labor-intensive job. I'm not blue-collar anymore, I'm—"

"Caish, you're—"

"No, let me finish. I'm a successful investor. I've made over a hundred million dollars. Most investors lose what they earned at one point or another and earn their way back. I know you laugh at it, even after I proved you all wrong, but I play the lottery, Caleb, and I'm good at it. Just the other day I won over five thousand dollars. I'll win big again. Statistics say that once you've won, you're more likely to win a second time. I'm not some schmuck mechanic anymore. You both need to respect that."

"We do, Caish, we just want to—"

"Thanks for dinner, this has all been quite pleasant, and Toni those brownies were to die for. Caleb, could you please get my jacket?"

Back in my Suburban, rumbling through the rain swept streets of Missoula, I mulled over our conversation. How could they be so patronizing? Offer me charity? They'll pay my mortgage? Who do they think I am? Have they not had a front row seat to my rise from poverty in Missoula to staggering wealth in Malibu? So pretentious. I gave them the financial security they have, and now they think themselves financial sages that can offer me a hand? So arrogant. Such hubris.

17

The more monotonous middle-class living became, the more it felt like I was trapped in a labyrinth of timeless boredom. Without much money, my options for business and pleasure were limited. For business, I didn't have enough money to invest in anything other than lottery tickets. I didn't have the resources or connections to create a new product or launch a new app. Plus, I didn't want to risk losing the last of my cash on another dud of a business idea (which, in that regard, was apparently the only type of ideas I had). Pleasure was limited to only those activities which were wholesome and cheap. Like sitting at home and watching every HBO, Hulu, and Netflix series ever produced. Then moving on to Amazon Prime.

Probation prohibited me from enjoying alcohol and cocaine. The world had been stripped of its color. The maximum level of enjoyment had been brought down from ten to six. The sober will never know the joys of those top four levels. And having lived most of my life at ten, six may as well have been high-functioning depression. Diet depression. Where once there were clear skies and fluffy white clouds, now there was forever a dark and brooding sky, threatening to rain at any moment.

Happiness is expensive, misery is free.

On paper I was doing fine. I paid most of my bills on time and stayed within the confines of my probation. My T-cell count returned to normal in a matter of months, and I was as healthy as I had ever been. I had settled into a new routine. Thanks to my drug testing, I was up at dawn's early light every morning. 8:00 a.m. sharp. If Miss Trunchbull didn't call, I would spend at least two hours searching Google for ways to make money that didn't require much capital. I considered this to be the first part of my job. Research. The second part of my job was driving to a gas station and buying lottery tickets. Action. Since my last big win of $5,212 I hadn't won anything. But I could feel a win coming soon. For lunch I would go somewhere cheap, like Taco Bell, Wendy's, or KFC. By around 2:00 p.m. I was back to work on the third and most important part of my job, networking. I spent hours on Facebook, LinkedIn, Twitter, and Instagram. I had a multipronged approach. First, I would post about how well everything was going in my life; it was important that everybody know I was still on top. Second, I would message old friends. Sometimes acting interested in their personal lives, and sometimes probing for any business opportunities. Third, I would make new connections by messaging people that looked successful

My "research, action, network" plan of attack was slow to bear fruit, but I don't give up easily. You don't get rich by giving up in the face of adversity.

Usually by around 5:00 p.m. I ordered dinner from somewhere cheap. I stayed at home most nights because I had no choice. I couldn't go to bars or clubs—to the extent that clubs existed in Missoula. There was also the added complication that I had HIV. It didn't feel right picking up on people when even if we used protection I could still give them a terminal illness. At this point I was living without sex, cocaine, or alcohol. If it weren't for cigarettes I'd wither away.

I spent evenings watching TV and feeling despondent. Cocaine was no longer there to lift me up in times of sorrow. Without liquor to dilute the cares and pains of my middle-class existence, I often slipped off the path of aspiration and slid down the rain-soaked slope of hope. At the bottom, I am forced to confront Hopelessness. Its slimy tentacles snare me into its black lair, its beak whispering words of despair. Its bite reminds me of my plight. I struggle against its crushing grip, but feel my muscles begin to rip. The more I fight against my state, the clearer the picture of my fate. Hopelessness will not relent, it has my scent, there will be no argument. The dread of nonexistence, with all its dogged persistence, saps my final feeble resistance. Darker than black, heavier than lead, there is no returning back, I will soon be dead. This tunnel has no light at the end, just an eternal black descend.

Then I'd wake up the next morning and do it all over again.

When I had lived in Missoula for about a year, I received a letter from the bank claiming that I had defaulted on my mortgage loan. I had only missed two or three payments and they were acting like I had robbed them at gunpoint. They cited to an "acceleration clause" claiming that they could demand full payment for the outstanding balance of the loan. Without full payment in thirty days, they would have no choice but to foreclose on the property.

I was sick of the house anyway. I had been thinking about moving and the bank's letter simply reminded me of what I already was planning on doing. Most of the boxes from my move to Montana were still packed, so this move would be easier. For the next thirty days, I browsed local listings for something a bit smaller than this house (I just didn't need all the space). On the thirty-first day, a representative from the bank came to my home and told me that they were beginning foreclosure proceedings. The little man gave me a pile of papers that explained how the foreclosure would work and what my rights were. I could stay in my house during the proceedings, but as soon as it sold I had to be out. The sale was set for one week from now. A judicial foreclosure on the 18th.

I found a nice modern house on the other side of town that I could afford for a few years. Five if I kept my other expenses down. The bank that was foreclosing on my house refused to lend to me. They were evidently in cahoots with the other banks in town, because they wouldn't lend to me either. It's not even like I was asking for that much. They all said that my credit score was too low and that I needed to have a job before they would even consider taking the risk.

The ace up my sleeve was Mr. Valentini, the biggest banker in Southern California—physically, not figuratively. I gave him a call and explained my situation.

"Anyway, I only need three hundred and seventy thousand, and I don't care about the interest rate. Let's do a thirty year."

"Caish. Do you have access to a computer right now?"

"Yeah, yup, I'm sitting in front of my laptop right this moment."

"Great. Log in to your bank account, will you? I just have a couple of questions."

"Sure thing."

"Are you logged in?" Mr. Valentini was always in a hurry.

"Not yet... one second..." I said, "okay I'm in."

"Caish, can you tell me when the last time any of your accounts received a deposit?"

"Hmm..." I scrolled through the transaction history in my checking account. "Well I don't—"

"And we're talking about all of your account, right? Any deposit at all."

"Let me just pull it up..."

"No need. Caish, you don't deposit money into your bank account anymore. Only withdrawals, no deposits."

"..."

"You still there, Caish?"

"Yeah."

"Do you see what I'm getting at?"

"Yeah, but my deposit history isn't the only thing that matters, I have enough in the bank for years of payments."

"Not thirty years' worth of payments. Seventy—"

"But enough to—"

"Seventy grand in the bank is not enough to prop up a nearly four hundred thousand-dollar loan. And, Caish. We haven't even talked about your credit score."

"I was hoping that with our long history of good loans you'd be able to see past some of the numbers and know that I would be good for the loan."

"Sorry, Caish. Not the case. Give me a call when you've got some money coming in and we'll see what we can do for you." Mr. Valentini hung up. I was stunned. He refused to lend to me. After years of loyal patronage, he turned me down merely because I didn't have a traditional nine-to-five job.

Whatever, I could always rent. In fact, it would be better that way. Renting would give me the freedom to get back to California the instant I won the lottery again. Plus, I wouldn't have to deal with the expenses of homeownership. I found a new chic apartment complex that had just been built downtown. The Crown Lofts. The rent was more that I was planning to spend on a mortgage, but it included utilities, so overall I was probably saving money.

The landlord of the Crown Lofts was a woman that hadn't realized the 1990s ended. Her name was Candice Tolman. She had a blondish tomboy pixie cut (think Princess Diana, as Candice surely did) and painted her eyebrows with excessive attention to detail. She had a long face but a short nose. She wore a dark-blue and green plaid shirt that was tucked into light-blue high-waist jeans that buttoned a few inches above her belly button. She rounded off her look with a pair of leather loafers. No socks.

"Hiiiiiii! You must be Cesh!" she said when I walked into the Crown Lofts management office. She stood up from behind her desk and extended her hand with a smile that showed off her blindingly white, noticeably large teeth. This woman radiated enthusiasm. Her office was decorated with framed certificates that probably made her feel important. "Triple-A Rated Landlord 2002," "Missoula's Best in Property Management 1996," "Landlord Association Standard of Excellence Award 2016."

"Am I saying that right? Cesh?" she asked.

"Yeah, close enough," I said, shaking her hand.

"Very good, very good. We are so happy you are interested in our newest apartments." She motioned for me to sit in one of the chairs in front of her desk. "The Crown Lofts are the biggest thing to happen to Missoula in a very long time." She could smile and talk at the same time. Just like Mia…

"Yeah, they look great. I'm excited to move in."

"They are great! And we're excited to have you move in. Did you want to walk through one of the units?"

"Nah, I think I'm ready to sign on the dotted line."

"Oh! Very nice! You know what you want, I like that. Let's have a look at floor plans and see which one you like."

"I looked through them online, I think I'll just go with one of the two-bedroom plans. I don't care what floor I'm on. And I need a parking place in the garage."

"Okay, great. That's great. We can definitely do that. Let's get you started by filling out some paperwork." Candice pulled a stack of paper out of one of her desk drawers, set a Bic pen on top of the stack and slid the stack across her desk. "Let's have you fill out that top form, it's just basic contact information and background stuff, and then I'll talk you through the rest. Do you want any water or anything?"

"Nope, I'm doing fine, thanks."

Candice clattered away at the keys on her computer while I filled out the form she had given me. With that form done, she walked me through the other forms. This one said I agreed to pay rent by the fifth of every month, this one said I agreed to pay my last month's rent up front (along with a $1200 deposit), this one said I agreed not to sublet the apartment, this one said I agreed not to sue them if I fell down the stairs, and on and on. I signed and initialed, signed and initialed, signed and initialed. Date date date. With the pile of papers signed, Candice said, "Great! You're all set! Just swing by at the beginning of next month and we'll get you all set up with your key and parking pass and you will be good to move in."

"Beginning of next month?"

"Yup! On the third we'll have your unit ready for you."

"Oh, I need to move in right now."

"Mmm. Sorry Cesh, your unit won't be finished for another couple of weeks. The third is when you can move in. We are still installing smoke alarms and carpets in all of the units." Candice looked at me like you look at a three-year-old when you break the news that Heffalumps don't actually exist.

"Can I move into a different unit?"

"'Fraid not, the third is our move-in day. We're going to have free hotdogs and live music for all our new tenants. We're almost at full capacity already, so it's going to be quite the party."

"But I have to be out of my place on the 18th. I have to move in before that."

"Cesh, I'm very sorry to hear that, but these units just aren't done. It would be against the law for us to allow you to move in before the final inspection. Plus, you don't want to move in without carpet and smoke alarms."

"What am I supposed to do between the eighteenth and the third?" I asked.

"Hmm. Well. You could stay with family."

"Not an option."

"Friends?"

"Nope. Not an option."

"Well, I guess you could stay in a hotel then."

Oh. Yeah. Hotels. I had forgotten about hotels. I certainly could stay in a hotel. I could just move my stuff into a storage unit and have a two-week vacation right here in Missoula. Good thinking Candice.

"Ah, good thinking Candice. Okay, see you on the third. And do I come here or go somewhere else to pick up my key?"

"Yup, come right back here and we'll get you all set up."

"Great, thanks, see you then."

"Sounds like a plan, Cesh! See you next month! And tell your friends about us!"

I hired a moving company to move my stuff into a storage unit and booked a room at the Hilton. It was called the DoubleTree, but it was "by Hilton," so it was essentially a Hilton without the pompous price tag. I splurged because it had been so long since I'd had a vacation. Having room service and a fridge full of alcohol took me back to the days of my wealth. Not that I could drink the little bottles of alcohol, but I could look at them. The little liquors and beers. Types you only think about when you see the inside of a hotel room mini fridge. Like Bombay Sapphire, Stella Artois Beer, and canned bloody marys. I'd inventory the pint-size contents of the fridge, just for the hell of it. I had plenty of time. Two Fireballs, two Skyy Vodkas, two Jack Daniels, two Grey Goose, two Absolut Vodkas, two Bombay Sapphires, one bottle of Stella Artois, one bottle of Corona, one can of Heineken, two cans of Amstel Light, and one can of Miller Lite. And then there were also the sodas and waters to serve as chasers, and Snickers, peanut m&ms, and other overpriced snacks.

The pool was as cold as any other hotel pool, and the hot tub was at a low simmer. I relaxed as much as possible despite the ever-present screams of children and their pitter patter as they chased each other around the pool. In the hot tub I thought about where things went wrong with me and Mia. When we were relaxing in the hot tub at the Ritz Carlton she had lost it. That's just how people are. But she was one of my closest friends, and it would be nice to have somebody to talk to about the shitshow my life has become.

An overweight family joined me in the hot tub, all grins and "how ya doin'?"s. They'd been living the American life too wholeheartedly. The water level lapped up over the edge as they sank in.

I could have killed for a drink right then. But I didn't have to kill. I just had to walk up to my hotel room and have a sip. One sip wouldn't show up if I had to pee into a cup. Plus, I peed into a cup that morning. The chances of getting called in two days in a row weren't that great. Sure, it happened every now and then, but not often.

Back in my hotel room I showered for half an hour in the hottest water I could stand, then turned on the TV and sat in front of the mini fridge. Such a wide selection. I had to choose wisely though. This would be my first drink in over a year, and I could only have a sip, so it was more about the taste than anything else. Jack Daniels has always had a special place in my heart, and Fireball reminded me of my high school days. Then again, the vodkas were calling my name. Maybe they'd have an effect on me even though I could only take a sip. The beers were out of the question. If I am going to have a sip of anything, it is going to be liquor. To help make my decision, I pulled out each little bottle of liquor and lined them up on the counter above the fridge. Twelve bottles, six options.

No, never mind. I can't. I put all the bottles back in the fridge and climbed on the bed. I'd just watch a pay-per-view movie or some porn or something. No need to drink. Even though I wouldn't really be drinking, just tasting. And if I did drink, it would be out of my bloodstream by tomorrow morning. It was only 7:45 p.m., which meant that even in the off chance that my color was called two days in a row, I could still pee clean because it would be eight hours from now. I could also follow the alcohol with a gallon of water to flush it out.

I settled on Dateline NBC. A true crime murder mystery about a son who killed his parents for insurance money. I tried to focus on the show, but my mind kept returning to the mini fridge. I'm not an alcoholic. I can control myself. It's just that it has been so long, and they are right there in my fridge. There is nobody else in this hotel room, I don't have anywhere to go for a couple weeks, and I probably won't be called in to pee tomorrow morning.

Okay, just one sip. I lined up the bottles on the counter again. Jack Daniels. Just a sip though. I cracked the seal. There was no turning back now, I had bought the bottle. Since the whiskey was kept in the fridge, it didn't smell as strong as it should. I poured a neat dash into a glass and examined the dark golden-caramel liquid. After it had a chance to warm up, the smooth aroma of oak barrels stung my nostrils. Its sweet undertones inviting me to partake. I savored the first sip. The taste of charcoal blended with its earthy spice. I poured another dash. Hints of vanilla and burnt toffee rolled around on my tongue. I swished the splash of whiskey around in my mouth and concentrated on the aftertaste. Sweet corn and oily wood. I relished in the warmth that just two tastes could bring to my throat and stomach.

I had my sip, so it was time to put the bottles away. I took them off the counter and placed them into the fridge. But I left out the opened bottle of Jack Daniels. Just to let it warm up. On second thought, I should pull out the other whiskeys and let them warm up. Not for me, but because that's just how whiskeys are supposed to be stored. The gins and vodkas would be fine in the fridge, but not the Fireballs or the Jack Daniels.

Back to Dateline. Jesus, this kid really did a number on his parents. Killed them with chloroform then carried their bodies back into the woods behind the house and strung them up in trees hoping that birds would destroy the evidence. Some people.

The Jack Daniels was probably warm by now.

I clicked through the other channels to see if anything else good was playing before I committed to buying a movie.

The Jack Daniels hadn't moved. I could still taste its sweet sting. The glass was still in my hand. The smell was still there. So was a drop at the bottom of the glass. I tipped it back and watched the drop slide onto my tongue. The flavor was almost proof that a God existed somewhere.

One shot doesn't even show up on a breathalyzer test. I think.

So surely it wouldn't show up in a pee test twelve hours later. That's what I needed to quench my craving, just one honest to God shot of Jack Daniels. I went back to the counter, picked up the bottle, and brought it back to the bed with my glass. The liquid gold rolled out of the bottle and into my glass like it would in a commercial. It was perfect. I poured a finger and inhaled its sweetness. Having teased myself enough, I swigged the Tennessee sour mash and poured another couple of fingers. Maybe I'd just drink this one bottle. Just this one, tiny bottle.

There was no way I was getting called in to pee the next day. I had peed that very morning. Tonight I would enjoy myself like I deserved. Nobody has been through what I have been through. Certainly nobody has been through it sober. Even if I did have to pee, I would explain my situation to Jenny Trunchbull and she would understand. Even that cold-hearted bitch had to understand. She was probably drinking right now too. Who was she to tell me not to drink?

All too soon, the bottle of Jack Daniels had run dry. Maybe I'd polish off the other one too. Then the Fireball. Just the whiskey. Whiskey wasn't as bad as vodka. I was drinking fire. My throat begged for a chaser, so I cracked open one of the $6 orange juices and soothed my revirginized throat. When the whiskey ran out, I felt like a starving person that had been given a single slice of carrot cake. I *needed* more.

There were just two bottles of gin, and gin wasn't as bad as vodka, so I cracked open one of the Bombay Sapphires. This was a new drink for me. I didn't expect it to be so thick. Almost oily. It was also sweeter, fruitier than I expected. The juniper was front and center with a strong citrus flavor. Good enough for me. I drank both bottles. By this point I was no longer using the glass. I wanted to preserve the scent of the whiskey.

For the first time in months, my cares melted away. Completely out of mind. Pain's blade was blunted. I was cozy and warm. The only thing I was missing was somebody to share this king size bed with. Jesus, I was hungry. I ate the $13 bag of cashews from the mini fridge and pulled out another bottle of vodka. I tried to call somebody to come over, but I couldn't remember any numbers and the hotel phone looked strange and unfamiliar. Plastic. Analog buttons and a twirly cord. Why was the cord always twirly and curly? Then I remembered that I also had a phone. Right in my pocket. A little black square phone with a screen that lit up so bright. The TV was now so loud. My ears were being attacked. Everything moved in slow motion. I told my hand to turn the volume down, then waited while my arm and hand worked together to point the remote at the TV, or near the TV, at least at the same wall as the TV, and give the command. This felt right. This is how life should be lived. Everybody was drinking, and now, finally, I was too. Oh, I had to pee. The bathroom was over there, so that's where I had to go. I moved and the room rolled a few degrees to the left. Like the hotel had set sail on the high seas. The toilet had a tricky lid, but finally I got it open and peed fire. This was a good sign. Since I was already peeing out alcohol, I could drink more. Having successfully flushed and returned to the bed, I reached into my pocket and fished out the phone. My phone. I looked at my phone and told Siri to call Riley. I took another swig of the Absolut Vodka and listened to the hums my phone made.

"Caish?"

"Yeah, iss me."

"Okay..."

"Riley, do ya wanna meet me at the Hilton? I'm here and have a king size with your name on it."

"Caish, you're drunk."

"Maybe a lil' buzzed, yeah. Prolly wouldn't argue with ya there."

"Are you with anybody?"

"Noooooooope. Thass why I'm callin' you. Ya gotta come on over"

"Okay, Caish, where are you?"

"Didn' I say? The Hilton."

"Which one?"

"Oh! Oh. Iss not the Hilton. Well it is, but iss a lil' different. Iss... umm... iss called the... umm..."

"Okay, Caish, you need to stop drinking. It sounds like you've had enough. Go home and go to bed."

"Mmm... Can't. Don't have a home right now. Juss a shade shy a homeless. Can't you come over, Riley? Yur makin' me sad." Suddenly a wave of sorrow crashed on me. I couldn't hold back the tears. Sobbing. Sloppy sobbing. I needed a tissue but didn't see one within reach so I used the comforter.

"Caish, I don't even know where you are. I hope everything in your life is going good, but I think it's best if we moved on." There were those words again. Riley had been talking to Agent Palmer. Everybody wanted to move on.

I hung up. Riley made me sad. I didn't need sad. Alcohol was here to save the day. Alcohol made me happy. I didn't have a care in the world until Riley called me, tryin' to bring me down. I cracked open the second bottle of Grey Goose.

My phone was buzzing. I opened my eyes and was blinded. The room was full of light, like the sun wanted a closer look and was just outside my window. And what window was that? I would never put up such hideous curtains. And what is this headache? A headache in the morning? I lifted myself onto my elbow and looked around. Ah, that's right. I was at the DoubleTree by Hilton. Nine little plastic bottles were scattered throughout and around the bed I was laying in. My phone had stopped buzzing, then started buzzing again. My eyes still hadn't adjusted, but I answered anyway.

"Hello?"

"Caish, your color has been called. Be here in ten minutes."

18

"Oh, good morning Jennifer. Um, I—"

"Will be here in ten minutes."

"Wait, Jennifer, I can't this morning, I've got the flu. And it is awful. I've been throwing up all morning."

"Don't try it, Caish. You know that doesn't change anything. Get in here and pee. If you pee dirty, you violated your probation and we'll deal with it. If you don't show up to pee, you violated your probation and we'll have to track you down and deal with it. Do you understand?"

"I can't move without throwing up."

"Then bring a barf bag." Jennifer hung up.

Fuck. I stumbled into the bathroom and drained myself. After peeing I forced myself to throw up, which wasn't too difficult. The room still swayed a bit. I couldn't go in. Jennifer hadn't shown any leniency in my first year of probation, and she didn't sound like she was in the mood to show mercy this morning. I took my time getting dressed. Maybe I could tell her I was forced. Kidnapped and forced to drink. Ah, dammit. She wouldn't believe that.

Think. I had to think. I lit a cigarette and stood next to the window (this was a non-smoking room, so I had to blow the smoke out the window).

The upside was that Jennifer would never be able to find me. My house was empty and there was no way she could find me. She could send a sheriff but they wouldn't find me. The downside was that I would violate my probation and be thrown in jail as soon as they found me. I plugged my phone in and googled how long alcohol stays in the blood. Google told me: "Alcohol can show up on a blood test for up to 12 hours." Twelve hours. So if I stopped drinking last night at midnight, I would be good to go at noon. But I can't be sure that I stopped drinking at midnight. I remember first savoring that glass of Jack Daniels around 8:00 p.m., and then I remember diving into the rest pretty quick after that. By noon I should be good. I'll drink all the water in the fridge, order room service for a big breakfast and more water and orange juice and milk and coffee. Then I'll stagger into Jennifer's office just after noon and pee into a cup. Perfect plan.

Room service brought me scrambled eggs, hash browns, toast, bacon, sausage, and pancakes, along with tall glasses of orange juice and milk, a pot of coffee, and three glasses of ice water. Halfway through my breakfast, Jennifer called again. I knew she'd be angry, but I didn't dare ignore the call.

"Hello?"

"Caish, you didn't arrive on time for your testing, so you are in violation of your probation." She didn't sound any more mad than she usually sounded. "We have sent the sheriff to bring you in. Would you like to come in on your own, or in the back of a squad car?"

"Jennifer, I think I'll be able to come in at noon. I'm feeling better, but I still throw up and almost shit myself whenever I try to get out of bed."

"Back of the squad car then?"

"I'll come in at noon, I promise. I'm already feeling—"

"Save it, Caish. See you soon."

She hung up. At this point I really was starting to feel sick. I tripped over my tangled sheets on my way across the room toward the bathroom. I stumbled into the bathroom and fell to my knees in front of the toilet just in time. My stomach contracted and blasted vomit through my throat and out my mouth and nose. The porcelain of the toilet bowl was ice-cold in my grasp. The tile was about as comfortable as tile could be. My stomach squeezed and wrenched until there was nothing left. I spit and blew my nose into the toilet, then flushed it all away. I took the hottest shower I could tolerate, then returned to my breakfast.

Jennifer didn't call again. I drank everything in front of me, and ate almost all of the breakfast. I peed a few times throughout the morning and none of them stung. I was in good shape. I readied myself for the wrath of Jennifer. I had to look presentable, but still like I was sick.

I pulled into the parking lot and made it inside without being tackled to the ground and thrown in jail, so maybe everything would be fine. Jennifer's office door was open, so I walked in. It was 1:23 p.m.

In my sickest voice, I said, "Hi Jennifer," and coughed a couple times.

"Caish, you violated your probation this morning. I have filed a report with the court with my recommendation that your probation be adjusted accordingly. Now, let's see what the damage is. Here's your cup."

Without another word, I took the cup from Jennifer's hand and walked to the bathroom like a sick person walks. I peed into the cup and, just to be safe, sniffed my urine. Sure enough, not a trace of alcohol. My urine was nearly clear and hardly smelled like anything. I put the cup on the shelf and walked back to Jennifer's office.

"Wait in the hell. I mean hall. Wait in the hall," she said without looking up from her paperwork.

So far, so good. Everything was going as planned. Whatever she did to "adjust my probation" would be undone with my clean pee test. Even if not, I could just explain to a judge that I had the flu. The judge would understand. I still felt nervous, though.

Twenty minutes later Jennifer stepped out into the hall. She looked down at me like a teacher ready to scorn a pupil.

"Caish. Would you like to see the results from your urine test?"

"Maybe you could just tell me?" I asked.

"Sure. The test detected ethyl glucuronide metabolite. You've been drinking. That's another violation of your probation."

"No, I wasn't drinking. I just—"

"Wait here, Caish."

In the half hour that followed, I thought about making a break for it. I was not going to jail for five years. That was not an option. The tiled hallway was empty. A florescent bulb buzzed and flickered. There wasn't a police officer in sight. I could make it back to my car, stroll into my hotel room, pack everything, and be out of town in a matter of minutes. Then, once in Canada, I could call a moving company to bring me my stuff from the storage unit. I could lay low and—

"Caish." Jennifer was standing over me. "Follow me."

"Where are we going?"

"To Judge Kanter's courtroom."

"Who is Judge Kanter?"

"The judge that is going to approve my recommendation for an adjustment to your probation."

"What is the adjustment to my probation?"

"Mandatory testing every other day and mandatory enrollment in Alcoholics Anonymous for one year. We're going easy on you since this is your only violation in a year."

"But I'm not an alcoholic."

Jennifer didn't respond. We walked into the courtroom and waited ten minutes in silence. The bailiff examined me and didn't break eye contact when I met his gaze. We stood when Judge Kanter entered the courtroom, then sat down when the clerk of the court told us to. Jennifer spoke to the judge quickly and with a level tone. She told the judge that I missed this morning's test then showed up and peed ethyl glucuronide, which was detectable for up to three days after the consumption of alcohol, into a cup (thanks a lot Google, didn't tell me about that). The judge nodded along as Jennifer spoke. Probably thinking about dinner. When Jennifer was finished, the judge shuffled some papers, then said, "Approved," and stood up and left the courtroom. We went back to Jennifer's office where she gave me the address of the AA meetings, which I was required to attend twice a week. There would be a place for me to sign in. She also told me about mandatory testing every other day, and whenever else they felt like calling me in.

Back in the Suburban, I sat and thought about how well everything had turned out. A few AA meetings and a couple extra pee tests? No problem. The AA meetings started at the beginning of next week.

When the third of the month came, I paid movers to move my belongings into the Crown Lofts. Sure enough, there were free hot dogs, just like Candice said. The Crown Lofts were the newest, nicest apartments in Missoula. The exterior was that new style of putting as many different surface areas onto the building as possible: bricks along the bottom, siding over there, metal vertical siding over there, stucco on this side, rusted metal plates up there, and plenty of glass. Very contemporary. My unit was comfortable and spacious. 1600 square feet, nine foot ceilings, and an open floor plan. The appliances were the newest offerings from Samsung, black stainless steel. I had too much stuff to fit into this space, so I kept the storage unit. The only hiccup was that the Suburban wouldn't fit into the parking garage, so I had to park outside.

The AA meetings turned out to be the most productive meetings I had ever attended. The first week I was there, nothing of note happened. By my fourth visit, I had a breakthrough. The meetings were held in Missoula's First Baptist Church on Tuesdays and in Smokey's Diner on Fridays. It was a Friday when I first met Susie. After the meeting I stepped out to burn a cigarette.

From behind I heard, "Hey, Caish, right?"

I turned to see a skinny woman with thin hair and a broad smile. Obviously poor. She knew my name because every meeting when we went around the room and introduced

ourselves, I said, "Hi, my name is Caish, and I'm an alcoholic,"
even though I wasn't an alcoholic. It's just what everybody said.
They were all alcoholics, and I wanted to lay low, so I introduced
myself the same way.

"Yeah, Caish. Remind me of your name?"

"Susie, Susie Granger. Like Hermione."

"Hermione?"

"Yeah, ya know? Harry Potter?"

"Hmm… I didn't see the movies."

"Oh come on, ya know. Hermione Granger?"

"Oh! Yeah yeah. Okay, I'm with you. You get that a lot?"

"Enough to where now I just inoculate against it by leadin'
off with it."

I smiled at Susie and took another drag of my Camel. She
pulled out a pack of her own and I offered a light. My Led
Zeppelin Zippo was a good conversation starter. When that small
talk ran its course, Susie asked, "So, what brings ya to AA?"

"I violated my probation and got assigned mandatory
attendance. What about you?"

"Same. Drug charges?"

"No. Well, sort of, I guess. I was in an accident and somebody
died and cocaine was involved and all that, so they put me on
probation for five years. What about you?"

"Drug charges. Got fucked by an undercover cop."

"Literally?"

"Haha, I wish! Haha, no, just busted. I got AA and NA
assigned to me as part of my probation."

"Ah, I see."

"So they got ya pissin' in a cup too?" Susie asked.

"Every other day at eight sharp." I lit another cigarette. Susie
seemed thoughtful. So I asked, "What's on your mind?"

"Nothin' much. I just wanna help ya out."

"How so?"

"Well. How do ya relax now that ya gotta piss inna cup? Can't taste the syrup, can't chase the dragon, can't ride the lightning. Must be agony."

"Of course."

Susie dropped her cigarette to the asphalt and stepped on it, moving her heel side to side like she wanted to work the cigarette butt into the parking lot. "Here's what ya gotta do. Go to the ER one night and tell 'em ya got a splittin' migraine. Tell 'em they run in your family and they just been gettin' worse and worse, and that ya can't hardly even stand it's so bad. One of the doctors will prescribe ya Vicodin or OxyContin or Demerol or somethin'. Get your prescription filled, then pay a visit to your probation officer. Tell him that ya have a migraine from hell and that the doctor prescribed you such and such, and show him your prescription. Your probation officer's gonna give ya shit, but then he'll say, 'Yeah yeah, whatever, if a doctor prescribed it ya can take it.' He'll probably be proud that ya even asked."

"But what's Demerol going to do for me? I've had painkillers and they don't do shit."

"Well, maybe not if ya take the recommended dosage, but bump it up a touch and you're in business. Plus, this is just how it starts. We'll get you goin' on some real shit in no time."

"So, what's the catch?" I asked.

"Sell me some of your pills, and I sell you some of mine."

"Why don't you just go get a prescription of your own?"

"Oh I've got one of those. I've got fuckin' six. I'm just tryin' to help ya out, Caish. Ya get ninety percent of the benefit from this little charade, I just want to be your friend and get you some spare cash when you need it, and ya help me when I need it."

I flicked the butt of my cigarette into a bush and thought about Susie's proposition. It seemed like a loophole that the system couldn't possibly allow. I was absolutely forbidden from taking heroin, but I was allowed to take hydrocodone—heroin's twin sister? There's no way.

"There's no way, Susie. Why would it be a violation of

my probation to shoot heroin and not a violation to shoot hydrocodone?"

"Because a doctor prescribed you the hydrocodone."

"Bullshit."

"I'm not kiddin' ya, Caish. Go to the ER tonight and get your prescription. Talk to your probation officer about it t'morrow mornin'. Maybe even call t'night to make it seem like you're really in pain. If he says no, no harm no foul. Fill your prescription and I'll pay you twenty times what you paid for the pills. If he says yes, you have me to thank when you take your Vicodin and feel the pain of life loosen its grip."

"I'll think about it."

"Please do. And here, let me get your number," Susie said as she pulled out her phone.

I didn't have anything else going on, so I drove straight from Smokey's Diner to the hospital. The ER nurse gave me paperwork to fill out, then sent me to a room to wait for a doctor. Dr. Rupert heard me out, ran a few tests, then, just like Susie said, wrote me a prescription for Dilaudid. Just like that, I was given doctor's orders to take painkillers. On my way out of the hospital I called Jennifer. Jennifer saw right through the shtick, and told me that if I peed dirty the next morning she would request jail time from Judge Kanter. I told her that my head felt like it was splitting open and she first told me that it wasn't her problem, then told me to take an Ibuprofen. But the next morning when I showed her Dr. Rupert's orders, she begrudgingly relented, and had me fill out a form detailing what "medication" I had been prescribed. I drove straight back to my apartment, opened the Dilaudid, poured a few four-milligram pills onto my coffee table, and used a razor to chop them up into a fine yellow dust. The process brought back fond memories of wealth and the associated cocaine. I wondered if Dr. Rupert could prescribe me with that. I'll ask about it during my next visit. "I'm feeling a bit sluggish, Doc, got anything white that'll bump up my heart rate?"

Satisfied that my Dilaudid was as fine a powder as I could get it, I used the razor to organize the powder into two neat lines. I rolled up a fifty-dollar bill and hunched over the coffee table. I closed one nostril with my left index finger, inserted the bill into my right nostril, and inhaled my two lines. Nothing to it. I leaned back on my couch and waited for the euphoria. Heroin never worked as quick as cocaine, so I figured Dilaudid would take a few minutes to kick in. Other than dizziness, I didn't feel anything. But then, one by one, then in droves, the soldiers of joy came marching home. Calmness slayed the anxious beast growing inside me. Not even alcohol was this effective. I felt happiness that I hadn't felt since living in Spanish Hills. The pain was receding.

And from where did this happiness derive? Atomized hydromorphone, true. But how did I get that? Money. Money bought the Dilaudid. Money made the Dilaudid. Money researched, synthesized, manufactured, and marketed Dilaudid. Money paid the doctor to prescribe it and the pharmacist to count it. Money had returned to save the day when all else failed. Money had bought my happiness, just like old times.

"Hey, this is Susie."

"Hey Susie, this is Caish, how are ya?"

"Well hey there, how ya doin'?"

"Yeah, I'm good. Hey, I'm out of Lortab, ya have any?"

"Mmm, nope. Fresh out of those lil' gems, but I could get you some Vikes."

"What about Dillies?"

"Mmm…" I could hear Susie take a drag of her cigarette, "Haven't had those in weeks. You're the only one 'round here with a Dilaudid prescription. When you're out of those you're on your own. I got plenty a Vikes for ya though, come get 'em."

"Ah, I gotta get Tabs or Dillies, I piss tomorrow morning."

"Vicodin tests the same as Lortab, sweetie, you'll be fine."

"You sure?"

"Hun, you ain't the only one takin' piss tests. Come on over."

"Alright, I'll be there in fifteen minutes."

The Crown Vic made a clunking sound that I had been meaning to get looked at, but otherwise made the drive to Susie's trailer without any incident. It had been nine months since my first prescription, and life had dramatically improved. I had settled into my new apartment and made some new friends. Through Alcoholics Anonymous I met Crack-Hand Jack, Shanice, Tobie, Simple Ed, and, of course, Susie. Although I would never associate with these types of people under regular circumstances, I made an exception. True, your friends say a lot about you. But these people were more "friends" than friends. It was a mutualistic relationship. We were as much friends as the shark and its pilot fish.

These anonymous alcoholics introduced me to the perfectly legitimate world of painkillers. I'll be the first to admit that I used to look down my nose at users of heroin, morphine, oxycodone, and methadone. I only ever took opiates to help with my anxiety back when I lived in Spanish Hills. But I had been born again and seen the light. Doctors, judges, and law enforcement officers all approve. Not only that, they use, too. We all use these shortcuts to joy. There's no shame in it. An entire class of drugs with society's stamp of approval. Sure, some were arbitrarily outlawed (like heroin), but others, with a virtually identical chemical structure (like buprenorphine or hydrocodone) were legal enough to carry into a courtroom and swallow in front of a judge.

No longer did I spend my days in maximum boredom. I relaxed on clouds of euphoria and mingled with the fine folks of Missoula. They weren't so bad after all.

A few months ago my Suburban was wrongfully repossessed, so until I could get it back I was driving a souped-up 2011 Ford Crown Victoria Police Interceptor. It was completely murdered out and had a supercharger that could smoke the tires at any speed. Totally badass. With less than one hundred and fifty thousand miles on the clock, I basically stole it from the dealer for three thousand dollars. Now there was just that clunking that I needed to get around to fixing.

Susie lived in a double-wide at the Green Hill Estates Trailer Park in the south side of town. My Crown Vic crumpled a beer can as I shifted into park in front of her trailer. Part of me can't believe that I'm standing in a trailer park. Just a few years ago I would have scoffed at the idea that I'd have any business among these pastel-painted heroin hovels. Susie peaked through her bent plastic blinds then stepped out to meet me on her splintery wooden stoop. She was wearing pink shorts and a beige bra. Her hair hadn't been cared for in days and she was still wearing last week's makeup.

"Doin' alright, Susie?" I asked.

She spoke past the last of a cigarette, "Yeah, fuckin' swamp cooler's broke again though, so we all sweatin' our asses off." Susie lived with two of her five kids and a man named Tyler Ogden. Tyler's full-time job was muling drugs across the Canadian border. He was a member of the Montana Mayhem Motorcycle Club and had the tattoos and scars to prove it.

"Ya holdin' up alright?" Susie asked.

"Oh yeah, real good."

"Outta tabs huh?"

"Yeah," I said, "and my Dilaudid isn't up for a refill for a week."

"Why you ain't got more than two scrips?"

"My probation."

"Mmm…"

"Yeah. Couple more years a that then I'll be able to get more."

"Well ya look good, hun." She sucked the last of the smoke out of her cigarette and flicked the butt into the gravel road. "I got your Vicodin, ya got my scratch?"

"How are the markets today?"

"Up, but that ain't nothin' for your rich ass. Eight dollars a pill, five hundred milligrams each."

"Oh come on, Susie, eight dollars a pill? Tobie's sellin' Percs for five a pill."

"Then go buy his pills! Shit. Actin' like I ain't doin' you a favor scrapin' these hydros together. I got twenty pills, ya want 'em or not?" Susie's sass was almost too much to bear. I gave her a hundred and sixty dollars and she handed me a plastic baggie with a handful of white pills stamped "VICODIN." Susie scoffed at me when I counted the pills and let her screen door slam behind her when she stomped back into her trailer.

On my way home I stopped at the gas station and bought five lottery tickets: two Powerballs, two MegaMillions, and one Scratcher. I still hadn't won anything more than a couple bucks since my five thousand dollar win a couple years ago. Which, just based on the odds and statistics, meant that a big win was coming.

Back at the apartment things had gotten away from me. I had fallen hopelessly behind on the laundry, dishes were piled high in the sink, and the carpet had so many crumbs in it that it was becoming more food than fiber. I cleared a spot on the couch in front of the coffee table and sat down in front of my twenty Vicodin. Since I was peeing tomorrow, I didn't want to overdo it. So I pulled out four pills and ground them into fine powder, then inhaled them and let the bliss overcome me.

Jennifer gave me the usual scornful report the next morning: "Well, you peed mostly clean, other than boatloads of opioids." It was her backhanded matriarchal way of saying that opioids were in some way dirty and that I should stop taking them. She didn't understand the kind of pain I lived in.

"Yeah, my back was really bad yesterday. I could hardly get out of bed." I had learned that the back was a much better reason to take opioids than migraines. Migraines worked the first few times, but nobody believed you if you said you had migraines every single day. My doctor would only prescribe small batches of Dilaudid for my head, but for my back I could get a healthy daily dosage of Lortab. Back pain is also less conspicuous. *Everybody* says they have back pain. Usually lower back pain. Doctors hardly even look at you when you complain of back pain, they just give you a ticket to paradise and go about their rounds.

"Caish, you gotta stop using opioids," Miss Trunchbull said.

"I wish I could. I do. But I have so much pain. I can't even function without something to help."

She just shook her head and gazed at me. I was sitting in the hallway on the shitty chairs in front of her office. She was looking at me over the top of a clipboard. She knew that no matter how strung out on opioids I got, it was not a violation of my probation to take prescription medication. She looked like she was going to say something else, but then just walked back into her office.

This became my new routine. Through Alcoholics Anonymous I met all sorts of new friends, like Demerol, Norco, Xodol, OxyContin, Sufenta, and Ryzolt. Susie and Tobie usually had endless supplies of most of these. Crack-Hand Jack knew a guy who knew a guy and got access to Embeda—essentially morphine, the queen of opioids (or so I thought at the time). And Shanice had access to Codeine. Simple Ed, bless his heart, could only get prescriptions to Reprexain, but had a prescription from every doctor in town. He had something like thirteen prescriptions to Reprexain.

For years I restrained myself to just my prescriptions. I needed to take more than what was prescribed, but had only taken the prescribed dosage. Then, at long last, my probation ended. I was free. There were some forms to fill out, some time in front of a judge, and then Jennifer Trunchbull just said, "See you soon," and that was it. All done!

To celebrate I drained my bank account on two hundred grams of cocaine (which was easier to come by in Missoula than I would have expected), and a shopping cart full of alcohol. I invited the crew over to my apartment. My neighbors didn't mind the noise, so we made some. We got the pizza delivery guy to do a couple lines with us. We lived that night to its fullest. Some of us had sex, but I can't remember who. Or with whom. But I'm pretty sure we did. We passed out one by one.

Early the next morning we were woken by pounding on my front door.

19

Simple Ed shook my shoulders. "Caish, somebody bangin' on tha door."

I stumbled through my living room and looked through my peep hole. It was Caleb. I unbolted my deadlock and cracked the door.

"Caleb?"

"Can I come in, Caish?"

"Uhh... I wish you would've called first. I have a few guests that are still asleep."

"It's noon, Caish."

"Mhm."

"We need to talk."

"'Bout what?"

"About you."

"Me?"

"Yes, Caish, you. Can I come in?" Caleb was looking over my head and into my apartment.

"No."

"Okay, let me buy you lunch. It won't be long, I only have a one-hour lunch break."

"Umm... I'm pretty tired. I just woke up Caleb. I appreciate the offer, but I gotta shower and all that. Get dressed and stuff. Let me call you later, we'll talk." I had no intention at all of calling him later. Talk about me? What are we, children? I'm an adult living my life. Caleb should be worried about his own life.

"I'm going to bring you dinner tonight, Caish. With wine. Good wine. I'll come by at seven. Will you be here?"

"Yeah, sure, seven. Wine."

"Okay, see you then." Caleb said, then turned and walked down the hall.

I closed my door, and leaned my back against it. The shades

were closed but the stubborn sun found ways to spill into the room. I pulled a cigarette out of the pack sitting on my counter and surveyed the room. Liquor bottles were scattered throughout. Some empty. Clothes, cups, pizza boxes, pizza, pill bottles, plastic wrappers, and other random objects cluttered the floor. Tobie was asleep on the ground next to the coffee table. He was naked and had a rolled up ten-dollar bill in his right hand. It looked like he passed out before he could get to the last of the three lines of coke he had lined up. His upper lip was pasted with a smear of sweat and white powder. I stepped over him, plucked the bill out of his hand, and snorted the line.

Susie was lying face down on my couch with a blanket covering her legs. She was an ugly sleeper. My TV had a hole in it. Not a crack in the screen, a hole about the size of a ham sandwich straight through it. That was probably Simple Ed. I shuffled into my room and found Simple Ed fast asleep on my bed, hand wrapped in one of my white—now blood red—towels. Mystery solved. Shanice was also in my bed. Her naked body was knotted up in sheets, her leg dangled off the side of the bed. Crack-Hand Jack and a few new friends were in my guest room. They were sleeping like a ball of snakes. Crack-Hand Jack was cradling a bottle of Bacardi into his chest, like he was trying to breastfeed it in his sleep.

After finding some clean clothes, I went to the bathroom. There was another line of coke on the counter, so I inhaled it. I pulled the shower curtain back and almost stepped on a duck. Not a rubber duck, an actual feathered, breathing, quacking duck. We looked at each other in a confused silence. I tried to think of how a duck got here, but couldn't come up with anything. Tobie or Shanice probably brought it over as a joke.

I had to shower, but I couldn't with the bird standing there. I walked back into my room and nudged Shanice awake.

"Hey. Shanice. Shanice." She was coming to. "Shanice, is that your duck in the bathtub?"

"Hm?" Shanice stretched and rolled over.

"Shanice. Hey, Shanice, wake up. Is that your duck in the bathtub?"

"Mmm... Georgia?" She asked.

"I don't know its fuckin' name, but I need to shower."

"Mmm... then shower."

"I can't. There's a fuckin' duck in the bathtub."

"Umm..." Shanice's eyes were opening. She leaned up on an elbow and squinted at me. "Umm... then take her out of the bathtub."

"I can't. You do it. It's your duck."

"No, she's Tobie's duck. And her name is Georgia."

"Shanice, will you please just come take this duck out of the bathtub? I need to shower."

Grumbling, she wrapped herself in my sheet, walked into the bathroom, and walked out with Georgia under her arm. "Where should I put her?" she asked.

"Jesus. I don't know. The kitchen sink?"

"K. What if it's full though? I think there's dishes in it."

"Ugh, Shanice, I don't care where you put the fucking duck." I walked back into the bathroom and turned the shower on. I stepped in after the duck shit had washed down the drain.

By the time Caleb came over with dinner, the apartment was back in tip-top shape. After the others woke up and left, I called a house cleaning service to come take care of everything. I told them they could keep any alcohol they found. While I was at lunch and running errands they polished the place clean. I came home to a spotless apartment. They even did my laundry for me and brought it back later that night. They earned a huge tip.

Caleb brought takeout from Outback Steakhouse and a bottle of cheap wine.

"I know you like restaurant food, so I figured I'd bring some Outback." He helped himself to my cupboards and set places for us on my table. "Had quite the night last night, huh?"

"Yeah. Just a little get together with some friends."

"Sounds like a good time." He filled two of my glasses with water from the tap and poured red wine into two of my wine glasses. "I think we're ready to eat. Shall we?"

Caleb kept the conversation alive by asking about how I'd been in the last few years and informing me what he'd been up to. We had only spoken a few times since he and Toni had me over for dinner along with our other siblings. "What's new?" he wanted to know. A lot was new. Especially now that probation no longer chained me to the iron ball of opioids. Not that opioids weren't wonderful, they were. Oh God they were. But nothing could replace pure, white, glorious cocaine. And now that I could freely drink again the clouds were parting. Hopelessness was departing.

After dinner, as expected, Caleb began his intervention speech. He had been speaking with Jennifer and he was worried about me. Didn't want me to "fall off the wagon." He had heard that I was taking painkillers and "runnin' around" with Crack-Hand Jack—a known pusher.

Then he offered to pay my rent. The proposal came with a stipulation that I work for Toni's uncle as a mechanic. Caleb told me that he thought a nine-to-five would help me get acclimatized to middle-class living and would help me stay responsible with my drinking. He seemed to know that I was almost out of money. Maybe he was just guessing. If so, his intuition was right. I had enough to pay my bills for three more months before I had to sell more stuff. If he covered my rent, I could cover my car payment and other bills. "Just until you're back on your feet," he said.

Humiliated, but relieved, I accepted his offer.

Toni's uncle wanted to see me first thing Monday morning, Caleb told me. 9:00 a.m. sharp. Show up ready to work a full day. I gave Caleb a rent receipt on his way out.

Monday morning came quicker than expected. Still, I wasn't

too late. Toni's uncle was called Malcolm Patchett. He bore an uncanny resemblance to Michael Clarke Duncan. As I would soon learn, everybody at the shop called him John Henry. We got off to a rocky start since he couldn't get over the fact that I was a few minutes late. He was also treating me like I was some kid fresh out of high school. He obviously didn't know that he was interacting with an emeritus millionaire. I had a house in Malibu worth more than the entire city, cars that cost more than Malcolm's neighborhood, and servants I paid more than Malcolm makes in a year. And yet, he treated me like a child. Even after the first couple of weeks of working there, he micromanaged me. Hovered over me. Gave me orders then explained to me how to do every tiny task along the way. By the end of the first month I had a hard time hiding my contempt. Not just for Malcolm but for everybody at Courtright Automotive. Everybody disrespected me. Ordered me around. My paychecks were nothing. $748 every two weeks. I was working a labor-intensive humiliating job for $1500 a month. Hardly enough for ten grams of cocaine. But my bank account was down to $4,109.38. So I put up with Malcolm and the others at Courtright.

Caleb invited me over for another dinner with him and Toni, this time without the rest of the family. It was another pleasant evening in middle-classdom. After dinner we sipped coffee and told stories about mutual acquaintances. I excused myself to use their bathroom. Out of habit, I checked their medicine cabinet. Aha! I had forgotten Toni was also on the hydro train. Zohydro ER, a painkiller so powerful that thirty states begged the FDA not to approve its release in capsule form. Of course, money won that war, and now doctors are prescribing Zohydro in every state in the union. But even so, these were tough to come by. I pocketed a few to try out later that night.

Once home, I minced and snorted the Zohydro and began my mini vacation. I rode the high to drowsy town and stopped there for the night. It was no cocaine, but painkillers had their place. I resolved to only buy cocaine for special occasions and to make a more concerted effort to live on painkillers. After all, I had more pain than most people, so I had a legitimate reason to medicate. The next morning I called in sick. I went to the pharmacy and got my prescription for Lortab filled. Then I drove to St. Mary's Hospital and got a prescription for OxyContin. Then to Mountain Ridge Hospital for my Percocet prescription. Then to the university hospital for Vicodin, Summit Hospital for Demerol, and Valley View InstaCare for Lorcet. I had enough to relax, and enough pills to sell to pay the bills.

Courtright wasn't working out, so I quit. Not formally, but I stopped going in, so I'm sure that Malcolm got the point. I did the math and figured I could make more selling painkillers. Plus, I'd had enough of the disrespect. Susie and the others bought half my stock.

Crack-Hand Jack bought all my percs and invited me over to his place for what he promised would be a life-changing high. His trailer was down the gravel road from Susie.

Jack's trailer was near barren. Filthy and spotless at the same time. The stale air smelled like cheap tobacco and fried cooking. The front room had a torn imitation leather couch and an old TV balanced on a stool. The carpet had alcohol stains and a large stain in the middle that I told myself must have been from red wine. There were no pictures on the walls. Jack led me to a back room without any furniture and told me to wait there. There was a microwave plugged into the wall, just sitting on the floor. He pulled the door closed behind him and I heard him lumber through the trailer.

My fear receptors clocked in. Was I about to be another stain in the carpet? Why didn't Susie tell me not to go with Jack to his murder shack? Was she in on it? Fuck. I had to get out of here. I couldn't hear Jack's footsteps anymore. Jack's trailer was silent. Shit. This probably wasn't Jack's trailer. This thing was abandoned and now Jack just uses it to hack people apart.

He probably gets his nickname from cracking people's skulls. I tried the window and found that it had been screwed shut. The room had a tiny vent in the ceiling that not even a child could fit into. The only way out was the door. I held my breath and tiptoed across the room. When my hand touched the doorknob I heard Jack's steps coming toward the room. I stepped away from the door and thought about jumping through the glass of the window and taking my chances with whatever was on the other side. I could probably outrun Jack. But would the others be outside the trailer in case I tried to make a break for it? Would Susie be waiting with a chainsaw?

Jack opened the door and stepped in with a friendly and excited grin. "Alrighty, so this is—woah, Caish, ya alright?"

I had backed into a corner and was sort of half-crouched, ready to make a break for the door. Jack was carrying a small black leather case. Not big enough for a butcher knife. Or a chainsaw.

"Umm, yeah, sorry, just a little wired I guess."

"Yeah, looks like it," Crack-Hand Jack said. He stood there looking at me for a few seconds, then said, "Caish, maybe we autta head back to Susie's. You're kinda freakin' me out."

"Oh no no, I'm sorry. Really, it's nothing. Sorry." Judging by Jack's face, I was not about to get hacked to pieces. In hindsight, he probably just didn't want me to see where he hid his stash.

"Hm," he thought.

"Really, Jack, it's nothing. I'm excited to see what you have. Is it crack?"

"Haha, no. Ya know, I never actually dealt crack. Ain't never even done the stuff. The nickname came from a stint I did in county lockup. I got into a lil' scuffle and cracked a guy's skull with a judo-chop. It was a weird thing, I ain't usually one to judo-chop, but it just sorta happened. Ya know how things get in a scuffle. Ya do weird shit. Haha, anyway, that's why they call me that."

Jesus Christ.

"Nah, what I wanna show you goes by many names. Maybe ya heard of it." He unzipped the leather case and displayed the contents. Three pill capsules, a stack of small patches, two syringes, a spoon, a lighter, a razor, a small plastic cup (the kind that come on the top of cough syrup bottles), and some tinfoil. "Murder 8... TNT... China White... Dance Fever..." He paused after each name and invited me to sit on the ground with him. He was obviously proud of his vocabulary.

"... Apache... Goodfella. Ya heard of it?"

"I've heard those names from Susie before, but nah, I dunno."

"Fentanyl."

"Fenanail?"

"Fen-ta-nyl."

"What's Fentanyl?"

"Fentanyl is a painkiller just like all that other weak shit you been takin'. But Fentanyl ain't fuckin' around. This shit right here is a thousand times heavier than heroin. Dead serious. It is actually one thousand times more potent than heroin and morphine."

"Bullshit."

"Caish, it's science. Fentanyl is harder than black tar. By *one thousand fucking times*." Jack was laying out the contents of his pack as he talked. "But, you ain't gotta take my word for it, I got enough to level a rhino right here." He held up a few of the patches between his fingers.

"Oooh, damn," I said. "Nah, I've heard of this. Goddamn elephant tranquilizer, right? Nah, I don't want any of that shit. Sorry Jack, this shit is lethal." I stood to leave.

"Caish, nah, have a seat. This ain't elephant tranquilizer. That's carfentanil. I ain't insane. This is *Fentanyl* not *carfentanil*. Big difference, Caish. Them tranquilizers are a hundred times as potent as this here TNT. Trust me, Caish, I didn't bring you here to kill ya."

Well, that was a relief.

"Hm. If you say so." I sat and watched Jack get the rest of his kit organized on the carpet.

"Now, you can do this however you want. You can be a pussy and take it like a pill. You can grow a pair and snort it. Or, my personal preference, ya can shoot it straight into your veins." He looked up, "So, what'll it be?"

A couple years ago my doctor told me that my HIV viral load was undetectable, and therefore pretty much negligible. She said that I should still use protection when I have sex, but that either way I probably wouldn't transfer the virus. I took my medication as prescribed, and didn't have any symptoms from the HIV. With that in mind, I opted for the syringe. I hadn't injected anything in years. Not since my Malibu house party days.

"You nervous?" Jack asked.

"Haha, nah. Why?"

"Cause you lookin' nervous as fuck."

"Nah. I'm good. It's just been awhile since I've mainlined anything."

"Mmm." Jack opened up the patches and used the razor to scrape the gel off of the patches and into the plastic cup. Satisfied that he had two servings, he placed the gel cup in the microwave and set the timer for thirty seconds. He handed me a rubber tube to tie above my elbow. After twenty seconds he pulled the cup out and used the needle to stir. He pulled a water bottle out of his jacket and poured a few drops into the cup. He drew back the top of the syringe and pulled the light yellow liquid into the small plastic tube. With the last drop sucked up, he held out his hand and said, "Here, gimme your arm."

"Fuck, Jack, I dunno. I'm not a junkie."

"Ain't nobody callin' ya a junkie. I'm givin' you a valuable education right now, not to mention the greatest high of your whole goddamn life, all free of charge. Out of the goodness of my heart. Now, have a little trust and gimme that arm."

I held out my left arm and Jack's sweaty hand cupped my elbow.

"Will it burn?"

"What do you mean?"

"You microwaved it for a long time."

"Oh, haha, nah. It ain't gon' burn. Gonna feel nice and toasty though. Just relax."

The prick of the needle didn't sting as much as I had expected. It was a painless injection. He found a vein on his first try and slowly injected the warm liquid into my blood. He pulled off the rubber hose as he withdrew the needle. It felt like someone pushed my shoulder back, and then the rest of my body. I fell back to the ground as the warmth spread up my arm, into my chest, up my neck, and then throughout my body. Waves of warmth. Pulsating pleasure. My body melted. The room melted. Jack's voice was distant and cheery. I had become God. This was unlike anything I had ever felt. Time slowed down, and it too became warm then melted away. I stopped moving, because why move? If I held still I floated. The melted ceiling got closer, then dissolved. There was nothing, only rapture. I closed my eyes. Jack made a sound. I opened my eyes and rolled my head over to see Jack pulling the needle out of his arm. He was laughing and leaning back. He said something on his way back. Then we were gods. We floated around in the palpable perfection. I floated out of the room, through the perfection, and into my pool in Malibu. The sun glistened off the water droplets on my sun-kissed skin. I floated and heard muffled seagull squawks and the whir of the earth. Weightless. Careless. Nothing mattered because nothing existed. The only thing I could think about was the only thing I could feel: joy.

20

The rapture lasted for a while, I'm not sure exactly how long because time didn't exist. After the initial rush, there were several hours of deeper relaxation than I had ever felt. Who knew the body had capacity for such intensely incredible sensations? I hated everybody who had ever tried this and not forced me to take it right away. Selfish bastards.

"How ya feelin' Caish? Doin' alright?"

"Was I asleep?"

"Ya may've nodded off." Jack was folding up his black case. The room was dimly lit by a single bulb hanging from the ceiling. Night had arrived.

"What time is it?" I asked.

"'Bout eleven thirty. We were ridin' high there for six or seven hours. Not bad."

Crack-Hand Jack stood and offered me a hand. He pulled me up and I took a moment to regain my balance. The magic had faded, but I felt good. Great, even. But slightly off kilter. We walked through the empty trailer in the dark, not worried about stubbing our toes on furniture, and out into the night. Jack locked the door behind us with a padlock, then turned and offered me a cigarette. After a few silent puffs, he said, "So, not bad, eh?"

"Haha, I have never felt like that before. That was better than I knew was possible."

"Yup. Shit like that oughta be illegal, right?"

"Oh bullshit, that can't be legal."

"I shit you not, Caish. What you just had is prescribed in all fifty states. Totally legit."

"How do I get a prescription?"

"Mmm..." Jack took a drag and blew the smoke straight up into the night. "That's the tough part. Gotta get cancer."

"Hm." I thought about whether it would be worth it. How does one even get cancer? I mean, I was doing my level best with the cigarettes, but was there a better way? I knew about tanning beds and uranium, but tanning beds take years, and uranium is hard to come by. Then it occurred to me, "Ah, shit Jack, I'm so sorry. What kind is it?"

"Ha! Ack ach," Jack's laugh almost cost him a lung. "I ain't got cancer, Caish. I was just sayin', that if ya wanted a prescription of your own, that's what ya gotta have. Nah, I got my own hookups."

"How can I get it?" The most important question of the night.

Jack smiled, "Through me. I got plenty for ya. In fact, I could use your help movin' some of it."

"You mean selling it?"

"You could put it that way, sure. Think of it as a business opportunity."

"Ah, Jack, I'm not a drug dealer."

"'Course not, Caish. I ain't askin' ya to deal drugs. I'm askin' ya to bring this gift to the masses. So what if ya earn a little extra cabbage on the side?" Jack's cigarette ashed itself. Tiny specks of glowing carbon escaped into the wind. "You ain't gotta give me an answer right now, Caish. Don't stress it. Sleep on it. But next time ya want a high like that, hit me up and we'll talk."

The next time I wanted a high like that was right that moment. And later that night, and again as soon as I woke up the next morning. The next day I snorted four oxys, but those now seemed like an appetizer. As good as chips and salsa could possibly be, one craves the full enchilada. The high was wonderful, but not enough. I called Jack that night.

Jack sold me the Fentanyl at "wholesale prices," and we agreed that I would sell seventy-five percent of it and give him twenty percent of my earnings (give or take). I hosted "taste testing" at my apartment. I invited people from Alcoholics Anonymous over, and asked for referrals. Susie and the crew were already aware of Fentanyl and bought their supply from Jack, but there were still plenty of folks in Montana who hadn't heard of this heaven. In a week I was a needle pro. In a couple of months I was beginning and ending my day in pure ecstasy. Although it never felt quite as intense as the first time, it was a pleasure I could not afford to do without. Money was coming in, but it wasn't enough to cover all my expenses. For the time being, I cut back on lottery tickets.

"Caish, what the fuck?" Caleb yelled into the phone. I could tell he was doing his best to maintain his reputation as a level-headed rational individual, but the strain came through my phone as clearly as his voice.

"What?" I asked.

"What? Are you kidding me? Try guessing."

"Mmm... Is this about me quitting Courtright?"

"No. Although what the hell was that about? We try and help you, we stick our neck out for you, and you just stop showing up to work? How do you think that makes us look? That hurts our relationships, Caish."

"Hm. Yeah. You're probably right."

Caleb grumbled something under his breath, then went on, "Caish, you sold fucking Fentanyl to Toni?"

"She needed it, Caleb. Are you calling to thank me?"

"Fuck no, I'm not calling to thank you! Caish, do you have any idea how addictive and dangerous Fentanyl is? And what are you, some fucking drug dealer now? And you sold it to *my wife*? Caish, what the fuck is wrong with you?"

I couldn't understand why Caleb was so fired up. His soft-spoken wife was in pain and I offered her something to ease that pain. It all happened by design, anyway. A month ago I was praying for more clients. Jack had lots of Fentanyl to sell, but I couldn't off-load enough of it to make any real money. I asked the Lord God for some help. Later that same day I was at Walmart and ran into Toni in the pharmacy area. She was refilling her Zohydro prescription. God couldn't have been more clear if he'd placed his message on a billboard: Toni needed Fentanyl, and I needed more clients. He brought us together to be part of His plan. Truly, the Lord works in mysterious ways. Anyway, I struck up a conversation and told her that I too struggled with chronic pain, and that the best thing I had ever found was Fentanyl, had she heard of it? She said she had, but was nervous to try it. I told her that the bad reputation was ill-deserved, and that it was a very safe drug when taken as prescribed. She asked how to get a prescription, and I told her of the two routes: cancer or me. It took a little more coaxing, then we were back in my apartment having a taste test. I didn't want to scare her off, so I gave it to her in pill form. She took well to Fentanyl and bought most of what I had for sale. She must have been in a lot of pain. She was back in a week looking for more and feeling much better. A week later, Caleb called.

"Look, Caleb, first of all, you need to calm down. Sec—"

"Caish, calm down? You are selling drugs to my wife, do you even—"

"*Second of all*, Toni was in a lot of pain, now she's not. Really, you should be thanking me."

"Oh fuck you, Caish. Do you even realize what you've done? Can you even see the implications?"

"Implications?" I asked.

"Of course you don't. You never do. You just cannot think ahead, can you, Caish? All you ever think about is right this moment. Not tomorrow, not anybody else, not even your own goddamn long-term well-being. You probably don't even give a shit about how dangerous Fentanyl is."

"Well, it's only dangerous if you—"

"Caish, Fentanyl is the drug that killed Prince. Prince, Caish. He died taking Fentanyl."

"I understand you're upset, but really, you need to calm d—"

"Caish, I'm not paying your rent anymore. Obviously. Don't ever give anything to my wife ever again. Don't come near us. Please leave Missoula."

With a huff, he hung up.

I looked around my dark apartment. It was 2:00 p.m. on a Tuesday. My front room was cluttered with pillows, blankets, food boxes, beer cans, and clothes. On the coffee table lay the instruments of administration set out from this morning's treatment. My shades were drawn but slim beams of light barged in through the cracks. Golden bands making the rest of the place darker. I lit a cigarette and blew smoke into the cloud that was forming on my ceiling. Candice, my landlord, had told me that I had to stop smoking in the apartment, but this was my apartment. I'll do what I want in my apartment. I heard something fall off the nightstand in my room. The sound of a phone dropping to the ground. Then my bed creaked.

Tobie walked in from my bedroom, clearly having just woke up. He had joined me for this morning's bliss train. An unlit Marlboro dangled from his lower lip.

"That sounded dramatic." Tobie opened my fridge and bent into it. "You got a light?"

"Not in there," I said.

Tobie walked over to me and held his cigarette to the flame of my Zippo, then walked back to the fridge. "So what was all that drama? Woke me the fuck up."

"That was Caleb. My brother. Have you two met?"

"Nah," Tobie pulled out a doggie bag from Chili's and put the box into the microwave. Chicken and waffles.

"He's my oldest brother."

"Hm. What's his deal?"

"Nothing. Just typical Caleb, trying to control everybody else's life. Wouldn't let his wife live her own life. He'd rather have her in pain than taking TNT just because it has a bad reputation. He's completely risk averse. To the point of causing pain to those around him."

"Yeah, hm. Whatever." Tobie was back in the fridge. "Caish, you outta Bud?"

"I dunno. If you don't see it, then yeah."

Caleb had riled me up. He'd given me stress that I didn't need. Stress is pain. I dumped two Fentanyl pills onto the coffee table and razored them to pieces. Reduced them to a fine powder. Then I scraped the powder into a spoon.

"You already headed back in?" Tobie asked.

"Yeah, I need to chill out."

Tobie shrugged. "Well I might join ya after breakfast."

He must of read my expression through the dark, because then he added, "Don't worry, I'll use my own."

I held my lighter to the bottom of the spoon and watched the powder reduce itself to a brown bubbling potion. I used the syringe to sprinkle a few drops of water into the spoon and stirred the Fentanyl. I drew as much as I could into the syringe, pushed the air out of the chamber, found a vein, and injected the liquid joy into my arm. Before I settled back into the couch I put the spoon into my mouth and cleaned off the leftovers. In seconds I was weightless. My heart pumped the warmth through my arteries. As reliably as a Swiss train, the bliss train swept me away from the pain.

At around eight that night, my vibrating phone pulled me down from the clouds. My vision was blurry. I lit a cigarette and answered my phone.

"Mhm?"

"Caish?" Somehow I could tell that Candice, my landlord, was smiling on the other side of the phone.

"Yeah, hi Candice."

"Did I wake you up?"

"No, no I'm up. You're fine. What's up?"

"Caish it's about your smoking. Some of the tenants around your unit have complained that their apartments are beginning to smell like smoke."

"That's so weird, I haven't smoked in my apartment since the last time we spoke. Are you sure it's not somebody else?"

"Yes. Mind if I come over?"

"Mmm... When?"

"How does now work for you?" Candice asked.

"Well, it's a little late, maybe you could come by tomorrow sometime. Earlier in the day, if you could."

"Well, it's only seven thirty, and, as it were, I'm right outside your door, could you let me in?"

"Umm, yeah. Sure, no problem." I pulled up the shades and threw open the sliding door to my balcony. "I um..." I flicked the cigarette off my balcony and ran into my room to open more windows. "I'm just indecent at the moment." I packed up my kit on the coffee table. "Just give me a second to put some clothes on and I'll be right there." I used a pillow to fan out the smoke.

"Everything alright in there?"

"Yeah, no, definitely," I shook Tobie, "it's just late is all." Tobie had passed out on the other side of the coffee table. "Tobie!" I shouted through a whisper, "Tobie, wake up. Tobie!" Tobie grumbled back to life. I held my hand over my phone, "Tobie, my landlord is here, sober up." I turned on all the lights in the apartment.

"Caish?" Candice asked. I hung up.

I pulled out a garbage sack and filled it with all the boxes, cans, food, and ashtrays I could find, then flung it off the balcony into the parking lot below. I stashed my kit under the couch and put my pill bottles in the bathroom cabinet. Running through my room I spotted another ashtray and tossed it out the window. Returning to the front room, Tobie had tidied up the blankets and pillows. He was throwing a pizza box off the balcony. I sprayed Febreze into every room and onto every piece of furniture. Then doused Tobie. Candice knocked on the door. "Caish?" she said through the door. "Open up." I scrambled from room to room making sure the place was presentable. Kicking this under that, straightening this, getting everything just so. "Caish, I'm coming in." I heard her key slide into the tumblers of the deadbolt. "Tobie, sit on the couch." I ran into my room. I heard the knob unlock, then the door open. I walked out of my room pulling a shirt down over my head.

"Jesus, Candice, I said I was just getting dressed. What the hell?"

"Sounded like there was a bit more going on than getting dressed." Like always, Candice was smiling. She looked at Tobie and extended her hand, "Hi, I'm Candice, nice to meet you."

Without getting up, Tobie lifted his limp sweaty hand for Candice to take ahold of. "I'm Tobie" he said. She shook his hand, then let it flop down onto his lap. She tried to be couth, but I saw her wipe her hand on her skirt as soon as she let go. Tobie's hands can be sticky at times.

"Caish, you've been smoking in here," she said, turning to me.

"No I haven't."

"Okay, Caish. Despite your noble effort with the Febreze, it smells like smoke in here. Also," she stepped toward the balcony, "maybe you could come with me out to your balcony?" She walked out and leaned over the railing. Turning back to me, she said, "Come on out, Caish, have a look."

I walked out to the railing and looked down. An exploded garbage bag was on the roof of some shitty green car below. A few cars down from that there was an ashtray sitting next to a dent on the hood of some shitty truck. A breeze nudged beer cans through the parking lot. "Am I supposed to be looking for anything in particular?" I asked.

"Caish. This is your final warning." Candice wasn't smiling anymore. "You pull this shit again, and you're out. If you're late on rent by a day, you're out. If a neighbor calls complaining about anything going on in this unit, including your frequent visitors, you're out. Ya with me?"

"Yeah. Whatever."

"I'm giving your information to the owners of those cars that you vandalized, and you will be billed for the clean-up."

"I'll just go clean it up myself."

"No, you won't. My people will clean it up, and you will be charged." Candice walked back into the apartment, looked around, then walked out without another word.

"She seemed sorta pissed," Tobie observed.

Rent was $1,050 a month, and it was due in nine days. My bank account was down to $207.44. I still had that $5,212 in cash stashed, but I didn't want to use any of that. That was *mine*, not Candice's. I earned about a thousand a week selling pharmaceuticals, but I had to buy $1,200 a week for new inventory from Jack and to refill my own prescriptions. I also had to find a way to pay for cigarettes, alcohol, and food.

My storage shed hadn't been opened in months. The metal door slid up and revealed three hundred square feet of stuff I didn't use any more. There was no musty smell because this unit had circulated air conditioning and heating. The movers had stacked everything to the ceiling. Couches on top of bookcases full of antiques next to paintings above electronics. Bins full of designer clothing. Clearly-labeled boxes stacked neatly. Expensive luggage full of expensive shoes.

At my feet was a box labeled "coffee table toppers." It was full of decorative bowls with decorative balls to fill the decorative bowls, candles, photography books, small tactile games, and coasters. The box was light, and fit into the trunk of my Crown Vic with room for more. I loaded as many boxes as my car could carry. I found the box labeled "camera stuff" and pulled out my Nikon D5 DSLR camera along with a few lenses.

Back at the apartment I plugged in the Nikon battery and started unloading my boxes. On my laptop I pulled up Craigslist and a few local online markets and looked at what people were selling similar stuff for. When the battery was charged, I took a few pictures of every item and listed them for sale. The rest of the night my phone was buzzing with eager buyers.

My storage unit had enough stuff in it, and enough valuable stuff, to pay my rent and then some. I could afford to pay my rent and buy higher quality pharmaceuticals from Susie and Crack-Hand Jack. I was back to buying lottery tickets every time I went to the gas station. I even had enough to drive to Denver and buy cocaine and go shopping for new designer clothes—a simple luxury I had deprived myself of for too long. I made a weekend stay of it and indulged at the Four Seasons.

After five months my storage unit was empty, but I had eight grand in the bank. I sold what I could in my apartment and brought my bank balance up to $9,043. To get rid of my car payment I sold the Crown Vic (for a profit of $400, because I'm a hustler like that), and bought a $1,000 beater: a 2008 Dodge Neon. The used-car salesperson gave it to me for only $200 down, no credit check. It would have to do for now.

But the money I made selling prescriptions was not enough. When I ran out of things to sell (even sold the Nikon), I felt like the captain of a ship that had a hole in its hull. Taking on water and unable to bail it out quicker than it was coming in. In a matter of weeks, I was unloading the lifeboat. I had to cut back on everything except cigarettes and Fentanyl.

Candice made regular inspections of my apartment, and didn't seem to have much patience for any small infraction. So when I missed rent for the second month in a row, I wasn't too surprised to come home to a yellow piece of paper taped to my door that said: "NOTICE OF EVICTION: Three Day Notice to Pay or Quit" and told me that unless I paid everything I owed in rent, I'd be removed from the premises pursuant to Montana State Code sections 70-24-108, 70-24-422, and 70-24-427. Three days.

I still had my $5,212 in cash, and I had a few hundred in the bank. I could make rent. But for how long? Why was I keeping up this farce in Missoula fucking Montana? This place had been sucking the life out of me since the day I arrived. First Alex gives me HIV, then they took my house on Canyon River Golf Course, then these backcountry lenders wouldn't lend to me for another house so I was forced into an apartment like some college student. Probation knee-capped me. The Montana lottery was no good. Then the repo guys stole my Suburban. The only good that came from this barren wasteland was Crack-Hand Jack and the discovery of Fentanyl.

California called. I was a pinball desperate to get back to the hole at the bottom but kept getting bounced up through tunnels into bumpers around loops in and out of pockets and against flippers. Distractions and forces beyond my control were forcing me to live a life of slavery. All the while, gravity pulled me toward California. The peaceful rest at the bottom. The center of the universe. Paradise. Palm trees, warm breezes, and sex with azizs. Oceans of wine and beaches of cocaine.

I had done this before with much less experience and became a multimillionaire. This time I had $5,212 in cash and a little in the bank. I had the most valuable education: street smarts. I had enough opioids to last me for a couple weeks. I knew which lotteries to play and where to stay.

Excitement overcame me. I unlocked my apartment and began throwing clothes into a duffle bag. I filled a roller suitcase with my shoes and the rest of my clothes. I dumped my drawer full of pills into my backpack. My laptop, phone, and chargers fit snug in with the pill bottles. I put my $5,212 in a small inner pocket of the backpack. I looked through the apartment for anything else I'd need. Nothing that I could see. I had sold everything of value and was looking at an empty apartment. It reminded me of Crack-Hand Jack's trailer. The only thing left in my front room was a torn leather couch that wouldn't sell. Wires hung from the wall where my TV used to hang. Nails marked the places where my art used to hang. The cupboards in the kitchen were empty. I had three forks, a steak knife, a spoon, two mismatched plates, a bowl, a coffee mug, and twelve shot glasses. The fridge was packed with takeout boxes at various stages of rot. I pulled out a bottle of vodka that Shanice had left and slid it into my duffle bag.

After scanning the apartment one last time, I picked up my keys and pulled my luggage out into the hallway. I was locking the door when I realized that I wasn't coming back to this apartment ever again. I pulled the key off my key ring, opened the door, and tossed the key into the apartment. I left the door open and the lights on.

I pulled off the highway for gas on the way out of town and looked back in the direction of Missoula. My birthplace had failed to help me get back on my feet. Friends and family had let me down. In the end Missoula left me right back where I started so many years ago. Filling up a shitty car in a Texaco, anxious to get to California.

21

On my way through Utah on I-15 at about 1:00 a.m., I had a revelation. I had been praying, asking the Lord for some help. Not much help, just enough to get a few million in the bank again and I'd take it from there. God's finger lit my lightbulb. My route to Los Angeles would take me straight through Las Vegas, the city of opportunity. This must have been why I felt inspired to save the $5,212. Too many coincidences to call it chance. God had a plan for me and I was just now seeing it.

As the sun was rising I pulled into the parking garage of Treasure Island. I stepped out of the car and felt the brisk morning nip of the desert kiss my cheeks. I resolved to never see snow again. I left my roller bag in the trunk, put on my backpack, and slung my duffle over my shoulder. Treasure Island had a room available. I decided to freshen up before heading for the roulette table. After a forty-five minute scalding-hot shower, I took a nap. I slept until the early evening. All the better, the roulette wheel needed to be warmed up before I got there. Room service brought me a shrimp alfredo dish and coke with a bottle of cheap wine. I paid for the room and the food with my debit card, figuring that I needed all $5,212 for the casino downstairs. Plus, might as well clean out the account and start with a blank slate.

Rested, fed, and clean, I put on my nicest clothes and took the elevator down to the casino. On my way down, a small family boarded the elevator. Tourists. Dad had on a Hawaiian shirt and khaki shorts, mom had on an Old Navy flag T-shirt tucked into Levis. The three children were dressed like children. To think, people used to respect themselves and wear dresses and suits. Humanity has declined.

The elevator doors opened to the electric jungle of the casino. Rings, bings, whirls, and dongs. Hundreds of thousands of light bulbs of every size and color blinked to the beat of the jungle. Drinks girls sauntered about, balancing trays and smiles. Tourists lost their money playing slots and video poker. Pit bosses kept their eyes peeled and dealers kept their cards dealt. Treasure Island's casino floor had a lowish ceiling with a Tuscan theme. Comfortable. The type of place you could spend an evening. And a fortune. But the Lord had made my path clear. After exchanging my $5,212 in cash for chips, I walked straight to the roulette table.

For sake of prudence, I watched for a few minutes before placing my bet. The roulette wheel is a perpetually spinning wheel. Wood casing holds the ever-spinning wheel and has an inset in the top of it that the dealer spins the ball around. The dealer spins the ball around in a counterclockwise direction, and the wheel spins clockwise. The little white plastic ball then slides down into the wheel, bounces around for a couple seconds, and chooses the winner.

The ball was landing on red more often than black. And the house was losing. I watched a high school kid double her money, first spin.

The roulette table is more complex than what you see in the movies. Next to the wheel there is a felt board with thirty-six numbered spaces. Each number is colored either red or black. You can place bets on the numbers (and do tricky things like corner bets), or you can make column bets, where you bet on a third of the numbers on the board by placing your chips at the end of one of the columns. You can do the same thing by betting on different number batches of twelve. But the only bet that really matters involves two boxes at the bottom of the board, one colored red, and one colored black. If you bet that the roulette ball will land on red, and it does land on red, then you've just doubled your money. If you bet red and the ball lands on black, the house takes your money. It's a risky game without the help of the Lord.

Two other people were playing when I walked up to the table. The dealer had just flicked the ball around the wheel and it was riding the top rail around.

"Bets closed," the dealer said.

I nodded and waited until the ball bounced into the black 22 slot. There are thirty-eight slots that the ball can land in. Thirty-six of which are black and red, two of which are green. If the ball lands in either of the green (either a zero or a double zero), the house wins.

The dealer announced the 22 black and dealt out winning chips to the person standing nearest to the wheel. Small bets, it looked like. At the dealer's nod, I placed my $5,212 in chips on red. The other two players looked at me with bulging eyes, then turned to the dealer.

"Big money on red," the dealer said, seemingly without any emotion at all. "All bets placed?"

The two other players repeated their small number-specific bets by leaving their chips on the table.

The dealer flicked the ball around the top of the wheel. My stomach knotted. The ball rolled round and round, when it finally fell below the top rail, I thought I saw the hand of the Lord guiding it. It hit the first notch and began its bounce around the wheel. With each click of its bounce my stomach's knot notched tighter. Then, as if magnetically, it came to rest.

"Six black," the dealer said.

I almost threw up right on the table. The dealer used a wooden stick to scoop up my chips without leaving his chair. How could this have happened? The Lord had inspired me. Was this a trial? Of course! Of course it was a trial. The Lord was testing my faith! Looks like it would be the martingale strategy tonight. Double or nothing. I jogged back to the cashier's booth and bought $5,212 in chips and returned to the table.

"Big money on red," the dealer said. This was it. How could I have doubted the Lord?

The ball did its dance and came to rest in black slot 35. "Thirty-five black," the dealer said. Then he pulled out the wooden stick and took my chips. The other people at the table were trying to contain their excitement. Nothing like watching somebody lose ten grand to make you feel better about yourself.

The Lord works in mysterious ways, and clearly He wanted to see if I had faith enough to follow Him into the darkness before he would answer my prayers. I walked back to the cashier booth and maxed out all my remaining credit cards to get eleven thousand dollars in chips.

This time when I returned to the table there was a small crowd forming. For them it was a win-win situation. They either were about to get free drinks on me, or had front row seats to a self-immolation.

I had five light-blue chips, each worth $2,000 each. Two purple, worth $500 each. Three gray, worth $20 each. And a white, a $1 chip. I placed my small stack onto red. Since it had landed on black the few times before, it was more likely to land on red this time. It's statistics. I didn't get to where I am today playing it safe. You must take risks to make money. College doesn't make you money, perseverance and risk-taking makes you money. The dealer made his announcements then spun the ball. "Bets closed," he said. It began its quiet spin. Proverbs chapter three, verses five through six: "Trust in the Lord with all thine heart; and lean not unto thine own understanding. In all thy ways acknowledge him, and he shall direct thy paths." I gave one last silent prayer, thanking God for guiding my ways.

The ball bounced, bounced again, then clattered its way down to number slots. The crowd, myself included, stopped breathing as the ball rattled into its final resting place.

"Double zero, green," the dealer announced. The crowd let out its breath, then looked at me as if I had just soiled myself. They took sips of their drinks and filed back to their tables and slot machines. Calling me names as they walked. Tough break, one said. With a face that said better luck next time, the dealer took my chips like a greedy raccoon.

I had no moves left. My credit cards were maxed. My bank account was empty. My cash was gone. My net worth was something like negative sixteen thousand dollars.

I wandered back to my room. Dazed and unsteady. I stripped out of my evening wear and took the hottest, longest shower I could. Room service brought me two lobster tails, crab legs, and a jumbo shrimp cocktail. The card on file with Treasure Island was maxed out, so everything from here on out was free. They would try to charge me at checkout, but how could they charge a card that's maxed out? After dinner I injected the last of my Fentanyl and let the drama dissolve. Money marooned me, the Lord stood me up, but Fentanyl was there for me.

The TV woke me up at around 4:00 a.m. A commercial for a show in the Bellagio. I needed to think. The Lord had abandoned me on the road to Jericho. He used my trust in him to reduce me to nothing. I had fallen among robbers and the Lord looked on with indifference. From here on out there would be no prayer. No more revelation. Only me. My success had to be mine and mine alone. Just like last time. If God doesn't want to help, He can go to Hell. I don't need his help.

My backpack had enough prescriptions to earn enough to get by once I made it to California. But it was getting there that I didn't know how to do. The Neon's gas tank was half empty — yes, half *empty*. Not half full, not full of both air and fuel, half empty. I'd probably need to fill up in Baker. My debit card might still work. I could overdraw my account. The gas station attendant would probably be a young tweaker, so maybe I'd be able to trade Vicodin for gas.

Room service brought me twenty bottles of water, two bottles of Cuvee Dom Perignon champagne, four club sandwiches in to-go boxes, a glass of orange juice, a glass of milk, and an All-American Breakfast with extra bacon and a side of buttermilk pancakes. After finishing my breakfast, I loaded the beverages and food into my backpack and duffle bag. The mini alcohol bottles from the mini fridge fit nicely into the outer pockets of my backpack. My bags were packed to maximum capacity. The bathroom toiletries bulged in my pockets.

This early there weren't many people in the hallways. It wasn't even 6:00 a.m. The lobby was empty, but the concierge was busy helping a family of early-bird tourists. I made it through the lobby and into the parking garage without incident. Bags loaded, I made my escape.

Sure enough, the gas station attendant in Baker was a tweaker and was happy to buy my Vicodin. She bought my entire supply, which gave me enough for a full tank and at least two more fill-ups down the road. Back on the highway I had plenty of time to think. With only the heat of the desert to distract me (the Neon's air conditioning was broken), my mind worked without hindrance.

For the next little while I would need to live out of my car. The repo man wouldn't take it because he wouldn't be able to find me. Even if he did, I'd be sitting in it and just drive away. My income would be opioid based. I had enough supply on me to get by until I could get into hospitals in LA and get new prescriptions. That would replenish my reserves and get me enough cash flow to find a place to stay. I couldn't call any friends because they couldn't see me like this. That, and I didn't have any friends left. I couldn't call my ex either, that would only end in rejection and more humiliation. I had enough alcohol, cigarettes, pills, and food to last me a few days. Hygiene wouldn't be a problem in such a short period of time, but if I absolutely needed to shower, I could use the public showers on the beach. The Baker tweaker gave me enough cash to keep this Neon on the road for several days, so transportation wasn't an issue. Worst case scenario, Caleb could probably wire me some money. I'd call him as soon as I got situated. He mentioned that he saved most of the money I gave them, and I don't think it would be asking too much to get a little of that back. It was mine in the first place, after all. The biggest problem in my immediate future was getting more Fentanyl. Crack-Hand Jack was the only way I could get it. Unless I could get cancer, I'd have to find another connection.

In Barstow I stopped and ate one of my club sandwiches. Say what you will about Treasure Island, they know how to make a club sandwich.

Soon I was passing through Rancho Cucamonga, then Pasadena, then, at last, Los Angeles. The mighty mecca of all that is worth being. The center of the center of the universe. The city that doesn't give a shit about you, but still gives you 75 degrees and sunny, daily. Royal palms, blue skies, and sandy beaches. A melting pot of smiling faces and diverse (and sometimes battling) races. A common enemy behind which the city can unite: traffic. The true land of opportunity, the real heart of America. A city with everything you want (for the right price). Try as the elements might, this city can't be burned down, smoked out, or quaked to ruins. A city with the perseverance of a cockroach.

I parked in a Rite Aid parking lot and sucked down another cigarette. Susie's networking classes came to mind. The trick to finding buyers is to find circles of smokers. The best place to find these circles is at AA and NA meetings, but those can be tough to find at first. The second best place is behind call centers. In either instance, the same principles apply. Call centers just had a lower success rate. But, the bigger the call center, the better the chances. With huge call centers, the workers are used to meeting new people every time they step out back to have a smoke. The big call centers also have a better variety of workers. Many of them are temp workers — people who have little incentive to stick around, and who are likely to have an addiction. Approach the circle and ask for a light. Smokers are always friendly. Smokers in the back of call centers are desperate to off-load stories of how shitty their work is. Listen attentively, nod along, then ask them what they do to manage all that stress. They'll laugh and say, "I appreciate the offer, but I've got my own hookups." You tell them you're not a weed dealer and laugh along with them. You say, "Nah, I'm just curious if you've got something better than me." Then you tell them a story about how you get headaches and went to see a doctor about it. You tell them that stress is a form of pain, and that painkillers like Lortab actually help a lot.

This is an important part of the pitch. If they have seen some bullshit CNN special about the danger of opioids and have a mom who is addicted, you'll probably lose them here. If not, they'll say something about one time they were prescribed with Lortab after surgery and it didn't do much for them. What they're really saying is they need more convincing.

"Well," you say, "you might be surprised. I'm not a pharmacist, so it's not like I benefit from any of this, but really, just swing into a hospital and tell them you have splitting headaches. They'll give you a prescription, guaranteed, and then your life improves dramatically."

"Ah, I'm not really into pills. Anyway, thanks for the tip," some will say as they walk away. But, a few a day will say, "Oh yeah? Hm. Got any on you?" And there's your next client.

Quite simple, really.

But I needed a few days off before getting to work. I hadn't seen the ocean in years. I was in Lincoln Heights, so I took highway 110 to the 10, got off on the 405, then took Venice boulevard straight out. I parallel parked like a seasoned professional and made my way through the tourists and performers. With shoes in hand, I stepped into the sand. The sun was setting, but the sand still had warmth from the day's cooking. The fine grains massaged and exfoliated my feet with each step. A cool breeze was blowing in from the ocean. It's salty mist a lovers kiss, welcoming me back from the abyss.

I stood on the packed sand that high tide had smoothed, cooled, and darkened and looked out across the Pacific. The sun was below the horizon and the sky was a display of oranges and reds—packed full of high-altitude fluffs, puffs, and whiffs catching the day's last light. The clouds carried the colors over the water reflecting the spectacle.

A child down the beach from me was yelling to her friends and pointing frantically, "Dolphins! See? Out by the pier!"

Slick gray backs and dorsal fins were rolling through the water. Not a dolphin or two, but an entire pod of cousins, uncles, aunts, grandparents, and children. There must have been over thirty dolphin backs breaching. They weren't in a hurry, just enjoying the evening. They were moving up along the beach. Soon they were swimming between me and the epicenter of the sunset and their fins were cutting through glimmering orange water. Occasionally one would jump and show its mischievous smiling face. I thought I heard it say something to me. Something like, "We knew you'd be back, you can check out for a year or two, but you can never leave."

How could I have been stupid enough to leave this paradise? California. The home of motherfucking Disneyland.

When the dolphins were tiny bobbing specs in the distance and the sky's oranges had turned to purples and dark blues, I made my way back to the boardwalk and sold a bottle of Dilaudid to the first local I saw. When filled, there were thirty pills in that bottle, the prescription cost me $13 to fill, and, after taking twelve for myself, the leftover eighteen sold for $40. Venice, it occurred to me, may be the best place to set up shop. Call centers may be the way to do it in shithole Montana, but in this tropical paradise there were droves of buyers sitting on Ocean Front Walk. No spiel necessary. Just spot the junkie (easy enough—it's all in the eyes), make an offer ("Need percs?" or "Waiting for Captain Cody?"), and negotiate ("Ten each." "Make it five player." "You know these go for twelve, how about nine?"

"Eight." "How many you need?" "Everything you got." "Cool, your total comes to $88, will you be paying with cash, card, or Venmo?"). Why these people didn't just go and get prescriptions of their own was beyond me. Why pay retail when wholesale prices are so easy to come by? Only the big ones were worth paying street prices for. Prescriptions for morphine or Fentanyl were unobtainable.

My new money bought me Enchiladas Del Mar and two borracho margaritas at La Cabaña. This Mexican restaurant on the corner of Rose and Lincoln is one of Venice's crown jewels. It's been here for more than fifty years and sometimes a mariachi band plays on the roof. My piping hot plate of cheesy tortillas filled with shrimp and crabmeat and surrounded by rice and shredded iceberg lettuce arrived just as I was finishing off my bowl of perfectly crisped chips and salsa. I dipped my last few chips into the healthy dollop of sour cream and guacamole that was on top of the lettuce. My first margarita arrived with the meal. Such friendly service. They boxed up what I couldn't finish and I let them keep the change. Blessed La Cabaña.

When you're living out of your car, spending a little extra on a nice meal is the equivalent of having wealth and taking a trip to Barbados. We all need vacations. Not that I am living out of my car, of course. I am between living arrangements, but I am by no means *homeless*. I'm a millionaire that's down on luck. A hiatus from my high place.

I drove around looking for a place to park overnight. Ideally the spot would have a view of the ocean. I missed waking up to that view. Maybe it was the margaritas, or the Vicodins I took at dinner, but my head grew heavy and my sight grew dim. I had to stop for the night curbside in front of a house on Frey Avenue. I made it. I'm finally back. I crack my windows, recline my seat, and fall asleep smiling.

22

Even in the tentacles of Hopelessness, California can ease your pain. Just lay on the sidewalk, any sidewalk, and take in the sun. If that doesn't cheer you up, you're past saving. I'm in the middle of one such concrete therapy session when I decide to leave the Dodge Neon behind. It served as reliable transportation and shelter for two months, until I was pulled over for driving on expired tags. The officer saw that in the past few weeks I had accumulated a handful of unpaid parking tickets and towed the Neon on the spot. He gave me instructions on how to get the car out of LAPD's impound lot then left me standing on the corner of 28th and Maple with my backpack, roller bag, and duffle bag. Overcome with anxiety, I spread myself out on the sidewalk and let the sun heal my wounds. If I saved up enough money to pay all those parking tickets and get the Neon out of the impound lot, I'd still have to get safety and emission inspections. And register it. That would be a hassle. My income was just enough to pay my phone bill and buy nourishment: opioids, alcohol, cigarettes, and food. Until I could earn more lottery money, the car would have to wait.

I call the few friends I thought I had left in LA, only to confirm that I do not, in fact, have any friends left. They all give excuses like, "Ah, you know I would love to have you stay with us for a little while, but we just don't have the room," or "Sorry Caish, I don't think my spouse would be comfortable with that."

The $104 in my wallet would be enough for a room tonight. From there I can plan my next move.

Google Maps shows me the nearest and cheapest room is at the Southlander Motel on the corner of 23rd and Central. The mile-long, twenty-minute walk winds me. This is the most physical activity I've suffered in years.

Southlander Motel's foyer is small, dingy, and styled to pay homage to Beetlejuice. The woman behind the desk puts her cigarette out as I walk in and looks up at me from her chair. Her skin has a severe Californian-sun-and-cigarettes wrinkle and is tanner than a water buffalo.

"Hi. Just you?" she croaks.

"Yeah."

"Rooms are fifty-six a night, ten-dollar deposit for the TV remote, you get that back when you check out and give me back my remote. Sign this." She slid a form toward me. "You stayed with us before?"

"No."

"K. Few rules. No hookers, male or female. Street walkers, curb crawlers, and lot lizards bring us too much drama. No drug dealin'. We keep an eye out, so don't. If you're gonna have anybody else in the room with you, you need to tell us. Rates go up for additional people. Don't smoke in the room. No refunds. Check out is at 11:00 a.m. Your room number is... let me check... six. So just park in the spot in front of six. Any questions?"

"Um, yeah. I know the rooms are fifty six a night, but could I do two nights for a hundred? I'm down on my luck and that's all I have left."

"No."

"What?"

"No. Two nights will cost you one twelve. Fifty-six a night is the price of a room. You're welcome to find somewhere else that charges fifty bucks a night, but I charge fifty-six."

"Alright, fine."

"Fine as in you're staying here for one night, or fine as in you're gonna look around?"

"I'll stay here, could I get the key?"

"After you pay."

I handed the grumpy wrinkly woman three twenty-dollar bills and she gave me the key to room six along with my change.

"And did you want the remote?"

"Nah, thanks though." I have planning to do. Plus, I have my laptop if I want to watch any porn. Which reminds me to ask, "And what's the wifi password?"

The room key is an old-fashioned toothed piece of metal. I even have to jimmy the knob. The room is styled like the reception area. If you were to look up "bland" on Wikipedia, you'd probably find a picture of this room. The walls are glossy off-white and void of any artwork. A simple shelf holds a microwave and an iron. Under that is an empty mini fridge. Above the shelf is a small flat screen TV. The queen-size bed takes up almost all of the room's floor space. It has a floral print comforter with a stain that hopefully came from a spilled enchilada. No closet, and the hanger rod doesn't have any hangers. The only furniture in addition to the bed is a folding chair in the corner. A folding chair.

The shower's hot water lasts less than ten minutes and never surpasses lukewarm. No complimentary shampoo or body wash, just a single bar of soap. The towels scratch me dry. Freshened up, I flop onto the bed, which is as comfortable as it is chic. After a nap I snack on trail mix and beef jerky, then take stock of what I have.

My duffle bag is big enough to live out of. It's a large leather Louis Vuitton bag with a shoulder strap, but I can also wear it like a backpack with my arms through the handles. I can fit a week's worth of underwear and socks as well as several changes of clothes, with enough room to spare for my laptop, charging cables, pill bottles, kit, toiletries, food, a couple water bottles, and pepper spray. My roller suitcase is full of clothes, shoes, and accessories that I can sell. I have two pairs of sunglasses that I can get a couple hundred bucks for. I can also sell my suitcase and backpack.

I post those on Craigslist low enough to sell quick. While I'm fielding texts about those sales, I plan out my next week. Without a car I can't get to as many hospitals and pharmacies to get my prescriptions. I can't lose that revenue stream. Without it I can't buy lottery tickets. Or food. Tomorrow I'll buy a bus pass. With the cash I get from selling my stuff I can get my prescriptions filled. Once I have a steady customer base I'll be able to rent a room somewhere. That will last me until I win the lottery again. Last time I did this it took me several months, so I can't expect to win any time soon. I'd have to weather a storm that could last months.

The first people to buy my stuff show up around 10:00 p.m. As soon as they leave, the craggy lady from the motel's front desk is knocking on my door telling me I had to leave.

"What did I say? No drug dealin'. Get your shit, you're out. No refunds."

"I'm not dealing drugs, I'm selling clothes and shoes."

"Oh come on hun, you think I was born yesterday? You think I haven't heard that before? That you just went ahead and opened up a cute little boutique outta my motel room?"

"No, really, look, check the room. There aren't any drugs, I'm not sellin' drugs." I step aside from the door and invite her in with a sweep of my arm.

She walks in and says, "Well I can tell ya right now, you've been smoking in here."

"Not true. It smelled like this when I walked in." Maybe I had smoked a couple cigarettes, but I had flushed my cigarette butts down the drain. Not a trace of my smoking in the room. Except maybe the smell. "Look wherever you'd like, I have nothing to hide. I'm not selling drugs."

She lit a cigarette and glanced around the room. She poked around then approached me and looked into my eyes as if trying to find a mosquito on a headlight. "Hmph. Well. Alright then. Sell your clothes. But if I find out that—"

She's interrupted by a knock at the door.

A valley girl is standing in the doorway with a puzzled look on her face. "Um, sorry, but is this where the Neiman Marcus suitcase is for sale?"

"Yup! Right here," I point to the bed. Without turning toward me to acknowledge her defeat, the craggy lady walks out the door and across the parking lot. Back to her lookout post behind the desk.

"So, like," Valley Girl says, "I know you posted it for fifteen hundred, but would you take fourteen?"

"Why?"

"Um, well, ya know, it's a little beat up and all."

"Hardly. It is exactly as described in the ad. Fifteen hundred is the price. It's been online for two hours, and I've already gotten tons of texts about it."

"Um. Alright well, here you go," she hands me fifteen stiff one hundred-dollar bills. Still in the originally sequenced order that they left the treasury in. Not a spore of cocaine in them. I count it. Then count it again. And again. Valley Girl said, "Is there a problem?"

"Oh, no. Sorry. You're good. You can take it. Thanks."

I help her lift the suitcase from the bed and ask her if she wants a matching backpack. No but thanks, she says. She rolled the suitcase out to her BMW M3 and put it in the back seat. Pfff, M3. People who drive those are the type that want everybody to think they're rich. M3s are poor people's sports car. Anybody with even a little bit of money would have a Porsche 911. Valley Girl thinks we all think she's the bee's knees. But we know. We know it's not *that* nice.

The fifteen hundred dollars in my hand feels right. I don't want to fold these beautiful bills. Putting creases in these would be like folding up a picture of a loved one. The picture should be framed and cherished, not folded up and stuffed into some dirty pocket. The texture of crisp money is familiar. The sequenced hundreds bring back memories of emptying ATMs into my back pocket. The smell of the newly-printed ink reminds me of paying cash for cars. Of long weekends abroad exchanging stacks of

Benjamins for euros, francs, renminbi, yen, or pounds. All with their own distinct smell. All with the unmistakable weight and sturdiness of currency. Money doesn't care where you're from or where you're going, power is a language spoken by every nation.

Around midnight I stop answering texts. I'm feeling alright. I have a plan and enough money to make it happen.

No more Fentanyl at the moment, so I have to settle for oxys. My administration kit's leather is cold to the touch. The oxys grind nicely and melt easily. With a little trouble finding a vein in my arm, I inject behind my knee. It feels like I'm stepping into a hot tub as the warmth works its way up my thighs, through my stomach, across my chest, up my neck, and around my brain. For the rest of the night I don't have any problems. I round off my high with several swigs of gin, then lay back on the bed.

A vacuum next door wakes me up around 9:30 a.m. the next morning. I freshen up and pack what clothes and shoes I have left into my backpack and duffle bag. I can't stay in this hole another night. I didn't sell enough last night for it to all fit into my two bags, so I borrow a garbage sack from the garbage can and fill it with designer clothes. I snack on beef jerky while I Google where to buy a bus pass and a room for rent.

The bus pass is easy enough. I can buy a week pass for $25, and I can buy them from a grocery store down the street.

The room is the hard part. There is plenty of space available downtown, but all of the apartments rent for more than $1,600 a month. There are single rooms available for less, but then I would need to have roommates. As that is my only option, I start calling on the single rooms. Since I'm new to begging a person to take my money so I can live in their shitty room, I was honest during the first couple of phone calls. When asked if I had any felonies or evictions, I said, sure, one of each. Steady income? Define steady. References? Mmm... the motel receptionist from Southlander Motel? And that would be the end of the conversation. Even when I got the swing of it, lying didn't seem to help, they all asked for my social security number and said they'd do a background check and get back to me. I don't anticipate hearing back from those ones.

The only places I have a chance at were halfway houses. Any addictions? Maybe. Steady income? Hardly. Stable, contributing member of society? I'm a huge contributor to relieving the pain of those around me. Great, swing by later today and we'll get you all set up.

I check out of the Southlander (taking the complimentary bar of soap with me, thank you very much) and walk north. Instead of going through the hassle of buying a monthly pass, I find a bus stop and pay per ride.

Buses are grimy places. Full of babbling beggars and hissing hipsters. I sit by the back door and try to get fresh air each time the bus stops. After a few exchanges I'm in the neighborhood of the halfway house that said they'd accept me.

When I finally find the place, I feel the tickle of Hopelessness on the back of my neck. The house is presentable, but the folks on the porch are downright frightening. Four people, three of whom are sitting on plastic yard chairs, the other one dangling her legs off the railing-less porch. I can smell their cheap tobacco from the sidewalk. Their clothes are threadbare thrift store donations. The two men haven't shaved in days, and the two women haven't ever brushed their teeth (I could tell from the sidewalk!), or brushed their hair. But, they were smiling. It was, after all, Southern California.

"Is this the Hope's Haven House?" I ask from the sidewalk, half hoping that I'm on the wrong street.

"Ah! Ya got us! Hahaha, yup! Triple H, here it is. The Merry-Go-House."

"I called earlier about a room, is the landlord here?"

"You're talkin' to her, you Cash?" The skeleton-thin woman that was dangling her legs off the porch hops down and walks across the grassless yard with her hand outstretched. "I'm Kay, the one you talked to on the phone." Her hand is sticky and makes mine smell like cheap tobacco. "My full name is Kay-Lynn LaShay Reeves, but y'all can call me Kay. Not so much a street name, just kind of an easier way a gettin' my attention." I looked behind me to see if more people had joined me to merit the "y'all," but I was still standing alone on the sidewalk. Should I just walk away? This is no place for a millionaire. "Why don't ya come on in and let's get ya a room. We have two rooms available, the choice is yours! Although we ain't no Chuck-o-Rama, hahaha."

I sign a few forms and give Kay my one thousand-dollar deposit. She tells me the terms of my lease, which, for the good of us both, she says, is month to month. Rent of $720 is due on the fifth of every month. The toilet and shower are at the end of the hall; everybody in your hallway shares that bathroom, so don't go settin' up your toothbrush and leavin' towels in there. The shared kitchen is right over there. We're happy to have you. Welcome home. Hope's Haven House has these programs and those programs, and here is a brochure with those and some other clinics. Here are phone numbers you can call, these ones are the emergency numbers. Here are local employers we work with. Here is this and here is that.

Eventually I make it to my room. It's on the second level, last door on the left. The door has been painted so many times it looks more like plaster than wood. Like Kay said, the door sticks, so I have to bump it open with my shoulder. The sight of my new living quarters uppercuts me with a reminder of my current worth.

The ceiling is within arm's reach, no tip-toe required. The carpet is worn through with cigarette burns aplenty. The decades-old wallpaper is a smoke-stained beige and is peeling near the ceiling. A stained full-size mattress on a cot in the corner takes up a quarter of the room's living space. Folded sheets and a wool blanket are piled on top of a pillow at the foot of the bed. Kitty-corner to the bed is a small desk and chair combo—the kind like in high school where the chair is connected to the desk. The surface of the desk is carved into a relief of crooked lines, profanities, and gang names. A grease-caked hot plate sits on top of a mini fridge next to the desk. Probably no alcohol in the mini fridge. I check just in case. Nope, no alcohol. Just food residue, mold, and an expired jar of pickles. A chest of drawers next to the door is the only other piece of furniture in the room. It's missing a front leg, so it wobbles like an uneven restaurant table. There is a window above the bed with a clear view of the house next door's roof. Not even Spanish tiles—taupe asphalt shingles.

I set my duffle bag and garbage sack next to the bed and slump down next to them. I roll onto my side and bring my knees to my chest. My anguish wells up into tears. At first I try to control myself, fighting back tears and looking on the bright side, but I give that up without a choice. As I have now reached rock bottom, my emotions are taking control. Prayer and reason have failed me; my gut is all I have left. And right now my gut wants to air some grievances. It feels good to cry. Like it's something I need to do. A tension that I need to recognize. When the storm runs its course, I feel cleansed of some of the sadness of my situation. I dry my face on the bottom of my shirt and sit on the edge of the bed. I need a shower.

The shower is more complex than its three knobs would suggest, and the hottest the water gets is tepid. The pressure is comparable to getting peed on by a few people. Without warning the pressure and temperature drop and leave me freezing, then gradually return to their dismal levels. In less than ten minutes the water is running cold. Only after I shut off the water and pull back the curtain do I realize that I don't have a towel.

I use my shirt to dry off, then put it on along with the rest of my clothes and walk across the hall to my room. Back in my room, I hang my shirt off the corner of the desk and lay on the bed. I know there are probably bed bugs chewing up my back, but they're probably in the floor too, so what choice do I have?

I light a cigarette and listen to the sounds of the Hope's Haven House. Somebody is watching Judge Judy at full volume. My neighbor across the hall is yelling at somebody she hates, or loves. Yelling her voice box to shreds. I open my window to let the smoke out and feel California's warm breath on my face. We aren't far from the 101. The sound of traffic drones out my neighbors. I hear a small crowd talking on the porch. I can't make out their words, but I hear their voices get excited, then quiet, then fits of laughter followed by excited follow-up that builds the laughter into unconstrained whoops and hollers. Sounds like some real comedians down there. I envy their laughter, but refuse to join them. It has been said that you're only as good as the company you keep. The birds of my feather are millionaires and change makers, not the talkative slothful residents of halfway houses. Plus, they probably didn't have any money to buy my painkillers, so there was no reason to talk to them.

But they sounded cheerful. Maybe tomorrow morning I'd say hi. Maybe one or two of them were like me, hustlers down on their luck.

My clothes would fit into four of the drawers, but I keep everything in my duffle bag. I might need to leave at a moment's notice. Plus, if I left anything in my room, these people would probably steal it. I have to keep everything I own on me at all times. Especially my pills.

I wake up from my nap after the sunset. Hunger roused me. Until I could sell the clothes that wouldn't fit into my duffle bag, I didn't want to leave. Walking around town with a duffle bag is bad enough, and adding a garbage sack full of clothes would make it look like I was homeless. I couldn't leave them because they were worth a few hundred dollars. Texts are still trickling in from my online postings, so I stay put until I can off-load the clothes that won't fit into my duffle bag.

Rifling through my bag I find two Snickers bars and a can of tuna. Tonight's dinner. One of the Snickers is the first course. The second course, the tuna, is sealed inside a can, and I don't have a can opener. Tomorrow I'll buy a pocket knife with a can opener on it. Living at rock bottom, you need a pocket knife. For now, I have to use the can opener down in the kitchen. Which means I will need to leave the relative safety of this tiny dark room (two of the three lightbulbs are out). I put my laptop under the mattress and deadbolt the door on my way out.

The hallway is as poorly lit as the room. The other seven rooms on this floor are filling the hallway with blaring TV noises and smoke smells. The last door I pass before getting to the top of the stairs is opened a few inches. Loud music is playing. As I pass, I glance in (as you do). An old shirtless man is sitting on his bed, back against the wall, eyes closed, toothless mouth open, head tilted back. Another shirtless man is bent over the old man's lap. Head bobbing.

Why hasn't anyone invented one of those memory wipers from Men in Black? There needs to be a way to scrub stains from the brain. And why do our brains play repulsive memories on a loop? I consider wiping the image from my mind with a swan dive down the stairs, but decide against it and make my way to the kitchen.

By the tender mercy of the Lord, nobody is in the kitchen when I arrive. The communal can opener is easy enough to find and doesn't look like it will give me tetanus. With the can opened and drained, I walk back upstairs, keeping my head down and eyes averted. Safely back in the room, I bolt the door. I eat the tuna with my fingers and without any mayonnaise. I also have some trail mix and a granola bar on the side. The third and final course of my meal is the second Snickers.

My Netflix, Hulu, Prime, and HBO subscriptions expired months ago, so I was left to browsing Facebook for entertainment.

Everybody I know is living better than me. I don't know anybody in the rung of life I now find myself in. The friends I used to have are still living in mansions and driving sports cars. Kelsey is still having yacht parties, the Malibu Ferrari Club is still having sushi at Nobu, and Riley is still updating Facebook with pictures from expensive clubs and the passenger seats of exotic cars. Their luck has been better than mine. God is not giving them trials. But I'm better for it. That's the thing about these hard times, they build character. My story will be all the more remarkable when I make it out of this. Despite all the ill fortune in the world, I rise above it. I need to find a publishing agent and get this stuff into a book. Maybe it will even be made into a movie. Which of Hollywood's A-Listers would play me in the movie of my life? Would I have a cameo in the movie? Do they use real cocaine in movies? How much in royalties will I make?

The noises in and around this halfway house make sleep nearly impossible. I play the Eagles on my laptop next to the bed and focus on the music. After a few hours of tossing and turning I must have drifted off.

23

I can't stay here. Hope's Halfway House, or, the Merry-Go-House, as the residents call it, is sapping my ambition. Most mornings I walk to the gas station to buy breakfast and a lottery ticket. When I get back to the house, Maria and Ron are relaxing on the porch, smoking home-rolled cigarettes. One morning they asked me where I came from, and we spent the next three hours exchanging stories about our mothers. We watched palm tree shadows make their leisurely voyage across the porch. Kay joined us at noon with a pitcher of Kool-Aid and asked about Ron's surfboard. I walk to the same gas station at one or two and buy lunch (usually jalapeño and cream cheese taquitos with a coke). In the afternoons I try to get work done. There are four pharmacies within walking distance of the halfway house, and I have enough prescriptions to keep me busy. One of the tenants, Camila, became a regular client, but she can't afford much. I have to roam the streets and solicit to make enough for alcohol, cigarettes, pills, rent, and food. Kay says that the terms of the lease forbid me from bringing alcohol and "drugs" into the house, so I have to buy small bottles and sneak them in. This house must be one of the only places on earth to forbid prescription painkillers. Kay keeps an eye on me.

The morning conversations on the porch turn into all-day conversations. In a matter of days I knew all the tenants. Turns out they aren't so bad. Sure, Lenny likes prostitutes, Ted is a drunkard, Camila is a tweaker, Ron is a burnout, Maria is a manic depressive, JJ's brain is permanently fried, and Diego's brain never worked well to begin with, but these people were good company. We all have our weaknesses.

Out on the porch steps, California's sun could work its soothing magic and dispel any of the soul's melancholy. The porch became a therapeutic escape from dwelling on my dreadful situation. The pulverizing grip and piercing bite of Hopelessness was kept at bay by relaxing conversations with the nearly homeless.

I'm relaxing in a hammock that I bought yesterday after I sold the last of my designer clothes. The porch is big enough for a couple hammocks and a few lawn chairs. The stairs leading up to the porch serve as overflow seating. The sun is setting and the thermometer in the door jamb says it's eighty-one degrees. I've got a pack of cigarettes and a coke within arm's reach. A freshly lit Marlboro is pinched between my lips.

Ted is telling a story about his brother, Tino.

"So anyway, Tino's kid—I ain't remember the kid's name, he's like a ten year old—Tino's kid come runnin' into his room at like ten o'clock at night, right? And Tino's drillin' his girl—doggy style, I think, haha—so he yells at the kid to get lost. Haha, well the kid, says, 'Dad, I just heard the doggy door open, but Ralf'—that's their dog's name, he's a huge bullmastiff and his doggy door is big enough for a full grown robber to crawl through—'Ralf,' the kid says, 'was sittin' on the couch next to me.' So Tino says 'k, I'll deal with it, wait outside the door,' and finishes fuckin' his girl! Hahaha, took him like two or three minutes. Haha and he does this knowin' that a robber might be in his spot. And Tino's got his son and a daughter livin' with him, right? So after Tino blows his load he pulls on some clothes. He tells the philly to stay in the bed and pulls his shotgun out of the closet.

"Well, for reasons I ain't been able to figure out, Tino always dry fires his shot gun to make double sure it ain't loaded. Points it at the ground and dry fires it. He just plans on scarin' the intruder, not blowin' his head off. Seems strange to me that you'd have a shotgun and not use it like God intended it to be used."

"Right," JJ cut in, "I saw on 60 Minutes once that if you're gonna point a gun at somebody you gotta be ready to use it. Or that you gotta use it. Yeah, that you only point a gun at somebody if you're surely gonna shoot 'em."

"Cops say that too," Maria adds.

"Yeah, I dunno," Ted says, "but either way it's just somethin' he does. So, hahah, oh God, so he cocks his shotgun, steps out into the hall, and pulls the trigger. BLAM! Hahaha, I kid you not, he fuckin' shot straight through the ceiling! Hahaha, he had left it loaded from the last time he went skeet shooting. Didn't even check the chamber before pulling the trigger!"

At this point we're all rocking in laughter. Ted's story is funny enough, but when he yelled "BLAM!" JJ jumped so high he almost fell off the stairs. Then he had Sprite coming out of his nose from laughing so hard.

"Hahaha, second time that night he blew his load! Haha, but that ain't it, that ain't it," Ted insists. "So he looks up at this hole he just blasted in his ceiling and realizes he's right under his daughter's room. So he drops the gun and runs up the stairs. Not even thinkin'. At this point his dog is losin' its shit. Just barkin' up a goddamn storm. Loud, big barks too. I mean this thing is huge. So, he gets upstairs and sees that he missed his daughter by several feet, but she's ballin', of course, ya know she's like only four or five years old. Tino picks her up and he's sayin' like, 'Hey, hey, it's okay, calm down, it was just a bang is all,' and he's lookin' around at the damage he's caused to his place, right? And he's thinkin', damn, I'ma get evicted *for sure*. Haha, well, he looks through the hole in the floor and can see down into the hallway where he fired from. But he ain't see no shotgun! It's gone! And keep in mind, his son just told him that somebody broke into the house. So he takes his daughter into the bathroom and lays her in the tub, tells her to stay put, and—"

"Puts her in the tub?" Ron asks.

"Yeah, they're metal," Ted says.

"Oh, in case he shoots at her again? Hahaha."

"Haha, yeah, or in case anybody else starts shootin'."

Camila adds, "Ya know, they say to get into your bathtub if there is a tornado or somethin' like that."

"Camila, damn," Ron says. "When was the last time you saw a fuckin' tornado in Los Angeles."

"Well, I was just givin' an example. Tornados, earthquakes, forest fires. Ya know, whatever catastrophe is goin' on, they say you're supposed to get in the bathtub. 'Cause it's metal."

"So what are we supposed to do?" JJ asks after realizing that we only have half-baths with showers in the Merry-Go-House.

"We fend for ourselves, like we always been doin'," Ron answers.

"Don't matter," Ted says, "anyways, puts his daughter in the tub and tells her to stay put. Then starts creepin' down the stairs to see where his son is. When he gets to the bottom of the stairs he hears some rustling in his kitchen. And that's where the dog door is. The dog is still barkin' somethin' fierce in the living room, which is next to the kitchen, so Tino's thinkin' that the dog's probably got the robber pinned to a corner or somthin', just waitin' for backup. Tino makes his way down the hall, cautiously and all, ya know, and peaks around the corner into the living room. And... BLAM!"

JJ jumps back and hits his head on one of the porch pillars. Glowing ash falls from his cigarette and onto his shirt.

"Hahah, fuckin' wall next to him explodes and he falls to the ground. BLAM! Again! This time the floor in front of his face explodes like a land mine just went off. Then there's the sound of a different gun goin' off, fuckin' POW, POW, POW, POW, POW! He's gettin' showered in drywall and paint and glass and all sorts of shit. BLAM! A third time! He manages to slide back behind the wall in his hallway and crawls out the front door. His ears are ringin' and he can't see shit because he got drywall and dust in his eyes."

"Wait," Camila asks, "he's just leavin' his family in the house with the robber?"

"Ha, well, no. He's just tryina collect himself. I mean the guy was just takin' heavy fire, ya know? Can't help his family much if he's pumped full of birdshot. So he crawls out onto his porch and is immediately tackled to the ground. His face is shoved into his porch so hard he gets a black eye. He arm is bent back around his back and he's got like three guys sittin' on him. They're yellin' shit at him but he can't hear anything because of the shotgun blasts. Haha, ears are still ringin'. They cuff him— so now he's realizin' these must be cops, probably called by his neighbors—and they drag him off his porch, down his stairs, and out to his sidewalk, then just drop him there. Right on his face. Tino fuckin' loses two teeth on the sidewalk right then.

"So, what had happened was, his philly panicked when Tino shot through the hallway ceiling. She didn't know it was him that was shooting because he pulled the door shut behind him. Well she rolled off the bed and grabbed a 9mm revolver that Tino keeps under his mattress. She curled up in the corner of the room and had the revolver trained on the door. Well Tino's room is right next to the kitchen and the living room, so she's right in the middle of all this chaos. When the second shotgun blast ripped through the corner of the wall Tino was peeks around, that blasted right through the room Tino's girl was crouched in. So she panicked and emptied the revolver into the wall! Hahaha, just fuckin' opened fire into the wall that Tino was standing on the other side of. POW, POW, POW, POW, POW! If he wouldn'ta hit the deck he'd a been Swiss cheese! Hahaha! So, oh God, hahaha, so the police storm the place in full SWAT gear. They kick down Tino's bedroom door and almost smoke his girl because she's pointing this empty revolver at them. How she didn't get smoked, I just do not know."

"Was she white?" JJ asks.

"Um, yeah, Tino's got a Colombian girl... but I don't think... actually, yeah, that's probably it, now that you mention it. She's pretty light skinned."

"So wait, what about the kids?" Camila asks.

"Jesus, hold on, the story ain't over," Ted says. He had paused to replace his cigarette. "So SWAT goes into the livin' room after Tino's room and find a loudass barking dog and the ten-year-old kid hidin' behind him. And next to the ten year old? Hahah, the fuckin' shotgun! The kid was in the livin' room when Tino shot through the ceiling and looked around the corner when he heard footsteps running upstairs. He saw the shotgun on the ground and brought it back to the couch to protect himself. When Tino came back downstairs, the kid didn't recognize him because he was covered in dust from the first shot he fired into the ceiling. So the kid just opened fire. Hahaha, just about blew his pops to high heaven! Ahahaha!"

"So, did they catch the robber?" I ask.

"Oh! Haha, yeah, ha, that's the best part. So they comb the bullet-ridden house lookin' for the culprit that started this whole mess, and they ain't seein' nobody. They all scratchin' they heads thinkin' the kid made it all up when, I kid you not, one of the officers pulls a racoon out of the sink! Ahahaha!"

"Wait, what?" Ron asks.

"A racoon, ya know?"

"Yeah, I know what a racoon is, but why was a racoon in the sink?"

"Because, Ron," Camila answers, "the racoon was what went through the doggy door. The kid just heard the door flap but didn't see that it was just a racoon that came in."

"Ooooooohhh, ahaha. Oh man, that is good, hahaha." Ron holds his sides and bounces up and down when he laughs. It looks cartoonish. "So did they arrest him?"

"Ha! The racoon?" Ted asks.

Everybody on the porch is beside themselves in uncontrollable laughter. Camila accidentally spits her cigarette out, Diego spills his Kool-Aid, JJ is back to sneezing Sprite and sliding down the stairs. Kay comes out after a few minutes to make sure everything is okay (she lives in the house with us). Soon she's laughing too and she doesn't even know why. The whole scene is probably enough to send anybody watching into fits of laughter. The laughter dies out after a few resurgences, then Ted ties up the loose end.

"No, no Ron, they didn't arrest the racoon or anybody else. In fact, Tino sued the city for $250,000 for police brutality."

Diego then tells a story about a hunting trip gone awry, and Camila follows it with one about her sister accidently shooting herself in the face with mace. Then we get into a philosophical discussion about gun control.

At the end of the night Kay tells us we better get to bed. Some of the tenants call her "mom." She tells us that she doesn't want to get any noise complaints, so "let's hit the sack."

When I latch the deadbolt and turn around to the room I'm staying in, it's as if Hopelessness itself is sitting on the mattress. "Quite the night you had out there," I thought it said, "welcome back to the room that you live in. To the life that you're leading. To the mess you've made. So, I guess this is you now, huh?"

"This ain't me," I mumble to myself.

"Ain't? Boy, really getting cozy with the locals for not being you. Either way, sure seems like you're you, but maybe it's worse than that." Hopelessness sighs.

"I'm wealthy and influential. Bad luck doesn't change a person."

"But does good luck?"

"Everything I've accomplished has been the result of hard work, luck is just opportunity meeting preparation. I prepared myself and created the opportunity. I'm doing the same now. Wait and see."

"I *will* wait. And I *will* see."

I put on headphones and turn up the volume loud enough to where I can't hear myself think. My thoughts were turning toxic, I had to drown them out.

I make the first month's rent, barely. Month two I'm twenty dollars short, but Kay lets it slide on account of my good behavior. Humiliated, I apply for a few odd jobs within walking distance of the Merry-Go-House, but they won't hire a convicted felon. An industrial linen cleaning company gave me a job, but I fail the first two random drug tests and miss a day of work, so they fire me. The California Employment Development Department denies my claim for unemployment. I have enough pills to make half of rent, but I have to sell my laptop to cover the other half. I hardly have enough for cigarettes.

Most the tenants at the Merry-Go-House have their bills paid by the government. They get Supplemental Security Income on account of their age or some mental or physical disability that "prevents them from working." That's what I need to get into. They always have enough to pay rent, buy tobacco and food, and have enough left over to buy a few lottery tickets. I ask JJ to put me in touch with whoever it is in the government that provides the benefits. JJ has no idea what I'm talking about. So I ask Kay.

Kay lets me use her computer and shows me how to apply online. Since I'm not over 65 or blind, I will have to have a "disability." My bad back will probably count. The other requirements are easy to meet: little to no income and few resources, value of the things owned less than $2,000, and citizenship. I should be a shoo-in. The paperwork seems endless. I'm in Kay's office for a few hours a day clicking through forms and answering questions. After I finish, a week later I get an email confirming receipt of my application, and am told that the application process may take up to six months. Six months. For money I needed now. I call the number included in the email (for my "local Social Security Office") and tell them that I need my money now. They tell me they understand, and transfer me to the county social security agency, which they say is in a better position to provide immediate assistance.

The county social security agency tells me they understand.

For the most immediate assistance, all I need to do is come down to their office with my birth certificate or social security card, documentation of my medical condition (including names of doctors, hospitals, and clinics, results of medical tests, and proof of how the condition affects my daily life), documentation of my income (including a list of the types of jobs I've had over the past fifteen years and copies of tax records or W-2 forms), and documentation of my assets (must include bank statements). Kay helped me get as much of this together as we could find online and in my email inbox. All we can come up with is my dismal bank statement. Severely overdrawn. I also have my social security card and prescriptions. With that documentation, Kay gives me a ride to the county social security agency.

The agency is in a nice building, relative to other government buildings. But it still looks, smells, and sounds like the DMV. I tell Kay I'll call her when I'm done. I take a number and wait. They make me wait for a DMV amount of time, then call my number. I'm led to a desk with a plate-glass partition and am asked for my name and documentation. I slide my documents through a slot in the bottom of the window, and tell the social worker (I assume that's what she is) that I already filled out an online application, but that I was told to come here for emergency assistance. She nods without taking her sleepy eyes from her computer. She asks me for the rest of my documentation, and I tell her that's everything I have.

She asks me to wait one second and walks away. Many, many seconds later, she returns with pamphlets in her hands. She explains to me that since I am able to work, I will not receive any emergency assistance, but that my application for SSI benefits is still being reviewed (look for a letter in three to six months). I stop her right there and tell her that I am unable to work. My back, I say. She nods and looks down at the booklets in her hands. These are other ways you can receive assistance. CalFresh (like food stamps) and Medi-Cal (this can help you with your medical expenses). Additionally, she continues, here is information on food kitchens in your area, and shelters if you need somewhere to stay.

Shelters? I ask the government to help me out, just a little bit, and they give me booklets on *shelters* in my area? I tell the social worker I'm not standing for this bullshit and she tells me I'll need to lower my voice or be removed by security. I tell her she's a terrible, heartless social worker and that I just need some help. Just a thousand a month. That's all I need. Just give me a thousand a month.

A tall gentleman in black clothing is then standing next to me. He looks down at me and says it's time to go. I protest by staying seated, and he wraps his iron hand around my upper arm and lifts me out of my chair. With his other hand he picks up the booklets and my documentation that the social worker slid under the partition. He walks me out of the building and hands me my papers. He smiles the whole time. Like he lives for hurting people who need help. Sadist.

Kay picks me up and apologizes for being late. She's sad to hear things didn't go well in there. Probably because it means that I might miss rent soon, and then she'll be making less money. I ask her to stop by the gas station on the way home so I can buy a lottery ticket and cigarettes. I'm practically begging God to just give me a break, maybe another $5,000 win. Something small is better than nothing. But, please, God, let this ticket be a winner.

We get back to the Merry-Go-House and brainstorm. Kay suggests I apply for Section 8 help. Maybe I can get some money for rent, she says.

I apply, but the state wants me to submit tax information that I don't have. I haven't filed taxes since I fired my accountant years ago. Very few people have paid more taxes than me. I can't believe California or the federal government has the gall to ask for more. Are they not content with the tens of millions I've paid them? The system is broken when, after millions of dollars paid in taxes, the government won't help out because I owe them a few hundred thousand. They are just looking for ways not to help. The whole goddamn system is set up to screw you if you're down on your luck.

At the end of month three, I'm three hundred dollars short on rent. I had another seventy-six dollars, but needed that for living essentials. Kay said it would buy me to the end of the month, but then I would need to leave unless I could come up with the rest.

When the sun is up, all is well. I relax on the porch, smoke cigarettes, and tell stories. I've even picked up the way these people talk. I know when to say, "Okay," "Yuuup," "Right?," and "Nah, he/she said/did what?" The palm trees don't go anywhere, and you can count on the sun to keep on rising. At least we have the weather.

But when the sun goes down and we stub our cigarettes on the porch and go back to our rooms, Hopelessness is always waiting for me. I'm alone and defenseless. I don't fight it anymore. Sometimes I don't even cry. We don't talk. I walk into its damp dark lair, let its clawed tentacles wrap me, squeeze me, then crush me. It's black, I can't see a thing; not forward or backward. But I feel. My rib cage collapses under the pressure. Lungs deflate. Hopelessness hisses that there will be no relief, no reprieve. Money will not come to the rescue. Money has abandoned me for good this time. Money has better things to do, better friends to be with, better lovers to fuck. The grip tightens. Money doesn't even remember you. You're nothing. Breathing becomes difficult. Smoke burns my sinuses. Hell's smoke.

Wait, that actually is smoke.

I remove my headphones. The smoke alarms in the hallway are wailing. I sit up and look around. The room has a cloud of smoke in it, swirling around the ceiling. Puffs of yellow smoke seep in from the cracks around the door. I hear yelling down the hall. The room feels like a sauna. I open the window and take a breath of the outside air. Cool wind blows in from outside but the smoke in the room grows thicker. I grab my duffle bag and stuff in what I can grab. I was wise enough never to unpack, but I had a few things. I pull on my shoes and wrap myself in the wool blanket from my cot. The power goes out and I see the glow of fire from under the door. I'm coughing bad despite decades of practice inhaling smoke. I tie a shirt around my face and stay low. The smoke is getting thicker. Sirens in the distance. People are yelling things outside.

In elementary school they told us to check the temperature of the door knob before opening a door in a burning building. The doorknob is hot, but not scalding. I unbolt the deadbolt and turn the knob, which is harder than usual to turn. As soon as the latch clears the strike plate, a freight train of heat and smoke blows open the door and knocks me onto my back. A spinning column of flames leans into the room and spreads out across the ceiling. The flames reach for the window. The heat is unbearable. Like a waterfall's roar the fire drowns out all other sound. Cracks, pops, and hisses snap out of the rushing sound of the flames. It feels like my skin is on fire and my eyes are melting.

I roll over onto my stomach and army crawl to the window. I'm dizzy and my cough is incapacitating. I can't move. The window isn't far away (the whole room is only a few square feet), but I'm caught in the cloak of smoke. Blinded and suffocated. The carpet is like lava. Finally I'm at the window and leaning out, filling my lungs with cool fresh air. I have to jump. Maybe I can make it to the next house's roof. I have to try. It's either get a few broken bones or become spent carbon along with the rest of this place. I pull myself up and get my knee up on the window sill.

From behind I'm lifted by my armpits and thrown over a shoulder. A firefighter yells something to me and puts the wool blanket over my back. My stomach is bent over the firefighter's shoulder. He spins around and marches me through a flaming doorway and into the smoke-filled hallway. I can't stop coughing.

At the end of the hall he turns hard to go down the stairs and my head bangs against his oxygen tank. He bounces down the stairs and knocks the rest of the wind out of me.

The outside air is cold in my lungs. I'm dropped onto a waiting stretcher and an EMT straps an oxygen mask to my face. Other things are strapped or clamped to me as I'm rolled down the driveway and into the back of a waiting ambulance.

24

The hospital releases me the next morning. My blood-oxygen levels have returned to normal, and they're confident that the smoke didn't cause any permanent damage to my lungs. My foot was burned at some point, but they've treated that and given me another Vicodin prescription for the pain.

I am released into the care of the Red Cross. A rec center gymnasium has been converted into a shelter for the tenants of the Merry-Go-House for the next five days. We are given a cot, a blanket, access to second-hand clothes, and three warm meals a day.

Kay tells us that the fire started on the first floor in one of the back rooms, what would have been the room across the hall from mine if we were on the same floor. That's where Tyrone lived. Tyrone had always been an angry person. He was one of the tenants who were forced to live in a halfway house by court order, and he had more restrictions than those of us staying there by choice. Ankle monitor and all that. On the night of the fire, Kay had told him that his parents were short on rent this month, and that he would not be able to stay unless he made good on the rent. If he couldn't stay at the halfway house, he'd have to go back to county lockup.

So, as Kay should have expected, Tyrone acted out. He used his last forty-five dollars to buy a five gallon gas jug and five gallons of diesel fuel. He returned to his room after the rest of us had gone to bed. He soaked his bedding and mattress in fuel, and poured the rest of the jug all over his carpet and walls. Then, tapping into his inner lunatic, he lit a cigarette, dragged the mattress down the hall, leaned it up against the door to Kay's room, and dropped his cigarette on it. He then returned to his room, threw his bedding into the hall in front of his door, lit that on fire, then shut his door and ignited his room.

Since Kay was on the first floor, she climbed out her window easy enough and called 911. By the time the fire department arrived, everybody was accounted for except for me, Tyrone, Ron, and Maria. Maria lived in the room across from me, the one directly above Tyrone. She had climbed out her window and jumped to the ground, her pant leg caught a screw in the window seal and she swung around heels over head. She fell straight onto her face on the driveway below. Paramedics say she died on impact. That, or laid there on the cement with a cracked skull and writhed in pain for nearly twenty minutes then died from catastrophic hemorrhaging. Nobody saw her until the firefighters arrived.

Ron slept through the whole thing. His room was near the front of the building on the second story and he had a habit of sleeping under his bed (paranoid, I think). Firefighters kicked open his door, didn't see anybody in the room, and figured he had run off. Ron woke up the next morning soaked in water from the firefighter's hoses and wandered out onto the street, asking why firefighters were showering the house.

Firefighters found Tyrone's body curled up against his window, charred like a hotdog microwaved for a half an hour. Apparently his window was jammed.

Anyway, Kay told us, we need to find somewhere else to stay. The county authorities deemed what was left of the house uninhabitable and condemned it. The Red Cross has phones we can use to call family and friends. We can keep the blankets and clothes they give us. I asked, "What about those of us without family and friends?" She told about shelters in the area if we were unable to find a place to stay. Good Shepherd Center, PATH, The Midnight Mission, Union Rescue Mission, Weingart Center, and more. The Red Cross has brochures with contact information for each one.

Everything I owned, including my phone and scrip slips, was lost in the fire. My only possessions were the scratchy clothes given to me from the Red Cross, my Vicodin prescription, six Vicodin the hospital had given me, and the wool blanket I was sitting on.

How would the FBI get ahold of me if they tracked down my money? How was I going to build a client base and pharmaceutical operation? Stay in a shelter? A *homeless* shelter? Nope. Couldn't do it. Can't. I have Caleb's number memorized, so I use a Red Cross phone to call him.

"Hello?"

"Hey, it's me, Caish."

"What do you need, Caish?"

"Well, the house I was staying in just burned down, and I don't have anything. I was wondering if you could help me out."

The line was silent long enough to make me nervous, then Caleb asked, "Your house burned down?"

"Well, it wasn't my house, but yeah, the place I was staying."

"Mhm." He didn't sound convinced.

"No, seriously, Google it. The Hope's Haven House. The LA Times ran an article on it. Two people died. I was carried out of my room on the shoulder of a firefighter. I'm not kiddin' around. Everything I owned was lost in the fire."

"Hm. Well. Here's the thing, Caish. Toni is in a rehab clinic. We've had to dip into our savings to pay for that. We don't really have much we can spare."

He couldn't be serious. I gave them that money. That was mine, and I helped them. Now they wouldn't help me, with my own money? "What do you mean?"

"I mean I won't wire you money. Especially since you'd just use it for heroin."

"I wouldn't use it for heroin."

"Then you'd use it for rent and use the money you saved on rent for heroin. Either way I'm buying you junk."

"Caleb, I don't have any money. You can't give me back even a little bit of the millions of dollars I gave you?"

"Sorry, Caish. I can't help you."

That fucking selfish bastard. "Can I at least stay with you guys until I get back on track?"

"Stay with us? Caish, no. Toni overdosed on Fentanyl and almost died because of you, and now you want to live with us? No. Absolutely not."

"You fucking selfish bast—"

"Don't ever call me again, Caish." He hung up. Just like that. Left me, the one who had given him over a *million* dollars, out to dry. Out to die. People are so selfish.

Fuck. I have to call my ex. The last human I know. The house I bought my son and ex has two guest rooms, and right now I need one. Luckily, that's another number I have memorized.

"Hello?"

"Hey, it's me, Caish, don't hang up. Don't hang up!"

"What do you want?"

"I need to come stay with you and Mark for a few days, the place I was staying in just burned down and—"

The line went dead. I call back, two rings, call ended. I call again and it goes straight to voicemail. What more could I have done for these people? I gave them more than they could ever obtain on their own. More money than they should be able to spend in their lifetimes. And now that I need a little bit of help, just a place to stay, for Christ sakes, they turned their back on me. Heartless, black-souled, empty conscious, selfish motherfuckers.

When the Red Cross kicks us out four days later, I walk straight to the Downtown Disciples Mission. A Catholic shelter. A Catholic *homeless* shelter. Because I guess that's what I am now. My burned foot is in excruciating pain, but I don't take the Vicodin because that's the only way I can make any money. The government and everybody I know has abandoned me, so I have to crawl out of this hole without any help. Which I will. I'll bounce back. I'll overcome this. My grandpa used to say, "Keep your head up, it's darkest before dawn. When things seem at their worst and darkest, the sun will rise and everything will work out." Probably an easy platitude to believe when you're living a middle-class life in Missoula, Montana. His darkest pre-dawn was probably a toothache.

By the time I hobble into the shelter, my foot is bleeding through the shoe I got from the Red Cross. The shelter has a medical staff that sees to me and gets me bandaged up. I ask them for painkillers, and they give me Lortab. Four of them. I take two and slip the other two into my pocket for later resale. The shelter's intake paperwork isn't too bad. Without any assets, incomes, or relations, most of it is inapplicable. I'm given papers with directions to my room, the cafeteria, the chapel, and the washroom. Meal times are laid out for me. A nurse helps me to my bed in a room full of bunk beds. I get a bottom bunk near the center of the room. The nurse brings me a water and snacks, asks me if I need anything else (to which I respond more pain killers), then leaves me to my loneliness.

It's the middle of the day and a few people are milling about. Maybe they would buy my pills. Probably not. Of all places to sell something, a shelter has to be the worst. If anybody here had any money, they wouldn't be here. I need to get out on the street, take my product to the market.

There's no other way of putting it, this shelter is depressing. It smells like bleach, the lighting is half-ass, the cream colored walls are killing me with blandness, and all these pictures of Jesus are creeping me out.

There is a service tonight at 5:00 p.m. that the shelter recommends I attend. It's right before dinner. And although it's not required to get your dinner, it sort of is. I don't do anything to pass the time. I wallow in boredom until five o'clock. I watch children play, oblivious to their circumstances. Chasing each other around the beds, sitting close, complaining to an adult about the unfairness of their playmate, and then settling down with their face buried in a smartphone or a tablet. In a homeless shelter.

The service is shitty, of course. I am surrounded by hundreds of homeless people. Hundreds. All wearing gallons of cologne and perfume in lieu of using soap and water. The homeless men look like the roller brush taken from underneath a street sweeper. The grime and scraps that end up in the gutter have become animated and they are now surrounding me. Lest you doubt their authenticity, lean in and take a whiff. Or lean away and take a whiff, you'll smell the rancor either way. Most of the woman don't look completely derelict, just destitute. But some certainly have that street-sweeper-brush look.

And these people have children.

These people bring babies into these circumstances.

We, the damned, file into a chapel and take our seats in the pews. Half upholstered. As if they ran out of tithing money before they could wrap the backs of these benches with padding. We sit uncomfortably close. "Scoot in," we're told, "we have a full house tonight, so we're going to need to get cozy." We scoot and scoot some more until we are sitting arm-to-arm. I'm fresh deli meat between two pieces of moldy bread. The room is sweat-through-your-shirt hot, and the service hasn't even started.

Finally, at 5:17 p.m. a pastor walks in carrying a massive gold-leafed Bible. He stands at the pulpit and looks us over. He's silent at first, waiting for the crowd's murmuring to die down. When it's silent, he revels in the room's new focal point: him. He stays quiet and smiles, looking around as if proud of all of us for graduating from something.

He looks down at the Bible in front of him and pulls it open to its pre-marked page. He checks to make sure we're still there, then begins.

"'Yea, though I walk through the valley of the shadow of death, I will fear no evil: for thou art with me; thy rod and thy staff they comfort me.' This, brothers and sisters, is the beloved text of Psalm 23:4. We know it well. How often have we recited this very scripture, using it for strength, relying on it for guidance? But why do we stop there? Why do we quote one verse and not the next? King David wrote this famous verse with the inspiration of our Lord. Did he not have that same inspiration in scribing the next verse? The next chapter? Psalm 24 begins: 'The earth is the Lord's, and the fullness thereof; the world, and they that dwell therein. For he hath...'"

The pastor goes on but he's lost me. Too many questions. And I can't help but wonder about this guy. Does he get paid to do this? He must. Why else would he do this? But how? These people are poor. Maybe he moonlights as a pro bono preacher, and in the daytime he does his paid work in middle-class congregations. Does this guy actually know the Lord? Does the Lord know him? Does the Lord know me?

"Hey," the broom next to me whispers, "you don't actually believe this shit, do you?"

"What?" I ask.

"Ya know, this bullshit preacher man is spewing, you don't actually believe it, right?"

"Um, I dunno." I hadn't been listening for a minute, so I wasn't sure what the pastor was talking about or what the broom was referring to. "I wasn't really listening."

"I'm Sam." The broom holds its hand out in front of it like it's a robot about to dice chives with its palm. I reach over and shake its hand.

"I'm Caish."

"Here's the thing," Sam whispers loud enough to get the woman sitting in front of us to turn around with a scowl, but he presses on, "religion is a virulent contrivance to subjugate the masses to 'virtuous'"—here he used air quotes—"obedience. An obedience that requires one to give up money, time, and free thinking to tax-exempt institutions and corporations claiming divine endorsement." Sam looks at me out of the sides of his eyes with a look of satisfaction. His face was asking me to thank him for giving me the truth.

"Okay," I mumble.

"The ontological fallacy of anthropocentrism and megalomania is the product sold by the preacher. The preacher—"

"Sam, I appreciate the insights, but I'm just here for the food and bed."

"Aren't we all."

Sam smiles, then looks forward, aware that maybe he came on too strong. We sit through the rest of the half-hour sermon, then file into the cafeteria. Sam stays next to me as we wait in line, then continues his bombardment.

"Caish, genuinely though, religion is bullshit. Think about it. It's all so obvious from the outside looking in. The preacher man commands the respect of a demigod, encourages capacity for illusion, then declares obedience and faith in illusion to be virtuous. And it's his own virtue that he's displaying by standing up in front of the crowd with his smugness and contentedness living the chaste life." The line is long and Sam seems to be enjoying this, so I don't interrupt, I just nod along. Now that we're standing, I can get a look at Sam. He's probably in his mid-forties, around 6'3," and as thin as a pin. He has scraggly hair and beard, but doesn't have the same look of senility that many of his peers so evidently display. He's wearing dirty clothes and a black beanie. He twitches when he talks. His left leg looks like it is receiving random shocks of electricity while he talks, and it looks like an invisible string pulls his head to the left at random times. He blinks violently.

"… the individual is encouraged to think of themselves as empowered, ordained, and destined for grand purpose," Sam is saying, "this capitalizes on humans' disposition to obedience and compliance. Humans harbor fear and dread of death. Religion has effectively relegated the fear to the subconscious. But it's still there. A paralyzing fear of the end. Religion offers catharsis. It tells them that they'll survive their own death. Not only that, it gets better after they die. 'This life,' as they call it, is the hard part. Religion absorbs the dread. Like a dry sponge of hope in a puddle of panic. Because of this, the religion is effective in proportion to the amount of complexity, certainty, and sincerity it can project. The more complex the dogma, the more convinced the sheep. Of course, this product comes with a price. Some religions ask for what you can spare, others ask for an absolute ten percent of patrons' income and create social structures and status symbols out of the payment of tithes. Membership fees of tens of thousands of dollars that patrons can either pay, or be shamed by their flock and guilted by their imaginary god. But the price is much higher than money..."

We are at the front of the line now. We hold out our trays and the people on the other side of the glass plop slop into the recessed plastic sections. The food doesn't look horrible, all things considered. Some sort of meat, probably ham, with a scoop of mashed potatoes on top, slathered in gravy. Green beans, packaged peach slices, a roll, lettuce, an apple. There's even a little chocolate brownie. At the end of the line we're given a water bottle. I see an empty seat, but decide to find a place with two empty spots. I don't want Sam to feel like I'm ditching him just because he's crazy and has a twitch.

"... the ideological trap of superstition binds the mind to unquestionable answers to questions that would otherwise provide a lifetime of growth and productivity..."

I sit at an empty spot near the door. This place reminds me of my elementary school. The only thing that's missing are those tiny cartons of milk. They would never give us enough milk. And they'd stamp my hand when I was behind on my lunch money. One stamp, two stamps, three stamps, and then they'd stamp my forehead so even if I forgot to tell my mom, she'd see that I was out of lunch money.

Sam was still talking. "... entrenchment in religious thinking dulls capacity for critical thought. The religious, in an attempt to rid themselves of the anxieties associated with the certainty of death and mediocrity, cash in their critical thinking for conformity, complacency, and the bliss only ignorance can buy. Death is terrifying, but convincing oneself that death is avoidable ignores everything we know about the universe. We will not survive our death." Sam bit into his roll.

"Wow," I say, "sounds like you've really given it some thought."

"I'm not done."

"Well, maybe for tonight? You've given me a lot to process."

"But you need to know. We all need to know. We need to rid the world of this pestilence. This cerebral virus." Sam was devouring his food. His tick either stopped or was lost in the fury of his feasting. "Because, Caish, it is the hope of a god and heaven that is keeping all these people poor."

"You included?"

"Huh?"

"I said, you included? Is the hope of a god keeping you poor?"

"Oh, me? No. People won't hire me because I have Tourette's. I take marijuana to calm my nerves, and employers don't like that either. They don't like the weed, and they don't like my incessant blinking. So my purpose in life is to spread truth and light to those in the menacing shadow of religion."

"And what do you think God thinks of that?"

"Ha! See? You're caught in the shadow! You are assuming the premise that there's a god."

"Of course there's a god," I say.

"Have you been listening to anything I've been saying?"

We went on like this for all of dinner, and into the evening. He followed me to my bunk and took the bed next to mine. Propped up on his shoulder, he explained again to me how the more complex the preacher can make the religion's doctrine, the more likely the religion is to survive. If the only piece of dogma was that an all-powerful magic being exists, it would fall like Santa.

The illusion of complexity encourages the masses to consider such complex rule and dogma structures as beyond the ability of a human to conceive. Further, the more stilts of doctrine used to prop up the religion, the more likely the religion will be to withstand the rising tide of external scrutiny. All the while, Sam is twitching like a jumping bean.

At some point in Sam's anti-homily I drift off. I wake up in the night with my foot burning in pain. Hopelessness is sitting on my foot at the foot of my bed. Bigger, darker, with more tentacles and a deeper voice. Its beak clicks as it speaks.

"Settling in alright?" it asks.

I don't answer. I close my eyes but I know it's there. Waiting. It can't kill me when there are other people around. The room is dark, but there are nightlights around the edges of the room. The room was filled with wheezing slumbering poor people. All unable to function in society. And then there's me, a millionaire in their ranks. Like a spy from the upper class to see what the masses are up to.

"Ha! A spy from the upper class?" Hopelessness screeches. "You are one of them, Caish. You always have been. You were an imposter among the rich. A fluke. This is who you are. Stop denying it. The plot is thinning. You are fucking worthless, Caish." Its tentacles tighten. "Ah, feels good doesn't it? The truth, that is. You are worth less than the clothes you are wearing. Truth, truth, truth. Speaking of which, ol' Sam here seems to be on to something. Death being the end and all. Won't that be nice? The peaceful darkness of death snuffing out your worthless existence."

I don't have my phone or headphones anymore, so I have nothing to drown out Hopelessness. I look around the room. Looking for anything that could help. The darkness was drowning me. One of Hopelessness's tentacles slides across my face. "Shhhhh," it whispers. Its beak, dripping blood, is less than an inch from my ear. "The only way out is death. We both know it."

I'm shaking, sweating, and can't take a deep breath. I'm leaking tears. The darkness fills my lungs.

"Scared?" Sam asks. He's propped up on an elbow looking over at me.

"Yeah."

"First night in a shelter?"

"Um. Yeah."

"Hey, it's alright. It's alright." He sits up, then kneels next to my bed. He finds my hand and takes it. Holds it with both of his grizzled, sticky hands. "You're safe. Everything is going to be alright."

"How is everything going to be alright? Look at me. I have nothing. I am nothing." Embarrassingly, I can't stop the sobs. I keep them quiet, but I'm overcome with the terror that this is who I am now. This is how the rest of my existence will be. But, with Sam patting my shoulder, I feel marginally better. At least Hopelessness has returned to Hell for the time being.

"Let's go for a walk, you up for that?" Sam stands up and helps me to my feet. We were both sleeping in our clothes, so we just slip on our shoes and shuffle out of the sleeping quarters. "We can't leave the shelter, but we can walk its halls."

We walk from one dark hallway to the next. Two graveyard shift volunteers eye us as we walk past their counter. Sam could knife me and leave me for dead in any one of the dark corners, but I trust he won't. Something about him tells me he's not a murderer. Godless, sure, but probably not a killer. There's a gentleness about him.

"So, how'd you end up here?" Sam asks.

"That's a long story."

"Plenty of hours left in the night."

"It's a sad story."

"Most are. But we gotta find a way to smile about it. Surely there's something we can laugh about. Let's hear it."

"I wouldn't even know where to start."

"How about at the beginning? Where were you born?"

I tell Sam everything. Once I start I can't stop. My upbringing, my adolescence, my lottery win, the failed marriage, my life as a millionaire, the theft of my money by Jamie Fucking Lowell, and the bad luck that has plagued me ever since. Sam nods along, asks questions, and encourages me to give greater detail. Our conversation lasts into the morning and through breakfast. Sam keeps twitching and blinking, but watches me with sincerity.

"I can understand why things seem dire, coming from where you've come from," Sam says, "but, you're in Los Angeles. The land of the endless summer and boundless opportunity. And now that you don't have anything to worry about, you can finally live free. Do you want to sleep on the beach? Do it, it's yours. You don't answer to anybody and you have nothing but yourself to lose. So, live freely."

Sam shows me the ropes of living on the street. Shelters are fine, sure, but the real living happens on the streets. On the urine-soaked sidewalks. Under the pigeon-filled viaducts. In the jungle of Los Angeles.

Shelters all have curfews, and many of them have lines so long that there's not hope of getting in unless you stand there for hours in advance. They fill up, then close their doors. We have no choice but to live off the land. We are the nomads of the metropolis.

Provisions are easy to come by. There are all sorts of giveaways in the city. Charitable organizations that transfer perfectly good stuff from the rich to the poor. Clothing, bags, tents, sleeping bags, tarps, tools, shoes, and everything else you need to live out here. Food is easy. Soup kitchens are all over the place. You just walk in and take whatever you want. Some places send you on your way with bags full of expired groceries that haven't yet turned. Sleep is easy once you get used to the ultra-firm support of asphalt and concrete. Always sleep with everything you have in a bag that you use as a pillow. And loop your arm through one of the straps. Anything else goes with you in the sleeping bag.

The essentials, however, are tougher to come by. Alcohol and cigarettes are never given out at soup kitchens or shelters. Neither are opioids. For those, you need money.

For all his preaching against money, Sam knew how to get it. Step one: get a stray dog. They're all over LA, and they're happy to live with you for a few scraps of food. Step two: wear your worst clothes, pack the good stuff away in your bag. Step three: skip the cardboard sign and hold out a cup. That's how they do it in Europe and they see much greater success. Step four: be injured. Limp, hunch, cough, and act sore. The fifth and final step is to put them all together in a place where the lower- and middle-class people shop. The upper class won't give you the shit from their toilet, so don't waste your time at The Grove or anywhere near Beverly Hills. Go to a Walmart. Shoppers there usually believe in a god and karma and are more likely to use cash when they shop. You're there to collect the spare change. The dog will do that for you. People are much more likely to give a dog money than a human. Starving humans are repugnant, starving dogs are in need of care and affection.

A day of work can bring in anywhere from twenty to a hundred dollars. Variables will impact your take; rain helps, another nomad anywhere in sight hurts.

Cash flow worldwide is down, so Sam and some others set up bank accounts and bought card readers. Now, if anybody says, "Sorry, I don't carry cash," Sam says "No problem, I take credit and debit." I bring in enough to buy a phone and card reader, but I can't set up a bank account to link it to. Banks want all sorts of information to open an account, and my social security number has debt painted all over it. So I only accept cash. It's best I stay off grid until I make enough to pay off the debt collectors (I'm sure they're looking for me).

Fentanyl is hard to find, but there's plenty of heroin to go around. And heroin can still make me float. Heroin can banish Hopelessness and help me feel like money used to make me feel. I don't make enough to use daily, but alcohol and other prescriptions get me through the time between hits.

Life isn't so bad on the streets. Plenty of time to reflect. Sam is fascinated by my life as a millionaire. He often asks about the details. What was it like to smell the exhaust of a Lamborghini? What did the inside of a private jet sound like? How heavy is one million dollars in cash? This evening's conversation is no different. We're eating Kipper Snacks in Pershing Square and Sam asks me how I got so lucky. That's how he words it: "How did you *get so lucky*?" As if it was something that could have simply been got.

"I earned it," I respond. "Plain and simple. Hard work. Determination. Grit. Cunning. The same way all rich people make their money."

"And how did you lose it?"

"I didn't lose my money, it was stolen from me. Remember?"

Sam smiles, twitches, and drops a piece of smoked herring from his fingers into his mouth. "So whose fault is it that you're rotting away on the streets instead of snorting lines of coke off of models in your Malibu mansion?"

I pause and look at Sam to see if he's serious. Usually he's not mean, but he can have bouts. He gets embarrassed when his Tourettes get bad and takes it out on others. Maybe this was one of those times. I don't take offense and give Sam an honest answer: "We've talked about this. Jamie T. Lowell. The government. The Marquez family. Bad luck. But, there—oh, and God."

"A god took your money?"

"Well, Jamie and the IRS took most my money, the Marquez family sort of finished me off with that whole lawsuit I told you about. In Pismo. But God is definitely givin' me a trial."

"A trial?" Sam asks. Blinking violently.

"You know, a tough time to humble me. A test of faith. What doesn't kill me only—"

"Yeah. Got it."

"Anyway. I know I'll rise above this someday and come out stronger. Richer. I'll work at the lottery harder than I did the first time. Did you know that people who win the lottery once are more likely to win a second or third time? There's this guy in Florida that—"

"Yeah, won a lot?"

"Yeah like four times."

"Why don't you just get a job, Caish? You don't have Tourettes, you're sane, you're attractive. Why are you living in the streets?"

"Because jobs pay you nothing and are for people who don't know how to make real money. I mean really, Sam, $10 an hour? We make that. And plus, what if Steve Jobs would've just gotten a job? I can't limit myself."

"But you're broke. And you could be making honest money in a McDonalds or something."

"Only 'cause I'm down on my luck. I didn't do anything to deserve this."

"Maybe by doing nothing you earned this."

I take a bite of my Kipper Snack and look Sam in the eyes. "I'm tellin' you, just watch, I'm gonna win again."

"But what if you don't? I mean, what if, and just hear me out on this, what if your chances of winning the lottery are, say, one in five hundred million? Then what do you do?"

"Are you sayin' you don't think I can do it?"

"I'm saying it's not in your control." Sam's arm twitches so hard his Kipper Snack dumps into the grass.

"Oh, shit, here, have mine," I offer.

"No thanks, I was done with it anyway," Sam says. "Caish, I care for you. I do. But you gotta stop thinking of yourself as a millionaire with magic abilities when it comes to lotto tickets. No, let me finish. You aren't ever going to win again. Know that. You won't. Now, think about what you need to do to survive knowing that."

Sam was like a father to me these past couple months, but now I see that he is just another hater. He doesn't hate me, he hates that I'm a rich person in hobo's clothing. He's trying to break me down to build up his own self-esteem. This is the end of the adventures of Sam and Caish.

Sam gives me some speech about helping others and leaves me to go find others he can help. If it weren't for my stray, Bosco, I would be completely alone. Nobody knows me. Nobody knows what I'd been through, or how much I was worth. To the people of Los Angeles I'm a roach, only worse because I take up more space. Even to my fellow roaches, I'm nobody.

For all its bright sides, even Los Angeles can be Hell. Demon ridden. Los Demonios.

Even if Sam is right, and money and I just aren't meant to be, I have to fight it. When your lover has cancer you don't just abandon them, you try everything. When they run out on you, you chase them. Let them know you care. I'll never give up on money.

More fervently than ever, I pray. As I stand, crouch, hunch, and sit on corners I pray for the Lord to soften the hearts of these my fellow Californians. When I curl up in my sleeping bag under my tarp on 5th street, I pray that the Lord will watch over me as I sleep. "Let me not be the object in a Good Samaritan parable." But above all, I pray not that the Lord will help me get through the day, but that God will grant me the life back that He took from me. I don't want merely to survive, I want my house in Malibu back. I pray not for loose change, but for real wealth. And I've heard the stories about us needing to put the work in, and only then will God help us out, so, I buy at least one lottery ticket every day. Every day I give God an opportunity to answer my prayers and reward my faith.

Alas, I'm still sleeping under a tarp in Skidrow.

666

The best course of action moving forward is selling my soul. God is not helping, so what choice do I have? I've seen enough movies and heard enough stories to know that Satan is always in the market, and he usually pays well. Plus, with my business acumen I'm confident I can negotiate a great deal.

When night falls, and in the privacy of my hut, I draw a pentagram on the cardboard and kneel down in prayer and supplication to Lucifer:

"Dear Devil, I know there have been times in my life when perhaps I was not as evil as I could have been, and for those times I ask for your forgiveness. I come to you tonight as a humble believer seeking to sell my soul. As you are probably aware, I am a person of charisma and charm that has the potential of leading many followers into your flock. By way of payment for my soul, I only request that the rest of my life be filled with the wealth and happiness that existed before I was robbed of my fortune. I am not picky, and I will take any route to this prosperity that you deem fit. Beelzebub, please know that I am thankful for all you have done for me so far, and consider this an offer of my undying commitment to your cause for the remainder of my days. In the name of Jes—er, um. In your name. Satan. Amen."

Then I wait. Surely a figure in a dark suit wearing a black fedora will enter my hut any second now. Satan is probably a man. A goat-man. He'll probably be smoking a cigarette and have flames in his eyes. Red hair probably. Or black. Actually yeah, I bet it's black hair, slicked back, with a black goatee. Either way, he'll be well-dressed and have a contract in hand that he will want me to sign. I will review the terms and conditions, making any necessary annotations, then I will sign with a quill pen that Satan provides me. Perhaps we'd also shake hands just to seal the deal. His hand will be scaly and his grip will be tight but gentlemanly. I imagine that as soon as I'm done signing he will laugh in a frightening deep chortle with bobbing shoulders and disappear in a plume of smoke and fire. Then I will either hear voices in my head or just be inspired to make certain decisions that will restore my wealth. I'll see the signs.

After a few minutes of waiting, I add another short prayer:

"Dear Devil, my hut is on the corner of San Pedro and 5th. It's the one with the black tarp and the cardboard porch. It's the only black tarp with a cardboard porch on the corner. In Satan's name, Amen."

Nothing happens. Not even a diabolical raven, black cat, or talking snake. What the Hell? In the Bible Satan was all over the place, invited or not. And now he won't even show up to buy a soul? I thought this was his bread and butter. Maybe I did something wrong. Maybe he went out of business. First thing in the morning I will go to the library and see what I can find on selling one's soul to Satan. I'm running out of options and I need this guy to pull through.

I crawl into my sleeping bag and lay awake for what seems like hours. The sounds of the night make sleeping on the streets tough. It's not like the movies, there aren't usually gunshots. But people talk and yell and cry. Sometimes people make sounds that sound like all three at the same time. Two or three times I hear people talking just outside my front "door." Cars are always driving around, sometimes with loud music or exhaust pipes. The drone of traffic on the 10, 101, and 110 is ever-present. Bottles rattle and break. Cats fight. And of course there are sirens. There are always sirens. At some point I drift off.

The din of LA wakes me up with the sun. The noises outside grow louder as the sun peeks over the horizon behind the city. I break down my hut and pack it neatly into my backpack—which is one of those hiking packs with a metal frame. My tarp folds up nicely, and the ski poles I use for support slide into side pockets. My sleeping bag is strapped to the top of the pack. I fold up my cardboard and slide it between the frame and the bag. If I leave anything behind, even cardboard with a pentagram on it, it will be stolen.

The library won't be open for a few hours, so I make my way to the soup kitchen on 6th for breakfast. A horrendously lengthy line circles the courtyard and extends down an alley. But it is breakfast, so I wait. The volunteers are always kind and the bread is usually decent. As an added bonus, we don't have to listen to a sermon while we eat (most soup kitchens preach Jesus with urgency). Crowded, stinky, and dirty, this morning is the same as any other. The line moves steadily and eventually I'm inside. Donated art and potted plants dot the walls, and most surfaces have been recently scrubbed. I get my food (in a Styrofoam bowl and a tiny plastic cup) and look for a place to sit in the courtyard. I squeeze into an empty spot on a picnic table and eat in silence without taking off my backpack. Breakfast is some sort of warm vegetable stew with a stale roll and a cup of cider.

While at breakfast I'm offered $30 for Bosco. He's been a loyal dog, but I can always find another stray if I need one. Bosco will be happy with his new owner.

After breakfast I take the two-shoe express for several blocks on 5th over to the library. I don't have a library card, so I have to wait in line to use one of the computers that are available for fifteen minutes at a time. When it's my turn, I open Google Maps and type in "satanic synagogues." Maybe I can get connected with people who worship Satan and they can give me instructions on how to sell my soul. Google Maps says there are no results. I search Google for "how to sell my soul to Satan" and get mixed results.

I jot down a couple of addresses on library stationery and set off in the direction of the nearest… church? I don't know what they call them. Place of worship, maybe.

The nearest place of worship, Spectra's, is across town. I walk. Hours later, I am standing in front of a black, windowless, one-story building. It is in need of a new paint job. The structure screams dingy. Which isn't inspiring. If the prince of darkness can't even afford adequate commercial real estate, what does that say about his ability to pay top dollar for my soul? But I walked all the way here, and I don't have many options left, so I walk around the building until I find an entrance.

The doors are in the back of the building. Two large oak slabs with a relief of half-goat Satan carved into them. I try both handles, but they're locked. I knock. Nothing. I check the info I wrote down at the library: open 10:00 a.m. to 5:00 p.m. daily, closed Sundays. It's about three-thirty. I stuff my paper back into my pocket and step forward to knock again, then see that a slot has opened in one of the doors and I'm being watched.

"Yes?" said the eyes on the other side of the door.

"Hi. You're open, right?" I ask.

"Depends, what business do you have at Spectra's?"

"Well, I'd be happy to discuss that inside, but aren't you open to the public? Your website said so."

The eye latch slides closed and I hear bolts and latches on the other side being unfastened. The door swings open and reveals the owner of the eyes.

I expected some black clothing, naturally. In hindsight I should have expected the black eyeliner. But the cape? And the black lipstick? The python draped around his neck? Is that really necessary? Not to mention his Nazi Death Head hat and black leather platforms. It all seems puerile in light of communing with the dark lord of the universe. Then again maybe Satan also dabs on eyeliner every morning, I still haven't seen him yet. The Satan zealot/Hot Topic model introduces himself as Astaroth. I assume the name is made up and has some dark meaning. Probably lifted it from some Latin book about demons.

"Nice to meet you Astaroth. My name is Caish. Like your hat." That's the best conversation I can manage.

"Thank you," Astaroth says. He invites me in, closes and

locks the door behind me, then leads me down a tenebrous hall. "'Tis an authentic Nazi General cap from 1941. 'Twas worn in battle and used in Satanic rituals since the early fifties."

"Wow," I nod.

Astaroth leads me into a large room full of pews. This is probably the chapel. There is plenty of open space at the front of the room for rituals. There aren't any torches, bats, or alters that I can see. Bit of a disappointment there. Just the snake curled around Astaroth's shoulders, tasting the air next to his face. Was that Satan? Was the snake about to talk?

We sit in the pews, Astaroth on a pew in front of me. He turns, arm over the back of the bench. "So what brings you to Spectra's?"

"I have a soul for sale that I'd like to talk to the Devil about." No time for small talk.

A stilted grin crosses Astaroth's face. He looks like he is trying to make it look mighty evil. But he doesn't say anything.

I prompt, "Have you ever brokered somethin' like that before?"

"Oh, but of course. Yes. 'Tis a common request. We can help. The members of our congregation will be delighted to hear we have another joining the ranks."

"Well, I'm not really interested in joining the ranks, no offense, I just want to sell my soul."

"Oh, indeed, indeed. You needn't dedicate your life to Lucifer in terms of attending service regularly with us. I but meant joining the ranks of the damned."

I joined the ranks of the damned long ago. "Sure. So, how do I do it? Because I already tried praying to him, and didn't get a response."

With another attempt at an evil smirk, Astaroth stood and bade me follow him. We walk through a door at the side of the chapel and enter what is evidently Astaroth's office. Black wallpaper, red shag carpet, black leather furniture, and plastic skulls on every shelf in the room. I sit across from his desk as he pulls a book off his shelf that looks to be from the early 1400s. Possibly carried across the Atlantic by Columbus. It is huge. Unabridged 1960s dictionary huge. It has a leather cover and worn pages. Just like in the movies. Finally we're getting somewhere.

He set the book on his desk and began thumbing through the pages. "The ceremony is an ancient one," Astaroth said, "dating back to the Salem witch trials, where we lost so many of our sisters."

"Hm," I say.

Settling on a page, and pleased with himself, Astaroth leans back in his chair, fingers interlocked, and asks, "So, before beginning the ceremony, I must query, would you be willing to make a contribution to the building of the Devil's domain on earth?"

"What?"

"A donation, such that we can perform the ceremony."

"I'm selling my soul, and you want me to pay for it? How about a commission. I'll give you one percent of whatever I get for my soul."

Astaroth laughed, startling himself and his snake. Then stopped when he saw that I wasn't joking. "Oh, we can work out a commission, but of course. But mightn't you be willing to make a small donation before then? Only to demonstrate your faith."

"I'm broke. Homeless. Literally. Do you think I'd be in here if I had money to donate?"

"Oh, indeed. Okay, that's fine. Let us forget the matter."

"So when is the ceremony?"

"I must make a few phone calls, but why don't we plan on tomorrow at noon?"

"Shouldn't it be at nighttime? I always imagined something like this happening at night."

"Understandable," Astaroth says, "but many of our patrons

have a hard time finding babysitters for their kids. Noon usually works best because they can come during their lunch breaks."

Come during their lunch breaks? What was this, some fucking box social? I'm selling my goddamn soul here. I guess it's a good sign this has become so mundane to Astaroth and the other patrons. This is a run-of-the-mill soul-selling. Nothing out of the ordinary.

"Okay, tomorrow at noon works for me."

"Most excellent," Astaroth stands and opens his office door. I follow him back through the chapel and down the hall.

"So, do ya have any clients that I'd know?" I ask.

"Pardon?"

"Who else have you brokered the sale their soul? Ryan Gosling, Elon Musk; any names I'd recognize?"

"Oh, indeed, there are names you'd recognize. But of course we keep their identities entirely confidential. You will receive the same amount of secrecy."

Back on the street, I stay local for the evening. No use hoofing it back to Skidrow just to come back tomorrow. With the thirty bucks I got from selling Bosco, I walk to a gas station and buy dinner, two packs of cigarettes, and a lottery ticket. My total comes to $29.31—a sign that everything is going to work out.

A couple blocks down from Spectra's there's an alley with a comfortable nook. A low pipe between dumpsters gives my tarp something to hang on, and there's extra cardboard for added lumbar support.

The next morning I'm back at Spectra's at 11:55 a.m. I put on my best clothes and find a public bathroom in which to get cleaned up. Today is the most important day of my life. The sunrise on my long, dark night. The end of Hopelessness. The return of money. And cars, and sex, and cocaine, and beach houses, and vacations, and long hot showers, and expensive wine, and sushi, and on and on. Finally, I was making my comeback.

Astaroth does the same slot in the door routine as yesterday, then welcomes me in. After stowing my backpack in the coat closet, he leads me into the chapel. Fifteen to twenty people in black cloaks are seated on the front two rows of pews. Hoods on and humming. The room is lit only by the multitude of candles on the walls and in the front of the room. The bouquet of candles at the front of the room, in front of the dark wood lectern, is burning like a campfire. Center left of the front of the room is a large metal bowl elevated by three legs shaped like snakes. Center right is a massive upside-down crucifix that almost touches the ceiling. It looks like it's made of marble. They probably stole it from a nearby catholic church.

Astaroth has me stand in the front of the room, then walks behind the lectern. "Followers of our great and dark lord and king, today we have before us a soul willing to enter eternal servitude. Caish Calloway stands before you, the disciples of Satan, wishing to exchange eternal salvation for earthly, material gain. Today, Caish Calloway joins the army of the damned!"

"Hail Him, the Lord of Darkness!" the cloaked patrons chant.

"Let us make haste and begin the ceremony," Astaroth says, stepping out from behind the podium, "remove your earthly clothing, Caish."

"What?"

"Remove your earthly clothing. You must make yourself bare before the Devil and his witnesses."

I should have known this would get strange. Whatever. What do I have to lose? My dignity? As I strip naked, one of the cloaked patrons stands and takes my clothes. Naked, I turn toward Astaroth, who is rummaging through a trunk next to the metal bowl. He pulls out a bag and tube that looks like it belongs in a hospital.

"Let your arms fall to your sides, Caish, you must present yourself to Satan and His witnesses. Be not ashamed nor fearful."

I let my arms drop.

"Now, face the witnesses."

I turn toward the witnesses. After I stand naked in front of a small crowd of cloaked strangers for a few minutes and hear rearranging behind me, Astaroth stands at my side. "Caish Calloway, do you wish to sell your eternal soul to Lucifer, the god of darkness and ruler over all that is evil and wicked?"

"Yes."

Astaroth tilts his head back, closes his eyes, and mumbles to himself for what must be two full minutes. All the while, I stand naked in front of a small crowd of humming, hooded strangers.

"Lucifer, Satan the Devil, accepts your offer," Astaroth says, tilting his head forward, "now, lay on the sacred tiles upon which you presently stand."

"Lay down?" I ask.

"Yes, lay down."

"Well, before I do, what did Satan say? What is he offering?"

"To purchase your eternal salvation, of course."

"But what are the terms? How much is he buying it for?"

Astaroth paused, as if he forgot to hammer out the details and now had to make something up. Then said, "Caish, Satan does not deal in dollar amounts, Satan deals in wealth. In true and everlasting power. You will be rewarded with wealth beyond your imagination so long as you shall live on this earth."

"But Satan didn't give you any numbers? No ballpark?"

"No, Caish, Satan doesn't operate like us earthly beings. Now, lay yourself, let us continue the ceremony."

The dark gray tile was cold on my bare feet and is just as cold on my bare backside. As I lay in the center of a large circled pentagram, the patrons stand and light candles. They place the candles on the circle around the pentagram and stand shoulder to shoulder looking down at me. Still humming. Now swaying.

Astaroth brings the tube and bag over to me. "We need your lifeblood to demonstrate your willingness to sacrifice for the Devil."

"What? I'm sacrificing my soul, why would you need my blood?"

"Satan wishes to see that you are committed. Your lifeblood is a necessary part of the ritual. It is so written."

Fucking hell. This is some serious bullshit. "K. Fine. Take my blood." Goddamn vampires.

One of the cloaks crouches down to my arm and finds a vein quicker than I've ever been able to. And in such low light. My dark red blood slides down the tube and fills the plastic bag. Satisfied, Astaroth removes the needle. Blood trickles out of my arm. I reach over to plug the bleeding, but Astaroth stops me. "Let your lifeblood spill into the pentagram." I watch my arm drain blood around my elbow and onto the tile. These people are lucky I'm not a hemophiliac. They'd have a serious lawsuit on their hands if I were. Then again, I guess not. I'd just die and be forgotten. Nobody would bring a wrongful death case. They'd just dump my body off a pier and the world would forget about me. The small puddle of my blood tickles my ribs.

Astaroth flicks a switch on the side of the bowl and flames climb out of the coals.

The chanting is getting louder, and the cloaked patrons are shuffling around the pentagram. Counterclockwise. Over their shoulders and in the gaps between them, I can see Astaroth standing next to the flaming bowl. He has the bag of my blood open, and he's dipping his fingers in and flicking my blood into the flames. Over the chanting I can hear him shouting at the flames. Maybe Latin? I wouldn't know it if I heard it, but it certainly isn't English and Latin seems appropriate for the circumstances.

"Roll onto your stomach, Caish, prostrate before Hell and its Lord," I hear.

I roll over, naked and slippery with blood and sweat, and lay face down on the tile.

Hands reach out and spread my arms and legs. I try to pull

them back but leather straps wrap around my wrists and ankles and hold them fast. "Do not fight the sacred ritual," someone whispers in my ear, "Satan will reward your humility."

26

Hours later, I limp out of Spectra's, contract in hand. At the end of the ritual I was helped to my feet and made to sign several papers. One of which was my copy of the contract with the Devil (although he never did show up (that I know of), apparently Astaroth has power of an attorney to sign on His behalf). The contract is on old-fashioned parchment and states that in exchange for my eternal servitude in the caves of Hell, Lucifer has agreed to supply me with earthly wealth. To receive this wealth, I simply need to follow the promptings of the Devil. They would be clear.

My first prompting is to destroy Spectra's. Even Satan wouldn't condone what they did to me. Astaroth told me to act on any strong urges, listen to every evil whisper, and move with determination when inspired. Will do.

I make it back to last night's nook and rest. I have enough trail mix and beef jerky to hang out for a day and let my body recover from that diabolical experience. I'm running low on water, but I can fill up in the public bathroom around the corner. For now I need to sleep.

The next morning I walk downtown to get money. On my way, a soup kitchen gives me lunch. At the corner of Broadway and 6th, I curl up on a sidewalk and place a cup on the ground in front of me.

At the end of the day, I've made $13.27. Enough for dinner, a pack of cigarettes, and a couple lottery tickets. Inspiration prompts me to buy a Scratcher and a Powerball ticket. I listen closely for Satan's revelation. Which numbers would He have me choose? I tell the teller I'll take a Powerball and panic when she lets the machine randomly generate my numbers. Then I see the hand of Satan in my numbers. Lots of threes and sixes. Of course, for Satan will not be mocked. And a four; four corners of the earth, four seasons, four horsemen of the apocalypse. Twenty-five—my lucky number.

25 30 33 46 60 03.

Satan's immaculate Powerball. The jackpot is up to $251,000,000, so this very well could be my ticket back to Malibu. It's a Friday, so the next drawing is tomorrow.

After a restless night on Skidrow, the sun rises on the first day of the rest of my life. I rush to the gas station and check the winning numbers. First number in the draw: 25! Next number 30. Yes! This is it. I knew it. Then 33! I knew I could do it. Then… 87. Eighty-seven? I check my ticket again. Maybe a mistake? Did I make a mistake? It should have been a forty-six. Next number 49. Goddammit. Satan dammit. Have I not paid the price? First God, and now I've been forsaken by Satan. Powerball number: 03. Oh? Well let's see. If I have the first three numbers, plus the power number, that means I have won… $197. Not bad, not bad. Maybe this is just Satan's way of testing my faith. Satan works in mysterious ways.

Two hundred dollars is enough to stay in a motel for a couple nights and get myself cleaned up. I'll refill my prescriptions, make some sales, and buy myself time at the motel until my next inspiration arrives.

But first, Spectra's.

I walk across town and get to Spectra's as the sun is setting. I stash my backpack in my alley nook and look through the dumpster for milk cartons. Four of them. That will do it. Behind the wall at the end of the alley are the backyards of lower-middle-class houses. When the glow of sunset gives way to the blackness of the night, I hop the wall and creep up to the base of a house, crouching under the windows. Wouldn't want the happy family inside to see me lurking around in their backyard. Their hose is rusted to the spigot. Their neighbor's hose isn't attached. It's lying in the overgrown grass like a dead snake. I hop the fence dividing their yards and put the hose over my head and across my chest. The neighbor's lights aren't on. I run across their yard back to the wall, which I scale and drop over back into the alley. Then I wait. This next part is best done when cars are no longer roving.

At what must be 2:00 a.m., I walk through the neighborhood until I spot an old truck parked in a backyard. Milk jugs and hose in hand, I hop the fence and run up to the truck. A porch light turns on and lights the yard. I crouch behind the truck and wait to hear the click-clack of a shotgun cocking. After a few seconds with my heart in my throat, pounding in my ears, the light goes off. Motion light. Nothing to worry about. I line up the milk jugs and unscrew the truck's gas cap. The hose slides into the gas tank without a sound. The other end of the hose tastes like rust and rubber. I suck and suck until my mouth is filled with gas. I spew out the gas and shove the end of the hose into a milk jug. I spit and spit, but the poison clings to my tongue. Spilled gas is soaking into my face and clothes. When the first jug is full, I move the hose to the next, then the next, then the next. I pull the hose out of the gas tank and lift it over my shoulder. I'm careful to keep both ends above the rest of the hose. Now that it's full of gas it may as well be lead.

In the bed of the truck is a two-foot length of rebar that will come in handy. The motion light goes on again when I take the bar. I tie the hose, ends up, around my shoulders, then sneak over to Spectra's. I try to stay in the shadows, but I take the long way (there's no way I'm climbing that alley wall loaded with all this gas).

I get to Spectra's without being spotted. Once behind the building, I set the four milk jugs down and rest the roll of hose upright against the wall.

The back door is fortified beyond what a rebar could ever pry open. But the plywood over the windows peels off like a corn husk. I set the board under the window without a sound. The window behind the board isn't even locked. Silence. No alarms.

Cheap bastard.

I lift the jugs and hose into the window, then climb in.

As thrilling as it is to be in a building at night without anybody else around, I'm not interested in sifting through files or rummaging through Astaroth's personal property. Then again, I might as well look for cash or liquor laying around. The opportunity makes the thief, as they say. I check that the velvet curtains are closed over the window I just climbed in and turn on the hallway light. The building is small, and finding Astaroth's office is easy. Down the hall, through the chapel, first door to the right. Lazy fuckers didn't even clean-up. My blood is still on the tile in the pentagram, polluted by Satanist clam sauce.

Astaroth's drawers are empty except for a few worthless pieces of paper. One drawer in his desk has a bottle of Fireball; I take it out and keep looking. No cash. There's a safe behind the desk (right where you'd expect it). It's about the size of a microwave. But I can't break into safes. Especially not with a piece of rebar. It's either bolted to the ground or too heavy to lift. Damn. That's probably where the money is. I press my ear to the cold metal of the safe's door and see if I can hear clicks when I turn the knob. Nope. I try the handle. The safe door swings open. Didn't even lock his safe! Oh Astaroth, what are we going to do with you?

Sure enough, there is cash. Three large and a couple hundred in checks. I sit behind Astaroth's desk and count it. $3,351.00 to be precise. The rest of the safe is full of legal documents. The cash barely fits into my pockets. With the Fireball in hand, I return to the room at the back of the building with my gas jugs and hose.

Now I have butterflies. What if Astaroth's cronies are on their way to beat me up? A camera somewhere I didn't see. A silent alarm. A nosy neighbor. I move quick. I pour the first jug out in Astaroth's office. Splash some in the safe, on and round the desk, on the couch, and I make a trail of gas back to the chapel. Two jugs for the chapel. I unravel the hose in the hall, connecting gas in the chapel to the back rooms where I empty the last jug of gas. I clamor out of the window, pockets bulging with cash and Fireball in hand, and crouch down. I hear a car pulling up on the street.

I peak around the building and see that it's a squad car. Fuck. Must of been a silent alarm. I rush back to the open window, pull off my gas-soaked shirt, and light it on fire. I toss it into the back room and run for it.

I don't hear any shouting, I'm not shot in the back, and no police officers tackle me. From a shadow half a block away I watch Spectra's. An officer steps out of the patrol car and turns on his Mag light. He takes his time inspecting the front of the building, then the side, then the back.

My shirt must not have landed in the pile of gas I left in the room, because smoke wasn't billowing out of the building yet. Let alone the flames of hell-fire. The officer checks the back door, then sees the window open and peaks in, pulling the curtain back.

A cumulonimbus cloud of black smoke rolls out and over the officer. The cop stumbles back, then jogs back to the squad car, talking into a shoulder walkie-talkie. While the officer is retrieving a fire extinguisher from the trunk, the smoke starts to billow. By the time the cop makes it back to the window, the curtains are a wall of fire and the pops and cracks of a structural fire are beginning.

I know I should be running away. If caught, how would I explain being soaked in gas and loaded with cash? But the fire demands my attention. I pull myself away when I hear sirens coming. Spectra's has flames coming out of all its openings, so even if they put it out now, I've succeeded.

My bag is where I left it in the alley two blocks down. I change into dry clothes and throw my fuel-soaked pants into the dumpster. Headed out of the alley in the opposite direction of Spectra's, I look back to check on the fire's progress.

Spectra's is a brilliant display of Hell's wrath. Of my wrath. The skeleton of the building stands in black contrast to the bright orange blaze leaping out its windows and through its roof. The flames reflect off the sides of the polished fire engines. Firefighters are hooking up a hose to a fire hydrant across the street and raising their truck ladders into the air. Police are watching, helpless. You can hear the fire's roar. Its voracious appetite for more fuel. Two blocks away and I can feel its heat. Black smoke twists into the night sky, bottom-lit by the flames to look more ominous. I can almost make out Satan's face in the smoke.

Then I get the hell out of there.

We've all heard it: it takes money to make money. Now that I had a few grand, my downward momentum has been stopped and my upward momentum is beginning. My rise is taking root. For truly, money is the root of all happiness. My downward momentum was stopped by hitting bedrock at the very bottom, and my upward momentum seems to be a result of me selling my soul to Satan. Now that I have enough money to make money, I can take advantage of lucrative opportunities.

After one more night on the street (just to lay low), I walk up to West Hollywood and check into Malibu Motel. The place is seedy for West Hollywood, but their showers are hot, their management is laid back, and their rates are low. It's a small place, two stories with maybe thirty rooms total. West Hollywood is right where I want to be. This is the platform from which I launch back to wealth. No better place to do it than Hollywood—the subsidiary of LA dedicated to making dreams come true. I just have to listen to the revelation and inspiration. So far it has worked quite well.

Malibu Motel has an extended stay program. You can pay up front for up to a month at a time. Like renting an apartment. So for $2,100 I have a room for twenty-eight days. A real bargain.

At the end of the twenty-eight days, you have to clear your stuff out, but then you can buy another twenty-eight days that same day.

I check in, take a shower hot enough to ignite the gas soaked into my skin, then order pizza and watch TV. I grind up the last of my Oxycodone, melt it down, and mainline it. Ah, the comfort money buys. I'm back. At least for now. At least for here. Right now I'm safe, full, and floating in the warm soft clouds of euphoria.

The next morning I get back to work. Networking is the most important part of any profession, including pharmaceuticals. Motels are great places to meet potential clients and suppliers. Unlike hotels, motels are usually full of locals. People who live, or used to live, in the area, and who need another spot to stay for a little while. Motels with long-stay options become their own little communities. There are usually a few rooms with people who have lived there for months, even years. These people are the ones who can point you in the direction of whatever you need. Meeting them is easy, most motel folks are easy going and smoke lots of cigarettes. Since most motels forbid smoking in the rooms, small packs of smokers form on porches and in the parking lot. Approach one of these groups with a cigarette between your lips, and they're sure to smile and introduce themselves.

This morning, well, early afternoon, there aren't packs of smokers around. Just a couple tenants mulling about. Across the parking lot from my room, a young mother, pregnant with what looks to be her fourth, is on a white plastic lawn chair with her legs and arms crossed. Elbow perched on one hand, fuming cigarette in the other. She looks at me with a look that says "so?" and "fuck you" at the same time. Three children play on the curb in front of her, oblivious to their portentous circumstances.

To my right, a local is leaning against a pole that supports the walkway above. Thin, middle-aged, and as blonde as a

Norwegian newborn, this person was ripe for conversation. I check to make sure I have my pack of cigarettes and lighter, and walk over.

"Smoke?" I hold out my pack with two cigarettes sticking out.

"Thanks." The local slides one out and leans forward, letting me light it. "I seen ya move in yesterday, welcome aboard." The local takes a healthy first drag and demonstrates a mastery of the art of smoking. The grip of the cigarette is delicate, the fingers are bent in a natural position, as if unaware they are cradling a cigarette. The lips don't purse or pucker, but close around the paper tube with ease, letting the teeth do the gripping. The inhale isn't some cheek-hollowing vacuum, it's as subtle as inhaling the scent of a new candle. The local blows the smoke out in a steady breath, then looks at the cigarette, as if in approval.

"I'm Golden," the local says, extending a hand.

"I'm Caish. Nice to meet you."

"Where ya comin' from, Cash?"

"Malibu."

"Oh, wow. Malibu? Shit, what'd ya do to end up here?" Golden chuckled.

"I got robbed. Everything I owned, stolen."

"Nah, you serious?"

"Yup, serious. Got conned."

"Damn, Cash. Well, like I said, welcome aboard. I guess ya could consider me this ship's captain. Been here longer'n anybody except Marbles, who has been here longer than even management. She lives up on 204. She's nuts though. Government pays her bills and she just stays up there in 204 with her cats. Management don't even make her move in and out every month. So if ya need anything, I'm the one to come to. I help most people 'round here get comfortable for as long as they're aboard. It can get tough livin' here sometimes, but I'm always here to help."

"Good to hear," I say, "it's nice to have a friend in tough

times."

"Essential, I'd say."

"So what's her deal?" I ask, nodding in the direction of the mother.

Golden looked across the parking lot, taking another drag of the cigarette. "Mmm," Golden blew the smoke out, "that's Topaz. She ain't in a good way."

"Why's that?" I ask.

She's strung out, addicted to everything under the sun, and due in three weeks, Golden tells me. Never had to work a day in her life, became reliant on her abusive boyfriend, then couldn't pay the mortgage when he was picked up for selling crack. She's now selling herself to make ends meet. Golden knew her life story. Every detail. Last week the baby stopped kicking.

We walk over to a bench with an unobstructed view of the sun and smoke through the rest of my pack of Marlboros. Golden tells me the stories of each of the long-stay residents. When Golden asks about my story, I begin what feels like a therapy session. During my telling, Golden asks me questions like, "And how did that make ya feel?" and, "Why do ya think that happened?" It reminds me of the way Sam used to ask questions. The truth is, I don't know why these bad things happened. I believe in karma, and have always been a good person. I tipped generously, donated tons of money to charities, and gave millions to family. Sam would say bad things happen because karma doesn't exist, but entropy does. Golden doesn't offer a solution. Golden just nods, says, "Mhm."

We talk away the afternoon, then walk down to Pink's and get burgers.

Afterwards, we're walking back to Malibu Motel, smoking cigarettes, when I tell Golden that I need to get pain killers. Golden smiles. Of course you do, we all do, Golden says. We have ways.

Over the next few weeks, Golden introduces me to both

suppliers and clients. A few are residents of Malibu Motel, including Topaz, but most are in the surrounding neighborhood. Rich people too. People who pull their Range Rover up to the curb and hand me crisp one hundred-dollar bills for a few pill bottles full of opioids. I reinvest the earnings in more inventory and lottery tickets. By the end of my first twenty-eight days at Malibu Motel, I have enough money to buy a laptop. So I do. It's a business investment. So I can network better.

But that investment makes it so I can't afford another twenty-eight days at the motel. Golden talks a friend into letting me stay in her garage—a one-car, unfinished, roach-infested wooden box of depression. But she let me stay there for $500 a month, so I can't complain.

One night on Facebook I see that Riley died. Two months ago. There aren't many details, but AIDS was the cause of death—another crash in the fast lane. Riley was too young to die. And too good-looking. Truly a tragedy. But at least Riley wasn't living in a garage. Nothing but a laptop, flip-phone, clothes, pills, and heroin in my possession. *There's* the true tragedy. But, all the better story when I make it back to wealth.

My story!

My story is my greatest asset! That's how I make it back! Now I even had the death of a lover. Hollywood will pay me millions for my story. For the screenplay. They love true stories! Then I'll get royalties from the film for the rest of my life. Hell, maybe I'll even become a full-time screenwriter. Hopelessness whispered to me that it would never work, that nobody would want to watch such a depressing movie. But Hopelessness doesn't know the human heart. We love to watch burning buildings, crashing cars, and sinking ships. Destruction stops us dead in our tracks. We love home videos of people hurting themselves. This is who we are. My movie will captivate the audience with the calamity, then reward them with the happy ending of me becoming a successful screenwriter.

The next morning I buy ten notepads, a pack of pens, and stop by FedEx Kinkos and print photos from the last several years of my life. The notepads are for this story. I can't risk typing it on Word then losing the laptop or having to sell it. I need my story in hardcopy from the first word to the last. The photos are for proof. Hollywood will want to see that this really happened. They will also help the director of photography get an idea for how to frame the cinematography. And they will help the director cast the right actors. Who is going to play me? Probably an A-Lister with a perfect build that doesn't mind committing themselves to the role. A method actor. They'll need to spend hours and hours with me to learn what I'm like. We'll become good friends and establish a lifelong connection.

I sit on my cot and begin writing. I start from the beginning. Well, the beginning of the end. My meeting with Jamie T. Fucking Lowell. My life in Malibu. My life in wealth. Writing is easy, I just scribble the words that come to me. No writer's block here. I'm not making it up. This is how it happened.

27

I keep at my screenplay day and night for weeks. I write until my hand cramps and my fingers shake. The story—*my* story—is my purpose. Deciding on a name for the story is tough. "Riches to Rags and Back," "Life, Liberty, and the Pursuit of Wealth," and "The Cost of Free Cash" became my working titles. The studio will probably come up with one anyway.

I even write a few poems. I didn't know I had it in me, but once I get into it, they just flow out.

Now I wasn't a homeless wretch, I was a starving writer—a perfectly respectable profession. I joined the ranks of the many screenwriters before me who had nothing, but would rise to fame and wealth by sheer act of will and profound storytelling abilities. By myself. Without any help from anybody. Neither Satan nor God came through, so I had to bootstrap my way back to wealth.

In the meantime, though, I still need money. Golden's friend is a nice lady, but she wants her "goddamn $500," and I don't have it. I need all the pills I have. I have enough for a few nights at Malibu Motel, so I pack my backpack and suitcase—a recent thrift store acquisition to hold my kit and screenplay materials— and check into the same ground floor room I stayed in last time. It feels like home. Golden even brings me a bottle of Jack Daniels as a welcome home gift. We sit on the nylon comforter of my bed, shoulder to shoulder, and pass the bottle back and forth.

I tell Golden about my million-dollar idea with the screenplay. Golden is excited about it and willing to help with editing. Golden claims to have a degree in creative writing from UCLA ("You can see where that got me!"). I also tell Golden about my predicament with cash. Namely, that I'm once again out of it.

"Can ya refill any of your scrips? There are always buyers." Golden takes a graceful swig.

"Nah," I say, "none are up for refill for another week. And I think I've been to every hospital within walkin' distance complainin' about head and back pain. I don't know how to get more."

"And ya don't have enough money to buy anything else right now?"

"Right."

"Well, Cash, we could always go the ER route." Golden set the bottle on the nightstand. "Let's step out and have a cigarette."

I follow Golden out to the porch and ask, "What's the ER route? Just asking ER nurses for something for your headache? Can I bum a cigarette off ya? I left mine in the room. Thanks."

"With the ER route, ya walk into the ER with a real injury." Golden blows smoke into the sunset and looks down, kicking a pebble off the porch.

"A real injury? My back really is injured. And I really do get headaches."

"Oh, sure, sure. I wasn't saying that. I'm just sayin', if you walk in... say... bleeding, or with a broken bone..."

"What? Like, get fake blood or something?"

Golden keeps looking down. Like an ashamed child. "No, not fake. From time to time, people in your position can get more painkillers—stronger painkillers—by injuring themselves... I know it sounds pretty bad, but it works."

"Oh, fuck that Golden, I can't break my own arm."

"Well, ya don't have to break your arm, you could just look like you got into a fight. Just roughed up. And have a couple cuts. That would do it. They'd give ya hydrocodone, probably. Maybe a Suboxone scrip."

"Ah, damn. I don't know, Golden."

"Well, think about it. I know Topaz is looking for hydros, so if you can get 'em, she's buyin'."

"Oh yeah, whatever happened to her baby?"

Golden looked pained by my question. "Lost it. Late

miscarriage."

"Fuck. That's terrible. How's she doin'?"

"She's in the market for hydros, so, I guess she's doin' about as bad as the rest of us."

Golden's plan is a good one. We'd give me a few cuts, rough me up, then dump me in an emergency room. The cuts and roughing up didn't have to hurt, Golden was armed to the teeth with heroin and alcohol. We agreed to split my profits 60/40. They would take my blood at the hospital and see that I was on heroin, but they wouldn't arrest me. They'd probably just give me methadone in addition to whatever painkillers they prescribed me.

Golden fills my veins with heroin and my stomach with alcohol, then hands me a glass from the kitchenette in my room. I brake the glass and drag the shard across the top of my knee. Blood gushed around my fingertips and down my leg. I must have squeezed the glass too hard, my finger is cut. Bad.

"Shit," Golden says, "that was pretty deep. Let's go."

"Wuddabout roughin' me up s'more?" I slur.

"No need, we got what we needed, come on." Golden lifts me by my arm and helps me out the door and onto the porch.

"Lock my door, Ima meet you at th—" I fall to my knees into the parking lot, hands extended to break my fall. I'm still holding the glass shard in my left hand. The asphalt plunges the shard into my fingers. I see it, but don't feel it.

Golden helps me to my feet, "Fuck, Cash, you alright? Your knees are scraped up. Oh fuck! Your hand is bleeding! Sweet mother of Christ."

Golden lifts me into the backseat of a friend's shitty van. "Yeah, I fell off th' curb," I explain.

The driver puts on the van's hazard lights and speeds to the hospital. La Riqueza Medical Center. We pull into the ER entrance and Golden helps me in. Golden tells the nurse that some guy—some fuckin' bastard—just beat me up. Tried to rob me, then got pissed when I didn't have anything on me. Cut me up. Cut my hands when I tried to defend myself. Hit my thigh with his knife. Fucking bastard.

I drift off when they stitch my fingers. My left pointer finger and right middle finger took twelve stitches. My knee needs more. Seventeen stitches to close that one.

But it's mission accomplished. They give me three different kinds of painkiller *and* methadone. I even get to stay the night and have hospital food.

Golden takes me back to the motel the next morning and makes the rounds with my new inventory. Even after Golden's cut, I make over three hundred dollars. Enough for a few more days at Malibu Motel. I buy heroin from Golden for the pain, and Golden is kind enough to throw in some marijuana. Weed is a superb side dish.

My writing hand is obtrusively bandaged, but I can still write. I make progress on my screenplay. Each day Golden tends to me to make sure I'm comfortable, and keeps an eye on my inventory. Golden takes care of the selling during the days and nights, and spends the evenings editing my manuscript. I've promised Golden thirty percent of the profits I earn from the screenplay. Golden believes in me. Believes in the screenplay. Golden knows this is going to be a money maker. I can see it in the way Golden works on the manuscript. Fervent. Always asking me clarifying questions. Giving suggestions on how to tell certain stories. Which stories to include, and which to leave out.

Golden even offers to write. At least until my hand heals. Golden sits at the foot of my bed and I dictate the story. We fill all ten notebooks and Golden buys more. We settle into a routine. We're both charged with the excitement about what this manuscript means for us.

Golden also comes up with the wise idea of novelizing the

screenplay. That way, when the movie comes out, we can ride the wave of fame and sell tons of books.

Before my big break I want to tie up a few loose ends. I email Caleb and apologize for any pain I may have caused him or his wife (although I'm still convinced I was just helping her). I send a Facebook message to my ex and Mark, apologizing for not calling more often, and promising to be a better parent when I get back on my feet. I email Agent Palmer, just in case.

At the end of the evening, after Golden has left for the night, I heat up a frozen burrito and take a few painkillers. After dinner I find a vein and inject euphoria into my arm.

The local news is droning on the TV. It's too loud. I'd rather float in silence. Where is that confounded remote?

"Our next story is one you have to see to believe," the plastic news anchor is saying, "luckily, we've got it all on tape."

The camera cut to the other anchor who was smiling and nodding. "That's right Kristen. Video surveillance footage from nine banks shows former lottery winner Timothy Eric Rayburn sliding a note across to tellers demanding money and telling them that he was armed."

Slack-jawed, I fall off the side of the bed.

"Jacob Handley is live at the scene of the most recent robbery. Jacob?"

A split screen of Jacob appears. He's standing, well lit, in front of a US Bank. He's smiling, waiting for his turn to talk. When Kristen, from the newsroom, stops talking, there is an awkward pause and then Jacob begins to talk.

"That's right Kristen, we're here in Burbank in front of the US Bank on Olive Avenue." The split screen gives way to his screen. "This was the ninth and final bank robbed by Timothy Rayburn. Local news and radio stations have been calling him the Brazen Bandit. As a former lottery winner with nothing left to lose, he walked into banks without a mask or disguise and demanded cash. His weapon of choice: a piece of paper. He simply slid a note across the counter that told the teller he had a gun and demanded money. When the teller gave him what was in the till, he'd walk out of the bank in full view of the cameras. Police say they had difficulty tracking the man because, even after releasing images to the public and receiving tips as to the man's identity, Timothy Rayburn did not have an official address. He and his wife, Selina, were living with a friend in Orange County. Police state that..."

Tim Rayburn. Fucking Tim Rayburn. Bank robber. Not once or twice. *Nine* times. I pull out my laptop and Google him. Reports say he pulled in an average of $4,000 from each robbery. He spent the money on a Honda Element, then bought wheels and a sound system, clothes, and heroin. The FBI raided the room the Rayburns were staying in and discovered nearly twenty grams of heroin. The news reporter droning on the TV is giving details about how Tim won the lottery twenty years ago, but then lost it all over the years. He and his wife were destitute, and he determined that robbing banks was the only way to survive.

Robbing banks.

Why didn't I think of that? You don't even need a gun. You just need to tell the teller that you have one. One robbery would be enough to get by until my manuscripts were purchased. Golden had been taking my hard copies and typing them into a Word document so we could send it to agents. Golden was almost caught up with me, and I was almost caught up with real time. A couple months, max, and the screenplay would be purchased. Tim robbed nine banks before getting caught, and he didn't even wear a disguise (did he want to get caught?). I could rob just one, using the same MO, maybe two max, and have enough to make ends meet for the foreseeable future.

Golden knocked, then poked in (always so polite). "Caish?" Golden asks. Golden started pronouncing my name correctly after I handed over the manuscripts to be typed up. Seeing it written helps.

"Yeah, come in."

"Hey, here's your take of what I sold tonight," Golden handed me a roll of bills, "and I have a ride lined up for ya tomorrow at eleven to take you to get your scrips filled."

"Thanks Golden, I truly appreciate how great you've been to me. Always watchin' after me."

"Well, we're friends. What else do we have, right? How are ya doin' on smack?"

"Good, I could use more though. Runnin' a lil' low. Oh, Golden, check this out," I turned up the TV. "I know this guy, Tim Rayburn, he's the one in the story with the Aventador that Mario Andretti drives. He's the only other lottery winner I know."

"No shit," Golden says, staring at the TV and sitting on the foot of my bed. "And he's robbin' banks?"

"Well, was, he got caught."

"How many?"

"Nine."

"*Nine?*"

"Yeah, got away with eight bank robberies, then got caught when an off-duty cop was at the teller station next to him at a US Bank in Burbank. Saw the teller's face and pulled out his concealed. Had Tim on the ground with his arm bent behind him for twenty-five minutes until Burbank's finest finally showed up."

"Damn. So did he lose everything too?"

"Yeah, but I don't think he got conned or anything. I think he was just bad with money. But Golden, I think I might give bank robbery a try. Just one to bridge me over until my manuscript gets picked up."

"Haha, sounds good, Caish, let me know if you need a getaway driver."

"Haha, will do. But I'm serious, Golden. I'm going to do the same thing Tim got away with eight times. I won't have a gun or anything, I'll just use a note."

"You're not actually serious though, right?" Golden asks, turning more fully toward me and examining my face.

"Yeah, I'm serious. He averaged four grand on every robbery. That would last me a couple months."

"But, Caish. That puts everything at risk. What about our screenplay? Our novel? How will you work on that and get that to publishers if you're behind bars? Publishers won't even look at you if you're locked up."

"I won't get caught. Tim did it eight times without even using a disguise. I'll change my look entirely. And imagine what that will do for the story!"

"Caish, you'll doom the story. This is too soon. You're not done with the story yet. You can't do this. I can't let you do this. We've put too much into our screenplay to risk losing it all."

"I've made up my mind, Golden. I'm doing this. Tomorrow morning. I'm a little behind with motel management too, so this will help me get current."

"Plus, the screenplay is basically done."

"Done?" Golden asks.

"Basically, I just need to write about the last couple of nights. It's all here."

"And you're starting your robbing tomorrow?"

"Yup!"

Golden sat at the end of the bed, looking at me. Reaching over, Golden turns off the TV. "So, I can't talk you out of this?" Golden asks.

"This is the answer. It's meant to be. You can't talk me out of it," I say. "This is how the story goes."

Golden thinks on my words, then stands and walks to the door. "Well, then tonight's a big night. The night before your foray into bank robbery. I think it calls for a celebration!"

"Haha, what?"

"I'll be right back. Sit tight." Golden pulls the door closed on the way out.

I sit on my bed, imagining how the next few months will go. This is perfect. I'll rob a bank, just one. Two tops. And have enough to get myself looking presentable in meetings where I'll be pitching my screenplay to agents and production studios. I even have a photo album that goes along with the manuscript. Visual aids are helpful with these production types. After they buy the rights to the story, I'll be set. This time I'll live more conservatively. Depending on how much it sells for. And how much the royalties are. Either way I'll for sure move back to Malibu.

That's when it comes to me, my magnum opus:

I am the score, the reminder of more;
the ambition that man makes his mission.

The woman of the hour, with her braids of power.
The sign of status, the aspiring vine's lattice.

The white clouds of bliss and the black abyss.
The endless sea, the omnipotent key.

I am the fire behind desire.
Money is me and I am thee.

Golden walks in with a smile and a kit. "Tonight's on me, Caish. One last ride into the sky before your high-stakes day tomorrow." Golden sits on the edge of the bed and pulls out a small ball of cellophane-wrapped heroin. "Pull the curtains closed, would ya?"

I finish writing the poem, then get out of the bed, pull the curtains closed, and lock the door. "I wanna float high tonight, Golden. Ya sure you don't mind me usin' up your junk?"

"Relax, Caish. Like I said, this one's on me. My own supply of the finest heroin in town. Pure, safe, and warmer than Fentanyl. As much as you'd like."

I walk around the bed and sit next to Golden, who had set up an administration station on my nightstand. Golden is already melting down a spoonful of carmel-colored syrup. A big spoon. Not a soup spoon; almost a serving spoon.

"Let's get that jacket off."

"I'm kind of chilly," I say.

"We'll put it back on after." Golden helps my arm out of my jacket. I tie the rubber tube over my bicep. The syringe sucks up the liquid and finds its way into my arm. I hardly see it happen. Certainly don't feel it. The warmth moves through my shoulder and I melt onto the bed.

"Give me a pinch more to go on," I ask Golden through the clouds of bliss below.

"Ah, better not. You're pretty high right now. Better safe than dead."

But I insist, and won't relent until Golden begrudgingly agrees.

"Just a pinch." I feel a faint pinch in my thigh. I look down to see Golden pulling away the syringe and packing up.

I want to ask, "What about you?" but my mouth doesn't move. My body is numb with warmth.

Golden stands up, takes my deadbolt key from the nightstand, and walks to the door. "Just relax, I'll be back in a minute." Golden pulls the door closed and latches the deadbolt.

Golden will be right back. I trust Golden with my life and know that Golden is always looking after my best interests. Golden is a gentle soul, and has no motive whatsoever to do me any harm. Golden only did what I asked.

Golden will be right back.

My soul is floating.

My mind is at peace.

My arms aren't working.

Neither is my back. I try to roll off the bed. My legs swing off the side and my torso stays put. My arms are spread in front of me. I'm kneeling next to the bed with my face buried in its itchy nylon. I can move my neck enough to see one of my poems. I try to read it, but my vision is blurring and tunneling at the same time. My breathing is shallow. I can't catch my breath.

From under the bed a tentacle twists around my leg. Hopelessness slides another up my back. Its beak clicks. It whispers but I can't make out the words.

I need my phone. This isn't right. I need to call Golden. I need help. 911. My heart hurts. My body is not responding. Not even my lungs.

My neck lets go and my face drops to the mattress. I can't feel my body. It's hard to hold onto thoughts. This can't

Epilogue

COUNTY OF LOS ANGELES		CASE REPORT			DEPARTMENT OF CORONER

	APPARENT MODE			CASE NO	
1	ACCIDENT/ SUICIDE				
	SPECIAL CIRCUMSTANCES			CRYPT 163	

LAST, FIRST MIDDLE		AKA	#

ADDRESS				CITY WEST HOLLYWOOD	STATE CA	ZIP 90069

SEX	RACE APPEARS	DOB	AGE	HGT	WGT	EYES	HAIR	TEETH ALL NATURAL TEETH	FACIAL HAIR NONE	ID VIEW Yes	CONDITION FAIR

MARK TYPE	MARK LOCATION	MARK DESCRIPTION

NOK	ADDRESS	CITY	STATE	ZIP

ID METHOD
FINGERPRINTS FROM FBI

LA #	MAIN #	CII #	FBI #	MILITARY #	POB

IDENTIFIED BY NAME (PRINT)	RELATIONSHIP	PHONE	DATE	TIME
@FBI				06:58

PLACE OF DEATH/ PLACE FOUND HOTEL/MOTEL	ADDRESS OR LOCATION MOTEL,	CITY WEST HOLLYWOO	ZIP 90069

PLACE OF INJURY MOTEL	AT WORK No	DATE	TIME	LOCATION OR ADDRESS WEST HOLLYWOOD, CA	ZIP 90069

DOD	TIME 14:50	FOUND OR PRONOUNCED BY LACFD SQ 8		

OTHER AGENCY INV. OFFICER LASD WEST HOLLYWOOD - DEP.	PHONE	REPORT NO.	NOTIFIED BY	NO
TRANSPORTED BY MICHAEL	TO LOS ANGELES FSC	DATE	TIME 19:15	

FINGERPRINTS? Yes	CLOTHING Yes	PM RPT No	MORTUARY
MED. EV. Yes	INVEST. PHOTO # 7	SEAL TYPE NOT SEALED	HOSP RPT No
PHYS. EV. No	EVIDENCE LOG Yes	PROPERTY? Yes	HOSP CHART No
SUICIDE NOTE No	SSR NO.	RCPT. NO. 269528	PP NO.

SYNOPSIS
ACCORDING TO THE AVAILABLE INFORMATION, THE DECEDENT IS A ▮▮▮ WHO WAS FOUND DEAD ▮▮ MOTEL ROOM. MULTIPLE PRESCRIPTION MEDICATIONS, MARIJUANA AND HEROIN WERE FOUND IN THE ROOM. THE DECEDENT HAS A HISTORY OF DRUG ABUSE. ▮▮ WAS RECENTLY TREATED FOR TWO LACERATIONS. ▮▮▮ DRUG OVERDOSE.

	DATE	TIME 16:31	REVIEWED BY	DATE	TIME 18:38
INVESTIGATOR					

FORM #3 NARRATIVE TO FOLLOW? ☑

County of Los Angeles, Department of Coroner
Investigator's Narrative

Case Number: ███████████   Decedent: █████████████████

Information Sources:

- Deputy ██████████ – Los Angeles Sheriff Department - West Hollywood, 720 San Vicente Blvd. West Hollywood, CA 90069 ██████████

- ████████████   ████████████

Investigation:

On ██████████ at 1610 hours, Los Angeles Sheriff Officer ██████████ reported this death to the Coroner's Office. Acting Supervisor ██████ assigned this case to me at 1621 hours. I arrived at the location at 1709 hours. I cleared the scene at 1837 hours, after completion of the field portion of the investigation. I utilized the above sources and my on scene investigation to obtain the information contained within this death Investigation. I have requested copies of the decedent's medical records from ██████████ Medical Center where the decedent was recently treated. The ██████████ an apparent overdose. See Coroner Case ████ ██████ I have also requested a copy of the police report from the ██████████ altercation at the decedent's department.

Location:

Motel – ██████████ Motel – █████████████████████ West Hollywood, CA 90069

Informant/Witness Statements:

According to Deputy ██████████, the decedent is a █████████████████ who has been living at the above motel since ██████████. On ██████ at approximately 1430 hours, the manager of the motel went to the room to collect the rent for the day. The decedent had only been paying by the day and was only paid through the night of the 16th. The manager knocked on the door and got no answer. The manager had not seen the decedent leave the motel. He attempted to use the pass key, but found the door locked on the inside. The manager forced open the door and observed the unresponsive decedent kneeling on the floor with ██ face and arms resting on the bed. The motel manager called 911 and Los Angeles County Fire Department Squad 8 responded to the scene. Paramedics examined the decedent and found no signs of life. Paramedics pronounced death on ██████████ at 1450 hours. Los Angeles Sheriff Deputies responded to the location and observed numerous prescription medications and some intravenous drug paraphernalia scattered around the room. Some hand written notes were found in the room. The notebooks, papers and photos scattered around the room indicate that the decedent's ██████ died. ██ was apparently in the middle of writing a screen play about ██ ████████████. The decedent has a history of drug abuse including heroin. On ██████████ the decedent was involved in a physical altercation with an unknown male at the apartment that █████████████. This resulted in the decedent being transported to ██████████ Emergency Room with lacerations to ██ thigh and hand. After being released from the emergency room ██████████ at the motel where ██ had stayed previously.

According to ██████████ the decedent has a history of drug abuse and is on numerous prescription medications. Although ██ was upset from the death of ██████████ ██ expressed no suicidal ideations. ██ was keeping busy with writing a screen play and poems about ██████████. ██ was also keeping busy with the putting together a photo album. The decedent was also looking forward to █████████████ to Los Angeles. The decedent sent an email to ██████████ at 0049 hours.

County of Los Angeles, Department of Coroner
Investigator's Narrative

Case Number: ███████████ Decedent: ████████████████████

Scene Description

The scene is a small motel room located on the ground floor of an older two story motel in West Hollywood. The room contains a bed, table, dresser and night stands. The room is cluttered with prescription medications noted on the nightstand, on the bed and in a suitcase. The decedent's clothing is piled in a chair next to the table. The decedent's computer, numerous notebooks, multiple photographs and a scrapbook are spread on the bed. Some syringes, a cooking cap and multiple small balloons are noted on the dresser. Two wooden boxes containing additional paraphernalia and balloons were also on the dresser. Several handwritten notes to the decedent's ████████████ were found on a chair. The decedent is in a kneeling position on the south side of the bed. ███ knees are resting on the carpet. ███ chest, head and arms are resting on the bed.

Evidence:

Several prescription medications, a vial of marijuana, some balloons of drugs and some paraphernalia was found at the above motel room. These items were booked as medical evidence at the Forensic Science Center.

Body Examination:

The body is that of a ████████████████ who was observed kneeling by the bed at the above location. ███ has ████ eyes and ████████ is wearing a ██████████ and a black jacket. ███ has no trauma, scars or tattoos noted. ███ has bandages on ██ left knee and right hand from recent medical treatment. Rigor mortis is rated at three throughout the entire body. Lividity is fixed and consistent with the position found. The ambient air temperature was 73.0 degrees at 1745 hours. The decedent's liver temperature was 92.2 degrees at 1749 hours.

Identification:

On ██████████, at 0658 hours, the Federal Bureau of Investigation identified the decedent as ████████████, (DOB ██████████) by fingerprint comparison.

Next of Kin Notification:

██

Tissue Donation:

The decedent is not a candidate for tissue harvesting due to the length of time since death.

Autopsy Notification:

No notification is needed for the examination in this case.

SUPERVISOR

Date of Report

12

AUTOPSY REPORT
ADULT FORM PROTOCOL

COUNTY OF LOS ANGELES

DEPARTMENT OF CORONER

No.

163

I performed an autopsy on the body of

at ___ the DEPARTMENT OF CORONER

Los Angeles, California ___ on ___ @ 1050h

(Date) (Time)

From the anatomic findings and pertinent history I ascribe the death to:

(A) Heroin intoxication

DUE TO OR AS A CONSEQUENCE OF

(B) ___

DUE TO OR AS A CONSEQUENCE OF

(C) ___

DUE TO OR AS A CONSEQUENCE OF

(D) ___

OTHER CONDITIONS CONTRIBUTING BUT NOT RELATED TO THE IMMEDIATE CAUSE OF DEATH

Anatomical Summary:

☒ As listed below
☐ See form #16 under gross impressions

① Cardiomegaly. Heart ___ grs with left ventricular hypertrophy 1.6 cm

② Visceral congestion

③ No recent external or internal evidence of injury.

④ Healing scars on right hand and the left knee

⑤ History of drug use
   A) see toxicological examination report.

76A890H-Rev 12/11

ADULT FORM PROTOCOL

page 2 of 17

name

163

IF A TRAUMA CASE STATE:

Injury date: _____ Hospital Date(s): _____

CIRCUMSTANCES:

☒ See Investigator Report form #3
☐ As listed below
☐ Source: _____

EXTERNAL EXAMINATION:

The body is identified by toe tags and is that of an unembalmed/embalmed refrigerated,

☒ adult
☐ elderly
☐ teenage

who appears
☒ about the reported
☐ older than the reported
☐ the reported
☐ younger than the reported
age of _____ years.

The body weighs _____ pounds,

measures ____ inches and is
☐ cachectic.
☐ mildly/moderately/extremely obese.
☐ poorly nourished.
☒ thin.
☐ well-built, muscular and fairly well-nourished.

Malibu Motel

163

☐ The skin is free of abrasions, bruises, lacerations, scars and burns.
  or

☒ SEE DIAGRAM OF SCARS AND LACERATIONS IN FORM 20

Wrist scars are ☐ present.
                 ☒ absent.

Tattoo(s) are: ☒ not present.
                ☐ present and identified as _____
_____
_____

☐ Rigor has presumably been altered/abolished.
☒ Rigor mortis is present.
☒ Livor mortis is POSTERIOR AND FIXED.

The head is normocephalic and   ☒ covered by   ■ black   hair.
                                ☐ partly covered by   blond
                                                       brown
                                                       red
                                                    ☐ _____/gray

There is   ☒ no   balding and the hair   ■■■■■■■■■■
           ☐ complete   can be described as   ■■■■■■■■■■
           ☐ frontal   ■■■■■■■■■■
           ☐ mid-biparietal
           ☐ occipital
           ☐ temporal

Mustache is (absent)/present. Beard is (absent)/present and described as _____.

Examination of the eyes reveals

☒ Irides that appear to be ■■■■■, in color and sclerae that are NON-ICTERIC
☐ Corneal removal (eye bank).
☐ Eye shields in place.

There are/(are no) petechial hemorrhages of the conjunctivae of the lids and/(or) the sclerae. The oronasal passages are unobstructed.

Chaunceton Bird

ADULT FORM PROTOCOL

page 4 of 17

name ‾‾‾‾‾‾‾‾‾‾ 163

☐ Lower	teeth are	☐ absent.
☐ Upper		☐ carious.
☒ Upper and lower		☐ partly absent and uncompensated.
		☒ present.

Dentures are: _____

The neck is (unremarkable) or _____

There (is/is no) chest deformity. There is (no/an/a mildly) increased anterior-posterior diameter.

The abdomen is
- ☐ distended.
- ☒ flat.
- ☐ not unusual.
- ☐ obese.
- ☐ scaphoid.

☒ The extremities show no edema, joint deformity, abnormal mobility, non-therapeutic punctures or needle tracks.
or

☒ POSSIBLE NON-THERAPEUTIC PUNCTURES IN RIGHT ANTECUBITAL FOSSA.

EVIDENCE OF THERAPEUTIC INTERVENTION:

☒ There is no evidence of any previous recent hospitalization.

☐ The following are present and are in proper position:
- ☐ Airway mouth piece
- ☐ Central intravenous lines
- ☐ EKG Pads
- ☐ Endotracheal/nasotracheal tube
- ☐ Esophageal obturator
- ☐ Intravenous lines
- ☐ Nasogastric/orogastric tube
- ☐ Urinary catheter
- ☐ Other _____

ADULT FORM PROTOCOL

page 5 of 17

name ▮▮▮▮▮▮▮

163

☐ There are signs that the following surgical procedures have been done:
  ☐ _____ sided craniotomy.
  ☐ Cerebral ventricular pressure monitoring tube placement.
  ☐ Tracheostomy.
  ☐ _____ sided chest tube placement.
  ☐ _____ sided thoracotomy.
  ☐ Laparotomy.
  ☐ Peritoneal lavage procedure.
  ☐ Vascular cutdown procedure(s).
  ☐ Repair of injuries to _____.

☐ Signs of cardiopulmonary resuscitation are as follows:
  ☐ Brown arc shaped paddle marks over the chest.
  ☐ Rib fracture located at _____
  ☐ Serosanguineous pericardial fluid.
  ☐ Signs of intracardial injections.
  ☐ Focal areas of red hemorrhage in the posterior wall of the left ventricle.

☐ There is evidence of old surgery. Scars are present at the _____
and the following organs are missing:
  1.
  2.
  3.

☒ There has/has not~~has not~~ been post mortem intervention for organ procurement ~~which can be~~

~~described as~~ _____

_____

_____

EVIDENCE OF EXTERNAL TRAUMATIC INJURY:

☐ Diagrammed on form(s) # _____
☒ None

Healing superficial cuts (medically treated)
on Dorsal surface Right hand — + over the left
knee. Healing well.

_____

_____

_____

CLOTHING:

The body   ☐ is clothed   and I   ☒ did not see the clothing.
           ☒ was not clothed   ☐ inspected the clothing.

ADULT FORM PROTOCOL
page 6 of 17

c ████████████
name

163

The clothing can be described as _____

_____

_____

_____

INITIAL INCISION:

The body cavities are entered through _____

> ☒ The standard coronal incision.
> ☒ The standard "Y" shaped incision.
> ☐ Additional incisions are _____
> _____
> _____

☒ No foreign material is present in the mouth, upper airway and trachea.

EVIDENCE OF INTERNAL INJURIES:

> ☐ Diagrammed on form(s) #
> ☒ NONE
> _____
> _____
> _____
> _____
> _____
> _____
> _____

NECK:

The neck organs (are)/are not removed en bloc with the tongue. No lesions are present nor is trauma of the gingiva, lips or oral mucosa demonstrated. There is no edema of the larynx. Both hyoid bone and larynx are intact and without fractures. No hemorrhage is present in the adjacent throat organs, investing fascia, strap muscles, thyroid or visceral fascia. There are/(are no) prevertebral fascial hemorrhages. The tongue when sectioned shows no trauma/or _____.

Malibu Motel

name   163

CHEST/ABDOMINAL CAVITY:

The right/left/both pleural cavity/cavities contain(s) no fluid blood, or adhesions/or
☐ Blood
☐ Fluid measuring _____ cc   RT_____   LF_____

No tension pneumothorax is demonstrated. The parietal pleurae are intact.

The lungs are
☐ partly collapsed.
☒ poorly expanded.
☐ voluminous.
☐ well-expanded.

Soft tissues of the thoracic
and abdominal walls
☒ are well-preserved.
☐ have early/late postmortem softening,
   discoloration and crepitation.

The subcutaneous fat of the
☒ abdominal wall measures 5/16 "
☒ chest wall measures 4/4 "

[redacted] are examined and sectioned in usual manner and show no abnormalities, or _____

The organs of the abdominal cavity have a normal arrangement and none are absent.
There is no fluid collection. The peritoneal cavity is without evidence of
peritonitis. There are no adhesions.

SYSTEMIC AND ORGAN REVIEW

The following observations are limited to findings other than injuries, if described
above.

MUSCULOSKELETAL SYSTEM:

☐ No abnormalities of the bony framework or muscles are present.
☒ Kyphosis/scoliosis
☐ Wasting
☐ Other _____

CARDIOVASCULAR SYSTEM:

The aorta is elastic/fairly elastic/inelastic and of even caliber throughout with
vessels distributed normally from it.

ADULT FORM PROTOCOL

page 8 of 17

name _____

163

The abdominal/thoracic aorta has

☐ discrete plaques that are not elevated.
☒ lipid streaking
☐ minimal/moderate/severe atherosclerosis.

There is no tortuosity or widening of the thoracic segment. The abdominal aorta has

☐ diffuse		☒ focal	☐ intimal	
☐ extensive	atherosclerosis	☐ marked	☐ mural	calcification.
☐ focal	with/without	☐ minimal	☒ ulceration and/or	
☒ minimal		☐ moderate		

There is/is no dilation of the lower abdominal segment. No/An intact aneurysm is present, measuring _____ cm. The major branches of the aorta show no abnormality.

Within the pericardial sac there

☐ are _____ cc. of _____ fluid.
☒ is a minimal amount of serous fluid.

The heart weighs ████ grams.   It has

☒ a normal configuration.
☐ an infantile configuration.
☐ biventricular hypertrophy.
☒ left ventricular hypertrophy.
☐ right ventricular hypertrophy.
☐ _____

The right ventricle is 0.4 cm thick
and the left ventricle is 1.6 cm thick.

The chambers are normally developed and are without mural thrombosis. The valves are thin, leafy and competent.

Circumference of valve rings are:

T.V.	9.5	cm	A.V.	6	cm
P.V.	8	cm	M.V.	10	cm

There is/are

☐ endocardial hemorrhages of _____.
☐ hemoglobin staining of the endocardium.
☒ no endocardial discoloration.

There

☐ is/are
☒ is/are no

☒ infarct(s)
☒ lesion(s)

of the myocardium.

Malibu Motel

CC#

name ████████████

1b3

There is/is no ☒ abnormality
☐ atrophy
☐ hemorrhagic necrosis
☐ necrosis
☐ scarring
of the apices of the papillary musculature.

There are/are no defects of the septum. The great vessels enter and leave in a normal fashion.

The ductus arteriosus
☒ cannot be probed.
☐ is obliterated.
☐ is widely patent.
☐ measures _____

The coronary ostia

☐ are narrowed. ☒ are widely patent.	☐ The left coronary artery is the dominant vessel. ☐ The right coronary artery is the dominant vessel. ☐ There is a balanced pattern of coronary artery distribution. ☒ There is a normal pattern of coronary artery distribution.

There is/are

☐ extensive ☐ minimal ☒ no coronary ☐ segmental	☒ atherosclerosis, ☐ atherosclerotic plaque(s)	☐ with _____ % ☐ with mild to moderate ☐ without ☐ with severe

☐ narrowing ☐ occlusion ☐ stenosis	of the	☐ anterior descending branch of the left coronary artery. ☐ circumflex branch of the left coronary artery. ☐ left/right coronary artery. ☐ major coronary arteries.

No focal endocardial, valvular or myocardial lesions are seen. The blood within the heart and large blood vessels is liquid/clotted.

RESPIRATORY SYSTEM:

☐ An extremely large amount of ☐ Considerable ☐ Moderate ☒ No ☐ Scant	☐ blood is ☐ bloody fluid is ☐ edema is ☐ exudate is ☐ gastric material is ☐ glairy fluid is ☒ secretions are

found in the
☒ lower bronchial
☒ upper respiratory
passages.

ADULT FORM PROTOCOL

page 10 of 17

cc#

name

163

The mucosa
- [ ] has _____ postmortem discoloration.
- [ ] is focally hemorrhagic.
- [x] is intact and pale.
- [ ] is severely injected throughout.
- [ ] is ulcerated.

The lungs are
- [ ] atelectatic
- [ ] crepitant
- [ ] emphysematous
- [x] subcrepitant

and there is
- [x] dependent congestion.
- [ ] postmortem softening.

The left lung weighs _____ grams.
The right lung weighs _____ grams.

The visceral pleurae
- [ ] are punctured.
- [ ] are scarred.
- [x] are smooth and intact.
- [ ] are thickened.
- [ ] contain marginal blebs.

The parenchyma is
- [x] congested.
- [ ] congested and edematous.
- [ ] consolidated.
- [ ] hemorrhagic.
- [ ] nodular.

- [x] The pulmonary vasculature is without thromboembolism.
- [ ] Thromboemboli are/are not present in the distal tertiary branch.
- [ ] Thromboemboli are/are not present in the extrapulmonic portions of the pulmonary artery.

GASTROINTESTINAL SYSTEM:

The esophagus is/has
- [ ] corrosion.
- [x] intact throughout.
- [ ] terminal postmortem erosion.
- [ ] ulceration.
- [ ] varices.

The stomach is/is not distended by AIR OR FLUID . It

contains 10 cc of GREEN-YELLOW LIQUID .

The mucosa IS UNREMARKABLE.

381

cc ▇▇▇▇▇▇▇▇▇▇

name

163

☒ Portions of tablets and capsules cannot be discerned in the stomach.

☐ Residual medication materials seen in the stomach _____

_____

☒ The external and in-situ appearance of the small intestine and colon are unremarkable.

☒ The small intestine and colon are opened along the anti-mesenteric border and ____

ARE UNREMARKABLE ·

☐ The small intestine and colon are examined by inspection, palpation and multiple

incisions and _____

_____

The appendix is (present)/absent surgically.

The pancreas occupies a normal position. There is no

☐ early autolysis.
☒ necrosis.
☒ trauma.

The parenchyma is lobular and firm. The pancreatic ducts are/(are not) ectatic and there is no parenchymal calcification.

HEPATOBILIARY SYSTEM

The liver weighs ▇▇▇▇▇ grams,

☐ is enlarged.
☒ is of average size.
☐ is smaller than normal

and is

☒ red-brown.
☐ tan-brown.
☐ yellow-tan.

The capsule is

☒ intact
☐ thickened
☐ thin

and the consistency of the parenchyma is

☐ firm.
☐ greasy.
☐ increased in resistance.
☒ soft.

The cut surface is

☐ macronodular.
☐ micronodular.
☒ smooth.
☐ fatty.

There is

☒ a normal lobular arrangement.
☐ acute passive congestion.
☐ chronic passive congestion.

Chauncton Bird

page 12 of 17

name 163

The gallbladder is ☐ absent. ☒ present.   The wall is ☒ thickened and rigid. ☐ thin and pliable.

It contains ☒ 10 ___ cc of bile ☐ no bile   and   ☐ calculi which are ☐ mixed. ☐ pure. ☒ no calculi.

There is no obstruction or dilation of the extrahepatic ducts. The periportal lymph nodes are enlarged/not enlarged.

URINARY SYSTEM:

The left kidney weighs ___ grams. The right kidney weighs ___ grams. The kidneys are normally situated and the capsules strip easily/with difficulty, revealing a surface that is SMOOTH.

The corticomedullary demarcation is ☐ obliterated. ☐ obscured by congestion. ☒ preserved.

The pyramids are/are not remarkable. The peripelvic fat is/is not increased. The ureters are without dilation or obstruction and pursue their normal course.

The urinary bladder is ☐ contracted. ☐ distended. ☐ trabeculated. ☒ unremarkable.   It contains ☒ SCANT cc of ☐ amber ☐ brown ☐ hemorrhagic ☐ no urine.   ☐ clear ☐ cloudy urine.

The urine is/is not tested by the dipstick method and the results are ___

GENITAL SYSTEM: (Cross or X out one — fill in the other.)

383

163

HEMOLYMPHATIC SYSTEM:

The spleen weighs _____ grams and is ~~enlarged/for average size~~. *enor* ⑩

The capsule is
- ☒ intact.
- ☐ lacerated.
- ☒ smooth.
- ☐ wrinkled.

The parenchyma is
- ☒ dark red.
- ☐ firm.
- ☐ mushy.
- ☐ pale.

There is an/no increased follicular pattern.

- ☒ Lymph nodes throughout the body are small and inconspicuous.
- ☐ There is generalized lymph node prominence and enlargement.
- ☐ There is focal enlargement of lymph nodes in the following areas: _____

_____

_____

The bone is <u>brittle</u>/<u>not remarkable.</u>

The bone marrow of the <u>vertebra</u>/<u>rib</u> is
- ☐ red and moist.
- ☐ the usual appearance for the age.
- ☒ unremarkable.

CC#

name

163

The ventricular system
- [ ] has a normal appearance
- [ ] is symmetrical
- [x] is unremarkable

without dilation and/or distortion.

Pons, medulla and cerebellum are unremarkable. There is no evidence of uncal or cerebellar herniation. Vessels at the base of the brain have a normal pattern of distribution. There are no aneurysms. The cranial nerves are intact, symmetrical, and normal in size, location and course.

The cerebral arteries
- [ ] are moderately sclerotic.
- [x] are without arteriosclerosis.
- [ ] have advanced/mild arteriosclerosis.
- [ ] have arteriosclerosis at points of bifurcation.

SPINAL CORD:

- [x] The entire cord is/is not dissected.
- [ ] A segment of
  - [ ] cervical
  - [ ] lumbar
  - [ ] thoracic
  spinal cord is examined and is unremarkable/or _____

- [ ] The spinal fluid is clear.

NEUROPATHOLOGY:

The brain and/or spinal cord is placed in formalin solution for further fixation and later examination.

HISTOLOGIC SECTIONS:

Representative sections from various organs are preserved in one/two/three storage jar(s) in 10% formalin. Sections of _____
_____ are submitted for slides.
The slide key is _____

TOXICOLOGY:

- [x] Bile
- [x] Blood
- [x] Liver tissue
- [x] Stomach contents
- [x] Urine
- [x] Vitreous humor
- [ ]

have been submitted to the lab.

- [x] A comprehensive
- [ ] A homicide
- [ ] A traffic
- [ ] A drugs of abuse
- [ ] No

screen was requested.

ADULT FORM PROTOCOL

page 16 of 17

163

SPECIAL PROCEDURES:

☐ Biopsies of _____ have been submitted
☐ Cultures of _____ to the lab.

☐ Anesthesiology _____ consultation(s) was/were requested.
☐ Anthropology
☐ Criminalistics
☐ Odontology
☐ Ophthalmology
☐ Pulmonary
☐ Surgical

PHOTOGRAPHY:

☐ At scene photos are/are not available.
☑ No photos are taken.
☐ Photographs have been taken prior to and/or during the course of the autopsy.

RADIOLOGY:

☐ The body is fluoroscoped _____
☐ No x-rays are obtained.
☐ The body is fluoroscoped and x-rays are taken of the head/chest/ _____

WITNESSES:

☑ None
☐ _____ of
    ☐ DA
    ☐ LAPD   witnessed the autopsy.
    ☐ LASO

DIAGRAMS USED:

Diagram form(s) # ███████████████ were used
during the performance of the autopsy. The diagrams are not intended to be facsimiles.

ADULT FORM PROTOCOL
page 17 of 17

163

OPINION:

The demise of this ▮ year old ▮ is the result of the depressant effects of heroin. This drug is a powerful opioid derivative, that produces a profound depression of the nervous and cardiorespiratory systems which can produce a lethal depression at anytime.

The ▮ present is old and appears to have been medically treated + healing well. There is no recent trauma.

After careful review of the circumstances, autopsy and toxicological examinations, the death is modeled as accidental due to the role played by the drug in its occurrence.

SIGNATURE
RESIDENT IN PATHOLOGY

PRINT NAME
DATE:

SIGNATURE
DEPUTY MEDICAL EXAMINER

PRINT NAME
DATE:

Malibu Motel

COUNTY OF LOS ANGELES   **PRELIMINARY EXAMINATION REPORT - FIELD**   **DEPARTMENT OF CORONER**

6

WAS ORIGINAL SCENE DISTURBED BY OTHERS? Y [ ] N [X]
IF YES, NOTE CHANGES IN NARRATIVE FORM #3.
DATE _____

AMBIENT #1 ___73___ F   TIME ___17:45___
AMBIENT #2 _____ F   TIME _____
WATER _____ F   TIME _____

LIVER TEMPERATURE #1 ___92.2___ F   TIME ___17:49___   THERMOMETER # ___12-01___

LIVER TEMPERATURE #2 _____ F   TIME _____

DATE & TIME FOUND ▓▓▓ @ 14:50   LAST KNOWN ALIVE ▓▓▓ @ 8:00

APPROX. AGE ▓ SEX ▓ EST. HEIGHT ▓ EST. WEIGHT ▓ CLOTHED ? YES [X] NO [ ] IF YES, DESCRIBE:
▓ Black Jacket

DESCRIPTION AS TO WHERE REMAINS FOUND AND CONTACT MATERIAL TO BODY:
Kneeling at side of bed

SCENE TEMPERATURE REGULATED? YES [ ] NO [X] IF YES, THERMOSTAT SET AT _____ DEGREES F.

LIVOR MORTIS: TIME OBSERVED ___17:40___   RIGOR MORTIS: TIME OBSERVED ___17:40___

NECK FLEXION:
ANTERIOR ___3___
POSTERIOR ___3___
RT. LATERAL ___3___
LT. LATERAL ___3___

JAW ___3___   HIP ___3___
SHOULDER ___3___   KNEE ___3___
ELBOW ___3___   ANKLE ___3___
WRIST ___3___

SCALE
0 = ABSENT / NEGATIVE
1 +
2 +
3 +
4 = EXTREME DEGREE

USE SCALE TO DESCRIBE INTENSITY OF RIGOR

SHADE DIAGRAMS TO ILLUSTRATE THE LOCATION OF LIVOR MORTIS.

DESCRIBE INTENSITY OF COLORATION AND WHETHER LIVOR MORTIS IS PERMANENT OR BLANCHES UNDER PRESSURE

Fixed consistant

Investigator

NOTE: ALL DATA COLLECTED FOR THIS FORM MUST BE COLLECTED AT SCENE.

388

MEDICAL REPORT

COUNTY OF LOS ANGELES   DEPARTMENT OF MEDICAL EXAMINER-CORONER

15

AUTOPSY CLASS: ☐ A ☐ B ☐ C ☐ Examination Only D

☐ FAMILY OBJECTION TO AUTOPSY

Date: ▓▓ Time: 10:50 Dr. ▓▓ (Print)

FINAL ON: ▓▓ By: ▓▓ (Print)

DEATH WAS CAUSED BY: (Enter only one cause per line for A, B, C, and D)

IMMEDIATE CAUSE:

(A) Heroin Intoxication

DUE TO, OR AS A CONSEQUENCE OF:
(B)

DUE TO, OR AS A CONSEQUENCE OF:
(C)

DUE TO, OR AS A CONSEQUENCE OF:
(D)

OTHER CONDITIONS CONTRIBUTING BUT NOT RELATED TO THE IMMEDIATE CAUSE OF DEATH:

☐ NATURAL ☐ SUICIDE ☐ HOMICIDE
☑ ACCIDENT ☐ COULD NOT BE DETERMINED

If other than natural causes, HOW DID INJURY OCCUR? Intake of the drug

WAS OPERATION PERFORMED FOR ANY CONDITION STATED ABOVE? ☐ YES ☑ NO

TYPE OF SURGERY: DATE:

☐ ORGAN PROCUREMENT ☑ TECHNICIAN: m▓

PREGNANCY IN LAST YEAR ☐ YES ☐ NO ☑ UNK ☐ NOT APPLICABLE

☐ WITNESS TO AUTOPSY ☐ EVIDENCE RECOVERED AT AUTOPSY
Item Description:

COMMENT:
▓▓ No DRUG USE FOUND, UNRESPONSIVE IN HOTEL ROOM C DRUG PARAPHENELIA. NO FOUL PLAY SUSPECTED.

PRIOR EXAMINATION REVIEW BY DME
☑ BODY TAG ☐ CLOTHING
☐ X-RAY (No.) ☐ FLUORO
☐ SPECIAL PROCESSING TAG ☐ MED. RECORDS
☑ AT SCENE PHOTOS (No. 7)

CASE CIRCUMSTANCES
☐ EMBALMED
☐ DECOMPOSED
☐ >24 HRS IN HOSPITAL
☐ OTHER:

TYPING SPECIMEN
TYPING SPECIMEN TAKEN BY:
SOURCE:

TOXICOLOGY SPECIMEN
COLLECTED BY: ▓▓
☑ HEART BLOOD ☐ STOMACH CONTENTS
☑ FEMORAL BLOOD ☐ VITREOUS
TECHNIQUE
☐ BLOOD ☐ SPLEEN
☐ BLOOD ☐ KIDNEY
☐ BILE ☐
☑ LIVER ☐
☑ URINE ☐
URINE GLUCOSE DIPSTICK RESULT: 4+
TOX SPECIMEN RECONCILIATION BY: ▓▓

HISTOLOGY
☑ Regular (No.) ☐ Oversize (No.)
Histopath Cut: ☐ Autopsy ☐ Lab

TOXICOLOGY REQUESTS
FORM 3A: ☑ YES ☐ NO
☐ NO TOXICOLOGY REQUESTED
SCREEN ☑ C ☐ H ☐ T ☐ S ☐ D
☐ ALCOHOL ONLY
☐ CARBON MONOXIDE
☐ OTHER (Specify drug and tissue)

REQUESTED MATERIAL ON PENDING CASES
☑ POLICE REPORT ☐ MED HISTORY
☑ TOX FOR COD ☐ HISTOLOGY
☐ TOX FOR R/O ☐ INVESTIGATIONS
☐ MICROBIOLOGY ☐ EYE PATH. CONS.
☐ RADIOLOGY CONS.
☐ CONSULT ON:
☐ BRAIN SUBMITTED
☐ NEURO CONSULT ☐ DME TO CUT
☐ CRIMINALISTICS
☐ GSR ☐ SEXUAL ASSAULT ☐ OTHER

WHITE - File Copy   CANARY - Forensic Lab   PINK - Certification   GOLDENROD - DME   (Rev. 9/13)

Malibu Motel

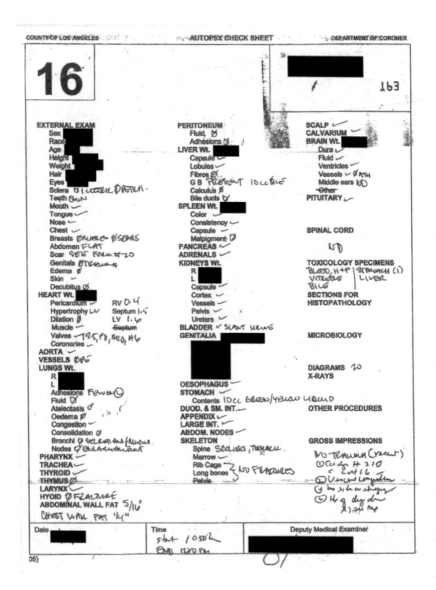

390

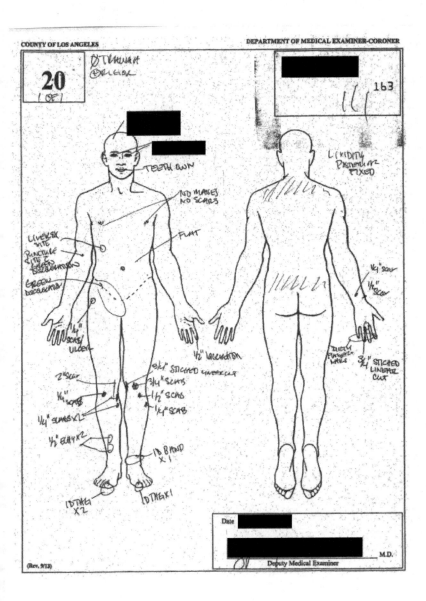

Malibu Motel

Department of Medical Examiner-Coroner, County of Los Angeles

FORENSIC SCIENCE LABORATORIES

1104 North Mission Road Los Angeles, CA 90033

Laboratory Analysis Summary Report

Deputy Medical Examiner
1104 North Mission Road
Los Angeles, CA 90033

☑ PendingTox

The following results have been technically and administratively reviewed and are the opinions and conclusions of the Analyst:

Coroner Case Number: ██████ **Decedent:** ████████████

SPECIMEN	SERVICE	DRUG	RESULT	ANALYST
Blood, Heart				
	Alcohol-GC/FID-HS	Ethanol	Negative	
	Bases-GC/NPD &/or MS	Duloxetine	ND	
	Bases-GC/NPD &/or MS	Propranolol	ND	
	Bases-GC/NPD &/or MS	Quetiapine	ND	
	Bases-GC/NPD &/or MS	Quetiapine Metabolite	Present	
	Benzos (Free)-GC/MS	Diazepam	< 0.10 ug/mL	
	Benzos (Free)-GC/MS	Lorazepam	7.9 ng/mL	
	Benzos (Free)-GC/MS	Nordiazepam	< 0.10 ug/mL	
	Benzos (Free)-LC/MS	7-Aminoclonazepam	25 ng/mL	
	Benzos (Free)-LC/MS	Clonazepam	ND	
	Cocaine-GC/MS	Benzoylecgonine	ND	
	Cocaine-GC/MS	Cocaethylene	ND	
	Cocaine-GC/MS	Cocaine	ND	
	ELISA-Immunoassay	Barbiturates	ND	
	ELISA-Immunoassay	Fentanyl	ND	
	ELISA-Immunoassay	Methamphetamine & MDMA	ND	
	ELISA-Immunoassay	Phencyclidine	ND	
	LC/MS	Zopiclone	15 ng/mL	
	Opiates-GC/MS	6-Monoacetylmorphine	Present	
	Opiates-GC/MS	Codeine, Free	0.11 ug/mL	
	Opiates-GC/MS	Hydrocodone, Free	< 0.03 ug/mL	
	Opiates-GC/MS	Hydromorphone, Free	ND	
	Opiates-GC/MS	Morphine, Free	1.1 ug/mL	
	Opiates-GC/MS	Oxycodone, Free	ND	
	Opiates-GC/MS	Oxymorphone, Free	ND	
	Outside Test	Buprenorphine	4.6 ng/mL	
	Outside Test	Norbuprenorphine	7.9 ng/mL	

Chaunceton Bird

SPECIMEN	SERVICE	DRUG		RESULT	ANALYST

Coroner Case Number: ████ **Decedent:** ████████

Legend:

		mg/dL	Milligram per Deciliter	PP	Presumptive Positive
g	Grams	mg/L	Milligram per Liter	QNS	Quantity Not Sufficient
g%	Gram Percent	ND	Not Detected	ug	Micrograms
Inc.	Inconclusive	ng/g	Nanograms per Gram	ug/g	Micrograms per Gram
mg	Milligrams	ng/mL	Nanograms per Milliliter	ug/mL	Micrograms per Milliliter

In accordance with the Department's Evidence Retention Policy, the blood specimen(s) will be retained for one-year and all other specimens for six-months from Autopsy.

Administratively reviewed by: ████ , M.S., PTS-ABFT, D-ABC

Supervising Criminalist II
TOXICOLOGY
████

Malibu Motel

3A

CASE #

DECEDENT'S NAME:

DOD:

INCOMING MODE:

Page 1 of 3

Drug Name	Rx Number	Date of Issue	Number Issued	Number Remaining	Form	Dosage	Rx Directions	Physician	Pharmacy Phone/ Comments
BUPRENORPHINE	▮	▮		17	TABLET	8 MG	BID SL	▮	BLOODY LABEL
BUPRENORPHINE	▮	▮		1	TABLET	8 MG	DAILY		WORN LABEL, SOME PILLS CRUSHED
CEPHALEXIN G	▮	▮	30	26	CAPSULE	500 MG	TID	▮	
CLONAZEPAM	▮			1	TABLET	1 MG	1.5 DAILY PRN		BLOODY LABEL
CLONAZEPAM	▮		45	0	TABLET	1 MG	1.5 TABS DAILY	▮	BLOODY
CLONAZEPAM	▮	▮	45	0.5	TABLET	1 MG	1.5 TABS DAILY	▮	
CLONAZEPAM	▮	▮	12	0	TABLET	1 MG	1/2 DAILY	▮	▮
CLONAZEPAM	▮	▮	45	37	TABLET	1 MG	1.5 TABS DAILY	▮	▮

Paraphernalia Description

2 SYRINGES, MULTIPLE BALLOONS, 1 GLASS PIPE, COOKING CAP, VIAL OF MARIJUANA, 2 SMALL BOTTLES OF LIQUID

Investigator:

Date:

COUNTY OF LOS ANGELES   MEDICAL EVIDENCE   DEPARTMENT OF CORONER

3A

CASE #:
DECEDENT'S NAME:
DOD:
INCOMING MODE:

Drug Name	Rx Number	Date of Issue	Number Issued	Number Remaining	Form	Dosage	Rx Directions	Physician	Pharmacy Phone/ Comments
CYMBALTA	██	██	30	0	CAPSULE	60 MG			
HYDROCODONE	██	██	20	9	TABLET	5-500 MG	Q6H PRN		NO RX INFO ON LABEL
LUNESTA	██	██	30	0	TABLET	3 MG	AT BEDTIME	██	██
LUNESTA	██	██		18	TABLET	3 MG	AT BEDTIME		
LUNESTA	██	██		21.5	TABLET	3 MG	AT BEDTIME	██	
LUNESTA	██	██	30	15	TABLET	3 MG	AT BEDTIME	██	██
LUNESTA	██	██	30	0	TABLET	3 MG	AT BEDTIME		BLOODY LABEL
NITROFURANTOIN	██	██	10	0	CAPSULE	100MG	BID	██	██

Paraphernalia Description
2 SYRINGES, MULTIPLE BALLOONS, 1 GLASS PIPE, COOKING CAP , VIAL OF MARIJUANA, 2 SMALL BOTTLES OF LIQUID

Investigator:
Date:

Malibu Motel

MEDICAL EVIDENCE

DEPARTMENT OF CORONER

3A

CASE #
DECEDENT'S NAME:
DOD:
DOB:
INCOMING MODE:

Drug Name	Rx Number	Date of Issue	Number Issued	Number Remaining	Form	Dosage	Rx Directions	Physician	Pharmacy Phone/ Comments
PROPRANOLOL	472889	3/25/2013	60	58	TABLET	20 MG	Q6H PRN ANXIETY		
QUETIAPINE			30	2	TABLET	300 MG	AT BEDTIME		
QUETIAPINE			30	28	TABLET	300 MG	AT BEDTIME		
QUETIAPINE			30	3	TABLET	300 MG	DAILY		
QUETIAPINE			30	17	TABLET	300 MG	AT BEDTIME		WORN LABEL
SULFAMETHOXAZOLE TMP			20	17	TABLET		BID WITH FLUIDS		

Paraphernalia Description
2 SYRINGES, MULTIPLE BALLOONS, 1 GLASS PIPE, COOKING CAP, VIAL OF MARIJUANA, 2 SMALL BOTTLES OF LIQUID

Investigator:
Date:

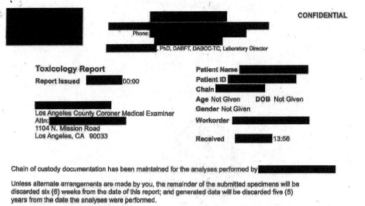

CONFIDENTIAL

Phone:

, PhD, DABFT, DABCC-TC, Laboratory Director

Toxicology Report

Report Issued _____ 00:00

Los Angeles County Coroner Medical Examiner
Attn:
1104 N. Mission Road
Los Angeles, CA 90033

Patient Name
Patient ID
Chain
Age Not Given   **DOB** Not Given
Gender Not Given
Workorder

Received _____ 13:56

Chain of custody documentation has been maintained for the analyses performed by

Unless alternate arrangements are made by you, the remainder of the submitted specimens will be discarded six (6) weeks from the date of this report; and generated data will be discarded five (5) years from the date the analyses were performed.

Sample ID
Matrix Blood
Patient Name
Patient ID
Container Type Red Top Tube

Collect Dt/Tm _____ 13:45
Source Cardiac Blood

Approx Vol/Weight 2 mL

Receipt Notes   None Entered

Analysis and Comments	Result	Units	Reporting Limit	Notes
0801B Buprenorphine and Metabolite - Free (Unconjugated), Blood				
Analysis by High Performance Liquid Chromatography/Tandem Mass Spectrometry (LC-MS/MS)				
Buprenorphine - Free	4.5	ng/mL	1.0	
Synonym(s): Buprenex®				
When a single 0.4 mg sublingual dose was administered 3 hours after a 0.3 mg intramuscular dose, the plasma levels following the sublingual dose were: 0.45 - 0.84 ng/mL at 2 hours 0.36 - 0.58 ng/mL at 6.5 hours 0.25 - 0.36 ng/mL at 10 hours				
Norbuprenorphine - Free	7.9	ng/mL	1.0	
Synonym(s): Buprenorphine Metabolite				

LA CORONER
OK to Release
LABORATORY

Page 1 of 1

CULTURE, SOCIETY & POLITICS

Contemporary culture has eliminated the concept and public figure of the intellectual. A cretinous anti-intellectualism presides, cheer-led by hacks in the pay of multinational corporations who reassure their bored readers that there is no need to rouse themselves from their stupor. Zer0 Books knows that another kind of discourse – intellectual without being academic, popular without being populist – is not only possible: it is already flourishing. Zer0 is convinced that in the unthinking, blandly consensual culture in which we live, critical and engaged theoretical reflection is more important than ever before.

If you have enjoyed this book, why not tell other readers by posting a review on your preferred book site.

Recent bestsellers from Zero Books are:

In the Dust of This Planet
Horror of Philosophy vol. 1
Eugene Thacker
In the first of a series of three books on the Horror of
Philosophy, *In the Dust of This Planet* offers the genre of horror
as a way of thinking about the unthinkable.
Paperback: 978-1-84694-676-9 ebook: 978-1-78099-010-1

Capitalist Realism
Is there no alternative?
Mark Fisher
An analysis of the ways in which capitalism has presented itself
as the only realistic political-economic system.
Paperback: 978-1-84694-317-1 ebook: 978-1-78099-734-6

Rebel Rebel
Chris O'Leary
David Bowie: every single song. Everything you want to know,
everything you didn't know.
Paperback: 978-1-78099-244-0 ebook: 978-1-78099-713-1

Cartographies of the Absolute
Alberto Toscano, Jeff Kinkle
An aesthetics of the economy for the twenty-first century.
Paperback: 978-1-78099-275-4 ebook: 978-1-78279-973-3

Malign Velocities
Accelerationism and Capitalism
Benjamin Noys
Long listed for the Bread and Roses Prize 2015, *Malign Velocities* argues against the need for speed, tracking acceleration as the symptom of the ongoing crises of capitalism.
Paperback: 978-1-78279-300-7 ebook: 978-1-78279-299-4

Meat Market
Female Flesh under Capitalism
Laurie Penny
A feminist dissection of women's bodies as the fleshy fulcrum of capitalist cannibalism, whereby women are both consumers and consumed.
Paperback: 978-1-84694-521-2 ebook: 978-1-84694-782-7

Poor but Sexy
Culture Clashes in Europe East and West
Agata Pyzik
How the East stayed East and the West stayed West.
Paperback: 978-1-78099-394-2 ebook: 978-1-78099-395-9

Romeo and Juliet in Palestine
Teaching Under Occupation
Tom Sperlinger
Life in the West Bank, the nature of pedagogy and the role of a university under occupation.
Paperback: 978-1-78279-637-4 ebook: 978-1-78279-636-7

Sweetening the Pill
or How We Got Hooked on Hormonal Birth Control
Holly Grigg-Spall
Has contraception liberated or oppressed women? *Sweetening
the Pill* breaks the silence on the dark side of hormonal
contraception.
Paperback: 978-1-78099-607-3 ebook: 978-1-78099-608-0

Why Are We The Good Guys?
Reclaiming Your Mind from the Delusions of Propaganda
David Cromwell
A provocative challenge to the standard ideology that Western
power is a benevolent force in the world.
Paperback: 978-1-78099-365-2 ebook: 978-1-78099-366-9

Readers of ebooks can buy or view any of these bestsellers by clicking on the live link in the title. Most titles are published in paperback and as an ebook. Paperbacks are available in traditional bookshops. Both print and ebook formats are available online.

Find more titles and sign up to our readers' newsletter at http://www.johnhuntpublishing.com/culture-and-politics

Follow us on Facebook at https://www.facebook.com/ZeroBooks

and Twitter at https://twitter.com/Zer0Books